TAKE DOWN

A MASON SHARPE THRILLER

LOGAN RYLES

INKUBATOR
BOOKS

Published by Inkubator Books
www.inkubatorbooks.com

ISBN (eBook): 978-1-83756-079-0
ISBN (Paperback): 978-1-83756-080-6
ISBN (Hardback): 978-1-83756-081-3

For Jason Kasper - Thanks for cutting the trail.

1

"**Y**ou're all clear. Go!"

The radio crackled, and the boy left the shadows. He sprinted across the quiet north Phoenix street, the pavement still baking hot even though the Arizona sun had long since set. Hitting the bar's gravel parking lot, he flipped across a split-rail fence and made straight for the motorcycles.

There were six of them—two Kawasakis, three Hondas, and one Ducati. All expensive race bikes, driven by airmen stationed at nearby Luke Air Force Base. Young guys with guaranteed housing and money to burn.

The bikes were their prize property. On a hot Friday night like this, they drove them into the city to show off to girls at the local military bars.

The boy had seen it before—he'd scoped out both the routine and the bikes for a month straight. After an hour of waiting in the shadows, he knew the airmen would be four or five beers in, zeroed in on female targets, and no longer thinking about the bikes.

Leaving a window of opportunity.

The boy chose the Ducati. Not because it was the easiest to hot-wire, or even the most valuable. The brand-new Honda Fireblade sitting next to it was almost certainly worth more. The Ducati Streetfighter, by comparison, was a couple of years old and a little sandblasted by desert life.

But he'd never jacked a Ducati before. And new bikes were part of the thrill.

He slid to his knees next to the Streetfighter and thumbed the radio. "Check?"

"Still at the bar. You're gold."

A dry smile crept across his face as he reached behind the bike's forks, just forward of the engine block, and traced wires toward the handlebars. There would be three running out of the ignition switch—beneath the gas tank and down to the starter. He found them and worked along the wiring harness until his fingers stopped at what he was looking for—the plastic coupling that joined the ignition system with the primary electrical harness. Even on a nice bike, the part was rarely more complex than a simple plastic plug, and with a quick flick of his finger he disconnected the ignition system altogether.

That was the hard part. The rest was downhill. Pulling a short piece of copper wire from his pocket, he bent it into a U shape and prodded each end into separate slots of the plug. There were three of them, providing for only three possible combinations. It wasn't rocket science.

He hit pay dirt on the second combination, and the bike clicked on. The dry smile spread to a full grin, and he scrambled to his feet.

"We're good!" he called into the radio.

"Hey, move it. One of the guys just got up."

The boy threw a leg over the bike and clamped the clutch. He'd never driven a Ducati before—he'd never so much as sat on one. But the controls were familiar. They weren't so different from any of the eighteen bikes he'd jacked in the last three months alone.

Kickstand up. Clutch in. Starter pressed. The eleven hundred CC motor grumbled to life with a cough of exhaust, and then two things happened at once—both bad.

The airman who owned the bike exited the bar's front door, and a cop car rolled into the parking lot.

"Hey! What the hell are you doing?"

The boy's head snapped back over one shoulder. He saw the airman breaking into a sprint, twenty yards away. Saw his partner in crime standing in the bar doorway, the radio hanging uselessly at his side. Saw the cop car sliding to a stop, the officer behind the wheel catching the airman's eye and following his pointing arm.

And then the boy knew he had a choice.

He slammed the gear shifter into first, gunned the throttle, and released the clutch. The Ducati screamed and threw a hail of gravel right into the face of the nearing airman. Rocks pinged off car hoods and the bar's front steps.

And then he was off—over the curb, onto the highway. Reaching second gear and not hesitating for a second. The motor roared like a caged beast, and the front wheel left the pavement. Hot desert wind swept back his hair and stole the air from his lungs. Heart thumping, adrenaline surging, he hit sixty. Then eighty.

Behind him a siren screamed, and blue lights flashed. Ahead the empty Arizona sky beckoned him on, the grin still plastered across his face.

There was nothing like it. The thrill. The excitement. The momentary escape from hungry nights in the roach-infested government housing complex he called home.

This was living.

And then it wasn't. He saw the intersection and the blazing red light only half a mile ahead and didn't plan to slow. It was a quiet part of town, so far removed from the outskirts as to barely be counted as Phoenix metro. This light was automatic, switching from red to green on a timer. There might not even be a passing car.

But there was—and not just a car. A semitruck, dragging a long flatbed, rolling across the intersection.

The boy grabbed the clutch and hit the brake. Tires screamed, and the bike shook. The truck barely seemed to move—still crawling at the pace of a snail. The intersection flashed closer as the bike dropped back into double-digit speeds, but still hurtled on.

Panic overtook his mind. He calculated the shrinking distance and knew he'd never stop in time. If he missed the truck, he'd hit the trailer, or worse still, the bike would slide beneath while he was decapitated by the trailer's edge. He saw it all in a microsecond, and he made a decision.

Rolling left, he shot his leg up toward the handlebar and dumped the bike on its side. Sparks exploded as metal met asphalt and his body left the Ducati. That same asphalt tore into his elbows and arms, ripping at jeans and the shoplifted leather jacket he wore. He wrapped both arms instinctively around his head and kept rolling. The bike spun into the darkness and slammed into the truck. Stars and asphalt alternated as he continued to tumble.

And then he hit the ditch. Dry desert dust and small cacti. It was a swirling mess of speed and pain, wrapping around his body and smashing into his face.

Then it was simply over.

He lay on his back in the ditch, face up. Breathing hard.

And still grinning.

Boots pounded the pavement, and the truck driver called to him. The cop car slid to a stop at the edge of the road, blue lights still flashing but the siren off. In a second both the cop and the driver were on top of him—no time to run.

Not even a prayer of escape.

The boy didn't care.

"Are you all right?" the trucker shouted. "Geez, son. Didn't you see the light?"

The boy sat up with a pain-filled grunt. He didn't even look for the Ducati. That bike was history. He just looked to the cop. Hard lines framed cold eyes, the officer's right hand resting on his gun. There was no panic in that face—no urgency or particular concern. Only resigned frustration.

The boy's grin faded, and nausea flooded his stomach.

The cop reached for his cuffs. "Well, Mason, I finally got you."

2

TWELVE YEARS LATER

I sat next to the diner window and watched the kid steal my truck.

He began at the driver's door, where a rotten window gasket left ample room to slip a lockout tool through. A quick manipulation of the implement and the heavy door swung open.

I took a bite of my burger and wondered how many kids these days knew how to use a lockout tool. Probably not many, which meant this kid was either smart or else associated with an old-school car booster, and that meant he probably knew how to hot-wire the truck, also.

I bet myself he could and ordered a milkshake.

The kid tossed the lockout tool into the passenger seat and clambered into my '67 GMC. He shut the door, and even through the diner window I heard the heavy-metal *thunk* of steel-on-steel, like a tank hatch slamming closed.

They don't make them like that anymore.

The kid went to work on the ignition, and I went to work on the milkshake. The ignition wasn't mounted on the steering column like modern cars. Instead, it was built into the dash, beneath the radio. The wires were inaccessible unless the kid ducked completely beneath the dash, and to do that, he'd need to leave the truck and lean in from the side.

But if he was smart, he wouldn't bother, because the truck was over fifty years old and the ignition was original, which meant the tumblers inside the keyhole were worn to the point of compliance with a manipulation as crude as a screwdriver. I knew that, because I once lost the keys and used a screwdriver to start it. That implement now lay in the glove box, ready for an encore performance.

The kid bent low beneath the windshield, presumably fiddling with the ignition. I gave him two, maybe three minutes before he simply twisted it, but I underestimated him. He resorted to the screwdriver in less than ninety seconds.

The old motor groaned, and the truck lurched forward. I always parked it in gear, because the parking brake was shot, and leaving it in first was the best way to keep it from rolling.

I pulled the cherry from the top of the milkshake and sucked icy, chocolaty goodness off the surface, then crunched down. I had an Army buddy who could tie knots in the stems of cherries with his teeth, and for a moment I contemplated giving it a go, but I didn't have time. The show was about to start.

The kid stared down at the dash with an alarmed contortion of his face. He looked at the gear shifter shooting out of the steering column, and then looked to the floor.

Three pedals.

Recognition dawned across his face as he noticed the clutch for the first time, but confusion returned as his gaze settled on the column shifter again.

He'd never seen a manual vehicle with a column shifter before. No member of his generation had. Hell, I hadn't either before buying the truck three months earlier. It was a quirk of yesteryear—three on the tree, they called it.

I put the cherry stem in my mouth. The kid looked back at the shifter, and then he seemed to put it all together. His body twisted as he depressed the clutch, and then he felt around with the shifter, sliding it out of first and into neutral and then feeling out the remaining gears.

A smart kid. A lot smarter than me.

He returned to first. Then he reached for the screwdriver again.

Black smoke puffed from the tailpipe, and the engine rumbled to life. A satisfied grin spread across the kid's face, and he put both hands on the wheel.

But he wasn't home free yet. I indulged in a dry grin.

He let out on the clutch and depressed the gas—just like he was supposed to, except not at all like he was supposed to. The engine choked, the truck lurched, and everything went quiet.

I laughed and fiddled with the cherry stem. Over the years, I'd owned several vehicles with three pedals, and none of them were half as tricky as my '67 GMC. Whether by design, quirk, or age, the clutch on that truck was like a violin. Once mastered, it ran as smooth as a Mercedes. But until then it gave you hell at every shift.

That was why I wasn't worried when I saw the kid approach the truck, and I wasn't worried now as he started the engine and attempted to drive it out of the lot again.

The GMC lurched and coughed out, and this time real anger spread across the kid's face. He slammed his hand into the wheel, gritted his teeth, and bent to start the truck again.

I left a twenty on the table and slid out of the booth. By the time I made it outside, the kid had hopped the truck halfway to the damp street, but had choked it out again, and was angrier than ever.

I approached from the rear, spitting out the cherry stem on the way and digging my Victorinox Swiss army knife out of my pocket. I used it to tap on the driver's window and was gratified to see the kid lurch upward like he'd been blown out of a cannon. Smooth brown cheeks paled, and large dark eyes grew as big as the plate I'd just eaten dinner off of.

I opened the door and motioned him out.

"Leave it in gear," I said.

His gaze settled on the closed knife, and his face blanched a chalkier white. Then his eyes darted from the parking lot to the street.

Looking for an escape route. Just like they always do.

"First gear," I said calmly. "Back and down. It won't roll."

He released the clutch and dropped his feet through the door. I could tell he was about to make a run for it, but I put a hand on his shoulder.

"You wanna explain yourself?" I asked, taking a good look at him for the first time.

He was young. Maybe fifteen, but tall for his age. Skinny but not frail. His shoulder felt firm, and even caught red-handed, he held his head high. He wore stylish jeans and Nike sneakers, paired with a yellow Atlanta Hawks hoodie.

Not great camouflage for jacking a truck in broad daylight, but it looked good on him.

His lip lifted in a sneer. "Who are you?"

I actually laughed. "The guy who owns this truck."

I saw calculation in his face. Quick math, evaluating his options. Should he plead guilty and hope for mercy?

Maybe he should kick me in the groin and make a dash for freedom.

I hoped he didn't pick that option, because I really didn't want to rough up a kid.

"What are you doing?" I asked, lowering my tone.

He didn't answer. I pocketed the knife, running the back

of one hand across my forehead. It was hot in Georgia, even in early April. Not just hot—it was muggy. Far more humid than my Arizona blood appreciated. The gray clouds rolling over Atlanta certainly didn't help. I'd waited most of the thunderstorm out in the diner, but the break in the rain wouldn't last. I didn't want to be standing here arguing with an adolescent whenever it returned.

"Look," I said. "This can go one of two ways. Either you start talking, and we work this out man-to-man, or I call the cops, and you deal with them. Now are you a man or not?"

I knew that would get him. It hadn't been that long since I'd been a punk kid myself, surrounded by a big city, acting out for attention. And that was all this was—a punk kid acting out. He didn't target my truck because he liked it, or because it was worth anything. He targeted it because he was trying to prove something, either to himself or to his punk friends.

And that made him vulnerable to my manhood jab.

The kid held his chin up. He was still blocked in next to the truck, but he didn't act like it. I admired that.

"Yeah. I'm a man."

"Okay then. Slide over."

He looked confused. I motioned to the passenger end of the truck's bench seat. My duffel bag rested there, but he could move it.

"There," I said.

"You tryin' to nap me, bruh?" he asked.

I rolled my eyes. "I'm taking you home, *bruh*. Where you belong."

He hesitated again, glancing across the pothole-infested parking lot to a street corner nearby. I figured some of his buddies might be watching. I didn't care.

"I can call you a ride if you prefer. I'm sure there's a cop around." It was a bluff—I didn't have a cell phone. But he took the hint and scrabbled over, pushing my bag out of the way. I slid in and slammed the heavy steel door, reaching for the screwdriver.

"What's your name?" I asked, pushing the accelerator to the floor. In his attempt to overcome the clutch, he'd flooded the engine, but on a truck this old you can hold the gas down and the excess fuel will drain out.

The kid gave me side-eye, keeping close to his door but not reaching for the handle.

"Jalen," he said at last.

"You got a last name, Jalen?"

"Not for a stranger."

I returned the screwdriver to the glove box and used my key. The engine rolled over and rumbled to life.

"We're barely strangers. You seem well acquainted with my home."

"Your home?"

I jabbed a finger to the bed of the truck. It was empty save for a large plastic container, which housed my air mattress and various light camping gear.

Jalen looked a little embarrassed.

"I didn't realize you were homeless," he said.

"I'm not. I just live in a truck."

He nodded slowly. Then dropped his gaze, looking sheepish for the first time. "Powell," he said. "My name's Jalen Powell."

"Mason Sharpe," I said, shifting into first and rolling toward the street. "Where do you live, Jalen?"

3

J alen directed me to turn left out of the parking lot. I drove smoothly, managing the clutch with practiced ease as I navigated back into Atlanta traffic.

The city was massive—much larger than it looked on a map. After spending two months in the mountains of North Georgia, mostly open-air camping in the bed of my truck, I'd turned south and had just reached the city that day.

Then the rain started. Only one of the windshield wipers on the old GMC worked, and it skipped a lot, rendering wet-weather driving dangerous under normal circumstances. I quickly learned that Atlanta traffic was anything but normal. The massive girth of Interstate 75 that snaked through the heart of the city stalled to a near stop, creeping along for hours as the steady deluge continued.

By the time I reached the south side of the city, it was nearly five p.m., and I was starving. I took the first exit I saw and found my way to the Skyline Diner right off the highway.

That was where I sat, waiting out the rain and enjoying a dry burger when Jalen turned up. I knew he couldn't live far away, because he'd approached on foot, and I hadn't seen any buses serving this part of the city.

"So, you're a Hawks fan?" I asked, mostly to make conversation. We were stuck in backed-up traffic again, down on the surface streets. The rain had slackened off since I had stopped for dinner, but a steady spray still made driving an aggravation. All around us slouching houses endured the dank weather. It wasn't a nice part of town.

"Yeah," Jalen grunted, avoiding my gaze.

"Ever watch the Suns?" I asked.

I wasn't a big basketball guy. Football was always my sport. But I used to have a partner who was a massive Phoenix Suns fan. She never shut up about them.

Back when I was a homicide detective for the Phoenix Police Department. Back before I was homeless. Before the truck, the camping, the wandering.

Before...

"Yeah, bruh," Jalen said, jerking me out of my thoughts. "Shaq was a beast!"

I grunted in agreement. "There was also this Barkley guy who was pretty good. But I guess that was before your time."

"You from Arizona?" Jalen asked.

I nodded.

"What you doin' here?"

"Looking after my truck, apparently."

It was only half a joke, but Jalen smirked. Even now, riding next to me as a semi-hostage, he didn't appear particularly alarmed. There was a confidence about him. Like he would land on his feet regardless of what happened next.

We crept forward another ten yards, then stopped at a light. There was a wreck up ahead—a Kia had found its way into the ditch and was now being retrieved by a tow truck. The source of the backed-up traffic.

"You got anything to say?" I prompted.

Jalen looked out his window, arms folded. I gave him time, using a dirty T-shirt to mop fog off the inside of my windshield. Without climate control, it was a losing battle.

"I think you owe me an explanation," I said. "I was enjoying my dinner. This truck is my property. You could have wrecked it."

"All right." He rolled his head toward the ceiling, his voice heavy with irritation. "I'm sorry, okay? Is that what you wanna hear?"

"Not really. It's a useless statement, and you don't mean it anyway. I'm more interested in why."

"What do you mean, *why*?"

"Why you did it."

Jalen snorted. "Why do you care?"

"Because humans are rational beings. We do things for a reason. Not always a good reason, but always some reason. I'm curious about yours."

"Why does it matter?"

"It matters because so long as there's a reason, you'll try it again. The next guy might not be so magnanimous as me."

"I don't know what that means."

"It means nice. Predisposed to be agreeable or caring. It means I didn't pull a gun on your dumb ass, or call the cops, or watch you roll this thing into the street and get hit by a dump truck."

"Oh, so you *care* about me." His voice dripped with angst, and I knew I had hit a nerve.

"Not really," I said, mostly to throw him off. "I care more about the collateral damage you'll cause if you keep this up. If you want to piss your own life away, that's your business."

He glowered out the window again. The light switched to green.

"Which way?"

"Right," he muttered.

I turned down another busted street, crashing through potholes flooded with water. The houses surrounding me stood in shambles, many with busted windows and tarps covering portions of their roofs. Old cars rested on blocks, and others sat on spinner wheels. The people I saw on porches and standing in open doorways were all black. I knew a lot of African Americans lived in Atlanta, but I hadn't expected the neighborhoods to be quite so segregated.

It wasn't like that in Phoenix. There was segregation, sure, but it had more to do with net worth than race.

"I don't think you did it for the money," I said, restarting the conversation. "The truck is an antique, but it isn't worth much."

"What makes you think I'm smart enough to know that?" Jalen asked, still facing the window.

"Because you were smart enough to pick a '67 pickup instead of the mid-nineties BMW parked next to it, or the late model Honda in the back of the lot. You knew those cars had alarm systems and would be difficult to hot-wire. But not an old truck. Easiest thing in the world to jack a vehicle like this."

"How would you know?"

"Maybe because we're not as different as you think."

Momentary curiosity flashed across his eyes, but I didn't think he believed me.

"Here," he said, jabbing his chin toward a field of brick buildings sprawling up ahead. The windshield was fogged again, and the worthless wiper was doing little to fight the currents of water washing across it, but it didn't take a picture-perfect view to know what I was looking at. It was a government housing project—a big one, built of two-story brick buildings with metal roofs, connected by sidewalks and cramped parking lots packed with dinged-up old cars. The grass was tall and uncut, littered with trash and adding to the overall unkempt look of the place.

I stopped the truck. Jalen reached for the door handle.

"Thanks for the ride," he muttered sarcastically. The irony wasn't lost on him.

I put a hand on his arm. "Got school tomorrow?"

He glowered at me. "Why you care?"

"I'd just like to know that you aren't back on the streets, harassing innocent travelers."

Jalen yanked his sleeve free. "Bruh, I got better things to do than look at dusty old books."

The door groaned open, and a light spray of rain pelted the floorboard. I relaxed behind the steering wheel. Jalen dropped a leg out, but I called after him.

"Just one thing before you go."

He glanced over his shoulder, face still hard as stone.

"You're obviously a bright kid," I said. "You're going places. Make sure they're places you want to be."

Jalen hesitated, and for a moment I saw a hint of openness. As though whatever pain that drove him to take the truck was visible, just for a moment. Then that moment vanished, and he dropped onto the wet concrete outside.

"Man, you don't know nothing 'bout me."

He slammed the door. I watched him slog across the street, head ducked in the driving rain. Not bothering to look back, not bothering to change course as he crashed through a mud puddle.

He navigated for the last apartment in a weather-washed building, and for a moment I didn't see a young black kid in a yellow Hawks hoodie. I saw a young white kid in torn jeans and a shoplifted leather jacket, crouched on a corner, tugging on a joint with two or three of his friends.

Alone. Orphaned. Eager as hell to prove himself to

anyone watching. A chip on his shoulder the size of Sun Devil Stadium.

I shifted back into gear as Jalen disappeared inside, taking the moment with him. Then I rumbled back toward the highway.

4

I t didn't take a genius to know that I was on a bad side of town. Low-hanging clouds blocked out the skyline, and an endless web of raised highways crisscrossed over an urban sprawl of shambled houses, but the grit and age of this place wasn't lost on me. I'd been warned by a park ranger up near Lookout Mountain that I should restrict my tourism to tourist-centric areas of the city. He seemed to have an inflated view of the rampant danger of a major metropolis, but in my experience it's not unusual for rural people to feel that way. Phoenix was no theme park either, with plenty of rough neighborhoods and enough crime to keep my homicide department hopping.

That didn't make me afraid to live there, and it didn't make me afraid to visit Atlanta. But I hadn't planned to stop in the city. My intention had been to drive straight through before finding a roadside inn or a camping spot on my way to visit south Georgia.

There was this song my late fiancée used to like, by the Zac Brown Band. Mia was a great fan of all sorts of music, but particularly liked oldies, folk, and folksy country. The song was called "Homegrown", and the band sang about the smell of Georgia pines.

I'd heard it on the radio at a gas station about a week prior, and the lyrics reminded me of my days of Army basic training and then Ranger School—both at Fort Benning, just outside of Columbus, Georgia. I'd smelled plenty of pines back then and hated every one of them as long days of brutal marches under a blazing summer sun taught me to despise the Peach State.

Maybe hindsight had given me rose-tinted glasses, or maybe it was simple nostalgia, but the years had eroded my memory of the misery, leaving in its place only a strange desire to smell those pines again. So, after I heard that song on the radio, I turned south out of the mountains, made it to north Atlanta, and then got stuck in rain and traffic.

Now I was tired, wet, and more than a little irritated by my frustrating experience with Jalen. I was also sick of fighting through the slog. I might as well stop for the night in the city, then re-evaluate my travel agenda the next morning.

I followed green signs directing me toward Hartsfield-Jackson International Airport, which lay southwest of downtown. I was still new to traveling, but one thing I'd already learned was that cheap and plentiful accommodations are always located near airports. Without a cell phone to look anything up, it was a safe bet.

I found a row of motels just off the highway, joined by grungy gas stations and neon-lit liquor stores. Most of the accommodations looked like absolute rattraps, with deliberately misspelled or hyperbolic names like "Sleepy Nite Inn" or "Red Carpet Motel".

They were cheap places, but that was okay with me. I hadn't held a job since leaving the Phoenix Police Department late the previous year, and even though that sudden and traumatic departure had come with a ten-thousand-dollar injury settlement, my savings had taken a hit over the last six months.

I scanned my options before selecting the Peachtree Motel at the end of the street, advertising rooms for just $39.99 a night. I hurried through the rain to the front desk, where a fat old guy with bleach stains on his shirt sat behind bulletproof glass, fixated on a small TV set displaying a basketball game.

I recognized the red and yellow jerseys of the Atlanta Hawks and remembered that April was playoff season. It made me think of Jalen again, but I was too wet and irritable to fixate on the thought for long.

"Can I get a room?" I asked.

The guy didn't look up from the TV. "How long?"

"Uh...a night."

"$47.93."

"The sign says $39.99."

"Taxes, jackass."

He still hadn't looked up from the screen. I peeled two twenties and a ten out of my wallet and passed them through the narrow slot beneath the glass. He fished a brass key from a drawer, barely glancing at the tag before shoving it back at me.

"Room 211. Second floor, rear wing."

I took the key and waited. He fixated on the screen. I cleared my throat.

"What?"

"Change?" I asked, motioning to the cash still lying on the counter.

The guy jabbed a thumb toward the glass without looking up. I followed the gesture to a crude sign written in black marker.

NO CHANGE GIVEN.

I sighed and took the key, returning to the rain. The motel was built of three wings, all assembled in a rough U shape and opening toward the street. I found room 211 on the second floor of the U's base and parked the truck directly beneath it before lugging both my duffel bag and the plastic storage bin up the stairs. I wouldn't need anything from the bin, but I knew it wouldn't be there in the morning if I left it outside.

The room was small and smelled moldy. I found a lamp near the door to shed light over a sagging bed, a nightstand stained and marred by cigarette burns, and a bulbous TV that was probably outdated a decade ago. A bathroom vanity framed one wall, with a door leading to a toilet and shower next to it.

The toilet was grimy, and the shower uninhabitable. Mold grew between the tiles, and unidentifiable brown stains clung to the bottom. I grimaced and returned to the room, suddenly feeling uninterested in a shower, even though I hadn't had one in nearly a week.

I locked the door and fixed the chain, then settled on the bed and pulled my soppy shoes and shirt off, resting both across the top of the bin. For a moment I just sat and ran a hand through my hair, regarding my reflection in the black face of the TV.

I looked rough. Rougher than I'd looked in my entire life. A week's worth of razor stubble was starting to resemble a beard, and I was at least a month overdue for a haircut. The scars on my left shoulder from the bullet wounds of the previous November were white and swollen, still a little tender to the touch, but far less painful than they'd been only a few weeks prior in North Carolina.

But it wasn't the grime and long hair that I didn't recognize. It was the emptiness in my eyes. The slump in my shoulders.

I'd lived a relatively hard life, beginning on the wrong side of the tracks in Phoenix and leading through the Army. Afghanistan. The Rangers. Then the Phoenix Police Department, and all the ugly things I saw on those streets.

But none of that prepared me for what had happened in November. For the gunshots. The screams.

And Mia.

I fished through my duffel bag, past my meager supply of clothes and toiletries. Past the battered violin I'd collected in North Carolina. Right to the bottom, where the Bible was nestled.

I drew it out and ran my hands over the worn brown cover. My late fiancée's name was fixed to the bottom in curling gold script: *Mia Hayes.*

It was a pretty name. A name I almost hated to change when I proposed to her. Mia Sharpe just didn't have the same ring, but I really didn't care what her name was so long as she said yes.

I lifted the cover of the Bible and found her picture nestled safely inside. It was a little worn and creased. A little water damaged from an adventure in the Cape Fear River, where I lost her Toyota.

But her smile was as clear and radiant as ever. It shut out the grimy motel around me and withdrew into months gone by. Moments on the couch, nestled close to each other. Her head on my shoulder.

And the questions that I would never live down. Questions like, what if I had taken her to lunch that day instead of bringing her lunch to the school? What if I'd stayed to eat with her instead of hurrying back to work?

What if I'd responded just a little sooner, somehow? Fired just a little quicker? Thrown myself in the path of those bullets...

My eyes blurred, and I closed the Bible. I could sit here

another two hours and stare at that picture, as I'd done for most of the 164 days since I lost Mia. I could fall asleep cradling it, only to dream fitful dreams of her just out of reach, standing on the other side of an impenetrable wall.

But none of that would bring her back, and I was losing energy to maintain the fight.

Tucking the Bible back into the bag, I looked briefly to the violin, contemplating tuning it up. I'd been working on that Zac Brown Band song, and for whatever reason it was proving more difficult than most.

But I didn't have the energy for that either. Not tonight.

Instead I simply crawled into bed. I lay on top of the covers with both hands behind my head and stared at the water-stained ceiling.

I closed my eyes and saw Mia again, in that picture. Her smile as bright as the desert sun.

I remembered the day like yesterday, and I fixated on it as I drifted to sleep.

I was still dreaming of her when my motel door exploded open, and a storm of men hurtled inside.

5

Reflexes took over. I rolled off the bed and onto the floor, reaching for a weapon. There wasn't one, of course. Nothing but the Victorinox Locksmith—a pitiful defense against almost anything, but it didn't matter anyway. Long before I reached the knife, bright white lights flooded my face, blinding me. Men shouted. Weapons clicked.

I put my hands up, still crouched on my knees alongside the bed.

Boots struck the floor next to my face, and somebody shouted for me to lie still. My arms were yanked behind my back, and handcuffs ratcheted into place, then I was jerked to my feet. Two men stood behind me, and a short, ratty little man appeared in my face as my vision began to return. He wore a dark blue windbreaker with three yellow letters emblazoned above the left breast: DEA.

"You're under arrest," he snapped. "Where are the weapons?"

I didn't answer—not only because I was still disoriented, but because I knew better than to volunteer information to a cop even if I was innocent. And this wasn't a cop, anyway. This was a three-letter agent, busting into my ratty Atlanta motel room at...two a.m.? I checked the bedside clock as the two guys behind me wrenched me through the door, onto the landing. My truck sat surrounded by unmarked SUVs and a Crown Victoria, all with lights flashing. I noticed peeping faces in the windows of several motel rooms, watching in more curiosity than fear as I was hauled down the steps, across the rough asphalt, and shoved into the back of an SUV.

My head was clear now. I'd been sleeping hard, dreaming of Mia when they broke in. Now I was awake—confused, but alert. I remained calm as the door slammed; then two meatheads took the front seats. I didn't bother asking where we were headed or why. I'd know soon enough.

The ratty guy took the Crown Vic, and then we were off. Back onto now quiet streets, then the highway. Turning north, toward downtown.

That tracked. I was probably headed for a detention facility or maybe a DEA field office.

But why?

Part of me didn't care. I knew I hadn't done anything, and I also knew from my experience with the CIA in Afghanistan, and both the FBI and DEA in Phoenix, that three-letter agencies are some of the bluntest implements of democracy. The CIA had been tasked with hunting terrorist leaders. The FBI and DEA chased more domestic criminals.

But while the targets were different, the job was essentially the same, as was the method—brute force, usually. A "whatever it takes" mindset that often infringed on the law and produced inconsistent results. But none of that mattered to the bosses upstairs, so long as they got their man in the end.

Whatever man the DEA was looking for tonight, I wasn't

him. So I remained relaxed as the SUVs stopped in front of a squat block building on the east side of town. It wasn't a headquarters—probably not even a field office. In a city the size of Atlanta, the DEA would have a big field office someplace downtown. This building was something else. It didn't have any windows and was surrounded by a high chain-link fence topped with razor wire.

Not much curb appeal, even for a government building.

"Let's go," one of the big guys growled, hauling me out. I grimaced as my bare feet encountered loose pebbles in the parking lot. I wasn't wearing a shirt either—that was back at the motel. But the rain had stopped sometime while I slept, and it wasn't cold.

The two guys from the SUV rammed me through a front door, then immediately shoved me into an inspection room where what little clothing remained was stripped away, and I was subjected to a full cavity search. I wasn't sure what they were hoping to find, but they didn't find it. I pulled my pants back on and was offered cheap foam flip-flops before being marched down another hall, down a set of stairs, and into a windowless room with a metal table and two chairs.

A mirror ran along one wall. A single light blasted down from overhead. The floor was block, with a drain, and the walls stark white.

Classic.

They sat me in the chair furthest from the door, leaving my hands cuffed, and then they left. The door slammed shut and locked, leaving me staring at the empty chair across from me.

I let out a tired sigh and allowed my shoulders to slump. Any feelings of sleepiness were now driven from my body by a natural dump of adrenaline, but I wasn't nervous. If anything, I was simply annoyed.

Why the hell am I here?

I backtracked through the previous few weeks, sifting for an incident that might have put me on the radar of a federal agency. There were plenty of incidents, actually—all of them taking place in a little town on the North Carolina coast, where dirty cops and organized criminals had met justice at the hands of my own heartbreak.

But those events had nothing to do with drugs, and neither did the following weeks spent wandering around the mountains of north Georgia, sleeping in the bed of my truck, grilling bad steaks on a propane camp stove.

I wasn't the kind of guy who was overly concerned about coloring inside the lines, but I was pretty good at staying out of trouble, also. I really couldn't think of anything I might have done to land me here, which reinforced my opinion that this was simply a case of mistaken identity. *Get your man, whatever it takes.* Tonight, that zeal had spilled out of control, and pretty soon I'd be back at the motel with an insincere apology and a cheap pair of foam flip-flops as a souvenir.

Compliments of the DEA.

I closed my eyes, conscious of the fact that I was probably under surveillance. Minutes dragged into the better part of an hour, and nobody came. I expected that. Time, more than intimidation, was often an interrogator's best friend. I had used it in both Afghanistan and Phoenix, leaving my man sitting for hours or even days in a boring and uncomfortable place, sweating on whatever illicit information he was holding.

Thinking too much. Questioning himself. Letting his mind run wild about what might happen next.

It turns out there's no better tool in breaking somebody than their own neurosis. But I knew how the game was played, and that gave me an advantage. I also knew I wouldn't be left waiting much longer. Not with the way they'd hauled me in here, like I was a trophy elk brought down in the Arizona mountains.

I gave them two hours. I was only off by maybe thirty minutes.

The door busted open just as I was beginning to fall asleep sitting up. I kept my eyes closed as the chair across from me scraped back, and multiple pairs of shoes tapped the hard concrete floor. Something smacked against the table, and I opened my eyes slowly, as though I were half awake.

Two men had joined me. The first was tall, well built, and dark haired. He had bold features and wore a clean black suit.

He took the second metal chair, dropping a plastic bin on the table with a loud smack, and glaring at me. I guessed he was trying to be intimidating. I wasn't intimidated, and simply glanced at the second guy.

It was the ratty agent from my motel. He still wore the dark blue DEA windbreaker and stood with his arms folded, his hair a little disheveled, wire glasses resting on a pointed nose. He smiled, but it wasn't a warm smile. It was a "we got you" smile.

I rested my hands on the table and drummed one finger against the tabletop, looking into the plastic bin. It contained a wallet—my wallet—my Victorinox, and...Mia's Bible.

My fingers stopped drumming, and I felt suddenly hot. I looked back to the first guy, and he didn't blink. Didn't so much as budge. An instantaneous staring contest kicked off, and I didn't blink either.

Something about the presence of the Bible felt like a massive intrusion—worse than kicking down my door and wrenching me out of bed. Worse than hauling me down here and tossing me in this room in the middle of the night.

This jackass had brought *Mia* into this. But I still didn't speak.

The guy across from me reached inside his suit coat and produced a folded leather ID case. He flipped it open, displaying a DEA badge and ID card.

"Special Agent Mark Feldon, Drug Enforcement Administration. This is Special Agent Randy White."

I didn't look at the badge. I didn't need to.

Feldon flipped it shut and leaned across the table.

"You'd better start talking, Mr. Sharpe. Because I've got everything I need to bury you."

6

I sat quietly, my gaze locked with Feldon's, and didn't answer. He kept both hands on the table and maintained his condescending sneer, letting his previous threat hang in the air like an ax, probably assuming it would break me if only given enough time.

I sat with my shoulders loose, mouth closed. Not so much as twitching.

Feldon broke first, his impatience overcoming his desire to win a staring contest. He snatched back his badge, then turned directly to the bin and began to dig through it. He produced my wallet first, opening it and dispensing cards across the table. An Arizona driver's license, a regional bank debit card, and my Social Security card. The only three things I carried.

The cash was gone, I noticed. Seized, probably, in the name of whatever witch hunt Feldon was on. I'd deal with that later.

"Mason Lewis Sharpe," Feldon said, as if my name were the answer to a game show question. "Phoenix, Arizona. You're a long way from home."

Dropping the driver's license, he moved next to the Victorinox, rolling it around in his hand and opening a few of the tools. The puzzlement on his face appeared genuine, and I wasn't surprised. People are always confused by the Locksmith. It's not what they expect when they hear the term "Swiss army knife". It's much larger and more robust. I'd carried that very knife right through Afghanistan and back to Phoenix.

"What's this?" Feldon asked.

I didn't answer.

He rotated the blade outward until it locked in place with a click, stainless steel gleaming under the fluorescent lights. The knife was sharp—I kept it that way. His brow wrinkled into a frown.

"You know a knife this large is illegal in some districts," he said.

I held back a laugh. He might be right, but those districts weren't in the United States. I knew the law better than most.

Feldon closed the knife. He reached next for the Bible, and I spoke through gritted teeth.

"*Don't* touch that."

Feldon didn't move. White smirked.

"So you *do* speak," Feldon said.

I didn't answer. He interlaced his fingers, looking angry again. Angry, and cold, as if there was something burning deep inside him that somehow reignited when he looked at my face.

"Okay, Mr. Sharpe. We've got some questions for you."

Feldon withdrew a leather-bound notebook from his jacket and flipped it open, consulting his notes. He looked back up.

"You drive a 1968 GMC pickup, correct?"

It was a '67, not a '68, but I didn't contest the point.

"North Carolina antique auto plates," Feldon continued.

"Bill of sale found in the glove box with your name on it, dated for earlier this year. Did you forge that document, Mr. Sharpe?"

I didn't answer. I knew I didn't have to, even though nobody had read me the Miranda warning.

Feldon snapped the notebook closed, anger flashing across his face. "Why don't you tell me what you were doing yesterday afternoon at the Skyline Diner?"

The diner?

The question took me by surprise, but I didn't show it. I left my hands on the table, palms down, and stared back, unblinking.

Feldon gritted his teeth. "You'd better start talking, Mr. Sharpe. I'm the only man standing between you and a life behind bars."

Like hell you are.

"Did you meet with Jalen Powell?" Feldon demanded.

Another curveball. I thought of the kid in the parking lot, sloppily attempting to jack my truck. I recalled the protracted drive back to his apartment, irritated by rain and traffic and Jalen's perpetual attitude problem.

It was a weird encounter, in hindsight. But it didn't feel like the kind of thing that warranted interest by the DEA.

Something was missing here. Something significant. I was curious, but considering the way I'd been railroaded into this interrogation room, denied my rights, and now harassed by these fools, I was disinclined to admit to anything.

So I stayed quiet. Feldon watched me for almost a minute, then tilted his head to White. The ratty guy left the room, and Feldon folded his arms.

"You wanna play hardball? Let's play."

White returned quickly with a black plastic bag and a look on his face smug enough to land him a bunk in a sorority house. He reached into the bag and withdrew a single item, slamming it against the table with an anticlimactic thud.

"Care to explain *this*?" White said.

He withdrew his hand, exposing the item.

It was cocaine. An entire *brick* of cocaine, about a kilo in weight, wrapped in plastic shrink wrap and marked with black marker. Worth thirty to forty grand in Phoenix, but doubtless more this far from the Mexican border. The price went up the farther the cartels had to move their product.

"Look familiar?" Feldon asked. "It should. We found it in your truck."

I glanced from the cocaine to Feldon, then back to the brick. For a split second anxiety crept into my mind, and my heart rate accelerated. It was a natural reaction, given the shock of the situation. I hadn't encountered narcotics of any sort since leaving the Phoenix Police Department, but for just a moment I questioned myself.

Had I missed something? Had Jalen been carrying the brick and slipped it under my seat as he left the vehicle? Was the brick already there when I bought the truck in North Carolina?

They were absurd questions, and I shut them out. No, there hadn't been drugs in the pickup when I bought it. I'd cleaned the truck out immediately after purchase, including digging a slew of empty soda bottles and peanut wrappers from beneath the seat. But no drugs.

And the brick hadn't come from Jalen, either. I'd watched him closely from the moment he appeared in the parking lot outside the diner.

There was no cocaine then. No cocaine later. So...

"It was under your seat," White said. "Can you explain that?"

I squinted at the brick, fixating on the tight layers of plastic wrap. And then on the little numbers written in one corner in black marker. Just a short row, barely half an inch tall. A subtle thing, easily missed. But on further investigation, a critical detail.

I smirked.

"Something *funny*?" Feldon demanded.

I didn't answer.

Feldon glared at White. White rapped his knuckles on the stainless-steel tabletop.

"Hey, *asshole!* This is serious. Why did we find this in your truck?"

"You didn't," I said, more irritated than concerned.

White looked to Feldon, his eyes bulging with incredulity. "You believe this guy?"

Feldon smacked the table, seeming to reach the limits of his own patience. "This isn't a joke, Mr. Sharpe. This brick alone is enough to lock you up for a *decade*. If you don't start talking, I'll be on the phone with the district attorney so fast you'll—"

"Flip it over," I said.

Feldon broke off. He didn't move. White paled, just a little.

I gestured to the brick with my cuffed hands. "Go ahead. Roll it over."

Neither of them reached for the brick, but Feldon glanced sideways at White. The ratty agent's faced flushed.

Bingo.

I leaned across the table, not even trying to hide my grin now. "You forgot to pull the evidence tag, didn't you?"

Feldon's jaw clenched, and he rolled the brick so that only he could see the underside. His cheeks reddened, and he closed his eyes. White snarled a curse and reached for the cocaine. Feldon shoved his hand away, and the brick dropped, bottom up.

A bright yellow evidence tag was affixed to the underside, filled out in ballpoint pen. Dated for three weeks ago.

It was the black marks that gave it away. I'd seen them before, with the Phoenix Police Department. When narcotics are seized, they have to be processed and tagged. There's a critical chain of custody maintained to ensure no evidence is lost, but in the initial chaos of the seizure process, things can get messy. Especially when it's a large seizure. I'd seen cops lose their jobs for the simple pretext of evidence abuse.

So some of the guys used to carry permanent markers and number evidence as they counted it. It was simply a more methodical way to ensure the count was accurate, preventing an unintentional discrepancy that later led to a termination.

The little black numbers were my first clue that White had withdrawn this brick from an evidence locker. The evidence tag was proof, and the date on that tag was my exoneration.

"How did you know?" Feldon asked.

"Little black marks in the corner," I said.

Feldon glowered at White, as though it were his fault their little scheme hadn't worked out. It was still unclear to me what the exact nature of that scheme had been, but I was growing tired of being toyed with. This nonsense had lasted long enough.

"Phoenix Police Department," I said. "Badge number 4877. Look it up."

7

Feldon and White left the room, taking the cocaine with them. I was left alone for nearly fifteen minutes.

When the door opened again, only Feldon returned. His countenance had changed entirely. His shoulders were now slumped, and he looked very tired.

He scraped the chair back and sat down, then dug a key ring out of his pocket and unlocked my cuffs. I folded my arms but didn't get up as he spun the key on the table, looking a little sheepish.

"I'm sorry, Detective," he said.

I didn't answer. Not only because I was no longer a detective, but also because I was now seriously pissed off. Maybe Feldon had reviewed my distinguished Army file, or the numerous news stories about my recent losses in Phoenix, and concluded I couldn't be his man. Maybe I'd simply cornered him with the evidence tag, and he now felt the risk of holding me was no longer worth whatever objective he was trying to achieve by arresting me in the first place.

It didn't matter. Either way, I wasn't interested in his contrition.

"We'll get you back to your motel," he said. "I apologize for the inconvenience."

"A violent arrest followed by illegal detainment and a sloppy attempt to frame me is more than an inconvenience."

"Nothing about this was illegal," Feldon protested, a little too quickly.

"You never read me my rights. I was never offered an attorney. Or was that White's job?"

Feldon flushed.

I stood. He held out a hand.

"Just...wait. You're not being detained. But if you could answer a couple of questions, it would be a big help."

"I'm sure it would. But that's not happening."

I scooped the knife and wallet off the table, replacing the cards and pocketing them. "Your people took my money. Nine hundred and fifty-two dollars."

"We'll get it for you," Feldon said, still seated.

I retrieved the Bible next, dusting it off and then lifting the cover to ensure Mia's photograph was still safely nestled inside. It didn't appear molested.

Then I started for the door, my flip-flops smacking the cold concrete.

"It's not about you, Mr. Sharpe," Feldon said. "I just want to know about the kid."

I stopped at the door, my hand on the knob, about to plow through. Feldon didn't move behind me, and I almost pushed ahead.

Instead I just stood there, facing the door. I knew talking to Feldon was stupid. Not only because talking to any interrogator without a lawyer is ill advised, but also because this man had tried to frame me less than half an hour prior.

But when I thought of Jalen, my natural curiosity outweighed my better sense. I reviewed the interaction in my mind for the second time and still couldn't see how anything about the troubled young man warranted interest from the DEA.

I turned back. "What about the kid?"

Feldon motioned to the chair. I didn't sit.

He ran a hand through his already disheveled hair, looking more exhausted than ever. I wondered if this was a ploy—if White was on the other side of the mirror, watching and recording, while Feldon played good cop.

Probably.

I turned for the door again.

"His name is Jalen Powell," Feldon said. "He's the half-brother of one Anthony Cox, a local gang leader."

I stopped at the door again. Feldon looked over his shoulder. "Anthony is serving life for the torture and murder of a federal agent, but the gang he operated is still thriving here in Atlanta."

"So?" I prompted.

"So twice this month Cox has met with his attorney at the prison. Those conversations are confidential, of course. Attorney-client privilege. But after each meeting, Jalen turns up at the attorney's office."

I squinted, evaluating the trail of events and quickly reaching a logical conclusion.

"You think the attorney is funneling messages from Cox to Jalen."

Feldon nodded. "And through Jalen to the gang, enabling Cox to continue calling the shots from prison."

I chewed my lip, still not seeing where I fit in to any of that. If the DEA suspected Jalen of passing messages from his imprisoned brother to gang members around the city, it made sense for them to keep him under surveillance. That would explain why they knew about my interaction with Jalen outside the diner.

But it didn't explain why I was arrested.

I decided I didn't care. Feldon might still be playing games, and I was growing tired of being cold and shirtless in a bland interrogation room. In fact, I was growing tired of Atlanta in general. I figured I could return to the motel, forgo the remainder of the night sleeping, and get a head start on reaching those Georgia pines. Maybe make it south of the city and locate a state park where I could camp for a few days. Work on my fireside culinary skills.

I reached for the door. Feldon called after me.

"Please, Mr. Sharpe. I just want to know what Jalen said to you. It could be important."

"It's not," I said.

"Why was he in your truck?" Feldon pressed.

I ignored him, pulling the door open. White stood outside, blustering as he rose from a chair, clearly pissed to have been sidelined. I ignored him and made for the hallway. Feldon cut me off.

"Look," he said. "Cop to cop."

"I'm not a cop anymore," I said. "Or didn't you read the news stories?"

Feldon's face fell, just a little, confirming my suspicions. He knew all about my departure from the Phoenix Police Force.

The school shooting.

Mia.

It made me angry, somehow. As though I had been forced to expose my own most tragic moments just to liberate myself from what was clearly a sloppy and unjustified arrest in the first place.

"Man to man, then," Feldon said. "Give me ten minutes. I'll make it worth your while."

I glanced sideways at White. The little rat man was still lurking just behind Feldon, glaring at me. I wanted to punch him. This whole situation made me want to punch them both.

But the tone of Feldon's voice got to me, nonetheless. Maybe because I was still curious. Maybe because years of government service had programed me to want to help law enforcement.

Or maybe because I wanted to know how a fifteen-year-old kid had fallen under the crosshairs of one of the nation's largest and most powerful agencies.

I decided my exploration of south Georgia could wait a little longer.

"Ten minutes. But we talk in your office—no recording devices. And rat-face stays outside."

8

The office Feldon led me to was small, completely undecorated, and equipped with only a metal desk and two cheap chairs. A mess of wires and a laptop sat on the desk, alongside a lamp trailing a power cord across the floor. The sparseness and chaos of it all reinforced my opinion that this wasn't Feldon's primary office. This was some kind of field thing.

A temporary operations center.

Feldon shut White outside and offered me a chair, then settled behind his desk. He asked if I wanted coffee.

"I'm good," I said. "This time of day I usually like to be sleeping."

"Yeah." Feldon nodded. "Sorry about that."

He seemed unsure where to begin. I made a show of checking my watch.

"Are you familiar with fentanyl?" Feldon asked.

The question took me off guard. I shrugged. "I know what it is."

"Do you know what it's doing?"

I did. Any cop in North America with more than a week

on the job knew all about fentanyl. A synthetic drug able to be manufactured entirely underground, it was easy to make and almost impossible to track. Loads of it was being cooked up in Mexico and slipped across the border every day. They called them "M30s"—little green pills with an *M* stamped on one side, and a 30 on the other—thirty milligrams.

A member of the opioid family, fentanyl was similar to oxycodone in its roots, but far more potent.

And more destructive.

"Fentanyl is fifty times more powerful than heroin," Feldon said. "But the high wears off quickly, and withdrawals kick in early. So all the side effects—all the damage addiction can do—is infinitely worse with fentanyl."

"I saw it in Phoenix," I said.

"Then you know how bad the epidemic is," Feldon said. "There are nearly a hundred thousand overdose deaths in the US every year, and a majority of those are now due to fentanyl or fentanyl-laced drugs. The Mexicans are mixing it up in underground labs south of the border. They pack it in plastic wrap like cocaine, then slather those packages in food and household chemicals to block the smell. Keep the dogs off it. They hide it inside personal vehicles and drive it right across the border by the trunk load. Day and night."

"And you can't stop that?" I asked. I knew the answer, but I was still pissed and felt like throwing a barb.

"Fifty thousand vehicles cross the border every day at Tijuana alone," Feldon said. "Imagine hiding a few hundred aspirin tablets in the frame of your truck, all slathered up in laundry detergent so the dogs can't smell them. How am I supposed to find that without backlogging traffic all the way to Los Angeles?"

"You found my cocaine easily enough."

Feldon's lips tightened, betraying the first hint of frustration. I checked my watch again.

"Here's the point," he said. "I've been stationed in Atlanta for three years. I only have one job—shut down fentanyl. The problem began in California and the southwest, but it's spread now. We've got M30s pouring into the southeast and up the coast. Atlanta is becoming a hotbed for distribution. The cartels are tapping into local gangs to help move the product across the region."

"I still don't see what that has to do with a fifteen-year-old kid," I said.

"South Atlanta Squad," Feldon said. "Or SAS—probably a play off the British Special Air Service, or else just a coincidence. I really don't know."

"Local gang?" I asked.

"That's right. African American gang, specifically. A big one. Jalen's half-brother, Anthony, was somewhere near the top. A shot caller, at the least. Maybe closer to a boss. They operate all across south Atlanta, from downtown to the airport. Pittsburgh, Mechanicsville, Adair Park, Oakland City. There are a few dozen outfits running those neighborhoods, but the SAS is something else. They got their start shifting weed, then cocaine and heroin. The usual progression."

"But now it's fentanyl," I said.

"Right. And they're damn good at what they do. Most gangs around here are all about status. They want the local cops to see them trolling around. They put a lot of value on intimidation. The SAS is much less territorial, and they don't flaunt their identity. They operate more like a cartel than a street gang, making them almost impossible to pin down. Their network has exploded over the last eighteen months. We've found their drugs in half a dozen major southern cities. It's like a virus."

"And you think Anthony Cox is still calling the shots?" I said.

"We know he is," Feldon said, his eyes turning cold. "Cox

is a cold-blooded murderer. We had a guy on the inside—deep cover. He got busted, and Cox..."

Feldon broke off, swallowing hard. He looked away and chugged water from a bottle. "Cox killed him, cartel style."

I winced, not needing details. With Phoenix lying only a hundred and twenty miles north of the Mexican border, I was familiar with how the cartels handled rats and moles. It was something of a sport down there, inventing increasingly brutal methods of torture and execution. Videos leaked onto the internet highlighted the more gruesome examples.

Chainsaw beheadings. Prisoners burned or skinned alive. Others mutilated slowly, over hours or even days, before being fed to starving jungle cats.

There was no limit to cartel brutality. If some of that brutality had seeped onto American streets, I could understand why Feldon was so desperate for a lead.

But he was still on the wrong track.

"Jalen didn't mention his brother," I said. "I was eating dinner when he turned up and tried to steal my truck. I confronted him, then drove him home. Tried to talk some sense into him. That was the extent of our interaction."

"Why your truck?" Feldon asked.

I shrugged. "It's old. Easy to hot-wire. The kid is smart."

"We know the SAS network is growing," Feldon said. "Cox has a lot of contacts. People driving in from the east coast to negotiate distribution rights..."

He trailed off, and my back stiffened. Suddenly, I felt like a walking moron. It was so obvious I should have seen it a mile away, but I was distracted by Jalen's involvement and the sincerity of Feldon's pleas for help.

Feldon *still* suspected me. He thought I was from North Carolina, driving down to stage a plausible and excusable run-in with Jalen to negotiate my slice of the growing fentanyl trade.

Unbelievable.

And I fell for it.

I stood, shaking my head. "You people are something else."

Feldon's face grew hard. "You're a long way from home, Mr. Sharpe. With no good reason to be here."

"Try freedom of travel," I snapped. "Try the Fifth Amendment."

I turned for the door.

"Don't go far, Mr. Sharpe. We might need to chat again."

I stopped, the doorknob icy under my hand. I thought about every interaction I'd ever had with the CIA, FBI, and DEA.

Three-letter agencies. Eager to nail their man. Willing to push the envelope and blur the lines.

Whatever it takes.

Then I shoved through the door and made for the exit.

9

B y the time I got my money back from the DEA and hired a taxi to cart me to the motel, it was almost sunrise. Feldon offered to give me a lift back, but by that point I was sick of seeing his face. I figured I'd reach the motel in time to repack the truck, then grab breakfast at the Waffle House across the street before hitting the road south. My visit to Atlanta would be brief, but Feldon, the weather, and the traffic had conspired to kill any ambitions I had of further exploration.

I was still thinking about a quiet campsite and a burnt ribeye.

As it turned out, I reached the motel not a moment too soon. The manager was on-site, freaking out about the busted door and hurling my stuff over the railing into the parking lot. The plastic bin I kept my camping gear in was busted, and clothes were strewn across the hood of the pickup. I ran from the taxi just in time to catch my falling duffel bag, the violin wrapped in a sweatshirt inside.

"Did you do this?" the manager shouted, pointing to the busted door.

"What do you think?" I snapped, scooping up socks and underwear from the grimy parking lot.

"You're gonna pay for this! Your room—your responsibility."

I snorted a laugh, examining my shattered bin and the gear it contained. My camping stove was dinted, but everything else seemed relatively unharmed. I packed it all into the passenger side of the truck, leaving just enough room to fit the duffel bag and its delicate cargo on top. Then I slammed the door and left the busted bin on the concrete.

"Hey!" the manager shouted from the second-floor walkway. "You hear me? You owe me two hundred bucks for the door!"

"Bill the DEA," I retorted, circling to the driver's seat. "I didn't kick that door down."

The old GMC fired right up, the one windshield wiper scraping automatically across the glass. I allowed the engine a while to warm as the manager continued to scream curses. Carbureted motors aren't like modern fuel injection. They take time to heat up, forcing me to endure the grimy premises of the Peachtree Motel for another few minutes.

As the motor rumbled and the manager continued to shout, I thought about Jalen. It felt like days since our encounter at the diner, but that was only because I hadn't slept much. I remembered the momentary fear in his eyes when I tapped on the window, and the way he shrank back at the mention of cops.

Typical reactions for a fifteen-year-old kid. Perfectly logical.

Except that Jalen wasn't just *any* fifteen-year-old kid. He was a neck-deep participant in an advanced street gang, passing messages for an imprisoned brother and stealing cars on the side.

It was the carjacking that I couldn't reconcile with

Feldon's description of Jalen as an up-and-coming gangster. I remembered what it felt like to boost cars as an orphaned fifteen-year-old hanging out with the wrong crowd on the grungy streets of Phoenix. We stole plenty of things back in the day—usually motorcycles, and usually for no greater purpose than a short joyride.

It wasn't about money. It was about thrill. And respect. And attention.

I assumed the same was true of Jalen when I first met him, but now I wasn't sure. An established member of a profitable drug gang wouldn't be stealing trucks on the side. The gang wouldn't allow it—it was a needless risk for everyone involved. And Jalen wouldn't need the attention, anyway. He was already running with the big dogs.

So why had he attempted to take my truck?

I saw the manager crashing down the steps, headed my way, and I shifted into reverse. I wasn't sticking around to hear any more of his outbursts. Navigating toward the highway, I skipped the Waffle House and turned immediately south. The truck ran well, but I noted the fuel gauge slipping closer to the quarter-tank mark.

I'd stop south of the city, outside the crush of traffic. Refuel and load up on cheap food from a grocery store. And then...

I thought about Jalen again. His face popped back into my mind like the lyrics of a nagging song that simply wouldn't go away. I couldn't put my thumb on it, but something just felt wrong.

I remembered again my years on the streets populated by increasingly rash and risky criminal activity, beginning with petty theft and leading into minor drug dealing. Eventually that activity got me busted. I was picked up at seventeen for possession with intent to distribute, but I scored an old-school judge.

The kind of judge who believed that prisons built recidivists, but the Army built reformers.

He gave me a choice, and choosing a green uniform over an orange one was the best thing that ever happened to me. But Jalen might not get so lucky. Special Agent Mark Feldon had his sights on that kid like a trophy buck, eager to bring him down.

Not because he hated Jalen. Because he hated Anthony Cox. Because there was a score to settle between the DEA and the South Atlanta Squad. Regardless of Jalen's involvement, his life would quickly become collateral damage. The DEA would flatten him, like they flattened so many in the name of their multi-decade war on drugs.

Like the CIA flattened Afghani villagers in their quest to hunt Taliban leaders.

Like the FBI exploited personal communications in the name of hunting organized crime.

Three-letter agencies, eager to get their man. Willing to do whatever it took.

I hit the brakes at a red light, the truck rumbling gently beneath me. The sun was coming up now. It was still early, but the city was already alive with traffic.

I flicked my blinker on. In another thirty seconds I made the block and was pointed back north again—toward the apartment complex where I dropped Jalen off.

There might be nothing I could do for Anthony Cox's little brother. If Jalen was hell-bent on a life of crime, the law would catch him sooner or later. But I couldn't convince myself that things were as simple as Feldon believed.

I could spare a few hours to test that theory.

According to my watch, it was a Wednesday. In early April Jalen should be headed to school, but I remembered what he'd said before about dusty old books and having better things to do.

He might be still around.

The complex was a mess. It reminded me of things I'd seen overseas—tired buildings patched together, with dirty sidewalks and dusty foot trails weaving among them. Trash danced across the street and piled up next to overfull dumpsters. Some windows were broken and covered over with cardboard and duct tape. Others were blacked out with spray paint.

A couple of guys with low-slung jeans and headbands wandered down the sidewalk, casting me hostile glances as I puttered down the street to Jalen's place. I noted gunmetal gray handkerchiefs hanging from each of their front pockets and wondered if gray was an SAS color.

Probably not. According to Feldon's description of the South Atlanta Squad, they weren't the types to loiter on street corners, flashing colors. These must be some other local gangbangers.

I parked the truck a hundred yards from Jalen's apartment, pulling close to the curb behind a Chevy Caprice on blocks. Cutting the engine, I settled into the seat, keeping my head low and relying on the obliviousness of a fifteen-year-old to further obscure my presence.

I didn't want him to know I was here. I wasn't sure what I expected to find, just skulking in the background, but I didn't want to talk to him. I wanted to see him in his natural environment, maybe blowing off school to distribute messages to Anthony's lieutenants.

If I saw that, I could rest assured that Jalen was as guilty as Feldon assumed, and I could head south without any guilt of my own. I wouldn't relish in Jalen's impending demise, but at least I wouldn't feel party to an unjust railroading.

I embraced the stillness and rested one arm against the pile of camping gear next to me, my stomach growling. Skipping breakfast now felt like a dumb idea.

An hour dragged by. The truck cabin was small for my six-foot-two frame, leaving my legs feeling a little cramped as I slouched down. I still saw no sign of Jalen. I wanted to get out and stretch, but I didn't want to risk being spotted if he suddenly appeared.

I twisted to relieve cramps in my right leg, then froze as the screen door of Jalen's unit blasted open, and the kid appeared. I didn't recognize him at first, because his head was twisted toward the interior of the apartment, calling over his shoulder to somebody inside. Then he hopped the porch and hit the sidewalk, walking in a gentle roll.

The yellow Hawks hoodie was gone, now replaced by a red Hawks jersey and gym shorts. Jalen walked with a basketball clamped under one arm, brand-new Nikes navigating among the trash blowing across the sidewalk.

It was a little chilly for the skimpy wardrobe, but I didn't have to guess why he'd forgone the heavier clothes of the day before. Not long after leaving his apartment, he was joined by another boy about the same age, but a few inches taller. This kid wore a Heat jersey, and the two exchanged some manner of complicated handshake before disappearing behind a building.

I left the truck and set off down the sidewalk. The morning was brisk, and it felt good to walk. Within seconds I was far enough down the block to catch a glimpse around Jalen's building. The kid and his friend were passing around a corner, falling out of sight again.

I broke into a jog, reaching the end of the street at a cul-de-sac and taking a turn onto another sidewalk leading deeper into the community while keeping a couple of buildings between myself and Jalen.

I had a pretty good idea where he was headed. I'd lived in government housing on a couple of occasions as a kid, and knew they were mostly designed the same way—a field of identical brick buildings, each housing multiple units, with parking lots sprinkled among them. Somewhere near the heart of the complex would be a little green space with a small playground and a couple of picnic tables.

Or, in the case of a big complex like this one, a basketball court.

I was right about the park, and I knew I was right about the basketball court before I even saw it. I could hear the rhythmic thump of a ball against concrete, mixed with the shouts and laughs of young voices.

I stopped at the end of the sidewalk and poked my head around the corner, conscious of how conspicuous I looked to any legitimate resident of the community.

The basketball court lay fifty yards away, surrounded by a ten-foot chain-link fence. There was a goal on each end, with faded paint marking the free throw and three-point lines. The nets were long gone, leaving only rusting rims clinging to dented backboards.

The kids on the court didn't seem to notice. There were six of them—a three-on-three match, with Jalen in possession of the ball. I recognized him immediately by the red jersey. His buddy with the Heat jersey was joined by another kid in a blue T-shirt.

The other three were shirtless and already glimmering with sweat. An old-fashioned game of shirts versus skins, played by a crew of truants with better things to do than look at dusty old books.

I glanced over my shoulder to confirm I hadn't been busted by a watchful neighbor, then slipped around the building and made a beeline for the end of the park opposite the basketball court. There was a bench there, situated under an oak tree, about eighty yards from the court. It sat in plain view of the kids, but I didn't expect them to be paying attention. The game was heating up. Shouts now joined the dribble of the ball and the occasional thump of rubber against a goal's backboard.

I got comfortable on the bench, watching through my sunglasses. Somebody had committed a foul, and the Heat kid was making a free throw. He missed, and the game resumed. Skins took the ball, but Jalen committed a steal almost immediately before swerving past a defender and making a rush for the goal.

The ball moved like an orange flash, gliding behind his back and beneath his leg. One of the shirtless boys had a good six inches on Jalen and worked hard to dislodge the ball, but he was simply too slow.

Jalen gave him the slip, driving for the goal again. Another defender blocked him, but Heat was wide open. I watched for Jalen to pass the ball. His friend jumped and called for it, both arms raised, open for a scoring shot.

Jalen ignored him, twisting again, backstepping to the three-point line and taking a shot of his own.

He missed—by a lot. The tall kid swatted the ball as it passed overhead, knocking it off course. Then it was back in the hands of the skins, rushing to the other end of the court.

A missed opportunity.

I settled against the tree and observed for another fifteen minutes as the ball passed back and forth, scoring sometimes and being turned over others. Whenever shirts were in possession, Jalen was generally in control of the ball. He was good at moving it, gliding down the court and easily dodging defenders.

But he was bad at shooting and almost never passed it off to either of his taller teammates. Most of his shots bounced off the ring or hit high on the backboard, quickly landing in the possession of the skins.

It was a study in character, I thought. A lot of talent. And a lot of selfishness.

I was starting to think I'd wasted my time returning to the housing project when I saw the older kids round the corner. There were four of them, all late teens or early twenties, dressed in loose pants and loose shirts. I noted gunmetal gray headbands wrapped around three of their skulls and hanging out of the pocket of the fourth.

It was the same color I'd seen on the two guys I passed when entering the community. This complex must be established territory.

The four guys sauntered right for the basketball court, and one of them called out a jeer as Jalen took another shot. The shot missed, but nobody rushed in for the rebound. The ball bounced twice on the concrete before being recovered by Jalen, and the game froze over like a lake in Milwaukee.

Everybody stared at the newcomers. The bigger guys drifted into the court, hands in their pockets, sneering at the younger kids. I picked out the leader easily enough. He was taller than the rest and skinny. He wore the gray bandana like a hat, covering his entire head and tucked in at the back.

And he bore down directly on Jalen.

"Wassup, punk?"

The words were clear, even from across the park. The court was dead silent.

Jalen held the ball under one arm, his chin up. Defiant.

"I thought I told your boys not to roll around here?" Bandana Hat said.

Jalen sneered. "What, you think you king or something?"

Bandana Hat laughed, throwing a glance over one shoulder to his compatriots. They laughed also, spanning out in a semicircle around the shirts and skins.

I watched from the bench, still unmoving. For now.

"You got a lot of lip for such a little shrimp," Bandana Hat said. He took a jab at the ball, trying to punch it free of Jalen's grasp. Jalen released it and dribbled it once behind his back, recovering it with his opposite arm. The movement was a blur, just a flash of orange. Bandana Hat punched at thin air.

"Don't trip, homie." Jalen laughed.

Anger flashed across Bandana Hat's face. His shoulders squared, and one hand made a fist. But he didn't swing.

The kid in the blue shirt and all three of the skins backed out of the court, leaving only Heat to stand near Jalen.

"Look here," Bandana Hat snapped. "Deadline's coming. You gotta pick a side or get rolled, you feel me? I'm here to warn you."

The threat was obvious, but Jalen didn't look concerned. He held his chin up, defying the bigger boy without a hint of fear in his posture.

"*Bounce*, bruh," Jalen said. "Before I pop yo ass."

Bandana Hat's eyes grew wide. He glanced in disbelief to one of his companions.

"You hear this cat?" he said.

I stiffened, watching as the bigger boy's shoulders tensed —the precursor of a right hook. Jalen didn't notice. He was too busy staring the guy down. He took another step forward, and I sat up.

"I said *bounce*," Jalen growled.

Watch it, kid, I thought.

Nobody moved. Bandana Hat's fist remained clinched. Heat looked ready to piss himself. The other gangsters stood back, waiting for a cue from their leader.

Then Bandana Hat laughed, shoulders loosening.

"One week, Jay. That's all you got."

Bandana Hat turned, and I relaxed a little. Jalen held the ball under one arm, chin up, beaming. He glanced over his shoulder to see the four boys outside the court, still looking panicked. Something crossed over Jalen's face.

Don't do it, kid.

"That's right, bitch!" Jalen called after Bandana Hat. "Bounce!"

The bigger kid froze. Heat took a step back. Jalen didn't move, too stupid to understand what he'd just done.

Then Bandana Hat spun, his fist knotted, and took the first swing.

11

T he whole scene disintegrated within seconds. The four kids outside the court tucked tail and ran. Jalen took a right hook to his face and stumbled back, nose spraying blood. Heat rushed in to avenge his friend, but then the three other boys closed around Bandana Hat, and what started as a fistfight dissolved into a beatdown.

I jogged toward the court as Heat was thrown to the ground and Jalen took a kick to the gut. Blood splashed, and Jalen fought back hard. His arms moved like striking snakes, getting in a couple of good hits across Bandana Hat's face before two of the other kids grabbed him by the shoulders and wrestled him back. Heat tried to get up, but the fourth gangster put a foot on his chest and stomped him down.

Bandana Hat drove a punishing blow into Jalen's stomach as I reached the edge of the court. Jalen choked and struggled to break free. The two bigger kids held him suspended by the arms now. A helpless target for the next strike.

"Drop him!" I called.

Everybody froze. Bandana Hat stood with his fist cocked

back, ready to knock Jalen's lights out. He looked over his shoulder, his face a mask of rage.

I didn't move, framed by the gate, my hands loose at my sides.

"Move along, man," Bandana Hat snarled.

I took a step inside. "Drop him," I repeated. "Or you'll wish you had."

Bandana Hat wiped blood from his lip. His two compatriots remained frozen over their subdued prey. Heat was still pinned to the concrete, and Jalen's nose ran like a faucet.

"You better roll, white boy," Bandana Hat said. "This don't concern you."

"I'll be the judge of that. Put him down and move along. This doesn't have to get ugly."

Bandana Hat sneered. "You threatening me, old man?"

I smiled, just a little. But I didn't move. "I never threaten anyone. I'm just letting you know what's good for you."

"Is that right?"

Bandana Hat smirked at his boys. Then his right hand dipped into his pocket, and a sharp *snap* rang across the court, accompanied by the appearance of glimmering steel.

A switchblade. Three inches. Double-edged, dagger style. *Great.*

Bandana Hat pointed the knife at my face. "Imma give you one more chance. You roll now or imma spill your guts right here."

I sighed. Put my fingers together and gently stretched each one until the knuckles popped. The process was methodical, and I didn't hurry.

"Arms or legs?" I asked.

"Huh?"

"Arms or legs?" I repeated. "I never go for the back. Too much risk of permanent disablement. Seems cruel to cripple a man who's already mentally challenged."

Bandana Hat appeared genuinely confused—not the brightest bulb in the box. He looked to his compatriots for clarification, apparently unsure whether I was dissing him or somebody else. Then his cheeks flushed.

"Boy, you better—"

"Dealer's choice, then," I said, hands falling to my sides. "Don't say I didn't warn you."

He rushed me, leading with the blade just like I knew he would. I stepped calmly to the right at the last possible moment, letting the blade slice past my face before I grabbed his knife arm, pushing down and back, bending the elbow in a way it wasn't created to bend.

Bandana Hat's own inertia snapped the bone like a twig, and the knife hit the ground. I spun left, allowing him to tumble as momentum took over, then drove my right foot into his left calf just as the knee hit concrete.

Another snap of bone—a fractured fibula or a dislocated ankle. Who cared? Dealer's choice.

The entire exchange took less than three seconds. Bandana Hat lay on the ground, writhing in pain while his three soldiers stood slack-jawed, unsure what had happened. Then they all moved at once, rushing me as more knives flashed, and Jalen hit the concrete.

This time I didn't wait. I ducked and retrieved Jalen's fallen basketball, clamping it between both hands and using it as a shield as the first boy slashed at me with a folder. Blade met rubber and stuck, and I shoved the ball into his chest, throwing him off balance. The next guy made a pass at my face, and I ducked just in time, shooting out with my right foot and catching him in the shin.

The third guy got me. Pain flashed from my arm as steel bit flesh, but it was a sloppy and hurried slash, delivered from too far away.

I grabbed him by the back of his neck and jerked—hard.

He lost balance and hit the pavement. Before his face collided with the concrete, I was engaged with the first kid again. He had abandoned his knife in the fallen basketball and now swung at my face, fast and reckless. I caught his arm, driving an uppercut of my own straight into his chin. Teeth crunched, and his eyes rolled back. Then he was down.

Only one guy remained—the guy I'd shin-kicked three seconds previously. He ran before I could reach him, jumping his fallen comrades and breaking for the gate. The guy who'd face-planted on the concrete scrambled on his stomach for his fallen knife. I swept his legs apart with one flick of my ankle, then drove my foot into his crotch.

Not hard enough to end his family name. Just hard enough to end his summer.

He puked, and I retrieved his knife. It was a cheapo—some crap from Walmart. I tossed it over the fence and collected Bandana Hat's switchblade.

It was much nicer. A Microtech Troodon, all black with a three-inch dagger-style blade. A three-hundred-dollar knife, almost anywhere. Spoils of war.

I retracted the blade with a push of the double-action button and pocketed the knife. Then I looked for Bandana Hat.

He was limping out of the court, supported by the guy with the busted jaw, while the guy I had groin-kicked was crawling after them. I watched them go, shooting Bandana Hat a two-finger salute. His eyes blazed, but he didn't hang back for more.

Maybe he was smarter than I thought.

I turned to find Heat helping Jalen up, Jalen's face coated in blood and tears, and Heat's pants soaked with piss. I calmly held out a hand.

"You all right?" I asked.

Jalen spat blood, looking first to the crimson-stained concrete, then to his ball. Then back to me.

"What the hell?" he shouted.

I shrugged. "They started it."

"No, bruh. *I* started it. What are you even doing here, man?"

"Saving your ass," I snapped, not bothering to disguise my irritation. "But please, hold the applause. No thanks necessary."

Jalen mopped blood off his nose, hurrying to retrieve the busted basketball. He scooped it up and jerked his head toward Heat. Both boys started for the gate.

"Where are you going?" I called. "I want to talk to you."

"Yeah? Well, I don't want to talk to *you*, man."

I bristled, feeling suddenly flushed. I wasn't sure what reaction I expected after swooping in to save Jalen from a beatdown, but this wasn't it. I covered the court quickly, blocking the gate.

"Hey," I snapped. "You're not gonna storm off like this. I just saved you a good pounding. You owe me—"

"Man, I don't owe you nothing!" Jalen shouted. "What, you think you just *helped* me?"

He shook his head in disbelief, looking again to his ball. I saw tears in his eyes, and my stomach twisted. I softened my tone.

"I'm sorry about the ball. I'm happy to replace it."

Jalen slung the flattened rubber to the ground, dragging the back of his hand across his nose. "Man, forget the ball. This ain't *about* that. You think you can just roll up in here and pound people, and that makes things better?"

"They were going to send you to the hospital," I said.

Jalen cursed. "So they send me to the hospital. Don't you know nothing? This is my crib, bruh. My turf! I can't let them shove me around like that. I take the beating now, and maybe get some respect. But you just broke 'em, man. They're gonna be back, now. They're gonna hurt me for real!"

I shook my head. "No. I won't let them."

Jalen shoved me, so fast and so hard I stumbled back. "You ain't gonna do *nothing*, you hear me? I don't need your white ass causing problems for my boys. Get the hell out of here, and don't come back!"

"Jalen, wait." I held out a hand.

Jalen brushed me off. "*Bounce*, bruh. I got somewhere to be."

Jalen stomped through the gate. Heat followed, glaring daggers at me. I watched them go, a little stunned, a little disoriented. As the battle rage faded from my mind, I thought again about the exchange in the basketball court. The way Bandana Hat had approached Jalen.

He hadn't threatened Jalen personally—not at first. No. He'd said, *"I told your boys not to roll around here."* The beef was over Jalen's friends. Maybe kids from another neighborhood who were visiting Jalen's basketball court.

Jalen was sticking up for his people. For his territory.

And he was right—I hadn't helped anything. Maybe I'd forgotten more about life in Jalen's shoes than I was willing to admit.

I watched as Jalen exchanged an abbreviated form of his complex handshake with Heat, his eyes still red, his cheeks still puffy.

"See ya Friday night," Jalen said.

"You sure, bruh?" Heat questioned.

Jalen glowered back at me, wiping his nose. "Hell yeah."

Then the two parted ways, and Jalen disappeared around a brick building.

I was suddenly conscious of open windows all around me. I wondered how many people had witnessed the fight, and realized that it didn't matter. Nobody would take up for me against a local gang. But they might take up for the gang.

I jogged back to the truck, wiping blood from my forearm as I slid inside. I started the engine and reached for the shifter; then something caught my eye from the direction of Jalen's apartment.

A hundred yards away, a white and blue van was parked against the curb, lights on, rear hatch open. I recognized the stance of one of those medical minivans—the kind modified to accept a ramp and a motorized chair. A driver stood next to it, sipping on a soda while watching the apartment complex.

My gaze drifted to Jalen's unit, and I saw another man dressed in a light blue uniform assisting an old lady in a wheelchair to exit the apartment. She might have been seventy-five or a hundred. From this far away, it was impossible to say, but it wasn't difficult to see that she was frail. Snow-white hair adorned her head, and an oxygen bottle on a hand truck stood in the doorway behind her.

As I watched, Jalen appeared around the corner, waving to the medical guy but turning his face toward the apartment.

Shielding his battle scars.

The medical guy eased the wheelchair down the steps, and Jalen hurried to follow with the oxygen bottle. He placed a hand on the old woman's shoulder and bent down to kiss her on the cheek.

She beamed when she felt his hand. She said something, and both the medical guy and Jalen laughed. They wheeled the old woman toward the medical van, and Jalen followed with the cart, casting nervous glances around the complex.

Probably looking out for more of Bandana Hat's friends coming to avenge him.

My stomach twisted.

The old lady rolled into the medical van, and I shifted

into reverse. Backing out of the parking lot, I found my way onto the surface streets and then wound toward the highway.

In another minute I was lost amid a crush of Atlanta traffic packed around my truck like bees in a beehive. But I wasn't headed south, out of town. I was headed north, back into the city. My second interaction with Jalen had left me with more questions than answers, while reinforcing my gut instinct that Feldon was wrong about Anthony's little brother.

With blood on my knuckles and Jalen's frustrated outburst still ringing in my ears, I knew I'd stumbled into something. For better or worse, I couldn't just walk away.

12

I found the Atlanta Public Library's Central branch on Margaret Mitchell Square, not far from the heart of downtown. All around me tall skyscrapers reached into the murk of morning clouds, and traffic buzzed along in endless currents.

I parked my truck in the public parking garage across the street and ran my fingers through my hair before stepping inside. I didn't look great. My already disheveled condition was now exacerbated by a sleepless night spent with Feldon and dried blood on my sleeve from the superficial cut I'd sustained during the fight.

But I wasn't worried about my appearance. Later that day I could book a room at a hotel with a clean shower and wash up. For now, I had other things on my mind. Things like Jalen, who he really was, and what had happened to his family.

The interaction at the basketball court had reinforced my suspicions that Jalen wasn't a hardened gangster. None of the kids in the gunmetal gray headbands would have screwed with him if Jalen were under the active protection of a gang as large as Feldon claimed the SAS to be. Also, his dedication to impressing his friends and mouthing off to his enemies lent credit to my theories that he was a hotheaded kid, eager for attention, and eager to prove himself.

Which would also explain why he tried to steal my truck.

But even though most of my guesses about Jalen's personality had proven correct, my understanding of his situation was drastically underinformed. Jalen had been right about my actions at the basketball court. I'd only made things worse for him, in the end. Those kids would be back—probably with whatever older guys ran the gang.

And then Jalen would be lucky to walk away with a broken fibula. If I was going to help him—actually *help* him —I owed him the effort of better understanding his predicament.

I left the switchblade and my Victorinox in the truck, figuring the library might have a metal detector at the door, and jogged across the street. The building was unique, with sharp angles and a lot of glass near the entrance. Very flamboyant in a geometric way, like a retired art studio. I found my way up the steps and inside, greeted by an Atlanta policeman and the metal detector I expected.

The lobby was large, and my footsteps echoed across the tile. I pocketed my hands and approached the reception desk, where a happy-looking black lady with pink lipstick and an "I Love Books" T-shirt sat behind the desk. She offered me a cheery good morning, and I returned the greeting.

"How can I help you, sir?"

"I was hoping to use a computer."

"Are you a card holder?"

I shook my head. "Just passing through town. I don't own a cell phone."

"Oh." She seemed slightly surprised, and her large eyes surveyed my disheveled wardrobe. She probably assumed me to be homeless, or at the least transient, because her lips puckered into a sympathetic little smile.

"I'm sure we can help you," she said, reaching for a clipboard. "Just fill out your name, here."

I completed the clipboard with a fake name—an old habit born out of years of sniffing around unfriendly places on the wrong side of the tracks. She accepted it back and ushered me to follow her.

The computer lab lay inside a glass-encased room—a bank of forty machines all sat on desks in long rows, with cheap chairs resting in front of them. There was nobody else in the room, and the librarian led me to the first computer. It fired up slowly, and she input a passcode.

"We limit use to thirty minutes," she said. Then, casting a glance around the room, she smiled ironically. "But, you know, if you need more, it's no problem."

"Slow day," I said.

"Everybody sleeping off that nail-biter!"

Momentary confusion faded as I remembered the motel clerk watching a basketball game the previous night. Hawks versus...

I couldn't remember.

"Did Atlanta win?" I asked.

She beamed. "You know it, honey. On a last second shot! You follow the NBA?"

"Not usually," I admitted. "But I hear the Hawks are on a roll."

"Oh, we gonna take the gold. This is our year!"

She turned for the door. "Call me if you need anything."

I waited for her to leave before resting my fingers on the keyboard. Then I navigated to a search engine, and the inputs began.

Anthony Cox.

The South Atlanta Squad.

DEA investigations in Georgia.

Undercover DEA agent killed.

I wanted to know everything—from the press, not from the DEA. As much of the full story as I could find.

The information came in a flood. A deluge of news stories was joined by public record incarceration files and court proceedings. It was a long, bloody, sad story, beginning almost two years prior when DEA Special Agent Drew Martin, who had spent the past fourteen months working undercover inside the South Atlanta Squad, was discovered dead in a railroad ditch south of town.

Dead, and faceless. From the shoulders up, his head had been peeled like an orange. Lacerations around his wrists confirmed restraints, and medical examiner records obtained by the *Atlanta Journal-Constitution* alleged that Martin had been *alive* during the peeling.

In fact, there were no other wounds on his body. No gunshots, cuts, or internal damage.

He drowned in his own blood.

I felt the sudden urge for fresh air and clicked out of the report on Martin's death. The next several stories I cycled through followed the progression of the resulting investigation. The FBI took over, backtracking Martin's last known location on a ruthless hunt for the truth of his murder.

Obviously, the SAS was a top suspect. Martin was undercover, after all. Somehow his cover must have been compromised. The face-peeling was a known torture method of Mexican cartels, and the SAS was thought to be associated with gangs south of the border.

The DEA wanted blood. The FBI was eager to close the case. Anthony Cox became their target.

Jalen's older brother was a known member of the Squad and a suspected triggerman, if not a gang boss. A quick arrest was followed by a flood of indictments, all spearheaded by a charge of first-degree murder. In record time Cox was arraigned. He pled not guilty, but that didn't slow the roll of a district attorney's office thirsty for a big win in a now highly publicized case.

A trial date was set, and a jury struck. Then came the court proceedings.

The prosecution's case was built on a foundation of direct evidence. Not only had investigators recovered a bloody hunting knife smeared with Cox's fingerprints from the scene of the crime, but they had also found traces of Cox's DNA on Martin's body, and splatters of Martin's blood on a dirty shirt in Cox's apartment. In the face of such damning evidence, Cox's state-assigned defense attorney chose a Hail Mary pass and argued insanity.

It didn't stick. The jury found Cox guilty on all counts, and the prosecution requested the death penalty. Only then did the momentum of Cox's doom hit a roadblock—one of the jurors refused to vote for capital punishment, objecting on moral grounds. Without twelve votes, Georgia law prohibited execution, and Anthony was shipped off to USP Hartwell in South Carolina instead.

A maximum-security prison.

For the rest of his life.

I assimilated the facts quickly while fighting to ignore the images of Martin's faceless head my imagination had so quickly generated. It was a gruesome picture. I could see him choking on his own blood, gasping for breath, unable to blink without his eyelids.

Or maybe he passed out from the pain and suffocated while unconscious.

Either way, it wasn't hard to see why Feldon was on such a witch hunt. During my days in the Army, or with the Phoenix PD, if one of my people had been captured and tortured that way, God knows I would have burned the world down.

But that didn't make Jalen deserving of being burned in the process.

I scrolled back to the part about Anthony Cox's defense attorney and tore off a sheet of notepaper from the pad next to the computer. I wrote down the name and the corresponding address—some office on the northwest side of town.

It was a local guy, working predominantly public service cases. Not a great lawyer, probably, but then again how do you defend a man like Cox? The fact that he'd even tried told me he was dedicated. Maybe dedicated enough to continue working with Cox through the obligatory appeals process.

If so, he might well be the attorney Feldon suspected of passing messages from Anthony to Jalen. The middleman, hiding behind the guise of attorney-client privilege, facilitating the operation of the SAS.

Which made him not so much dedicated as corrupt.

I crammed the note into my pocket and cleared the search history on the computer. Feldon's theory wasn't a bad one. Public attorneys don't make much money. Maybe the guy needed the payoff from the SAS to clear up his student loans.

Or maybe not. Because I still didn't understand how Jalen could be at the heart of this scheme, yet so unprotected by his brother's gang that gutter punks harassed him at his own home. Just like his attempted theft of my truck, it felt like a puzzle piece that wouldn't quite fit, and that left a hole in Feldon's theory.

Maybe the lawyer could exonerate Jalen. If so, that would at least take him off the DEA's map. Then maybe I could do something about those thugs in the gunmetal gray bandanas before getting back on the road to south Georgia.

I owed Jalen that much for the mess I had made.

13

The law office of Albert Benjamin Colby sat on a grungy street situated between a Burger King and an abandoned shopping strip. The neighborhood was called Bankhead and looked to be no nicer than any of the south Atlanta streets I'd found Jalen in.

The office itself wasn't really an office at all. At some point it might have been a small store—one of those retail places that sell title loans or cell phones. Now the windows were tinted and grimy, with white letters pasted across the front door:

A. B. Colby, Attorney at Law.

Only one car sat in the parking lot—a ten-year-old Honda Accord with balding tires and a Georgia State University sticker on the back glass. An empty chip bag drifted across the parking lot as I exited the truck, and the air smelled of grease from the fast-food joint next door.

The office wasn't an expensive establishment. The car

wasn't a premium vehicle. If Colby was on the take from the SAS, he hid it well.

I left the truck and pocketed my hands, making for the door. Before I reached the sidewalk, a middle-aged, bald man dressed in a cheap department-store suit barreled out, fumbling with keys as the door swung shut behind him. A computer bag and four inches of documents in manila folders were clamped under one arm, and his socks didn't match. I could see one blue and one black from beneath the bottom edges of olive drab pants legs.

He dropped the keys and snapped a curse, bending to retrieve them. I saw the file folders slipping; then the whole pile left his arm and exploded over the sidewalk.

He screamed an angry curse and dove for the papers. I jogged in to help, kneeling and scooping them up as a gentle wind fought to distribute them across the city.

"Stop the receipts!" he called. I saw the folder crammed with stacked receipt paper flapping open and dropped a hand over it just in time to save the whole mass from being swept across the parking lot. The bald guy scrambled to gather the remaining papers, still clutching the keys in one hand, sweat glistening across his bare scalp.

In short order he packed everything into a wad. I handed off the receipt folder, and he took it without comment, not even meeting my gaze. The Honda's trunk popped open with a press of his thumb to the key fob, and he dumped everything in. Then he slammed the lid and stood motionless with both hands resting on the top. His eyes closed, and he breathed in short, angry bursts like an irate parent fighting not to rip their kid's head off after a snotty exchange.

I pocketed my hands, waiting for him to remember somebody else was present.

Maybe he simply didn't care.

He ran a hand over his forehead to scrub the sweat away, then marched to the office door, keys in hand.

"Mr. Colby?" I asked.

The guy laughed, shaking his head and still not facing me.

"Unfortunately," he muttered, jamming a key into the lock and twisting. He started toward the car, and I stepped forward.

"My name is Mason. I—"

"I'm not taking clients right now," Colby cut me off. "And honestly, I'm in a hurry. Thanks for the help."

"I'm not here about me. I'm here about Anthony Cox."

Colby stopped mid-step. He looked over his shoulder and subjected me to a piercing stare. Suspicious and exhausted, all at once.

"Who are you?" he growled. "Press?"

"No. I'm a friend of Jalen's."

Instant recognition washed across Colby's face. Recognition and annoyance.

"Look. I told that kid there's nothing I can do. I can't *make* the man file an appeal."

Colby reached for the door handle, and I blocked the door with one hand. He stiffened indignantly. I kept my voice low.

"What do you mean, you can't make him file an appeal? Make who?"

Colby squinted. The clouds were breaking up, and bright sun shone across his face. He was older than I first estimated. Late forties?

"Who are you?" Colby repeated.

"I told you. I'm a friend of Jalen's."

"Yeah, I got that part. What *kind* of friend?"

"The kind who's looking out for his best interests. The

kind who doesn't want to see him swept up in Anthony's mess."

Colby fidgeted with the car keys. He looked around the parking lot, almost as though he expected an army of gangsters to materialize out of thin air and gun us down.

Based on the look of the surrounding neighborhoods, I couldn't blame him.

"If you want to help Jalen, tell him to accept his brother's wishes. Tell him to focus on his own life."

"What wishes?" I pressed.

Colby squinted. "I thought you said you were his friend?"

"I'm a new friend."

"But you know about his brother?"

"Everybody does, apparently. He's in prison. You're his lawyer. Are you working the appeal?"

Colby looked away, snorting irritably. But he didn't reach for the door.

He *wanted* to talk. Or maybe to vent.

"Anthony's not filing an appeal, is he?" I asked. "Why not?"

"Oh please," Colby snapped. "Attorney-client privilege. You know I can't discuss that."

I frowned, more confused than when I arrived. I remembered what Feldon had said about Jalen visiting the lawyer, and glanced quickly around the parking lot, toward the abandoned shopping strip.

The surveillance car stuck out like a sore thumb. A dark blue sedan, parked a hundred yards away near a light pole. Too clean to have been sitting there long. Too new to belong to this neighborhood.

I looked back to Colby. "Jalen stopped by, right? You can talk about that."

Colby wiped his lip. "I really don't have time for this. But if you're a friend of Jalen's, do him a favor and kill this obsession. His brother isn't coming out. That's just reality. I can't change that, the ASJC can't change that, not even a miracle is gonna change that. Cox is *done*. Jalen should think about his own future."

Colby put a hand on the Honda's door handle. I kept my palm over the doorjamb.

"What is the ASJC?"

Colby rolled his eyes. "Atlanta Social Justice Coalition—local nonprofit working to revive impoverished communities. They have a pro bono legal wing. Overturning wrongful convictions, that kind of thing. I've got to go."

He yanked the door open. I stepped back, pocketing my hands. Colby folded himself in, starting the motor with a clanking whine. Then he paused, squinting up at me as the sun beat down.

"I did what I could, okay? I talked to Anthony. Twice. Jalen just has to accept that."

The door slammed. Colby rolled the window down and shifted into reverse.

"If you want to help him, get him out of here. That's the only way these kids survive. This city's a meat grinder...it'll kill us all in the end."

The Honda rolled out, and I watched him turn onto the highway. I thought again about what Feldon had said—about how the lawyer had visited Anthony Cox in prison twice over the past month, while Jalen had visited the lawyer.

It was a logical trail of events for a message-passing apparatus. But Colby's explanation felt just as logical. Had the DEA interviewed Colby to ask those questions?

I looked back to the sedan parked near the shopping strip, and knew they hadn't. Confronting Colby would tip their hand, and besides, they weren't interested in exonerating anybody.

They were only interested in decimating the SAS, once

and for all. Jalen would just be collateral damage, guilty or otherwise.

I walked quietly back to my truck, starting the engine but not pulling away. I sat with one hand resting on the steering wheel and thought about Jalen. Thought about what Colby had said.

"If you want to help him, get him out of here."

I knew what he meant. Atlanta wasn't the problem. No more than Phoenix, Detroit, or Chicago were. The cities were interchangeable. The realities of poverty, broken families, gang violence, and hopelessness were universal. If Jalen didn't find a way out of that cycle, he'd be broken down the same as Anthony—assuming he lived that long. With Feldon ready to roll over anything to bring down the SAS, and those gray bandana punks sure to resurface and exact vengeance on Jalen for the pounding I gave them, Jalen would be lucky to land in prison alongside his brother.

He'd be lucky to survive at all.

I looked toward the dark blue sedan and hoped they could see my face in a pair of binoculars. I held that invisible gaze as I turned the truck back to the highway; then I navigated toward downtown without hesitation.

If what Colby said was true, Jalen was innocent of the associations Feldon accused him of, but it would take time to prove that. In the meantime, the more immediate problem would be the amateur gangsters from the basketball court. Jalen was right—they'd be back for blood sooner rather than later.

I had to strike first.

14

I found a chicken finger restaurant called Zaxby's located just outside of downtown. It was built like a barn, with a metal roof and red siding, and a big chicken on the sign. I hadn't seen a Raising Cane's since leaving Arizona, and my existing hunger was now matched by a craving for my favorite lunch. So I parked the truck and went inside, figuring I would do my best thinking over a good meal.

I ordered the five-finger plate with slaw and sat in the back with a good view of the door. I wasn't expecting any of Bandana Hat's friends to track me across town, but I wasn't going to give them the chance to get the drop on me, either.

My chief problem now was intelligence. All I really knew about the kids at the basketball court was that they wore gray bandanas. I didn't have a gang name, a territory, or any idea where to find their bosses. Without that intel, my only other option would be to play bodyguard, indefinitely hanging around Jalen's apartment, waiting for them to turn up again.

And that wasn't happening.

I mopped chicken fingers through house sauce while contemplating the problem. The food was good—really good,

in fact. Different from Raising Cane's, but a suitable substi-
tute. I demolished the meal in ten minutes and sat staring at
the empty plate still smeared with ketchup and house sauce.

Red and brown, contrasting against each other. Like gang
colors.

I'd never been an official member of any outfit during my
teenage wannabe gangster phase, but I'd learned plenty
about street warfare as a cop. I knew all about the colors and
what they meant. It was something the Bloods and Crips
started back in Los Angeles. Red for bloods, blue for Crips.
Usually marked by bandanas, like some kind of uniform. A
way to identify friend from foe.

The gunmetal gray bandanas were probably the same. A
gang marker. Easy enough to identify, but that told me
nothing about the nature of the gang or what part of the city
they claimed. That was local intelligence, unique to Atlanta.
Something you wouldn't know unless you were in some way
involved.

I finished my Coke while studying the plate, still thinking
about that contrast. Then I shoveled everything into the trash
and found my way back to my pickup. Behind the Zaxby's a
strip mall ran the length of a sprawling parking lot, mostly
abandoned, with only a couple of discount stores and some
beauty shops remaining. I selected the nearest discount store
and walked to it, pushing through dirty glass into a faded
interior. It might have been a Kmart at some point, or a
Circuit City. One of those old department stores now long
dead amid the internet age. Now it was stocked with sagging
shelves, each loaded with scratch and dent products from
retailers around the nation. Toys, clothes, household products...and electronics.

I found a column of prepaid cell phones hanging from a
rack and scanned the length of them, selecting a model from
a brand I'd never heard of. It was a smartphone, like all

phones are these days, and it came loaded with a ration of talking minutes and internet data.

More than I needed.

I took the phone, along with a street map of Atlanta and a pack of cheap pens, and paid the cashier. Then I returned to my truck and used Bandana Hat's switchblade to slice the packaging open. The blade cut with a razor edge, and the phone spilled out alongside a charger. I powered it on and went through the obligatory setup process, registering the device under a fake name. Then I used the internet browser to look up the phone number for the Atlanta Police Department.

Not 911. I wanted to speak directly to the precinct.

"Atlanta Police Department, how may I direct your call?"

"I'd like to speak to your PIO, please."

"May I ask who's calling?"

"Chuck Barkley," I said, remembering my conversation with Jalen about famous Suns players.

"One moment."

I was put on hold, and boring music skipped and ground through the cheap speaker. I drummed my fingers on one knee and thought about the boneless wings advertised on the Zaxby's menu. Maybe I'd try those for dinner.

"Atlanta Police, Public Information Office," a flat male voice said. "How can I help?"

"Hi," I said again. "I'm Chuck Barkley. My family and I just moved into town, and I was hoping I could speak with you about local gang activity."

"Gang activity?" The guy sounded semi annoyed. Public information officers are usually designated by police departments to speak with local media, but they're also obligated to address the questions and concerns of citizenry. It could be a thankless, annoying job, usually passed down to rookies or officers who were otherwise unable to serve on patrol.

"Well..." I hesitated, trying to sound like a middle-class father of four who was distracted and overworked. I wasn't sure what that sounded like. "The thing is, Officer, my family and I just moved into a house south of town, and my son... he's fifteen. He's started wearing this gray bandana. It's got me worried."

"Gray?" The guy sounded ready to hang up.

"Yeah, you know. Like gunmetal gray. In his pocket or around his head. I asked him about it, but he won't talk. I'm worried he might be getting involved with a gang."

"You said you're on the south side of town?"

"Yeah, in Pittsburgh." I spouted off the name of one of the south Atlanta neighborhoods Feldon had mentioned. Stomping grounds of the SAS, apparently, but the SAS worked in the shadows. The guys in gray were something else.

The PIO tapped on a keyboard. The phone shifted against his shoulder, and he muttered to himself.

"There are quite a few active gangs in your part of town, Mr. Barkley. An outfit called Steel Mafia comes to mind. They've popped up around Pittsburgh a few times, and they wear gray, but they're an African American gang."

"What do you mean, *but*?" I knew the guy had assumed I was white, and I didn't care. But I wanted to keep him talking, and I wasn't above playing ignorant to do so.

"Gangs are very segregated here in Atlanta, Mr. Barkley. Unless he's black, it's unlikely Steel Mafia would accept him."

"Where do these Steel Mafia kids hang out?" I asked. "Is there someplace I should avoid?"

Another tired sigh. "They're not just kids, Mr. Barkley. Steel Mafia specializes in dealing crack cocaine. It's a highly addictive and very destructive drug, usually smoked with a pipe or straw."

I knew all about crack cocaine. Next to fentanyl, it was

one of the deadliest drugs on the streets of Phoenix. Even one hit was known to cause crippling addiction.

"Is this something I should be worried about?" I asked, again channeling the voice of what I thought a concerned father might sound like.

"If your son is wearing any particular color and won't talk about it, yeah, I'd be concerned. Steel Mafia works predominantly along Cleveland Avenue, near Perkerson Park and Sylvan Terrace. Pittsburgh is a little far north for them, but depending on where your son goes to school, they may have contacted him there. They're growing."

I made mental note of the neighborhoods he mentioned, scratching them down on the map with the pen.

"Are there any other gangs I should be concerned about?" I asked. "Any other colors?"

"There are at least sixty organized gangs in the Atlanta metropolitan area. All of them are dangerous."

"Anything specific I should look out for?" I pressed.

Another tired sigh. "You've got the Latin Kings and La Gran Familia—both Hispanic gangs. Bloods and Crips, of course. Red and blue, respectively. There's a new outfit working the Venetian Hills area called the Slash Crew. They're a hybrid gang—multiple races allowed. They wear orange, but I don't think they've really spread to Pittsburgh yet."

"Are they violent?" I asked.

The PIO actually laughed. "Mr. Barkley, this is Atlanta. Every gang is violent."

I thanked him and hung up, making another note on the edge of the map, then flipping it open and tracing my finger across south Atlanta. I found the neighborhood of Pittsburgh just south of the bypass, then moved west until I noted Venetian Hills, then south along Highway 75 until I found Cleveland Avenue.

Jalen's apartment complex was situated right in the middle of the three, like the heart of a lopsided triangle. The bullseye of a bloody target.

I scratched one cheek, feeling the rough razor stubble. I still looked like hell, but for a change, that might be useful.

Leaving the map in the truck, I returned to the discount store and navigated to their clothing section. I selected baggy jeans, a white T-shirt, a black jacket, and a bandana. An orange bandana.

I paid at the counter and changed in the bathroom. Then I returned to the truck, my new switchblade close to hand, headed back to south Atlanta.

15

I used the map to locate the neighborhoods of Perkerson Park and Sylvan Terrace, both communities running along Cleveland Avenue just west of Highway 75. The avenue itself was wide and smooth, rolling with steady traffic, and lined with convenience stores, check-cashing offices, and liquor dealers. A mix of new and old cars, some with spinner wheels and others with jet-black tinted windows, pulled in and out of parking lots, while an occasional police cruiser glided by along Cleveland and didn't stop.

I accepted that as a sign I was in the right place, and patrolled the streets north and south of Cleveland for a while, surveying the houses and taking note of drastically different levels of landscaping and repair from one to the next.

A house covered over by a worn tarp, with a PT Cruiser sitting on blocks in the driveway, was joined by a dressed-up craftsman next to it, with a brand-new Lexus sparkling in the drive and cutesy monogram letters on the mailbox. The next two houses were bashed and battered, with uncut grass and a couple of boarded-up windows.

Then there was another polished and restored family

home, with a Mercedes this time, and a San Francisco 49ers flag flapping in the breeze from the porch.

The flag told the story of this place as well as the inequality of home repair and landscaping. Atlanta must be a transplant boomtown, attracting young professionals from much more expensive cities in California and the northeast. Those transplants flooded in, flush with cash from the million-dollar shacks they had just sold in the Bay Area or metro New York City, and quickly snatched up "cheap" southern homes in fancy neighborhoods.

When those fancy neighborhoods were packed out and no longer cheap, those transplants looked elsewhere, navigating into increasingly undesirable neighborhoods, driving out low-income occupants ahead of them. Soon enough, rough neighborhoods became mixed neighborhoods. A rotting shack here, a remodeled McMansion there.

I'd watched the cycle in Phoenix. What I saw in Perkerson Park and Sylvan Terrace was no different—low-income, crime-heavy neighborhoods now invaded by 49ers fans with too much cash and not enough sense, convinced by some real estate spin doctor that these communities were the "up and coming" neighborhoods of the city, guaranteed to rise in value.

Well, the property values might rise. But in my experience as a beat cop, crime rates mirrored housing costs. When people couldn't afford a roof over their heads, they often defaulted to desperation.

I completed my sweep of the neighborhood, ensuring there were no cops around, and returned to the avenue. Parking at a check-cashing place half a block off the main drag, I pocketed both the switchblade and the orange bandana and left the vehicle, hiking up my baggy pants as I walked.

They weren't comfortable, but they didn't need to be. This wouldn't take long.

I'd noticed the three guys lurking outside the liquor store next to the check-cashing place on my second pass. They were older than the kids at the basketball court. Maybe early twenties, all muscle with tight shirts matched to loose pants, smoking cigarettes and passing around a bottle only partially hidden inside a paper sack.

All wearing gunmetal gray bandanas.

I mapped out the space next to the liquor store as I approached. The three gangsters loitered on the sheltered side of it, invisible to the traffic on Cleveland Avenue. A couple of cars were parked on that side of the store, and as I approached, a patron or two wandered in and out.

But behind the store, one turn around the brick wall, was complete quiet. Stacks of rotting liquor boxes leaned against the brick, with rainwater dripping off the roof and running across blackened concrete. A privacy fence separated the area behind the store from Sylvan Terrace, forming a darkened alley overhung by trees.

Perfect.

I ducked my head and tied the bandana around my skull as I stepped into the parking lot, flashing bright orange. Slash Crew colors—whoever the hell they were. Then I marched straight for the three guys smoking at the end of the building.

They noticed me as I stepped around the parking lot dumpster, walking smoothly, glaring right at them. One guy straightened, his hand dropping reflexively to his belt, probably for a gun. The two others faced me head-on, leering out of hooded and sleepy eyes.

It was only then that I smelled the smoke and realized they weren't cigarettes. They were joints—heavy ones.

All the better.

I stopped ten yards away and spit right between us. The oldest of the three bristled.

"What you want?" he demanded.

"You boys Steel Mafia?"

The leader smirked derisively. "If you have to ask, you don't belong. *Roll*, cracka."

I didn't roll. I took another few strides forward, reaching the curb and standing eye-to-eye with the middle guy.

"I asked you a question," I snarled.

The leader's shoulders bulged as he flicked his joint into the parking lot. Anger flashed behind the intoxication in his eyes, and he tugged up the edge of his shirt.

A Glock 22 was exposed beneath. A .40 caliber, fifteen plus one capacity. Not a bad weapon, if you knew how to use it. By virtue of the fact that he had allowed me to approach within two feet of him, I already knew he didn't know how to use it.

"You better *roll* before I merk yo ass."

I looked to either side, noting each of the other gangsters standing in similar fashion on the sidewalk's edge, exposing handguns in their waistbands. It was a dumb stance. If they had any sense, they would have already drawn those weapons, fingers ready near their triggers, sights hovering over center mass.

Rookie mistake.

I nodded once, as if I were admitting my mistake, and dipped both hands into my pockets. My right hand closed around the Microtech, my thumb finding the switch. I took half a step back, as though I were retreating.

And then I struck.

My hand left the pocket in a flash; the button depressed, the double-edged blade snapping out like a bullet. I slashed right at eye level, slicing the leader's forehead open just above his eyebrows.

The move was lightning quick and totally unstoppable. Blood gushed from the head wound, streaming into the guy's eyes before he could even scream.

I was already gone, rushing around the back corner of the building and into the alley, pressing my back against the damp brick with the switchblade still clamped in one hand.

The lieutenants shouted. Feet pounded the sidewalk as their leader screamed for them to gun me down. The first guy rocketed around the corner, gun raised, expecting to see me making an escape some twenty yards ahead.

Instead, I was right on him, too close to realign his weapon, already striking before he even registered my presence. The switchblade sank into his right bicep a full two inches before I wrenched it free. He screamed and fumbled the gun. I dropped the knife and tore the pistol free of his grip, grabbing it by the barrel and swinging it immediately to the left—right into the face of the third guy as he rounded the corner.

The butt of the heavy gun smacked him in the forehead, and he went down. Lights out. The second guy fumbled for my fallen knife with his right hand, his left hand still clamped over the wound to his right bicep.

I flipped the pistol around, still driving with the butt, and clocked him over the back of the skull.

He fell next to his comrade, both of them landing in a splash of mucky runoff water.

I spun the gun around, taking a quick note of the model in order to check for a safety. It was a Hi-Point 9mm—an absolute junker of a gun, available at almost any gun store for under two hundred bucks. It looked more like a science fiction movie prop than a real weapon, but for all that, it was reasonably reliable.

The last gangster rounded the corner, his gray headband pulled over the cut on his forehead to stem the blood flow, his right hand leading with the Glock. His face plowed straight into the muzzle of the Hi-Point.

"*Drop it*," I snapped.

He relinquished the Glock with a grinding of gold-plated teeth, his gaze falling over his two unconscious soldiers.

I'd hit them both hard. They'd be out for a while.

"Into the alley," I said.

I pushed him ahead with both guns, around a stack of rotting boxes to a sheltered spot invisible from the street. Then I stowed the Hi-Point in my back pocket, switched the Glock to my right hand, and smacked him across the side of the head.

The guy stumbled back, grunting and spitting blood across the concrete. I pressed the muzzle of the Glock beneath his chin, forcing his face up.

"You know who I am?" I snarled.

He blinked, still high as a kite and unafraid.

That chilled me, despite myself.

"A dead fool," he snarled.

I tugged my headband off and clenched it between my fingers, shaking it only inches from his eyes. "You see this? You know what this is?"

I pressed harder with the Glock, forcing his neck to strain.

"Tell your boys that Jalen Powell is *off-limits*."

Confusion clouded the gangster's face. "Who?"

"*Jalen Powell*," I snapped. "Your boys made a pass at him this morning. But he's off-limits, you hear me? He's *ours*."

The guy blinked hard as blood escaped his headband and ran into his left eye. It gave him a crazed, battle-wounded look, reminding me of dusty streets amid mountain villages. Chattering AK-47s.

Death on the air.

"You mean Cox's little brother?" he said at last.

I shoved with the Glock again. "That's right. *Back off.*"

I saw something flicker behind the intoxication in his eyes—anger or indignation. I decided to crush that spark before it became a flame, and rammed my knee straight between his legs.

He doubled over, and I let him slump to the ground, backing off a yard.

"Leave Jalen alone," I said. "Or else."

I turned for the end of the alley. Behind me I heard the guy gasping for breath, still doubled over from the groin kick.

And then I heard another sound. Laughter.

"Man, you some kind of fool," he rasped. "They gonna burn that kid like they burned his brother."

I stopped, gun frozen at my side. Then turned back. "What did you say?"

He shook his head, wiping blood off his face. I raised the Glock and crowded in, and he shielded his crotch.

"What did you say?" I demanded.

"I said the SAS gonna burn that kid! He's history, bruh."

"No. What did you say about his brother?"

He looked away. I pressed the Glock into his neck. "*Talk.*"

He held up a hand. "Chill, bruh!"

"What about Anthony?"

He looked away again. I put my finger on the trigger.

That did it.

"A brotha don't just fold, man."

"So somebody sold him out?" I asked.

He rolled his eyes. "Man, you slow for a thug."

"What, then?" I prodded.

"I'm *saying* they burned him. I'm saying that cat took the fall."

I froze, finger still on the trigger. He didn't move, his blood-filled eyes glaring up at me.

"You think a killa just gonna go down without a fight? Nah, man. Not in this hood."

"There was a knife," I corrected. "Anthony's fingerprints."

The guy laughed again. "Like that's hard to get."

My mind spun back to the evidence in Anthony's trial. Fingerprints, DNA, blood. All pretty damning stuff, but not impossible to fabricate.

I wasn't sure if I believed it, but what I believed didn't matter.

"Does Jalen know?" I demanded.

The guy looked away, reaching up to scrub blood from his cheek. I belted him across the face with the Glock, sending him reeling back before I grabbed his neck with one hand and pressed the pistol into his eye.

"*Does Jalen know?*" I hissed.

This time he didn't fight me. His neck relaxed, and he actually grinned.

"Why you think we wanted him? We was gonna use him against the Squad. Get our territory back. But you know what, bruh. I'm happy to let you fools do the killin' for us. That kid is all yours."

16

The words had barely left his lips before I heard shoes on the sidewalk alongside the liquor store, followed by a voice. "Deshaun? Where you at, dawg?"

The guy I had pinned down looked sideways, toward the end of the alley. His chest tightened, and his lips parted. I popped him in the temple with the butt of the Glock, and his eyes rolled back in his head.

I snatched up the switchblade as the voice called again from the sidewalk; then I turned for the privacy fence walling off the alley. There wasn't time to make for either end. The footsteps grew louder, as did the calls for Deshaun.

I grabbed the top end of a post and walked up the fence with my tennis shoes, flipping to the other side and landing in a shallow ditch. A dog barked from the yard adjacent to the fence, but I didn't see any people.

I withdrew the magazines from both pistols before scrubbing away my fingerprints and dumping the guns in the ditch. The Steel Mafia guys would find them, but they'd find guns anyway, and I wasn't interested in carrying potentially stolen weapons.

As I left the ditch and crossed back onto the sidewalk, I saw the guy looking for Deshaun reach the alley and encounter the first of the unconscious gangsters. A commotion erupted, but he didn't look for me.

I was already across the street, walking casually, hands in my pockets. Just another pedestrian.

I PILED BACK into my truck and sat with both hands on the wheel, breathing hard and staring at the dash.

Like they burned his brother.

The words echoed in my mind, and I immediately questioned them. Was Deshaun—or whoever he was—simply trying to throw me off?

I couldn't think of a reason why divulging that information would help Deshaun. He had no way of knowing my relationship with Jalen or my concern for the kid's future. For all he knew, I really was a rival gangster beefing over territorial nonsense.

But I still wasn't sure how to process the revelation.

If Anthony was innocent—if he had taken the fall for somebody else's crime—that changed everything. I thought again of my conversation with A. B. Colby and how the lawyer had advised me to kill Jalen's obsession. To convince him that Anthony was a lost cause.

I put two and two together, and suddenly Feldon's version of events seemed by far the least likely. If the rumor mill claimed that Anthony had been railroaded, and Jalen believed it, then his visits to Colby's law office were exactly what Colby claimed them to be—the dedicated hounding of a kid on the warpath to overturn an injustice.

That wasn't the kind of thing a rational adult would turn back from. Ever. Even if their own life went down in flames as a result. And Jalen was a far cry from a rational adult. He was like an adolescent rattlesnake, equipped with all the venom of its mature counterparts, but none of the control.

I tore the stupid orange bandana off and cursed myself for ever stopping at that damn diner—for ever interacting with Jalen in the first place. I could have simply run him off or called the cops.

I could have *not* played the hero. Been deep in south Georgia by now, practicing the song on my violin and searching for the answers to my own existential crises.

Everything I'd done since meeting Jalen had only made things worse or further served to unravel an endless tapestry of problems.

Cox can't be innocent.

I thought it, but I didn't believe it. Not only because I'd seen gangsters take the fall on behalf of bigger gangsters before, but because my mind traveled back to the evidence. Blood, fingerprints, and DNA.

Direct evidence. Hard proof. But if Anthony Cox was being set up by somebody who knew him well, how difficult would any of that be to manufacture?

I glared out my window, tapping the wheel slowly. I'd committed that I was going to make things better for Jalen. First by forestalling the Steel Mafia, and then by getting Feldon off the kid's back.

I couldn't back out now. If I did, I would be culpable for Jalen's inevitable demise. The DEA, the Steel Mafia, or the South Atlanta Squad itself would get him. One way or the other.

But that didn't give me the first clue how to unravel this mess.

I drove toward Jalen's apartment by default, recalling the

little old lady I'd watched him assisting earlier that morning. I had mentally convicted Jalen of blowing off school to play with his friends. For his friends, maybe it was that simple. But not for Jalen. He'd skipped the bus to help the old lady he lived with. A grandmother, perhaps? A great-aunt?

Somebody he cared for. That much was obvious in the way he followed her to the van, patting her shoulder and kissing her cheek.

I parked the truck in the same spot as before, behind the Caprice on blocks, eighty yards from Jalen's apartment. It was just now past two p.m., but I could see a light on through the window next to the door. Shadows passed behind that glass, and the door swung open.

It was Jalen, dressed in sweatpants with no shirt, carrying two bags of trash over one shoulder. He lugged them down the sidewalk to the dumpster, then hurried back, whistling as he walked.

Back inside I saw his shadow play across the window again; then he appeared on the narrow front porch with a broom, dusting off the concrete. He straightened the little stool set next to a low table, then used the broom to remove cobwebs around the door frame.

It was a careful, methodical procedure. More love and care than any of the surrounding units had seen in a long time, by the look of it.

After finishing, Jalen returned inside, but two minutes later the door opened again, and the old lady in the wheelchair appeared, pushed by Jalen. He got her situated on the front porch next to the little table, then sat down across from her and produced a small box.

Dominoes were arranged, and a game commenced. There was a lot of laughter between the two. Big smiles from Jalen, mixed with accusatory outbursts after the old woman made a play.

I watched behind my dirty window, transfixed by the two. Captured in a moment by their relationship. They were unweathered by their environment. Undamaged by the pressure of an imminent beatdown in Jalen's near future.

This wasn't a kid at all. This was a young man, wearing shoes much too big for him, but wearing them with style. Looking after his household.

Facing his problems.

I started the truck, steering out of the complex and once again taking the highway north, toward downtown. I remembered the Steel Mafia kids in the basketball court. The hungry fire in Feldon's eyes.

These assholes wanted to burn this kid, for no reason at all. Whether Anthony was innocent or not, if they wanted to get to Jalen, they'd have to go through me first.

17

I ran another search on the burner phone to obtain the address for the Atlanta Social Justice Coalition—the nonprofit Colby had mentioned while discussing Jalen's obsessive pursuit of his brother's freedom. The building was downtown, on the outskirts of the financial district, built of grungy concrete with street parking available along the curb.

I parked the truck and tilted my head back to survey the fifteen-story structure. The windows were dirty, and the flower beds choked by dead grass of the previous summer. The sign at the top read simply "ASJC", in tall black letters. Nothing more.

The simplicity of the building was a good thing, I thought. Whatever work this organization was dedicated to, they weren't wasting donation money on needless grandeur.

I paused next to my truck's sideview mirror to straighten my hair and shirt collar. I still looked homeless—which I kind of was. But hopefully I would appear legitimate enough to warrant an audience with whatever lawyer or paralegal had spoken to Jalen.

I wanted to know more about the case. More about what Jalen knew, and how Anthony had been convicted. If what Deshaun had said was true, there wouldn't be an easy way to overturn Anthony's conviction.

But overturning a gangster's conviction—just or otherwise—wasn't my goal. Right then I just needed information. Something I could use to get Feldon to piss off, and Jalen to calm down.

The lobby inside two tall glass doors was quiet, with worn carpet and outdated floral chairs lined against one wall. A receptionist hung up a phone and offered me a weary smile as she glanced sideways at a desk clock.

It was nearing four thirty. Quitting time, I figured.

"Can I help you, sir?"

I ran through my mental notes quickly, reviewing my planned pitch. It wasn't a great one, but on short notice it was the best I could manage.

"Hi, I'm Mason Sharpe. I'm a private investigator working the Anthony Cox case. I was hoping to speak to the attorney you have assigned."

It was a bold statement, and it assumed a lot. But I figured if there *was* an attorney working Anthony's case, they would only speak with me under the assumption that I was legitimate. Somebody of authority.

The receptionist swept her gaze over my wrinkled shirt and stained jeans. I shrugged apologetically.

"I've been undercover."

She swiveled to her computer and ran a search, polished nails clicking over worn keys. Then she shook her head.

"I'm sorry, sir. We don't have a Cox case on file. Who was the attorney?"

I thought quickly.

"I'm retained by Jalen Powell. He said he spoke with somebody."

A light bulb glowed behind her eyes. Recognition, but maybe not enthusiasm.

"You mean the kid?" she asked.

The kid. So, Jalen had made a name for himself. He'd been here a few times. More signs of an obsessed young mind running in overdrive.

"Right," I said, pocketing my hands and offering an apologetic smile. "He couldn't remember who he spoke with...an appeals attorney?"

"He spoke with Ms. Dalton, I believe. Only once. She's not taking his case...I'm sorry, who are you again?"

"Mason Sharpe. Sharpe, Thomas, and Smith—Private Investigators." I rattled the names off the top of my head, instantly regretting my use of Smith. People always choose Smith when they're making up a name. It's the obvious choice.

The receptionist simply looked at the clock again.

I stepped closer to the desk, lowering my voice. "There's been a development. About Jalen. I thought she should know."

Another calculated guess based entirely on instinct. Any attorney who forwent a lucrative career at a big Atlanta law firm in favor of nonprofit work must have a heart. Maybe enough of one to stay ten minutes late and talk about a troubled kid.

"I'll give her a call," the receptionist said at last. "No promises."

I retreated far enough to make her comfortable. The call lasted less than twenty seconds.

"Ms. Dalton can spare fifteen, but she has an appointment after work."

Of course she does. The woman was a good receptionist.

"Which floor?"

"Eight. Down the hall to your left."

"Thanks."

I took the elevator and avoided my reflection in the stainless-steel doors, resolving to spend a little more on that
night's accommodations. Broke or otherwise, I could only go
so long without a proper shower. Maybe I would find some
scissors and give myself a haircut.

The eighth floor was little better decorated than the rest
of the building. The sign outside the elevator read "ASJC –
Legal Dept." Two worn chairs sat in the lobby alongside a
table laden with outdated sports and culture magazines.
Nobody waited behind the narrow reception desk across the
room, so I took the hallway to the left, as directed.

I found the office of Sarah Dalton, Attorney at Law, at the
end of the hall. The door was open, and as I stepped inside, I
was greeted by tall windows overlooking the heart of downtown Atlanta. The office itself was spacious, but crowded by
stacks of legal boxes, a pile of empty take-out containers, and
enough books to stock a small library.

Sarah Dalton wasn't present, but the computer was still
on, so I knew she hadn't gone far. Pocketing my hands, I
walked to the windows and surveyed the city. It looked
cleaner from this angle than it did down on the street.

Cleaner and not as harsh. Almost picturesque in the late
afternoon sun.

"Mr. Sharpe?"

The voice was feminine and cheery. I turned and did a
double take.

Sarah Dalton was gorgeous. No, more than gorgeous, she
was stunning. Closer to six feet than five, with swept-back
blonde hair and crystal blue eyes. She wore a smooth
pantsuit without a wrinkle present, completely defying the
absolute chaos of her office. The suit was modest but failed to
conceal the natural curves of a toned body.

She approached me with an outstretched hand and a

warm smile, apparently not the least bit perturbed by an unwelcome, last-minute visitor. I took the hand and shook once, fumbling for words.

"That's right," I managed.

"Sarah Dalton. A pleasure to meet you. Please have a seat."

She motioned me to the single chair across from her desk, occupied by a file box. I shifted the box to the floor as she settled into her desk chair.

"Tracy said you're a private investigator?" Sarah said.

"Uh...right."

I glanced impulsively from Sarah to the pile of sour take-out trash next to the desk, completely confused by the absolute dichotomy of the flawless woman and her catastrophic environment. Sarah seemed unconcerned by my confusion and simply smiled again.

"May I see your license?"

"Um...sorry?"

"Your PI license."

I thought quickly. I hadn't expected an identification challenge. I hadn't expected any of this.

"I'm not that kind of investigator," I said at last.

"Oh?" Sarah opened a drawer and withdrew a pack of sandwich crackers. She commenced eating but didn't fill the silence. She seemed completely unhurried to put me at ease, and that only served to further confuse me.

I glanced around the office, noting diplomas on the wall from the University of Georgia at Athens, and Emory University in Atlanta. Expensive schools. A prestigious education. A beautiful woman.

And yet here she sat, consuming crackers like a lawn-mower eight floors into a dingy building. Probably earning thirty percent of what she was worth.

"This is about Jalen Powell," I said at last, ready to take

control of the situation. "Anthony Cox's little brother."

Sarah nodded once but didn't comment. She poked another cracker into her mouth and crunched down like a fifth grader on lunch.

"I understand he came to see you?" I prodded.

"Who?"

"Jalen," I said, irritation creeping into my voice.

Sarah said nothing. I made a show of dusting my pants legs off and sat forward. "Look. I'll cut straight to the point. I know Jalen thinks his older brother is innocent. I know he came to speak to you. I was hoping you could help me out with some details."

"Nope." She shook her head, reaching for another cracker.

"Excuse me?"

"Nope."

"Nope what?"

"Nope, I can't help you out with details."

"Why not?"

"Attorney-client privilege, for a start."

"Jalen isn't your client. The woman downstairs said he only met with you once."

She cocked her head, thinking and chewing. Taking her time doing both. Then she nodded. "That's true. But there's still reason number two."

"Which is?"

"You're lying to me. And I don't help people who lie to me."

I held her gaze. Sarah Dalton ate her last cracker, then dusted her hands off with a loud smacking sound and smiled. But she didn't say anything.

The woman was impossible.

I considered my options, scanning the room for any personal items I could use as a point of connection. It was a tactic I had used before, as a homicide detective. They taught us to find common ground with the people we interviewed. To look for an opportunity to connect.

But the only personal item in the room was a framed photograph of a middle-aged man pushing a little girl on a swing set. The little girl looked like the woman in front of me, leaving me to think that the man was her father. I'd never met my father. Not something to connect over.

I looked back to Sarah and found her still calmly sitting with her hands in her lap, smiling. She knew she had me cornered. If I was going to get anything out of this interaction, I would need to alter the status quo.

"Okay," I said. "Maybe I am lying. What then?"

"Well, you could start by telling me the truth."

"About?"

"Who you are and why you're here."

I thought about that for a full minute. I don't like volunteering information about myself. Not to anyone, especially not to people I don't know, and especially not to lawyers. It's a no-gain situation.

But again. She was holding all the cards.

"Okay," I said. "Start over, then. My name is Mason Sharpe. I'm a former homicide detective for the Phoenix Police Department. I was passing through Atlanta and met Jalen by chance. I've stumbled into some information about his personal life, and I find myself concerned. That's why I'm here."

"Why not lead with that?" she asked.

"Because people in your position are waylaid by concerned citizens on a daily basis. I didn't think you'd speak to me."

"You'd be correct. But I also don't speak to liars."

"Well, I'm not lying."

"How did you meet Jalen?"

"He was borrowing my truck."

"Borrowing..." she repeated the word as though it were part of a dead language. I said nothing.

"What information did you 'stumble into'?" She made air quotes as she said it, still relaxed. Still smiling.

"That Jalen believes his brother is innocent. And that he just might be right."

"He's not."

"You looked into the case?"

"Mr. Sharpe, I'm an appeals attorney working for a nonprofit firm, and the Cox case was the most publicized federal trial of the past decade. So yeah, I'd say I looked into it."

"What makes you so sure Cox was guilty?"

Sarah laughed at that, breaking eye contact for the first time since I'd sat down. She stared out the dusty windows, and her smile faded, leaving her looking suddenly tired.

"Are you in a hurry, Mr. Sharpe?"

"I've got nowhere to be."

"You hungry?"

I frowned. "You literally just ate."

"I suffer from hypermetabolism," she said. "I consume four to five thousand calories a day just to maintain my weight."

"Lucky you."

Sarah shut off her computer and stood. "Come on. There's a deli downstairs. They have great salami."

18

B efore I met my fiancée, I'd dated a lot of women. During my Army years, I could have reasonably been labeled a player, working the local bars and clubs for one-night stands or two-month relationships.

But I never remembered meeting a woman so absolutely at ease with herself as this attorney. Sarah seemed completely unconcerned with the fact that she had just invited a total stranger to dinner, even in context of my shabby appearance and the fact that I had just admitted to lying about my identity.

She exuded confidence. It was strangely likable.

The deli was dark and narrow, built into the bottom of a high-rise across the street from the ASJC. The heavyset Italian guy behind the counter greeted Sarah by name and asked if she would be having the usual. I scanned the menu quickly before requesting a pastrami on rye bread, with a bottled water. Then I reached for my wallet. Sarah beat me to it.

"My treat," she said, flicking out a credit card.

"I don't mind," I said. "You're making time for me."

"I was eating here anyway, and I enjoy having somebody to talk to. Besides, buying dinner is all about power for men. Power and sex. You'll be enjoying neither."

She swiped the credit card and shot me a coy wink. I pocketed my hands, getting used to the idea that this woman could not be made uncomfortable.

We found our way to the booth in the back, and the Italian guy brought our food—a thick pastrami for me, grilled in a panini press, and a foot-long Italian for Sarah, packed to the brim with salami. The sandwich looked bigger than her head.

She took a big bite and let out a satisfied groan, then reached for her drink. I was too fascinated by her enthusiasm to try the pastrami yet. I sipped water.

"So Jalen stole your truck." Sarah spoke through a mouthful of sandwich.

"He borrowed it."

"*Right*." She dragged the word out with obvious skepticism.

"Why would you assume he stole it?" I asked.

She shrugged. "Because I've seen his rap sheet."

"He has a rap sheet?"

"Half a mile long. Most kids in Jalen's situation do. The police are hard on them. Loitering, petty theft, noise complaints. Some old grandma calling the cops over two or three minority kids bouncing a ball near her house."

"I take it there's a lot of racial tension down here," I said.

"You could say that. Atlanta has a sad history of racial tension. The whole region does. Some things improve—some things stay the same."

"So Jalen is a victim?"

Sarah shook her head. "I don't believe in victimhood. It's a disabling mental construct. I'd rather see people empowered."

I grunted, both impressed and somehow surprised. I guess I expected a social justice attorney to be heavily involved in the concept of victimhood, but I agreed with her analysis. The judge at my teenage trial had said something similar. He'd been right.

"I'm not saying Jalen hasn't been *victimized*," Sarah continued. "Life has dealt him a brutal hand. Orphaned, estranged from his extended family, impoverished. I wouldn't wish that situation on anyone."

"Jalen lost his parents?"

She squinted. "For a guy who's poking around on his behalf, you don't know much about him."

"For a woman who only met him once, you seem to know a lot."

Sarah wiped her mouth, half the sandwich already consumed. She sipped her drink, then picked at her fingernails. For the first time, she seemed thrown off balance. Or maybe a little unsure.

"Three times," she said at last.

"What?"

"I met with him three times."

"The receptionist said you met only once."

Sarah shrugged. "Officially, yes. In my office. On the record. I took him to dinner on my own time. Twice. Right here, actually."

"Why?"

"Because I found his story compelling. And because... nobody listens to people like Jalen."

"So why didn't you take his case?"

"You saw my office."

"Yeah..."

"All those case files? All that paperwork? The ASJC is

funded in large part by government grants, Mr. Sharpe. I'm working seven cases right now—by myself. Every case I take, every meeting on my calendar, tells the story of our effectiveness. The more effective we are, the more funding we get, and the more effective we can be. It's a chicken-and-egg thing. I can't afford to clog my day with investigatory conversation."

"So you spoke with Jalen on your own time."

"Right."

"But you still haven't taken his brother's case."

Sarah shook her head.

"Why not?"

"Several reasons. Not least of which because Anthony Cox isn't filing an appeal. His public defender never processed the paperwork."

"A. B. Colby," I said.

"Right. Jalen thought Colby was incompetent, which is why he came to me. I spoke with Colby myself, and he's definitely in over his head. But that isn't why the appeal was never filed."

"Cox refused?"

Sarah nodded. "He's given up."

"Why?"

"Maybe because prison breaks you. Maybe because the appeal feels hopeless. But honestly? In my opinion?"

"Yes?"

"Because he's guilty as sin."

"You think he killed that guy."

"I know he killed that guy—as sure as any lawyer can know anything, and I say that as an appeals attorney who generally believes the justice system is corrupt. A lot of innocent people are behind bars, Mr. Sharpe. Anthony Cox isn't one of them."

I thought back to my conversation with Deshaun in the alley behind the liquor store.

"They gonna burn that kid like they burned his brother."

"What makes you so sure?" I asked.

Sarah took another massive bite of her sandwich. I still hadn't touched my pastrami.

"The evidence is damning. Cox's fingerprints on the murder weapon. Cox's DNA found on the body. Witnesses from the DEA who testified that Cox was one of the primary targets of Martin's undercover investigation. And, of course, Martin's blood on Cox's clothes. It's pretty overwhelming."

"And none of that feels too tidy to you?"

"What do you mean?"

"Prints on the weapon. DNA on the body. Blood on the clothes."

"Murder trials are rarely as complex as they appear on TV. And anybody who could peel a man's face off and watch him bleed to death is certainly out of his mind. Maybe insane, or at least whacked out on enough drugs to prevent him from properly covering his tracks. I think it adds up."

She wasn't wrong about murders. I was a homicide detective, after all. It always astounded me how brutally simple things often were. One guy gets pissed at another over an unsettled debt or an attractive woman, and out come the guns. Bam.

Another body hits the streets.

But that didn't mean the simplest explanation was always the correct one.

"What if Anthony was burned?" I said. "Set up?"

"What do you mean?"

"What if somebody else did the killing, then had Anthony take the fall for it. Manufactured the evidence."

Sarah chewed mechanically, thinking about that a minute, then shook her head. "Even if that were true, you'd need bulletproof evidence to overturn the conviction. But I'm telling you, this isn't like the movies. People don't take the fall for things they didn't do."

"Sure they do," I said. "These gangs are like massive families. They cover for each other all the time. I was a cop, remember?"

"Then you know how impossible it is to get a look on the inside. To prove that somebody set Cox up."

"Jalen believes it."

"Jalen is a lost kid with no strong role models in his life. Anthony is his hero. The two of them were extremely close. It's only natural that he would be in denial over Anthony's guilt."

"It's only denial if Jalen is wrong."

"And he's only right if he can prove it. Which he can't. I'm assuming the 'information' you stumbled into has something to do with local gangsters claiming Anthony was set up?"

I said nothing, caught a little off guard. Sarah smiled sadly.

"Jalen told me. I don't blame you for wanting to believe him, but kids on the street say all kinds of things, especially when they're wannabe gangsters. Without evidence it's just hearsay. Right? Smoke in the wind."

Yeah, except Deshaun wasn't a kid, and he wasn't a wannabe.

I thought it, but I didn't say it. Somehow it felt like information I wanted to hold for now.

Sarah returned to her sandwich, finishing the last few bites in record time before wiping her mouth. Still completely unfazed.

I leaned across the table. "I thought you cared about cases like this? Standing up for the little guy. Defending the helpless."

She flushed, just a little. The first sign that I'd got under her skin.

"I work for a nonprofit, Mr. Sharpe. I make seventy thousand a year. I could be making three or four hundred almost anywhere else in town. I work ninety-hour weeks, and I have no love life. I have no friends. I have no hobbies. When I go home, it's more time behind the computer—more time poring over files. Looking for some way—*any* way—to help these people. It's my life. Do you understand? The only thing I do. Don't you dare question how much I care."

"But you won't help," I said.

Her shoulders slumped, just a little. She looked down at her empty plate. "Take it from me, Mason. There are cases you can win. There are cases you can't. This one falls in the *can't* column. Hard."

I looked out the window and surveyed the street for a while, recounting my interactions with Jalen, beginning with the incident at the diner and flowing through the confrontation at the basketball court. I stripped away Feldon's vision of a kid caught in the middle of a vast gangland conspiracy, and built my own image of Jalen, filling in the gaps between what I knew to be true with what I guessed to be true.

An orphaned kid. No close family—except for Anthony and possibly the old woman he lived with. A woman he cared for and took tender care of.

But despite the tranquil picture of Jalen whistling while he swept the porch, then laughing while he played dominos with the old lady, Jalen was angry. Deeply so. He believed his older brother to be innocent, and those beliefs were fueled by the rumor mill he swam in. Whispers of Anthony being burned. Further whispers of Jalen being next on the chopping block. So he embarked on a private campaign to see an injustice overturned. He started with Colby, pushing the lawyer to meet twice with Anthony to provoke an appeal.

Colby failed. Jalen moved on to the ASJC, hoping for better luck. He met with Sarah to plead his case, and she took him seriously. At least enough to hear him out.

But she also refused, because in her own words, this was a hopeless case. She turned Jalen away, after which he...gave up?

No. Not a chance in hell.

"What did he say?" I asked.

"What?"

"Jalen. When you refused the case. What did he say?"

Sarah sipped her drink, looking suddenly tired. She smiled sadly. "Well, he wasn't happy. I believe his exact words were 'To hell with your bitch ass.'"

She chuckled, but the amusement didn't reach her eyes. I saw only pain there. Sadness. A woman who couldn't help empathizing with a broken kid.

"Did he say what he was going to do next?" I prodded.

"Oh yes. Told me all about it. He said he was gonna hire a *real* attorney. Some ambulance chaser he saw on a billboard. Get Anthony out himself. Not like he has the money."

An electric shock raced up my spine, and that final floating piece clicked. *The truck.*

I thought of it again, and it suddenly made sense. I couldn't reconcile Jalen's attempted theft of my truck with a life neck-deep in crime. But what if Jalen hadn't stolen the truck for attention? What if it *had* been about money?

The old pickup wasn't worth much. But it was a nice start.

Momentary elation at my unraveling of the mystery was replaced by instant, crushing defeat. Because if I was right, Jalen's situation was more hopeless than ever. A kid who would risk his entire future by stealing a vehicle in broad daylight would only make increasingly worse decisions, laying them like bricks along his own highway to hell.

There was no stopping this. No taming the angry beast raging inside him. Not unless...

"If I brought you hard evidence that Anthony was innocent, would you take the case?" I asked.

Sarah said nothing. I gave her time.

"Jalen isn't gonna last," I said. "The DEA are still on a witch hunt for the gang his brother ran. They're convinced Jalen is in the middle of it. There are other gangs trying to recruit him, meanwhile. Trying to suck him in. And he's neck-deep in his own criminal enterprises. That kid won't see twenty-one the way things are headed."

"And you think proving Anthony's innocence will change that?"

"I think it will help. I think it might just give Jalen a reason not to flush his life away."

Sarah sucked her teeth again. She glanced at the empty plate. Then she reached into her purse and withdrew a card. Flipping it over, she wrote down a number.

"This is my personal cell. If you find something...something *concrete*...I'll take the case."

"Pro bono?" I asked. "Like you said, he hasn't got the money."

Sarah rolled her eyes. "All our work is free. My salary is paid from those grants."

I pocketed the card and slid out of the booth, my sandwich still untouched.

"I'll be calling you."

I took a step toward the door. Sarah stopped me with a raised hand.

"Mason?"

"What?"

"I know you want to help. I admire that. Just be careful you don't cause more harm than good. It's a rough world Jalen lives in. One domino leads to another."

I thought about the Steel Mafia and those four kids I'd wasted at the basketball court. What Jalen had said about making his life worse.

You have no idea.

As I pushed through the door into the rush of city noise, I knew I wasn't leaving Jalen worse than I found him. I didn't yet know what that meant, but I would figure it out.

I turned for my truck, already reaching for my keys.

And then I saw the car.

19

The unmarked government sedan sat half a block away, illegally parked in a fire lane, its tinted windshield pointed dead at me. It was a Ford Taurus, late model, dark blue with those base-model plastic hubcaps that scratch and deform against curbs.

It was the same car I'd seen outside A. B. Colby's law office, in Bankhead.

I glanced once at the Taurus, then lowered my head and walked casually to the corner, turning left. Putting a building between myself and the sedan. As soon as I was safely out of sight, I broke into a jog, circling the building and navigating down an alley that split the block. Mud puddles and piles of cardboard boxes left a winding path to the other side, where I popped out fifty yards behind the sedan.

I approached quietly, moving with my hands in my pockets and remaining behind a mailman with a big bag over his shoulder for as long as I could. By the time the mail guy turned for his truck, I was only ten feet behind the car and headed for the driver's side. I slipped the Victorinox from my pocket and repeated the same procedure I'd used with Jalen —smacking the butt of the knife against the driver's window.

The Victorinox made a sharp snapping sound, and the guy sitting behind the wheel almost jumped out of his skin. A half-eaten burger fell across his lap while the man seated next to him reached for a pistol. Jammed inside the narrow interior of the car, he couldn't get his hand around the grip.

I rapped with the knife again. The driver made eye contact, and his cheeks flushed. He reached for the window switch.

"You're illegally parked, Agent," I said as soon as the glass was halfway down.

I didn't recognize either man, but it wasn't hard to smell the bureaucracy wafting out of the car along with the odor of greasy fast food. They were federal agents, absolutely. Feldon's people.

"What are you up to, Sharpe?" the driver demanded, regaining a bit of composure.

"Oh, you know. Just seeing the sights. Exploring a new city. More of that Fifth Amendment stuff I told your boss about."

"The Fifth Amendment protects against self-incrimination," the driver sneered. "It doesn't say anything about tourism."

"It says I'm not to be deprived of life, liberty, or property without due process. In the opinion of the esteemed William O. Douglas, such liberty includes the right to free travel."

The guy looked confused. I leaned down until I was at eye level and made a rolling gesture with one finger. "Douglas was a Supreme Court Justice...of the United States...of the Supreme Court."

The condescension in my voice was overbearing.

The driver flushed again. "You been talking to the lawyer?"

I didn't answer.

"We saw you go to the deli with her."

So you have eyeballs, good for you.

"We're watching you, Sharpe," the guy from the passenger seat said, speaking for the first time. His voice was colder than the driver's. More confident.

"I noticed," I said. "And you're wasting your time. Tell Feldon he's on the wrong track. Jalen has nothing to do with the SAS. Neither does Colby."

"We'll be the judge of that," the driver said.

"You really want to burn that kid's life down? Just for your pound of flesh?"

"It's more than a pound," the second guy snapped. "Martin was one of ours. They ripped his *face* off."

"Right. But Jalen didn't. So leave the kid out of it."

I straightened, pocketing the knife. I couldn't see the second guy any longer, but he called out to me through the open window.

"You're not helping yourself, Sharpe. An innocent man would get out of town."

"Give me a break. You're throwing spaghetti at a wall and you know it. But that's fine, go ahead and burn taxpayer dollars. That's what the feds do, right?"

I smacked the roof of the car with an open palm.

"Don't forget to stretch, boys. Stakeouts can really do a number on your glutes."

———

I took the truck back to the airport, but this time I drove a little farther down the strip of low-cost accommodation and selected a chain motel in place of a dingy independent joint. The rate was almost twice as much per night, and the rooms still had exterior access doors, but the bathroom was clean enough to scrub myself free of a week's worth of sweat and grime. I used a razor from a nearby convenience store to scrape my face clean, then lathered up in soap and spent a long time just standing beneath the hot water, enjoying the steam.

I still felt cold from my days in North Carolina. If I closed my eyes, I could still feel the crush of icy water washing through Mia's Corolla, rising up to my waist. Chilling me to the bones.

It had been nearly six months since I lost her. Six months since that eruption of gunfire at the Phoenix elementary school where Mia taught second grade.

Six months since a shooter's bullets tore through my back, and I collapsed to the floor in a puddle of Mia's blood. Only seconds too late.

But those seconds might as well have been hours.

I toweled off and dressed in a clean pair of clothes, then stood for a while in front of the mirror.

I didn't recognize the man I saw. Not just because, for the first time in fifteen years, I was late for a haircut. Not just because I'd lost ten pounds and spent enough time outside to turn my skin dark and leathery.

It was the look in my eyes that threw me off the most. A sort of haunting. Like I was staring at a ghost.

I turned away from the sink and grabbed my wallet. There was a Mexican restaurant attached to the motel, with colored jalapeño lights strung outside the front door. I was missing the pastrami sandwich now and thinking about tacos and salsa.

But first I walked to the business center built into the motel's lobby and got the password from the clerk to access the internet on one of the computers. It took me only a minute to find the .gov website dedicated to public information about the federal prison system. Only a moment longer to locate the webpage for the Hartwell Federal Penitentiary, just south of Greenville, South Carolina.

I used the notepad next to the computer to write down the address, then made further note of the phone number and visitation hours.

By the time I logged off and headed for the Mexican joint, I had everything I needed to pay Anthony Cox a visit the next morning.

It was time to hear the story from the horse's mouth.

20

"What do you have to say for yourself, young man?"

The judge was old and didn't have a hair on his head. He sat behind a raised bench, a pen in one hand, his loose cheeks bunched at the lips in a puckered frown.

Encased in black robes, he looked like the grim reaper himself, transmitting enough ire at the boy standing hand-cuffed behind the defendant's stand to melt any pretext of teenage defiance.

But the boy held his chin up, anyway. Swallowing hard. Sweating a lot. But not breaking eye contact. Not speaking, either.

The judge nodded slowly. "So it's gonna be like that, is it?"

The boy didn't answer, but he rolled his shoulders back, just a little. Alone in a darkened courtroom, his attorney vanished into thin air. The state prosecutor disappeared. Even the bailiff. Now it was just the boy and the judge, alone in a void, locked in a defiant staring contest.

And then the judge smiled. His voice softened.

"You know, son. I've seen a lot of foolishness in my time.

But pissing away your future at seventeen years old—now that may be the greatest tragedy this court could stand witness to. And I simply won't stand for it."

The gavel cracked like a gunshot, echoing in the void. The boy jumped despite himself. The judge stood, a swirl of black robes, and his voice boomed as though he were holding a loudspeaker.

"These streets won't set you straight, Mr. Sharpe. But Uncle Sam can!"

Lightning flashed. The judge vanished in a black cloud, and rain beat down. The boy hit his knees, no longer wearing a gray prison jumpsuit. Now he was clothed in a sopping wet ACU uniform, mud splashed across his face, a fifty-pound rucksack on his shoulders. His hands hit the dirt, and vomit spewed from his mouth. All around him boots pounded, sending muddy rainwater spraying into his face as he shivered in the cold.

"*Sharpe!*" The voice roared from the darkness, loud enough to shake concrete. Then the face appeared—a tall black man in a wide-brimmed hat, his muscled frame contained by a saturated uniform, his face stretched in an enraged glower. Across his chest a name tape read *Powell*.

"*What the hell are you doing? Get off my dirt!*"

The boy shook. He spat more vomit in the mud and dry-heaved. The drill instructor's boots slammed next to his face, and the wide-brimmed hat smacked against the back of his head.

"*Do you hear me, Sharpe? Do you speak English? Are you freaking stupid?*"

The boy put both hands beneath his chest and pressed up. He made it halfway and collapsed, falling face-first into the mud.

The drill instructor leaned low. He placed a powerful hand on the boy's shoulder and shook him hard.

"*Sharpe! You are gonna get on your feet and reach the top of this hill. Do you understand me?*"

"I can't, Drill Sergeant!" The boy lay in the mud now, his face milky pale, his arms shaking. The rucksack had fallen halfway off. The rain beat down in an endless blast—like a hurricane, drenching the hillside.

"*What did you say to me?*" the instructor screamed.

"I said I *can't!*"

"*Private, don't you ever say that word again! Do you hear me? You're dead set on pissing your life away, but I won't allow it. Get on your feet!*"

Thunder rolled. Rain sprayed from the instructor's lips. The boy looked ready to pass out, his body limp in the mud.

But then something flashed behind his eyes. Something like the lightning still streaking overhead—something hot and angry.

The boy gritted his teeth.

"Yes, Drill Sergeant!"

He scrubbed one sopping elbow across his face and scrabbled to his knees. Mud gave way beneath him, and his chin hit the ground again in a splash of rainwater, the rucksack pinning him down.

Then the drill instructor extended a hand.

"*Take my hand, Private. We're going up this hill.*"

I sat bolt upright, scrubbing rainwater out of my face and shaking like a leaf. My gaze snapped toward the sound of the drill instructor's voice, but he wasn't there.

Nobody was there. It was just my motel room, encased in shadow, the hum of the AC unit the only sound to join my shaking breaths. Sweat—not rainwater—ran down my bare chest. But as I placed my feet on the floor and looked down at the worn carpet, I still saw the mud. As real and tangible as it had been all those years ago back at Fort Benning.

Army Basic Combat Training.

I ran both hands through my hair and sucked down a long, slow breath. I closed my eyes and tried to see the drill instructor again, once more picturing his screaming face and iron-brimmed hat.

I saw the tape on his chest, but it didn't read Powell as it had in my dream. The man's real name had been Smiles— Sergeant Patrick Smiles. I remembered, not only because it was an ironic name, but because Sergeant Smiles had gone out of his way to enable my admission into Ranger School.

It was almost an unheard of thing for a guy like me—a guy with a juvenile criminal record—to make it into the Army's famed 75th Regiment. Smiles wrote me a recommendation letter following boot camp. Just three short lines—the very best words anybody had ever said about me.

Private Sharpe never quits.
Not on himself, not on anyone.
The Army would be well served to admit him into Ranger School.

Sincerely,
– Sgt. P. Smiles

I stared at the floor, and the memory brought a dull smile to my face. That judge had been right—Uncle Sam had set me straight. Electing to join the Army in place of going to prison was the best decision I'd ever made. Sergeant Smiles almost single-handedly turned my life around—taught me values, hard work, and self-worth. The will to overcome.

Powell.

Why had I seen Jalen's name on Smiles's uniform? It was

probably just the contortion of a tangled mind weaving together too many thoughts into a dreamscape of semireality.

And yet it felt so real. As though it had all happened only days prior.

I looked to the clock on my nightstand and saw that it was nearly six a.m. Standing from the bed, I walked to the window and peeled the curtains back. In the distance a jumbo jet was streaking toward the Atlanta Airport, tucking its nose in preparation for landing. It wasn't yet light outside, but the sky was turning gray.

I thought again of Smiles's recommendation letter and heard the words in his deep baritone voice.

Private Sharpe doesn't quit...not on himself. Not on anyone.

I closed the curtain and turned for the shower. I needed some cold water to jolt my body to life, and then some coffee to fuel my mind. It was a long drive to South Carolina, and I wanted an early start.

Because I wasn't quitting on Jalen.

21

I hit the road an hour later, referencing my road map for directions out of south Atlanta. I estimated it would be a three-hour drive to the prison. In a modern vehicle capable of modern highway speeds, it would have been a lot less, but the old GMC wouldn't do more than sixty on the highway and was more comfortable at fifty-five.

I was okay with that. As eager as I was to question Anthony Cox, I also needed time to think. And there was no better place to think than behind the wheel, cruising an American highway.

I phoned ahead to the prison using my burner phone and attempted to schedule a visitation with Cox. The woman who answered said that Cox was not accepting visitors, but she agreed to pass on a message to him. I asked her to tell him that I was a friend of Jalen's, and that Jalen was in trouble.

It was all true, and if Anthony cared about his brother at all, it would be enough.

The radio in the old GMC was unreliable at best, and with the windows down it was difficult to hear anything anyway. I'd learned to appreciate the hum of tires on asphalt and the unique creaks and groans of the aged chassis. It wasn't as pleasant as a good Johnny Cash song, but the symphony of an old vehicle told a different story. A story of generations gone by who used to travel these roads without the aid of GPS or unlimited music to stream.

I liked the simplicity. It gave me peace and allowed my mind to wander. It made me think that I never wanted to return to a life of so much speed and complexity as my existence in Phoenix. I thought I had never been happier when I was engaged to Mia, only months away from embracing a lifetime together.

So far as Mia was concerned, I *was* happy. But since leaving Arizona, I'd begun to wonder what a simpler life would have looked like with her. What it would have felt like to drive this same truck, down this same rolling Georgia highway, with Mia at my side.

My eyes stung a little, and I switched my mind away from the past. This wasn't the time to be dulling my intellect with emotion. There were problems at hand. Problems like what to do about Feldon, and how to prove Anthony's innocence.

There had to be a *reason* Anthony was refusing an appeal, but the only logical answer I could think of was that somebody had leverage over him. Serious leverage. Enough for him to embrace a lifetime in prison.

Still, something told me there was more to the story. I was willing to burn a couple of tanks of gas to investigate that theory.

I rolled into South Carolina just before noon. USP Hartwell lay fifteen miles south of downtown Greenville, deep in the countryside, safely out of sight for any worrisome soccer moms in the suburbs. I reached the front gate and stopped at the guardhouse overlooking a sprawling complex with fifteen-foot, electrified fences, guard towers, and block walls.

I'd visited prisons before—usually to interview known associates of homicide suspects. Arizona hosted several federal penitentiaries, but I'd never been inside a maximum-security penitentiary like Hartwell. The facility was impressive—just like in the movies, baking under a blazing South Carolina sun.

The last stop for the worst of the worst.

"What's the nature of your visit, sir?"

The truck idled next to the guard shack. I spoke to a gray-suited correctional officer holding a clipboard.

"Inmate visit," I said.

"Are you on the schedule?"

"Yes," I lied. I hadn't heard back from the prison, but hopefully Anthony had added me to his approved visitors' list. Inmates are usually permitted a limited number of discretional slots to list "friends and associates" as approved visitors. If Anthony believed my story about Jalen and was smart, he'd tell the prison he recognized my name and have them list me as a friend.

If he believed me. And if he was smart.

"Have you been here before?" the CO asked.

"No. First time."

"All right. You're gonna wanna follow the signs to the main entrance. Park in visitor parking. Make sure you leave anything metal behind."

He gave me a long, piercing stare, as if he expected a guy like me to be carrying a gun, but didn't want to go through the hassle of asking.

I nodded my understanding, and he motioned me forward.

"Sweet truck."

I shot him a two-finger wave and drove toward the complex. The road wound, with signs directing me past two intersections and through another fence line.

I left both knives and the cell phone in my truck next to the heap of camping gear, taking nothing but my wallet inside. The front doors of the prison were automatic, and a rush of cool air washed over my face as I entered. The lobby resembled a hospital ER more than a prison, with rows of waiting chairs, a vending machine, and a reception desk lined by bulletproof glass. I waited patiently for my turn to speak with a receptionist, then slid my Arizona driver's license through the slot at the bottom of the glass.

"Mason Sharpe to see Anthony Cox," I said.

The woman took my ID without comment and typed on a computer.

"Who did you say?"

"Anthony Cox," I repeated.

More typing. She squinted at the screen and double-checked my ID. Then she shook her head.

"Sorry, sir. You're not on his list."

"Can you double-check? I should be."

"I'm looking right at it," she said, her tone turning surly. "You're not on it."

She poked the driver's license back through the slot.

"Can you call him?" I pressed. "It's important that I see him."

"Sir, if you're not on the list, you're not on the list. Please move aside."

I leaned closer to the glass, conscious of a bulky security guard in the corner eyeballing me.

"Ma'am, please. It's about his little brother."

"Doesn't matter what it's about. Step aside before I call security."

The guard cleared his throat. I drew breath for one more attempt. Then another woman appeared behind the glass, short and heavyset, wearing too much makeup.

"Did you say Anthony Cox?" she asked.

I nodded.

"You called earlier?"

"I did."

"It's all right, Miranda," the new woman said. "I spoke with Cox. He's adding Mr. Sharpe to his list."

"But it's not—"

Miranda continued to splutter as the new woman motioned me down the counter. I passed my ID through another slot at her station, and she gave it a cursory glance.

"You must be special, Mr. Sharpe."

"Why do you say that?"

She handed my ID back. "Because you're the only person on Mr. Cox's list."

She motioned me to another waiting line, and I was slowly migrated through security, including a metal detector, a sloppy pat-down, and a brief interview with a security officer. I was then given a clipboard to fill out before finally being ushered into visitation.

Again, the room was just like the movies—large and cold, populated by metal tables with metal benches bolted to the floor. No color. No style or attempt at humanity. Prisoners sat with their families and friends around the tables, playing cards and talking quietly. Enjoying a portion of the four hours of monthly visitation they were guaranteed by the government.

I looked for Cox, but the guy leading me didn't walk to a table. Instead, he walked through another door, into a narrow hallway lined by benches, with little partitions between them. In front of each bench was a panel of reinforced glass, with telephone handsets mounted next to them.

The guard gestured to the last bench in line with a disinterested grunt. "Ten minutes."

I nodded my gratitude and rounded the partition.

A black man sat on the other side of the glass, dressed in

drab gray prison overalls that failed to conceal the bulk of his biceps. He was bald—maybe thirty-five, with a strong jaw and deep brown eyes. Clean shaven, clear-eyed. Staring at me without a hint of emotion.

Anthony Cox.

22

I made myself comfortable on the bench before reaching for the phone. There was an identical handset on the other side of the wall, but Anthony didn't pick it up.

He just stared at me, both arms on the table, unmoving. His eyes impenetrable depths of indifference.

I held the phone against one ear, waiting patiently. At last Anthony lifted his receiver, moving it slowly against his face. When he spoke, his voice was flat and toneless, but not the gruff growl I expected. It was a smooth voice. A clear voice.

"Who are *you*?"

"Mason Sharpe," I said. "I'm a friend of Jalen's."

"I seriously doubt that, white boy."

His words were still monotone, but they carried conviction, nonetheless. He didn't blink. I remained loose.

"We met recently," I said. "I'm here on his behalf."

Anthony didn't answer. I saw calculation in his eyes and wondered what he was thinking. He had requested the partitioned visiting arrangement—I knew that. Had he been handcuffed, I might have assumed that we had been placed here for my own security, but his free hands told another story.

He didn't know who I was. He wanted to speak to me, probably because of what I'd said about Jalen. But he was also ready for a trap.

A careful man, or maybe a jaded one. If Deshaun was right about the SAS burning him, Anthony had every reason to be cautious.

"Jalen is in trouble," I said. "He's brushing up with local gangs—Steel Mafia, specifically. But maybe you already knew that."

Anthony didn't answer.

"I'm doing what I can about the Mafia, but that's not why I'm here. I came because twice last month you met with an attorney named Colby, after which Jalen paid that attorney a visit. The DEA is convinced that you're passing messages through Colby to Jalen and then on to your gang. South Atlanta Squad, right?"

No answer. Not the hint of emotion flashing across his face. The man was made of stone.

"The DEA is going after Jalen," I said. "They've got a hard-on for him, big time. They think you're running the Squad. If they aren't proven wrong, they're gonna burn that kid. He'll be sharing your cell before it's over."

Anthony still hadn't blinked. And he still didn't answer.

"You gonna say something?" I let the irritation creep into my voice. I wasn't sure what I expected when I met the convicted killer of a DEA agent, but this wasn't it.

"Leave Jalen alone," Anthony said, his voice dropping a notch. "He don't need your help. Neither do I."

Anthony moved to hang up the phone. I spoke quickly.

"I had a chat with a gangbanger down in Sylvan Terrance yesterday. Wanna know what he said?"

Anthony hesitated, the phone an inch away from his ear. I leaned close to the glass.

"He said you got burned. Set up. By somebody in the SAS, right?"

The phone slid back against his face. Anthony's voice descended into a growl.

"*Who* are you?"

"Just a guy," I said. "A guy who's been where Jalen is, and has a strong intolerance for injustice."

Anthony's knuckles whitened around the phone, but he didn't speak. I could see things behind his eyes now—wheels turning. Thoughts conflicting, maybe. I decided to pour on the heat.

"Why are you refusing an appeal?"

No answer.

"They have leverage on you, don't they?"

No answer.

"Jalen's on the warpath, Anthony. He's stealing cars to raise money for a fancy lawyer. He's trying to get you out. And yet they tell me I'm the only person on your visitation list—I guess that means you aren't seeing Jalen, either. You can sit up here and play stone-cold gangster all you want, but you're only making things worse. If you've got half a spine, you'll man up and start talking before—"

"Back off!" Anthony barked through the phone, his eyes turning suddenly wide, almost as if they were about to pop from his skull. Spittle gleamed from his lips, and breath whistled between his teeth as a crazed fire consumed his gaze.

He looked like a rabid animal. A rabid, *cornered* animal.

"I'm right, aren't I?" I said, lowering my voice.

Anthony continued to breathe hard, but his gaze switched away from me. Glancing over his shoulder, around the room.

Up to the camera.

"Anthony," I said, "I can help you. But you have to—"

Anthony hung up. I heard the phone slam into the receiver even through the reinforced glass. He stood up fast enough to topple his stool and glowered down at me. Eyes still bulging. Chest still rising in strained breaths.

I placed my phone in the cradle but didn't stand. I just returned the stare.

Anthony ran his tongue across his lips, slow and methodical as his breathing began to slow. Then he mouthed a single word. I couldn't hear it, but I didn't need to. The body language was clear enough.

"*Don't.*"

I didn't blink, and I didn't move.

Anthony left the partition in a flash of gray prison uniform. A moment later the guard appeared at the end of the hall and called my name. I took my time leaving, looking over my shoulder to catch another glimpse of Jalen's older brother.

He was gone.

As I was signing out, Miranda appeared and smugly informed me that Anthony had removed my name from his list. I ignored her, tossing the pen down and exiting back into the bright April sunshine. My truck fired right up, still warm from the long drive out of Georgia.

I sat tapping the wheel, visualizing Anthony sitting behind that glass. The ice in his eyes and the bluster that had crept into his voice. The way he'd panicked when I'd hit too close to home.

It wasn't a natural reaction. Not for a stone-cold killer. It made me think Deshaun was right. It made me think Jalen was right. Anthony Cox might well have been burned.

But if that was the case, the burning wasn't over. Somebody was still breathing down his neck, holding something over his head. Something important enough to keep him quiet in prison.

And what do you hold over the head of a hardened gangster with no home, no wife or children? No parents or close friends?

The only thing he has left. The kid brother he loves more than anything in this world.

Jalen.

23

The needle on my truck's fuel gauge bobbed around a quarter tank as I returned to Greenville. I'd learned the hard way not to trust that gauge and decided to refuel before getting too far outside of the city.

I found a gas station just off the interstate, but within seconds of leaving the highway, I knew I'd picked the wrong exit. The streets were grungy, populated by boarded-up stores and abandoned parking lots, reminding me of south Atlanta. The fuel station itself was dilapidated, and the debit card reader on the pump was broken, so I peeled three twenties out of my wallet and headed inside, taking note of my dwindling supply of cash. There was maybe seven or eight hundred left, plus a couple grand in my bank account.

And then...

And then I didn't know. I hadn't made plans to support myself as a homeless wanderer. I hadn't made plans for anything beyond reaching those Georgia pines. Eventually I'd need to secure some more funds or else find a job, but just then I had more pressing problems on my mind.

Problems like how to prove Anthony was innocent when

he clearly didn't want to be proven innocent, and still might not be. Problems like how to keep Jalen alive if the SAS came calling to make good on their threats.

Maybe I'd bitten off more than I could chew.

I selected a Coke and a candy bar, then stepped to the cashier, still thinking about Anthony and Jalen. Part of me wondered if Sarah was right. Maybe this was a lost cause. The streets of America's biggest cities were a cold and unforgiving place, and Jalen might just be one of ten thousand Atlanta kids to be ground through the machinations of criminal life before dying young.

But the fact that he wouldn't be alone in no way assuaged the responsibility I felt. Maybe because I remembered what life on those streets was like. Maybe because my actions at the basketball court had made things worse for him.

Either way, I had to try.

"The rest on the truck," I said, handing the clerk the cash. He looked dumbly out the grimy window to locate the pump, his hands hanging over the register drawer. Then he froze.

"Um...dude. It's rolling away."

I glanced through the window to see the GMC gliding away from the pump, the driver's door open. There was a slight incline leading away from the gas station and dropping down a steeper hill. As the front tires of the truck caught it, the vehicle gained speed.

I sprinted from the counter, blowing through the door and past the pumps. At the foot of the incline sat a small apartment complex, with a row of aged vehicles lined up in the path of my solid-steel, old-school Detroit pickup.

I caught the tailgate just as the truck really began to gain speed. I planted both feet in the short grass barricading the space between the gas station's parking lot and that of the apartment complex, but momentum had taken over, and my tennis shoes simply scrubbed through the dirt. I almost fell as I clawed my way forward, half-running, half being dragged along. The driver's door still hung open as the GMC plowed headlong for the rear end of a minivan only forty yards away.

I reached the doorjamb and lunged for the wheel. I missed and almost fell. The truck hopped the curb, now hurtling along at fifteen or twenty miles an hour and dragging me along. I grabbed the emergency brake lever mounted beneath the dash and yanked it. It ratcheted back, but the truck didn't stop. In the heat of the moment, I'd forgotten that the brake didn't work.

The minivan was barely twenty feet away. I grabbed the doorjamb and slung both feet forward, stabbing blindly at the floorboard. The heel of my right shoe caught the brake, and the truck jolted.

It was too little too late. The front bumper of the old pickup slammed into the minivan, and my forehead smacked against the steering wheel. I saw stars as I tumbled back out of the truck and hit the concrete. Blue sky swirled, and my stomach convulsed. I probed the back of my head, searching for blood.

I didn't feel any.

"Hey! Hey, you! That's my van!"

The voice boomed from across the parking lot, heavy with outrage. I scrabbled to my feet and held on to the truck bed, washed with dizziness as I turned toward the speaker.

It wasn't one guy—it was three. Big, beefy black guys, dressed in black jeans and loose T-shirts. I identified the speaker as the man in the lead, both hands clenched at his sides. Meanwhile the two men standing just behind kept their hands concealed in oversized pockets—faces set in stone-cold glares.

I held up both hands, my back pressed against the bed of the truck. The three of them had come out of nowhere, responding so quickly to the crash they must have watched it happen. Their aggression still surprised me.

"My bad," I said. "It must have slipped out of gear. I'll pay you for the damages, all right? Is cash okay?"

I kept my hands up, not making any sudden movements. The lead guy was closer than I liked, but still far enough away to prevent me from getting a quick hit on him. His companions hung back a little farther, ensuring they had time to deploy whatever hidden weapons lay in those pockets.

I'd lost the tactical advantage before I even knew I was under attack. But maybe this could be de-escalated.

"Who are you, man?" the lead guy said.

"Just somebody passing through. Let's settle up about the van, and I'll be on my way."

I motioned to the damage. The guy didn't so much as look at the smashed minivan.

"That don't answer my question," he snarled. "*Who* are you? And what you doin' in South Carolina?"

I frowned. *What was I doing in South Carolina?* What was anybody doing in South Carolina? And who cared?

"Just passing through," I repeated. "Look, I've got a few hundred bucks on me. If that won't cut it, we can find an ATM. All right? No need to get ugly."

I kept my voice calm and peer-like. The same tone I'd used as a beat cop, talking down bar brawlers. This felt like a bar fight.

Except it also didn't, because the two guys in the background still hadn't spoken or even glanced at the minivan.

"I'll decide when it's time to get ugly," the guy snarled. "And you're gonna answer my question. Why are you here? Where did you come from?"

More strange questions. He took another step my way. I tensed, because as much as I wanted to de-escalate this, if he crossed another inch toward me, I'd have no choice but to turn violent. He'd be inside my safe zone. Too close to control.

Not something I could tolerate.

"Why do you want to know?" I said, lowering my tone.

He glanced over his shoulder toward one of his guys. That guy in turn looked over his own shoulder, scanning the parking lot.

And then I knew it was coming.

I ducked the first blow. It swung wide and high, missing my face and nearly smacking into the white cab of my truck instead. Dropping low, I threw a right hook into his stomach, hard enough to drive the wind right out of him. He doubled over, and I scrambled left, looking for open space behind the truck where I couldn't be pinned down.

Long before I reached the tailgate, the second guy was on me. His hand flashed from his pocket and gleamed in the sun, wrapped in a pair of brass knuckles. The first swing clipped my temple, only a few degrees away from knocking me out cold. I kicked out with my left foot, driving for his knee. Instead of stepping back, he swept my feet with his shin, catching me off balance. I tumbled, hitting the ground on my ass with my shoulders against the rear tire just as the third guy closed in, his own set of knuckles whistling toward my face. I leaned right, and his fist slammed into the bed of my truck, hard enough to leave a dent. I reached into my pocket, scrabbling for the switchblade.

Then I remembered I'd left the knife in the truck while visiting the prison. I'd left both knives in the truck. There was nothing in my pocket.

The next swing hit my shoulder before I could stop it. Shooting pain raced through my chest and down my back, igniting the barely healed bullet wounds from the previous November. I coughed and kicked out with both feet. I saw the first guy standing over me, his fingers wrapped in more shiny metal, his teeth gritted. He raised a fist.

Then a siren chirped, loud and harsh. All three men looked up, and I caught a glimpse of blue lights flashing from between their legs. The two guys in the rear pocketed their hands and turned quickly toward the tree line behind the gas station.

The lead guy took a moment longer, dropping the knuckles into his pocket and leaning over me.

"You one lucky joker, you know that?" he snarled. "You better get your nose out of other people's business, or it's gonna get worse for you. A *lot* worse."

Then he dashed around the rear of the truck and broke into a sprint for the woods. The patrol car rolling through the parking lot blipped its siren again but didn't accelerate to give chase. Instead, it stopped at the rear of my truck, and a petite female officer stepped out, wearing aviator sunglasses, with one hand on her sidearm.

"Sir? You all right?" She spoke with a heavy Southern accent. I sat up, my shoulder still inflamed with pain. Looking up to the gas station, I saw the attendant from behind the counter watching us with one hand shielding his eyes, the other holding a cordless phone.

He must have observed the impending beatdown and dialed 911.

"I'm good," I croaked.

The cop approached cautiously, still gripping the holstered gun. I grabbed the bedrail of the truck and hauled myself up, looking toward the woods just in time to see the last guy disappear.

Into the trees. Not into the apartment complex, where the presumed owner of the minivan lived.

"You wanna tell me what happened?" the cop asked.

I wiped my lip, still wondering myself what had happened, but already thinking I had a pretty good idea.

And it had nothing to do with a smashed minivan.

"Just a misunderstanding," I said.

She chewed gum, looking sideways toward the nose of my truck. The rear hatch of the minivan was dented pretty good, and the plastic bumper was cracked. The solid steel of the GMC was barely scratched.

"You been drinking?" she asked.

"No," I said flatly, dusting my shirt off. Then I walked to the front of the minivan and peeled another two hundred bucks from my pocket. I rolled the cash up and pinned it beneath a windshield wiper. It would probably be gone long before the owner found it, but it was the best I could do. I wouldn't be sticking around.

Returning to the truck, I piled in and slammed the door. The cop didn't move. I knew she wasn't going to stop me. Asking questions would lead to paperwork—a lot of it, maybe. Not how she wanted to spend her afternoon.

I started the truck and wiggled the shifter, placing it in first and testing the lockup.

It took effort to return to neutral. Just as it always had. Because the truck didn't pop out of gear—not without somebody manipulating the shifter.

"Stay out of trouble," the cop warned.

I ignored her, returning to the gas station to collect my fuel before navigating back onto the highway.

All the while wondering who had sent those guys, and how the hell they had found me.

24

The drive back to Atlanta felt twice as long as the drive out to the prison. My back ached, and the road jarred me as I pushed the truck closer to the limits of its outdated engine. It was nearly four p.m. before I reached the south side of the city again, and I made a beeline straight for Jalen's apartment.

During the ride, I had unpacked the incident at the gas station and concluded that there was only one possible explanation. The three guys who jumped me must have trailed me from the prison. I didn't know who they were, and I certainly hadn't noticed anyone following, but my truck was easy to identify and even easier to keep up with. On a freeway packed with ordinary white and silver cars, I probably wouldn't have noticed a tail even if I had been paying attention—which I wasn't. I had been too preoccupied with analyzing Anthony's response to my questions.

So they followed me from the prison, and while I was inside the gas station, one of them must have taken the truck out of gear and given it a little push. Hard enough to move the fight into the secluded parking lot next to the apartment complex, while also offering the pretext of a beatdown.

That also explained the weird questions about where I was from, and why I had come to South Carolina. But what it didn't explain was *how* somebody had picked me up at the prison in the first place. How had they known to follow my truck?

Anthony must have called somebody, I decided. But not after I left—he'd called them beforehand, alerting them that some unknown guy was coming for a visit, and that they were to wait outside and trail me after I left.

Following our unproductive conversation, Anthony must have called again, directing them to confront me at the first available opportunity. Which would have been the gas station.

In hindsight it all made sense and left me with only two possible conclusions about Anthony. Either he was a psychopath, irrationally obsessed with pounding me for bothering him in prison...

Or he truly was innocent and desperate to keep it a secret. Maybe the scumbags who had set Anthony up would skin his little brother alive just the way they'd skinned DEA Special Agent Martin if anyone questioned his conviction.

That would certainly explain why Anthony wasn't filing an appeal. It would also explain why he'd called in some favors from friends on the outside. Sent them to rough up and run off the stranger who was poking around asking dangerous questions.

Whatever it took to protect his kid brother. I couldn't say I blamed him. Given the hand he was dealt, I'd probably play it the same way. But I wasn't given his hand. I was on the outside of this thing, yet somehow in the middle of it, growing tired of the smoke and mirrors and dishonesty. I was ready to cut the bullshit.

I was ready to confront Jalen.

I parked in my now familiar spot behind the Caprice on blocks and marched straight to Jalen's door, the switchblade in my pocket just in case somebody else popped out of the woodwork. I didn't expect it, but I wasn't playing games any longer. If the gas station clerk hadn't dialed the police, I might be in a coma by now.

I pulled back the screen door and knocked on the bare metal behind. My knuckles rang like muted gunshots, and I cast a quick glance around the compound to see if anyone was watching. I didn't see anyone.

But that didn't mean anything.

Inside the apartment I heard a scraping on the tile floor, followed by a subdued female voice saying, "One moment."

I remembered the old lady Jalen had assisted the last time I was here. Maybe Jalen wasn't home.

The doorknob rattled, but the door didn't open. The voice called out again, "Who's there?"

"I'm Mason," I said, keeping my voice friendly. "I'm a friend of Jalen's."

The lock twisted, and the door swung open just a little. I saw a chain holding it from opening all the way; then the old lady's face appeared in the crack.

She was seated in a wheelchair, leaning out to make herself visible. That face was far older than I initially estimated. At least late eighties, with crinkly brown skin and the deepest brown eyes I thought I'd ever seen. She had a soft, kind look about her from the first moment our gazes met, and instead of looking suspicious, she smiled.

It was a warm smile. A very grandmotherly expression.

"Yes?"

"Hello, ma'am," I said, returning the smile and keeping my posture relaxed. "Is Jalen home?"

"No...he had something after school. Who are you?"

"I'm a friend," I said again.

She looked semi-suspiciously toward the parking lot. Maybe looking for a government vehicle or some other explanation for why a stranger was knocking on her door. I couldn't blame her for the mistrust. It was a dangerous part of town.

"He's out with his friends...I don't know when he'll be back. Would you like to leave a message?"

"That's okay," I said. "I'll stop by later if that's all right."

"Okay," she said.

I turned for the steps and made it back to the sidewalk. She didn't shut the door, still watching me. I stopped and pocketed my hands, looking first toward the setting sun and then back to the old lady.

"He's a good kid, isn't he?" I asked.

The old lady beamed. "He's my sunshine, that Jalen. I don't know what I'd do without him."

I thought about Jalen helping her into the medical van. That kiss on the cheek as he concealed his busted nose.

Protecting her. Caring for her. A good kid.

"Have a wonderful evening, ma'am."

She nodded once, and I returned to the truck. The motor rumbled to life, and I took the surface streets back to the highway, then turned north. I found the Skyline Diner right where I left it—right where I first met Jalen—and I ordered a burger, fries, and milkshake. I had barely eaten all day, and my stomach growled while I waited for the food, looking out the window and watching my truck.

It sat in the same parking space where it had been when Jalen found it. But I didn't see the kid now. I didn't see anyone.

My burger came, and I dug in while my mind spun through the events of the past two days, sorting through them and working to see the full picture. The burger was better than I remembered, or maybe I was just hungry and eager for something to be happy about.

I felt like I'd run straight into a block wall. If everything I now suspected was true—if Anthony was innocent, Jalen was hell-bent on proving it, and the SAS was dangling Jalen's life over Anthony's head—there was really only one way to proceed: Go to war with the SAS.

Their blackmail of Anthony was the lynchpin of this entire mess. The wrench binding everything up. So long as they held leverage over Anthony, it really didn't matter if he was innocent or not. He would maintain his guilt. Send his buddies after me and anyone else who attempted to help him.

Leave Jalen to piss his life away pounding against that same block wall I now faced.

And wasn't that the irony of it all.

I slopped my burger through a puddle of ketchup on my plate, frustration blurring into irritation. The farther I dug into this thing, the messier it got. A large part of me wished I'd dropped Jalen at his apartment and never turned back. I could be halfway to Florida by now.

The door opened behind me, and I instinctively looked over one shoulder. The diner had two entrances, making it impossible for me to sit anywhere without my back to one of them. It was a tactically inferior situation, but the man I saw shuffling inside with his head cloaked in the hood of a jacket didn't look threatening.

He didn't look like Steel Mafia or one of the guys from South Carolina or one of Feldon's people. He walked with his shoulders loose, hands in his pockets.

I returned to my burger, taking another bite as the guy sat down in the booth directly behind me, his shoulder blades only inches from my own. A menu shuffled, and his jacket crinkled against the booth's vinyl. The waitress came by, and he ordered coffee. I wiped ketchup off my face and subdued a burp.

"I'm gonna make this real simple." The guy behind me spoke, his voice a deep growl with a thick accent that blended between urban and Southern. Something in his tone made it clear he was addressing me, and I twisted toward him.

"You turn around and I'll pop your ass right here," the guy said. I froze. The waitress returned and deposited his coffee. She asked for an order, and he waved her away. I watched the interaction in the polished stainless steel of my napkin dispenser, the reflection blurry, my hand dropping toward the switchblade.

"Who are you?" I said, keeping my voice low.

"Don't matter," he said. "Don't matter who you are, neither. Only thing that matters is that you gonna get back in that truck, and you gonna get out of town. You gonna leave Jalen alone. You gonna leave Anthony alone. You gonna leave it all alone. Understand?"

I didn't answer. My hand was clasped around the switchblade now, the weapon free of my pocket. I was still monitoring the guy in the napkin holder, ensuring that he wasn't about to clock me. He hadn't moved, his back still turned, his hands invisible beneath the table.

"What if I have other plans?" I said.

He slurped coffee. The cup clicked against the tabletop. "Then I'll bury your ass out in the county, and you won't never be heard from again."

There was no bravado in his voice. No arrogance. Just cold resolve.

"I'm hard to bury," I said. "And so is the truth."

A cold snapping sound rang from his booth. My muscles tensed as my mind registered the click of a cocking revolver. I didn't move, my gaze still fixated on the napkin dispenser.

"Boy, I been burying things since you was in diapers. Don't roll those dice."

I glanced quickly around the diner using my peripheral vision. There was a family across the room. A dad, a young mother, and two kids. In the corner an old couple shared a meal. Somewhere near the counter a homeless guy was begging the hostess for scraps.

Innocent people. Collateral damage if this guy started shooting.

I didn't move.

He took another slurp from the coffee cup, then set it down and slid out of the booth. He kept his back to me, preventing even a profile of his face as he dropped a bill on the table. His left hand was buried in the pocket of an over-sized coat—concealing the weapon.

"Move along," he warned. "I ain't foolin' around."

Without another word he walked to the door. The moment I heard hinges groan, I shot out of the booth, the switchblade at my side, rushing after him. I saw a figure slide into a waiting car, and a motor rumbled. It was an old-school Cadillac, dark green with heavily tinted windows. I rushed into the parking lot as the tires ground across the pavement, and then the car shot out into the street.

Long before I could reach my truck, it was gone, lost in the crush of Atlanta traffic.

25

I watched the Cadillac fade, not bothering to give chase. I'd never catch up in my truck, even if I made it into the street before the car disappeared. It was a simple matter of horsepower.

I returned to the diner instead and finished my burger, ignoring the milkshake and paying in cash. Back in the truck I sat with the engine off and steamed, recalling the faceless man's threat.

Don't roll those dice.

Everything about the interaction was different from my collisions in south Atlanta and at the gas station in Greenville. The guy at the diner had the tone and style of an old-school gangster—not somebody interested in making a flashy appearance so much as getting the job done. That told me nothing about his identity or his motives, but the fact that I had been accosted twice inside the space of one afternoon put me on edge.

These people were serious. Anthony was serious.

He would do anything to protect his little brother. And somehow, he was keeping tabs on me.

I dug into my pocket and sifted past loose change, the switchblade, and my wallet until I found the card Sarah had given me. I dialed her cell using my burner phone and waited five rings for her to pick up.

"Hello?" I heard a shower running in the background, and Sarah's voice echoed a little the way a voice does in a tile bathroom, but she sounded as unflappable as ever. As though she expected my call. I checked my watch. It was almost six p.m. She must be at home.

"Sarah, it's Mason."

She didn't answer.

"From the deli," I clarified.

"I know who you are. Why are you calling?" Her voice remained relaxed. Somehow that annoyed me.

"I spoke with Anthony."

"At the prison?"

"Right."

"And?"

"He won't talk, and after I left, I was roughed up."

"Okay."

No concerns about my condition or safety. How nice of her.

"Somebody's leaning on him," I said. "Hard enough to keep him quiet and keep him scared. I don't know why he sent goons after me, but there's clearly something at stake if his guilt is questioned. I think it might be Jalen."

"Can you prove that?"

"I'm working on it. I need you to send me everything you've got on the Cox trial. All the depositions, evidence, transcripts. Whatever."

"What makes you think I've got any of that?"

"Because you knew a lot about the trial. And because you care too much for your own good. You wouldn't have turned Jalen away without digging into the case."

A long pause. "Pretty sure I'm not the one who cares too much for their own good."

Fair point.

"Email me," I said, adding my personal email address. I hadn't checked it in months, but I figured I could still log in using the motel computer.

"Those are confidential documents," Sarah said.

"So email me the public access ones. Just get me what you can."

"What's your play here, Mason? What are you roping me into?"

"I'm not roping you into anything. I'm just trying to find the truth before Jalen gets in too deep. Send me the docs and let me dig. If I can find something to exonerate Anthony, will you run with it?"

Another long pause. I still heard the shower in the background. An involuntary image of Sarah's unclothed body standing amid rolling steam flashed across my mind, joined by a rush of blood flow.

And then instant guilt.

I hadn't thought of any woman since I met Mia. Not once. And not since she died, either. The thought of Sarah outside the shower made me feel dirty and disloyal.

"If you bring me hard evidence, I'll run with it," Sarah said. "But your mental math is weak, Mason. If you're right, and Anthony took the fall for a bigger gang boss, that boss isn't gonna go down without a fight."

"Well, he's gonna have to fight me, then," I said.

No answer. I started the truck.

"Just send me the docs. I'll take it from there."

I hung up and used the web browser on the phone to look up listings of local rental car dealerships. There were several nearby, and I navigated to one just a few miles southeast of downtown. It was a chain store with a familiar green sign.

There was a Home Depot built in the parking lot next to it, and I parked the GMC in the back of the lot and locked the doors. Then I headed for the dealership.

I was growing tired of being so easily followed in such a recognizable vehicle, and even more tired of being unable to give chase in such an underpowered vehicle. I needed something fast and generic. Something nobody knew to look for.

I rented a black Dodge Charger with a V6 engine. Not the most powerful thing on the street, but much faster than my GMC and much more ordinary. The fee was seventy-five dollars per day—a steep price against a dwindling bank account.

Problems for later.

I took the keys and slid into the car, ratcheting back the seat to leave room for my oversized frame. The car started with a gentle rumble, and I used the touchscreen on the dash to manipulate a built-in map of the city. It wasn't difficult to pick out now-familiar locations: my motel near the airport, the Skyline Diner just off the highway, and Jalen's apartment complex.

I navigated to a sporting goods store first and purchased a compact pair of binoculars. Then I selected Jalen's apartment complex and let the GPS do the work. As I rolled back onto the highway, I switched the headlights on. The sky was darkening, and downtown lights glowed in my rearview. A constant crush of traffic pressed in all around me, but I didn't mind.

I felt invisible in the Charger. Just another one of thousands cruising around the big city. Nobody would notice me at the apartment, watching from a distance.

Jalen, least of all. I remembered that throwaway line he'd tossed at his buddy two mornings prior at the basketball court: *See ya Friday night.*

At the time I'd barely given the line a second thought. A

couple of teenagers could have a dozen innocent reasons to meet up on a Friday night. Video games, a favorite TV show, or more basketball. But there was something in Jalen's voice when he said it. A piercing look he shot the other kid as the words left his lips. It made me wonder if they were headed out of the complex, someplace else in the city. Maybe planning to jack another car to raise money for Anthony's legal fund.

If so, they might be trailed by whoever had accosted me at the Skyline Diner—the man looking after Jalen.

And that gave me an opportunity to do some accosting of my own.

26

I changed up my parking spot near Jalen's apartment, figuring that it was my visit to the old lady that had tipped off the man at the diner. He'd probably seen my truck parked behind the Caprice on blocks and might be on the lookout for it again. Maybe that was how he kept tabs on me—by looking out for the unique pickup.

Instead, I moved down the street to a little parking lot and sandwiched the Charger between two former police cars, both sporting spinner wheels and spotlights. The position only gave me a partial view of Jalen's apartment, but it was better than nothing. I leaned back in the seat and quietly monitored the tempo of the community.

It always amazed me how a place could have a heartbeat. Born of the people who lived there and the unique lives they led, every neighborhood developed a sort of tide that came and went with each cycle of that community's daily activities.

The government housing project Jalen lived in was certainly no different. I noticed people returning home in clusters as city buses pulled up to a designated stop outside the complex, and porch lights flashed on when they reached their apartments. Kids played in the overgrown grass between the buildings, and from someplace nearby a barbecue grill wafted the smell of burning charcoal toward the Charger.

Guys sitting on porch steps drank beer and laughed. Mothers shouted at children. A cop car rolled by, and everybody became quiet until it disappeared.

It was an entire social ecosystem built of culture and hardship, perspective and reality. All the things that made an entire group of people think and feel the same way about enough things to make them appear as a unit. A society.

And I was an outsider. It reminded me of what Sarah had said about me doing more harm than good. What the guy at the diner had said about me getting lost.

They had a point. But there was another side to that coin, also. Left alone, Jalen would keep ramming his head against the wall of Anthony's incarceration until Feldon, the Atlanta Police, or another gangster brought his freedom—and maybe his life—to an end.

It was an inevitable thing. The forces of nature, slowly consuming a young and ignorant life. Something I simply couldn't watch happen.

I pictured the fifteen-year-old in my mind, and like magic he appeared. He hustled around the corner of the apartment building, accompanied by the kid I had seen before—the one in the Heat jersey. Jalen's right-hand man, apparently.

They both wore backpacks and pushed bicycles. When they reached the parking lot, they swung into the seats and commenced pedaling, taking off toward the street.

I hit the Charger's push start and shifted into reverse. In short order I traced them out of the complex and into the city, hanging back and stalling at every stop sign and traffic light to avoid overtaking them. It was tricky business, and on multiple occasions I was forced to drive past them to avoid blowing my cover. The kids were fast though, working the bikes like absolute pros and gliding through intersections and past stop signs without any regard for traffic laws.

As I drove, I kept an eye out for the dark green Cadillac I'd seen at the diner. It was a coupe, I remembered. A late seventies or early eighties model, all stretched out and riding low. I figured that whoever the man in the diner had been, if he was looking after Jalen, he might be prowling nearby. If I could get the jump on him, I might have a shot at getting some questions answered. Maybe get some idea about how to unravel this mess without directly declaring war on a drug gang.

But I didn't see the Cadillac. I didn't see anyone patrolling the streets, keeping tabs on the boys. It was just me and the Charger.

We were now someplace east of Highway 75 and north of Cleveland Avenue, and the neighborhood around us was a mottled mix of aged and decrepit houses crowded by tall and skinny gentrification builds. The deeper into the neighborhood we moved, the fewer of those tall and skinnies I saw, now replaced by moldy old houses overhung by oak trees and surrounded by busted sidewalks.

Many of the streetlights were dead, and more than a couple of houses looked ready for demolition. I eventually switched my headlights off, figuring that now that traffic had thinned out, I should do all I could to blend into the darkness.

We had traveled nearly five miles before Jalen and his friend ground to a stop, and I still hadn't seen the dark green Cadillac. The boys leaned their bikes against a two-story brick building, standing right on the corner of a wide intersection. It was weathered and old, with all the windows either blacked out or boarded over, and a neon sign reading *lounge* mounted alongside a solid steel door. Large black guys in dark clothes slouched outside that door, smoking and laughing. The street was clogged by cars—dark sedans, some on spinners, others lowered. All of them heavily tinted.

Styled cars. Show cars. The building was a social hotspot, I judged. And not the kind of place for a couple of teenagers.

I stopped the Charger half a block away and pulled in front of a vacant-looking house. Cutting the engine, I sat quietly with a partial view of the club.

Jalen and his friend left their bikes and sauntered right up to the entrance of the big building like they owned the place. It made me think they had been here before, but the big guys near the door didn't bother to be friendly. They halted Jalen at the curb, and some manner of exchange ensued. I couldn't hear anything, but the body language was obvious.

Jalen wanted to go inside. Nobody was going to let that happen. One of the big guys motioned him back and said something. The other big guys laughed.

Jalen bristled.

I looked into my mirrors to ensure nobody had slipped up on me. When I checked the scene at the club again, Jalen and his comrade were reluctantly surrendering their backpacks.

It didn't look like a shakedown. The big guy stuffed both packs beneath his arm and made a calming motion with one hand. Jalen stood with his arms crossed, still fuming. But he made no effort to enter the building as the big guy disappeared through the door.

Five minutes passed. Then ten. The other guys at the door were ignoring the kids now, focusing on smokes and cell phones instead, exchanging jokes now and again. I could tell by the way they laughed, but Jalen and Heat weren't part of the exchange.

I dug the binoculars out of their packaging and used them to zoom in on the building. Dull light from a nearby streetlamp aided my view as the club door once again swung open. The big guy returned with the backpacks, but this time they weren't empty—he held both by their straps, and they dangled under the weight of new cargo.

He wasn't alone, either. A smaller guy joined him. Average height, dressed in sweatpants and a tight tank top, with a black skullcap stretched over his head, his hands in his pockets. He was muscular and fit. Late twenties or early thirties. And clearly in charge.

I could tell by the way the other bouncers straightened and pocketed their phones when he exited. The new guy approached Jalen and spoke calmly to him, motioning to the backpacks halfway through his spiel. Jalen held his head up, shoulders back. Confident, or at least projecting confidence.

Another motion to the backpack. Jalen made a dismissive wave of one hand and said something.

The new guy smiled. He didn't laugh. He didn't speak. He just smiled, and something about the expression chilled me.

It was cold. Heartless.

I reached instinctively for my burner phone and activated its built-in camera. It wasn't much of a camera, especially this far away. As I zoomed in, the picture blurred a little, but I snapped a few shots of the crowd on the corner anyway, centering around the guy in the skullcap.

A little documentation. Just in case.

The interaction at the corner seemed to be winding down now. The big guy handed off the packs to Jalen and Heat, and the two kids shouldered them with deferential lifts of their chins. Then they were hustling back to their bikes, leaving the guy in the skullcap to watch them.

Hands in his pockets.

Jalen and Heat swung astride their bikes and turned toward home, pedaling right by me without so much as glancing at the Charger.

I didn't bother to give chase. I already knew where they

were headed, and I already knew what was in the backpacks. Weed, probably. A few pounds of it. A gateway product for aspiring drug dealers.

I'd seen it before. Hard-hitting gangs in Phoenix often used children to hand off their product to passing cars, knowing that cops would be less likely to suspect or accost kids. When a promising young entrepreneur broke from the pack, proving himself to be clever about the art of narcotics delivery, that young man would be offered an advanced opportunity: taking control of a larger supply and distributing it through a small territory. Probably his apartment complex.

If he succeeded at that, he'd have a shot at climbing the ranks. Becoming an advanced dealer.

But I doubted seriously whether Jalen was thinking that far ahead. This wasn't about growing a career in narcotics distribution, this was just another way to raise money for that billboard attorney.

What bothered me now wasn't Jalen, or even the drugs he carried. It was the guy in the skullcap who continued to stand at the edge of the curb, that sinister grin on his lips. Watching him from a hundred yards away, nestled in the shadows, a new thought hit me like a ton of bricks. Something I'd never considered before, but should have.

If the SAS is using Jalen as leverage, they must be keeping tabs on him.

And what better way to keep tabs on a kid like Jalen than to have him working for you?

If I was right, and if the guys in the club were members of the South Atlanta Squad, Jalen didn't know. There was no way he'd associate with the gang he believed to have burned his brother.

But maybe they knew him. Well enough to trust him with

the weed. Well enough to keep him handy just in case they needed to put the screws on Anthony.

It was a shot in the dark, but the logic was sound enough for me to give up on trailing Jalen or hunting for the driver of the green Cadillac, at least for now.

Instead, I wanted to watch this club. I wanted to watch this gangster.

So I got comfortable. Skullcap went back inside, and I waited. An hour. Two. Four. I leaned back in the seat and squeezed my legs together when I had to piss, leveraging all of the patience and sustained alertness I had learned during my tenure as a homicide detective in Phoenix.

Embracing the slow crawl of the clock.

Skullcap finally appeared at just past three a.m., lighting up a smoke on the sidewalk. A moment later a Mercedes S-Class sedan pulled around the corner. It was jet black with aftermarket rims and tinted taillights, muting the glow of red as the driver stopped near the club door.

Skullcap got in, and I started the Charger.

27

We left the city quickly, navigating out of the neighborhood and onto the highway. The S-Class was fast, and the driver drove hard. I would never have kept up in the GMC, but with the Charger's three-hundred-horsepower engine, I had a fighting chance.

I cut through the traffic along I-675, monitoring our travel southbound on the Charger's built-in GPS. The blackened Mercedes took the interchange onto I-75, still headed south toward Macon, and accelerated.

I hit the gas, watching the digital speedometer tick up to ninety, the Mercedes cruising two hundred yards ahead.

The city vanished behind us. It grew darker off the highway, with only occasional passing lights of truck stops every couple of exits. The traffic began to thin, and I worried about being spotted.

Then the dull glow of flashing orange shone from behind the tinted taillights, and the Mercedes took the next exit.

I followed, hanging back as far as I could. The S-Class took a county road away from the exit, weaving amid sparse subdivisions separated by occasional rolling fields. If I hadn't just driven out of Atlanta, I would have had no idea we were so near a metropolis. Signs advertised local towns, eight and ten miles away. We passed a couple of gas stations, and I slowed to put another hundred yards between myself and the German sedan.

And then I saw muted taillights. They flashed on, and the Mercedes slowed. I stepped on the brake but allowed the distance between us to shrink. Just the way a late-night driver stuck behind a turning car might do.

I saw the Mercedes pull into a gravel drive with a tall chain-link gate blocking the path ahead. The Mercedes stopped, and I rushed on by.

Just another late-night driver, eager to get home.

A mile down the road I doubled back, passing the gate. The Mercedes was gone, and the gate was locked again. I slowed to barely twenty miles an hour and rolled by, noting the spot on the Charger's navigation system and double-tapping until a digital pin dropped in place to mark it.

Then I hit the gas and drove a quarter mile around the bend to the last gas station I'd seen, where I pulled the Charger in behind a pump and cut the engine. The gas station was closed, and the lights were off. The Charger blended into the dark. I took the switchblade and the binoculars, then locked the doors.

My tennis shoes crunched over short grass as I jogged the quarter mile alongside the road back to the turnoff. I could still smell dust on the air where the Mercedes's tires had disturbed the gravel drive. The gate was locked, wrapped in a chain with KEEP OUT signs wire-tied to the fence.

But fifty feet to the right of the gate, buried in under-growth, I saw a fallen tree lying across the chain link, crushing it toward the ground. Brambles tore at my legs as I fought my way through, clawing up onto the tree and crossing the fence with ease. It was pitch black and choked with briars on the other side. I knelt long enough to allow my eyes to adjust, listening for sounds of humanity.

I heard cicadas—giant flying insects native to the southeast that make a noise like a small helicopter. I remembered them from boot camp at Fort Benning. Sergeant Smiles used to call them Georgian candy bars, and threatened to make us eat them when anyone complained about hunger.

The memory brought a smile to my face, but just now I could do without their incessant buzzing. They made the already uncertain process of sneaking into unfriendly territory even more dangerous. I couldn't hear any footsteps. No disgruntled grumblings of a bored sentry. No warnings as to whether I was about to walk right into somebody.

I kept low to the ground as I navigated through the weeds and into a small grove of pecan trees, their limbs tangled with the dense nests of webworms. I chose each step carefully, avoiding direct collisions with last year's fallen pecans, and then I felt the ground rise beneath my feet.

I dropped to my stomach as I neared the crest of the rise, worming along between the brambles and enduring the superficial cuts they left along my exposed arms. Another ten yards and I reached the top, pushing grass aside to look down into a shallow valley below.

It wasn't a valley so much as a dish, maybe three hundred yards across, with the gravel drive leading down into it. At the bottom, about a hundred yards from my current position and just a couple dozen beneath me, sat a large brick building. Two story, with shattered windows and a number of brick smokestacks reaching out of the roof toward a star-filled sky.

The building was old—probably from America's Industrial Age. A factory of some type, now long abandoned with shattered windows and a busted parking lot. The driveway the Mercedes had entered through was some kind of secondary entrance. The main entrance was poured in concrete, leading out of the valley on the far side, now blocked by heavy chain-link gates.

I took note of the Mercedes parked near the building and one of the big guys smoking outside. There was a black SUV, also. An Escalade, sitting next to the S-Class.

I couldn't see Skullcap or any lights shining from the building. The entire place lay quiet and dark, only a few hundred yards off the highway yet completely invisible to the outside world.

It was kind of a sanctuary, I thought. And given the occupants of that Mercedes and the drugs I'd just seen them pass off on a couple of kids, I could only conclude it to be a sanctuary for bad things.

It brought to mind my weeks in North Carolina the previous January. The people I had encountered, and the bones I had broken. There was a house up there, buried in the woods, filled with illicit activity. In my experience as a cop, this was a standard arrangement. Someplace off the beaten path where operations could proceed unmolested.

And yet, this was different. Because if Skullcap and his associates were in the business of slinging drugs, they shouldn't *need* a place like this. Or want one. It was too easy to be detected by a DEA drone or satellite. Too easy to be discovered by a cop trailing them, the same way I had.

Having a place like this was a risk. And it begged the question: *why?*

I back-crawled out of the brush, enduring the cuts of the brambles again before using the fallen tree to circumvent the gate. I was back inside the Charger and picking thorns out of my clothes when the Mercedes passed. It rushed by my position behind the gas pump without pausing—a blackened ghost of the early morning.

I dumped the thorns out the open window and rubbed

my eyes. They burned. Weariness was setting in as I struggled to think of a next move.

Starting the engine, I turned back to the city and navigated for my motel. Deep in my gut an idea was beginning to form. Some way to break through the block wall I'd rammed up against.

Some way to pull the lynchpin of this entire mess.

It felt just out of reach, like a specific word I was searching for but couldn't quite remember. Something important that my tired mind couldn't quite compute.

I needed to rest. I needed to let the idea incubate and hopefully hatch into something useful.

Because with Jalen's newfound enterprise as a drug dealer, this train was gaining momentum.

I was running out of time to stop it before it ran completely off its tracks.

28

I parked the car directly outside my motel room and descended immediately into bed. I was exhausted, but sleep didn't come easily. The moment the lights were out and I was left to stare at a blank ceiling, I saw Mia.

My fiancée had been dead for nearly six months, but in my mind it felt like only yesterday when she was alive in my arms. Her bright smile, her warm lips on mine. I could still taste them, but the memory was starting to weaken. That thoughtless moment with Sarah on the phone, imagining her naked in the shower, had shaken me.

It left me feeling like I'd betrayed Mia, somehow, and the fading sensation of her head against my chest reinforced my desperation.

I took a cold shower and eventually found sleep a little before five a.m., catching five hours of fitful sleep before I put my feet on the floor again and ran both hands through my uncut hair.

I thought about North Carolina. About how I had weaponized an innocent woman's loss into an opportunity to avenge my own heartache. I wondered if that was happening all over again, right here in Atlanta. If once more I was looking for people to pound just to keep from pounding myself.

Maybe. And maybe that was a problem. But it didn't change the fact that I had walked into an absolute mess, and I wasn't a man to leave things worse than I found them.

Sergeant Smiles had taught me better.

I dressed in a fresh pair of jeans and a shirt, shaved, and repacked my gear. The violin still lay in my duffel bag, waiting patiently for me to have another go at that Zac Brown Band song. Mia's Bible felt worn in my rough hands, and I wanted to flip it open and stare at her picture.

I didn't. I couldn't look her in the eye after that fleeting thought about Sarah.

As if on cue, the burner phone buzzed, and a text message appeared on the screen. It was the first message I'd received since activating the phone, and it was from Sarah's number.

Check your email.

I pocketed the phone and put my shoes on, then stepped outside. Atlanta had been awake for hours, the sky hazy with clouds, a jumbo jet screaming overhead on its way to the airport. Across the parking lot a woman in pajamas screamed at a shirtless man in gym shorts, her stringy hair wrapped in a towel, a fresh bruise on his face. Even from the second floor, I imagined I could smell the alcohol on their breath.

I really had to find a better place to sleep.

I started down the steps, but stopped cold halfway, my gaze falling on the Charger. It sat right where I left it, facing my motel room, dusty from last night's trip into the country-side.

But something was wrong. I couldn't put my finger on it at

first. Something simply looked *off*.

I continued to the parking lot and rounded the nose of the car. Then I saw it.

The front right tire was slashed. As was the rear. I hurried to the far side and confirmed more of the same. All four tires were cut, and the car now rested on rims. I breathed a curse, then noticed the yellow sticky note pasted to the driver's window. I snatched it off and scanned the short message—only two words.

Last warning.

My gaze snapped up, and I surveyed the lot, the street, and the adjacent McDonald's. There was nobody. No DEA sedan staking out my position. No rolling Mercedes or dark green Cadillac.

But someone had been here. Somebody who must have trailed me from the night before. How else would they know where I was staying? Know that I'd switched vehicles?

I crumpled the note and stomped to the motel office, shoving through the door and waiting impatiently for an old couple to check out. The sour-faced woman behind the counter was the same one I had checked in with. She looked every bit as bored as before.

"Hey," I said. "Somebody slashed my tires."

She grunted, filing the old couple's electronic keys back into a dispenser.

I rapped on the counter with my knuckles. "Ma'am, did you hear me?"

She didn't even look up, pointing to the wall nearest the door, where a white sign printed in red letters declared:

NOT RESPONSIBLE FOR THEFT OR DAMAGE TO VEHICLES.

"Really?" I said.

She shrugged.

"You got cameras?"

"Yep."

"I want to see the tape."

"Nope."

"Why?"

"Because you're not a cop, and I don't see a warrant. Besides, my cameras don't cover the parking lot."

I gritted my teeth, but I knew it was a lost cause. I wasn't too worried about the tires anyway. My rental insurance would cover them. I was much more concerned about *who* had slashed them.

Returning to the lot, I briefly considered running a search for evidence around the car, then decided it was a waste of time. This would have been an easy job—roll up, pop open a knife, cut the tires and stick the note to the window. Twenty seconds, tops. If the guy had half a clue what he was doing, there wouldn't be fingerprints.

And even if there were, it wasn't like I could do anything with them. The motel clerk was right. I wasn't a cop.

I poured myself a cup of black coffee from the pot in the motel lobby, then proceeded to the motel's business center and plopped down in front of a computer. The clerk cleared her throat and pointed to a sign barring food or drink from the business center. I held her gaze, unblinking, and took a long slurp of coffee, smacking my lips like an absolute psychopath.

She bugged off, and I called the rental company. The girl who answered was spunky and helpful, promising to have a new car delivered within the hour and assuring me there would be no charge for the slashed tires due to my insurance. I hung up and logged in to my email.

It had been months since I had checked my email, and I

was unprepared for the deluge of messages that greeted me. Not just the usual slew of junk newsletters from streaming services and online memberships. There were messages from my mortgage company, warning of an impending foreclosure of the home I had abandoned in Phoenix. Emails from the human resources division of the Phoenix Police Department, inquiring about the expiration of my personal leave and whether I would be returning to duty.

And emails from friends. Dozens of them. All checking in or asking me to give them a call. One name stuck out from the rest—the name of my partner in the PPD, Jacquie Richardson. Her emails were blunt and used increasing amounts of profanity, all ordering me to call her before she sent out a search team.

The last message was dated for three weeks previously. I couldn't help but open it.

You're a real asshole, Mason. Call me. I deserve that much.

I was unsurprised by Jacquie's bluntness, but the last line stung a little—because it was true. I hadn't spoken to Jacquie since leaving North Carolina, and since I abandoned my phone, she had no way of contacting me.

I needed space. I wanted space.

But I also knew I was on the precipice of losing a friendship forever.

I closed out of the message, resolving to deal with it later, and opened Sarah Dalton's email. It contained only three words and a file.

Check it out.

I double-clicked on the attached PDF and was greeted by a four-hundred-and-fifteen-page document packed to the brim with everything related to the Anthony Cox case.

Court files. Submitted evidence. Depositions. Clerk notes. Testimony transcripts. Crime scene photos. Police reports.

And this was only half of it, I knew. Probably less than half. A trial of this magnitude could produce thousands of pages. But the fact that Sarah had assembled this much so quickly confirmed two things I'd already assumed about her: She was damn good at her job, and she had already taken a deep dive into Anthony Cox's case.

Instead of scrolling, I navigated straight to the top of the PDF viewer and selected the search bar. Then I went to work inputting key words—items I knew from experience would take me to the heart of the matter.

Crime scene.

Key witness.

Defense exhibit.

Victim photographs.

In twenty minutes I knew more about the Anthony Cox trial than a hundred news articles would ever tell.

It all began when Special Agent Drew Martin went offline while working undercover. His body was discovered in a ditch outside of town, hog-tied and...well, faceless. Pictures of the crime scene were included under the evidence section of Sarah's document, and it was all I could do not to choke up my coffee as I scanned them. With the skin stripped away, Martin's head was bloody red with shiny white glowing through in places where the knife had scraped right to the bone. His eyes looked inhumanly wide and full of pain, his lips missing, and his teeth caked with dried blood.

He hadn't suffocated. He had drowned, his windpipe flooded by his own body fluids.

It was one of the ghastliest things I'd ever seen, and I'd seen more gore than most. My stomach turned, and I scrolled quickly away, blinking to remove the images from my mind. It was too late; they were already seared in place.

I knew they were seared in the minds of the jury, also. Anthony Cox had been doomed before the trial even began. All of the evidence I had already read about—the fingerprinted knife, the DNA, the blood—was now described in painstaking detail. Enough proof to smother even the most ardent presumption of innocence.

As for Cox himself, he had been picked up in Greenville, South Carolina, a day after Martin's body was found. An anonymous caller tipped off police. Anthony was extradited immediately back to Georgia, and later that year the trial commenced.

I scanned through a paragraph of key witnesses for the prosecution and noted that Mark Feldon topped the list. Apparently, he was a leading member of the task force involved with managing Martin's undercover work—a link that didn't surprise me. It perfectly explained his rampage against the SAS. I knew if I lost a fellow Ranger or cop to a death like this, I'd certainly burn the world down in my pursuit of anyone and everyone responsible. One confessing killer wouldn't be enough. I'd want them *all*. The entire gang. The whole army of them.

Whatever it took.

The prosecution's key physical evidence consisted of the murder weapon. It was a skinning knife like you might buy at a sporting goods store—a short, razor-sharp blade and a wood handle, both stained with Martin's blood.

I moved on to the defense testimony, but there wasn't much to see. A few psychiatrists testifying that Anthony was verifiably insane. Some questionable character witnesses. An expert attempting to diminish the DNA evidence.

Nothing that would make any difference, in the end. Anthony was on his own. Despite mentions of relations in Greenville, only two family members had showed up for the trial. Some uncle named Reginald James, who only appeared the first day...and Jalen.

I sat back in the squeaking business center chair and rubbed my chin. I'd never considered myself anything of a legal mind, and I certainly hadn't had extensive training in the subject. But I'd sat in the witness box at enough homicide trials to know a slam dunk when I saw one. Sarah had been right—Anthony Cox never stood a chance. The prosecution came at him like a battalion of Marines storming a beach, and he was done.

And yet...

And yet something in my gut told me the story wasn't complete. Not just because of Deshaun's snide declaration in the alley, or Jalen's own instance that his brother was innocent. Because of my interactions with Anthony. I recalled the way he'd exploded when I touched on his guilt. The force with which he and several others had attempted to run me off.

I closed my eyes and pictured a generic courtroom. Anthony behind the defense table, sitting next to a flustered and overwhelmed A. B. Colby. The prosecutor pouring on the heat in front of a transfixed jury.

And Jalen sitting in the gallery. Wide-eyed and terrified. He'd shown up *every day* of Anthony's trial. Blowing off school and maybe hitching rides. Putting his own life on hold to support his brother.

Yes, the two of them were close. Very close. There were no parents mentioned on those court records. No other family standing behind the defense table as the verdict was read. Just Anthony and Jalen against the world.

I heard tires grind on the concrete outside the motel lobby and opened my eyes to see a white Charger pull in. Two guys in polo shirts featuring the rental company logo got out, and one pointed to the car with the slashed tires.

I leaned back in the squeaking chair and watched them, cradling my coffee and thinking.

Thinking about Jalen and Anthony. Thinking about the Squad's blackmail—the lynchpin of this whole problem. Nothing would change for Jalen until that lynchpin was pulled. Until the morbid threat of Anthony's former associates was neutralized.

But how could I neutralize it without launching a one-man war against an entire drug gang? It was a noble idea. I liked the mental image it generated. But I didn't have the resources. I didn't have the personnel.

But somebody else does.

The thought cracked in my mind like a shotgun blast. It was the idea I had felt dancing in the back of my consciousness earlier that same morning, just out of reach, but loud enough for me to know it was a good one. Two items, apparently unrelated, with a connection that now seemed blatantly obvious. So perfectly plain.

I had an entire *army* at my disposal. They just needed a target.

Turning back to the computer, I closed out of the files and logged out of my email. Then I navigated to a web browser and ran a search. Found a number and wrote it down on a scrap of paper.

Meeting the rental guys outside, I transferred my meager luggage into the new Charger, then sat behind the wheel with the engine running and dialed the number I took from the computer.

"Drug Enforcement Administration, Atlanta Office. How may I direct your call?"

"Get me Special Agent Mark Feldon, please."

"Who may I say is calling?"

I buckled my belt and shifted into reverse. "Tell him it's Sharpe. Tell him I've got something."

29

I used the Charger's built-in GPS to select a hotel right in the heart of the city: the Sheraton Atlanta, a twelve-story building nestled amongst Georgia's skyscrapers. It would be quite a bit more expensive, but I already knew I'd be staying another night in the city, and I needed a place with valet parking to protect my car from further vandalism. A nicer bed and a cleaner shower were icing on the cake.

By the time I reached the highway, rush hour had commenced, and apparently there was a wreck. It took me over an hour to drive the ten miles from the airport district into the heart of downtown, where I found the Sheraton and checked in immediately.

I was right about the room—two fifty a night, and the clerk claimed that was some kind of special price. I paid with my debit card, then asked for a recommendation on a local restaurant. It was almost noon, and skipping breakfast was catching up with me.

Besides, I needed a rendezvous.

"There's a café about a block down Andrew Young. The Metro."

"Perfect."

I left the bag in my room, surveying a clean king-size bed and a spectacular view of the sprawling cityscape through a tall window, then returned downstairs and took the front door back onto the street.

City clamor echoed between buildings, and I scanned quickly to either side of the Sheraton, noting each of the parked cars sitting on the street near the hotel. Most were taxis and Ubers.

But one was a dark blue Chevy Impala. Unmarked. Cheap hubcaps.

I pocketed my hands and jaywalked across the street, turning down Andrew Young Boulevard, which was really just another city street. An illuminated sign advertising the *Metro Diner and Bar* stuck from the side of a building fifty yards away. Breakfast, lunch, and dinner. Since 2006.

I crossed the street again to reach it, not bothering to look over my shoulder.

Glass doors lined in chrome greeted me, followed by dark blue carpet and a set of stairs. A hostess stand sat at the top of the steps, and a woman in a black apron greeted me.

"Good afternoon, sir. How many?"

"Two," I said.

She selected a pair of menus and gestured for me to follow her to a line of booths situated under a semi-glass ceiling. The restaurant was quiet, and I took a seat with my back to the stairs and the door below, as though I were blind to both.

"What can I get you to drink?" the woman asked. She spoke with a slow drawl, making me think hot summer days in the Old South.

"Got any sweet iced tea?" I asked.

"We got a peach tea that'll make you slap your mama."

I wasn't sure what the quality of the proposed beverage

had to do with committing an act of violence, but I took a risk and assumed the expression was a positive one.

"I'll take it," I said.

She bustled off, and I flipped through the menu. It was diverse, with everything from burgers to pasta to fried catfish on offer. My stomach growled. It all looked good.

Footsteps hit the carpet behind me, too heavy to be the waitress. I didn't look up from the menu.

"Hello, Feldon."

Another two steps, and the man stood next to me. I fixated on the menu, purposefully ignoring him until he took a seat. When I finally looked up, I didn't see the brash and abrasive special agent I remembered from my interrogation only two nights previously.

Feldon looked like hell. Tired, with black bags beneath his eyes, and a permanent slump in his shoulders. He wore a suit that was either identical to the one he interrogated me in, or else the same one. I smelled a little body odor, and it dampened my appetite.

"You ever shower?" I asked.

Feldon's lip twitched, but he didn't bother to answer. When the waitress returned, he ordered black coffee, and I thought he needed it. I stirred the tea with my straw, noting swirling particles of fresh peach as I sipped.

It was delicious, but I felt no need to slap anybody.

"Why am I here?" Feldon demanded as soon as she left.

I set the tea down and folded my arms, just watching him for a while. He'd sounded tired on the phone, but his tone now slipped closer to defeat.

"You're here because we need to talk," I said at last. "About Jalen Powell."

"Still poking your nose where it doesn't belong?"

"You know I am. Those half-assed agents of yours have

been stalking me since I left your interrogation room. That's why you took my call."

"I took your call because you said you had something." Feldon's voice tightened. I remained loose.

"I do have something. But first there's some things we need to clear up."

"What things?"

"Things like why you've been stalking me."

"I told you before, Sharpe. You're endangering a federal operation."

I shook my head. "That's not true. If it were, you would have already found a way to detain me. We both know there's another reason."

He didn't answer.

"I had a look at some trial docs," I said. "It seems you're a reasonably big deal around here. You were the agent in charge of the task force running the undercover op against the South Atlanta Squad. Drew Martin was your man. You testified against Cox during his trial. I guess it makes sense why you'd want to see him burn."

The waitress brought his coffee and asked for our order. I requested the fettuccini alfredo. Feldon waved her off.

"What's your point?" Feldon said as soon as she left.

"I don't have a point. Just a theory."

I sipped tea, poking my straw amid the ice and forcing him to ask.

"And that is?"

"Well, for starters, I don't think Drew Martin was just one of your agents. I think he was a friend. Maybe an old partner. Somebody you knew well. Somebody you cared about in greater than a professional capacity."

Feldon didn't so much as blink. I pressed ahead.

"I think when he died, you took it hard. I saw the crime scene photos—I can't say I blame you. It's one of the worst things I've ever looked at. I'm sure you called headquarters and asked for additional agents. More resources to burn the SAS to the ground. But you didn't get them, did you? They denied you for two reasons. First, because this was now a gruesome homicide, not a drug case. So the FBI would be taking over. And second, because your bosses believed you to be too emotionally compromised. I'm guessing they pulled you off the Squad altogether."

Feldon's lip twitched, just a little. The only sign he was even listening to me. I set my glass down.

"They probably tasked you with some trivial nonsense. Busting pot dealers in high schools. Little league stuff. But a guy like you, losing as much as you have...you weren't just gonna accept that. Which is why you rounded up a posse of people you could trust. Agents who knew and cared about Martin as much as you did. That ratty guy who helped interrogate me, and the two eggheads you've had following me. Together, the group of you have been running your own little investigation off the books. Hunting down any and every lead you can find. Trailing a kid and harassing a stranger in a pickup truck. Desperate to bust the entire SAS for what happened to Martin. Ready to bend some rules to make it happen."

Another twitch of his lip. His eyes rimmed a little red, and he fixated on his coffee.

"That's why you pulled me in," I said. "I wondered at the time what you were doing, because nothing was protocol. You didn't even read me my rights, and then there was that business with the cocaine. Trying to rattle me, I guess. But you know what really gave you away?"

Feldon couldn't resist. "What?"

"You *let me go*. Just like that. Right after you learned I was an ex-cop, you loaded me up with information about the case and turned me loose."

I sipped tea. It was almost gone already. I'd take a refill.

"I didn't give it a lot of thought at the time," I said. "I figured I had caught you red-handed with the cocaine, and you didn't want things to get out of control. But that wouldn't explain why you so freely shared with me about the case, or why your guys continued to trail me. Which leads me to my final conclusion."

He looked over the rim of the coffee cup. "And that is?"

"You aren't trying to stop me, and you never were. You're having me tailed because you're hoping I'll crash around and uncover something. And you want to know about it when I do."

Dead silence. Feldon didn't so much as blink, and I knew I'd hit pay dirt.

"Do you have something or not?" Feldon growled.

I sat back. Folded my arms. "Oh, I have something. And it's all yours if you want it. But nothing comes for free. You and I are going to make a deal."

———————

efore Feldon could respond, the waitress turned up with my fettuccini, depositing it on a hot plate and asking again if he'd like to order. Once more Feldon waved her off, and I went to work on my meal, leaving him to sit and fester.

Time was now my weapon. Just like Feldon had left me to sit in that interrogation tank, betting on my own neurosis to wear down my better judgment, I could now slow-walk this pasta and leave him to crack first. I knew I was right about his predicament—his off-the-books investigation, his lack of results. His obsession with burning the SAS to the ground.

And I had something he needed. I didn't have to wait long.

"If you have something, you are legally *obligated* to turn it over," Feldon growled. "Withholding information is an obstruction of justice."

I actually laughed. "So arrest me, why don't you? I'll call a lawyer this time. Or better yet, I'll call your bosses. Tell them all about your little side hobby."

He said nothing. I set my fork down.

"Here's what I want. I'll bring you the SAS on a silver platter. And you'll take your thumb off Jalen Powell. Permanently."

Feldon snorted. "Seriously? You're still worried about that damn kid?"

"I'm worried about a lot of things, Feldon. World hunger. The stability of the economy. Whether or not the Cardinals are ever going to win a Super Bowl. But frankly none of that matters if I can't address the injustice right in front of me. That's how the world is meant to work. We take care of our own little piece of it, and next thing you know, it's a better place for everyone."

"Look at you. Gandhi meets Batman. Rampaging around, overturning apple carts."

"Only when they need to be overturned. Don't pretend you're any less pragmatic. If you were, you wouldn't be here. We wouldn't be having this conversation."

Feldon took a while to respond. I saw his mouth twitch as he chewed the inside of one cheek. Undecided. Concerned about something.

"I can't have a vigilante rolling around harassing people," he said at last. "It could bite me in the ass."

"Maybe. But so could operating this underground investigation of yours. And you're already rolling those dice, aren't you?"

Feldon leaned forward, both hands on the table, his voice low. "Let's say you're right. Let's say I'm running my own op, using my own people. Let's say Martin was an old friend. In that case, you'd want to help. You'd want to tell me what you know. One cop to another."

"I'm not a cop anymore. I'm just a guy."

"All right. Man to man, then. Human being to human being. You saw what those monsters did to Martin. Tore his face right off. Drowned him in his own blood. You've *got* to want to see justice done."

"Oh, I do," I said. "Which is why I want you off Jalen's back."

Feldon turned rigid, sitting back and folding his arms. His face fell into a series of hard lines, and I knew I'd pushed him as far as I could. It was time to play my hand.

"Do you actually have something, or are you just wasting my time?" Feldon demanded.

I laid the fork down. Wiped my mouth. Sat back in my seat.

"Cox didn't do it."

Feldon didn't move. Crimson crept up his neck, and the edges of his eyes turned red. He looked like a stick of dynamite just as the last of the fuse burns away.

"Are you freaking kidding me?"

I held up a hand. "I'm not here to argue with you, Feldon. I don't expect you to believe me. But the fact remains, Cox was burned."

"Why would you possibly think that? His prints were on the damn knife. His DNA on Martin's *body*."

"None of that would be difficult to fake. Not for somebody who knew Cox well. Somebody on the inside."

Feldon continued to boil. "Where is this coming from? Who have you been talking to?"

"Several people. Including Cox."

"Of course *he* would say he's innocent."

"Except he didn't. He maintained his guilt, and then he had some goons rough me up immediately after. Told me to bug off."

"That doesn't prove anything."

"You're right. But it gives me cause to question the status quo. Did you ever wonder why Cox was arrested in Greenville?"

"He's from Greenville. He has family there. He must have fled there to hide."

"Why would he hide with family? It's literally the first place the FBI would look."

"So he's dumb as a rock," Feldon growled. "He's a gangbanger. What do you expect?"

"You can't have it both ways, Feldon. Either Anthony is smart enough to build and operate a complex drug distribution empire that you yourself admitted was impossible to pin down, or else he's dumb enough to leave prints on the murder weapon, then get caught hiding with family. Which is it?"

Feldon's face flushed a dark crimson. He clenched a fist on the table.

"Anthony Cox *butchered* my agent. Tortured him to death. If your whole crusade is to get a guilty man out of jail—"

"My crusade is to keep your rogue investigation from obliterating the life of an innocent *kid*," I said. "But if Anthony Cox is innocent, I won't deny taking issue with that. I don't like injustice, Feldon. And I don't like bullies."

"And what do you think I am?"

I took a while answering, the fork in one hand, loaded with fettuccini.

"I don't know yet," I said at last. "But it may not matter. I know you want the rest of the Squad. I have some leads on where you can find them. So that's my offer—the Squad for Jalen. I help you take them out, and you piss off."

Feldon didn't move. I saw the gears turning behind his exhausted gaze, and I couldn't tell whether he was confused, frustrated, or just finished with life. At last he just snorted a derisive laugh and shook his head, staring into his coffee.

"Well?" I demanded.

"I thought you actually had something."

"I do. It's me. You see, I was never very good at being a

cop. It turns out I'm too much a pragmatist to appreciate the slow game. I like to break bones when the need arises. That's not something you can get away with. But with me on board, you won't have to."

"You're out of your mind."

"Maybe. But from where I'm sitting, you seem to be short on options. And this is a low-risk, high-reward arrangement. If I wind up strapped to a chair, choking on my own blood, you get to deny you ever met me. Life rolls on."

"And if you find something?"

"Then I call you. You call the cavalry. The SAS goes down in flames, you get promoted, Jalen is left alone, and I get back in my truck and roll out of here. The world is a better place for everyone."

Long pause. Feldon looked back into the coffee as though it were a crystal ball, one hand wrapped around the cup. But not drinking.

"Why?" he said at last.

"Why what?"

"Why do you care about Jalen?"

"Does it matter?"

He looked up. Set his jaw in a hard line. Finished the coffee in two long gulps, then reached into his pocket and flicked out a business card. I caught it without looking down. Feldon stood up.

"If you make a mess, I'll hang you out to dry."

I pocketed the card, and Feldon turned for the door.

"One more thing," I said. Digging the burner phone from my pocket, I called up the picture of Skullcap—the snapshot I'd taken the night before.

I passed the phone to Feldon.

"Recognize him?"

Feldon squinted at the image, rotating it and using his fingers to zoom.

"Where did you get this?"

"I took it. Last night."

"Where?"

"That's not important. I need to know if he's SAS."

Feldon put the phone down. Pocketed his hands. "I don't know his name, but I recognize the face."

"So he's a Squad member."

"Yeah. Not sure what rank. Possibly a boss."

My stomach sank. I realized I'd been holding out hope that Jalen was dealing pot from an unrelated group. Maybe another gang. People who weren't keeping him on a string with an invisible ax hanging over his neck.

No such luck.

I turned the phone off and reached for my fork. The fettuccini was mostly cold, but I was still hungry. Feldon looked once around the café to make sure nobody was near enough to hear, then leaned low over the table.

"I want them all. You understand? You tell me how to split them wide open, and I don't give a rat's ass what happens to that kid."

I stopped with the fork halfway to my mouth. Didn't say anything. The tone of his voice mixed with the sour breath of a man who hadn't showered or brushed his teeth in two or three days reminded me of a hungry wolf growling from the shadows. Overlooking a herd of sheep.

Feldon straightened and buttoned his coat. Then he was gone, back down the steps and out onto the street. Still on the warpath. Ready to do anything to get his man.

But I was going to get there first.

31

There was a drugstore built into the bottom of a high-rise not far from the Sheraton. I stepped inside and bought a comb and scissors, then returned to my hotel room and cut my hair in front of the mirror. It wasn't a professional job—far from it. But with a little work I looked like one of those hipsters who keeps disheveled hair as a style choice.

Then I showered again, enjoying the cleanest bathroom I'd used in months. The hot water soothed my shoulder, which was still aching from the impact of the brass knuckles outside of Greenville. I remembered what Feldon had said about Anthony having family there and wondered if the three guys who jumped me at the gas station were members of that family.

That tracked, anyway. If an SAS boss had burned Anthony, it was reasonable to assume that same boss had called in the anonymous tip to the Greenville cops the night Anthony was arrested.

Which meant the whole thing had been a setup from the start, not a cover-up.

I toweled off and dressed, then sat on the bed and stared at my battered hands. The fight at the gas station was the first I'd lost in a while—and only because I'd let somebody sneak up on me. It made me question my mental edge and what other mistakes I might be making.

I knew I was depressed. I'd been depressed for months, and had good reason to be. But it was more than the loss of my beautiful fiancée, or the complete upending of the life I had built in Arizona. It was something deeper. The tragedies in Phoenix had only served to trigger an identity crisis. Without the Army, without the police department, and without Mia...I found myself with no better identity than what I had given Anthony and Feldon.

I'm just a guy.

I looked into the reflection of the blackened TV and saw black bags under my eyes from too many nights spent barely sleeping. I saw tousled hair that would have made the Army freak.

I saw disheveled clothes that the PPD would never have tolerated.

Turning to the duffel bag next to the bed, I sifted through dirty clothes and reached for the violin, but my fingers touched Mia's Bible instead. It was small, only about six inches tall, bound in brown leather with her name printed in gold.

I lifted it out and traced the edges of the battered cover. The Bible had sustained more abuse in the six months following her death than in the entirety of Mia's ownership. I'd done my best to take care of it, storing it amid my socks, but never once reading it.

I wasn't much on religion. I never had been. Mia was the first religious person I ever met who didn't feel fake and contrived. She used to say she wasn't a religious person at all, but a person of faith.

Whatever that meant.

I thumbed the cover open and flicked through the thin pages. They crinkled as they turned, and I recognized some of the book titles as they passed.

Exodus. Ruth. The Prophet Micah. And then the New Testament.

There were markings here—highlights and little notes in Mia's immaculate handwriting. Someplace in the book of Hebrews a verse was both highlighted and underlined, with three little exclamation points written next to it, and a heart.

Like the kind Mia used to write on sticky notes left next to my dinner when I came home late.

Let us hold unswervingly to the hope we profess, for He who has promised is faithful.

My eyes blurred a little over the line, and I read it again. A third time. The words ran together and didn't really mean anything. I saw Mia on an early Sunday morning, a coffee in one hand, this Bible spread across the table. Reading this text. Poring over it. Investing herself in a higher power.

And what had that got her? A shotgun blast to the gut, drowning in a pool of her own blood.

I shut the Bible, tossing it back into my bag, and ran both hands through my hair. The room around me turned a tinge of red, and I realized I wasn't the Ranger anymore. I wasn't the cop. I certainly wasn't her fiancé. Maybe I wasn't even the vagrant hero, running to the aid of a lost kid who reminded me of myself.

Maybe I was just another angry thug, looking for something to pound.

The South Atlanta Squad would be that something.

32

I slept until the sun went down; then I pulled the Charger from the valet parking and drove out of town. I wanted a department store—someplace that sold both cheap clothes and various household goods. In the end I settled with splitting the difference, stopping at a uniform supply store for black pants and a black jacket, then pulling into an Ace Hardware for the rest—black grease, a small LED flashlight, a can of lubricant, and a shortened pair of bolt cutters.

The clerk at the counter was a middle-aged woman with tired lines in her face. She didn't so much as make eye contact as she shoveled the items into a bag. I guessed she'd never lived on the other side of the tracks, or the correlation between the four items might have been obvious.

Back in the Charger, it was now almost eight p.m. and dark out. I used a restroom at a gas station to change into the black clothes, then navigated south, manipulating the GPS to find the abandoned factory from memory. I had saved the location in my previous Charger but neglected to transfer that information into the new car. Luckily, there weren't a lot of turns involved.

The highways were clogged again, and progress through the heart of Atlanta was slow. As I passed the exit for the Skyline Diner, I thought about Jalen and wondered what he was up to.

Slinging weed, probably. Whatever Skullcap had given him would have been issued on credit. Jalen would have a deadline to distribute the product and pay off his account.

It was a harmless racket, in the grand scheme of things. I'd never been particularly opposed to weed. It was what came next that did the real damage. Cocaine. Heroin. And now fentanyl.

I thought about what Feldon had said about Mexican M30s pouring into the States, and how the South Atlanta Squad was positioned to become a primary distributor. Feldon's intel on the SAS situation had proven faulty at best, but if he was right about the fentanyl, and if Jalen's weed broker was associated with the Squad as I assumed, then Skullcap was only prepping Jalen for bigger and greater enterprises.

The day Anthony's little brother loaded M30s into his backpack, everything changed. Feldon was right about one thing—fentanyl was poison. Literally. The complete societal breakdown brought on by the opioid crisis would bring Atlanta to its knees just like Los Angeles and Chicago before it.

Jalen would be just another casualty.

I pulled the Charger off the road at the same gas station as before, parking behind the building and checking the clock. It was nearly ten p.m., but that was still too early. I kept the radio on low and ground through another ninety minutes, bouncing between local country music stations in search of Zac Brown Band songs.

At a quarter to midnight, I killed the radio and pulled the tube of grease from the Ace Hardware bag. Flicking my Victorinox open, I cut a slit in the tube and squeezed out a dollop of black grease. It was synthetic and sticky. I rubbed it between my fingers, then used the car's rearview mirror to apply it to my face.

Cheeks, neck, nose, and forehead. I worked until my entire head was black, leaving nothing but the flash of my teeth and the whites of my eyes. The grease stank up the car, but I ignored it, cleaning my hands on my black pant legs before installing the Victorinox, lubricant, and binoculars in one pocket, the switchblade and flashlight in the other, and the bolt cutters in the small of my back.

Then I checked the time. It was just after midnight—as close to dead quiet as any place this near a major city would become. I left the car and circled to the front of the gas station, checking both ways for cars before jogging alongside the road, back to the gravel drive where Skullcap's Mercedes had pulled in the night before.

My shoes crunched on loose rocks as I turned off the road; then I waded into the weeds and found the fallen tree right where I left it. Crossing the fence, I found myself back in the tangle of briars and thorns, but this time I was prepared for them. The thick canvas of the black work jacket shielded my skin from injury. I descended to my stomach, worming my way to the top of the hill just as I had the previous night.

I was less hesitant to raise my face over the crest than before. I knew what lay below, and I knew the black grease muted my white skin from shining in the moonlight.

The factory building lay quiet beneath me, but it wasn't unoccupied. The Escalade I'd noted from the previous night was present, and I noted a dim light behind one grimy window on the ground floor.

Digging the binoculars out, I swept the length of the

building, straining my eyes to see in the dim light. This far away, most everything was clouded in shadow, but the binoculars collected enough light from the lone window for me to make out smashed pizza boxes piled near a door on the near side, along with a heap of empty beer bottles.

Whoever was inside had been inside for a while. Maybe a permanent installment of local muscle left to ward off any careless trespassers.

I lowered the binoculars and thought again about the vulnerability of using a large headquarters like this. I'd never been a drug dealer, but I'd encountered plenty of them during my days as a beat cop, and the successful ones are always the most subtle. They don't build elaborate production facilities or marijuana gardens. They plant in basements under grow lights and distribute out of car trunks and small storage units.

This building was ideal in a way, because it was off the beaten path and provided a safe place to assemble. But it couldn't be a permanent arrangement, or else the pile of trash outside the door would likely be much larger.

No. This was a temporary thing. For a special purpose.

But what was that purpose?

I wriggled down in the weeds and waited, checking my watch every so often to mark the passage of time. Over the next hour I saw somebody leave the building only once—a tall guy in low-slung jeans, stepping through the door and pissing on the pile of pizza boxes. Then he stumbled back inside, and all was quiet again.

It was nearly two a.m. before Skullcap arrived. Headlights flashing into the valley were my first warning; then the Mercedes S-Class rolled in, windows jet black, tires churning up dust. It parked next to the Escalade, and I watched through the binoculars as Skullcap stepped out.

He was dressed much differently than the night before.

Now in black jeans, a black leather jacket over a tight black T-shirt, with a heavy gold chain hanging around his neck. He wore rings, too. Also gold and gleaming even in the dim light.

The skullcap was still there, though. As were the trio of goons accompanying him, dressed in similar leather and expensive jewelry.

I watched them enter through the side door, and a moment later the guy who had pissed on the pizza boxes ran out and began to collect the trash in a rush, stuffing it into a black bag.

I chewed my lip, checking my watch again.

Two fifteen. Rolling up in fancy clothes. Worried about the trash by the door.

Something was going down, tonight.

I pocketed the binoculars and climbed to my feet, turning along the ridge and working through the tall weeds. I circled to the end of the building, where shadows hung thick against the factory and I was safely secluded from the door. Then I started down the side of the valley, weaving amid brush and short trees, keeping close to the ground and taking my time. There was nothing significant about two fifteen, and it was unlikely Skullcap would roll up so close to an important event.

Three o'clock was my mark. I had time.

As I neared the gravel lot outside the old factory, I dropped into a crouch and waited behind a bush, scoping out my next move. The brick building lay fifty yards away, across open space with no place to take cover should an emergency arise. At the end of the building a concrete loading dock was built, with a busted rolling metal door hanging down at an angle, blackness beyond.

A possible entrance, but what caught my eye was the fire escape bolted to the corner of the structure, leading from the ground all the way to a metal door on the second floor. There was a gate at the bottom of the fire escape, and a chain held it closed.

But that chain would be no match for the bolt cutters tucked into my pants.

I waited another two minutes, listening for noises from the building and watching for lights behind the busted rolling door. Then I sprinted for the fire escape.

I was right about the chain—it snapped under the bite of the bolt cutters. I sprayed small amounts of lubricant on the gate's hinges and then swung it open without a sound. The stairs were metal and groaned a little under my weight.

I wasted no time ascending to the second floor. The door there was windowless, with only a simple metal knob, which was locked.

I placed the flashlight between my teeth and sprayed the hinges as before, then dug into my pocket for the Victorinox. Sorting through the knife's tools, I found the large flathead screwdriver/bottle opener and flipped it open with a soft snap.

The screwdriver tip fit easily into a gap between the hinge and the hinge pin. I pried, and the pin slid up smoothly, slick with lubricant. I wiggled it out with my fingers, then repeated the procedure on hinges two and three. Then I pressed the screwdriver tip into the gap between the doorframe and the door and pried outward.

The door dropped out of the hinges and into my hands, slumping against the doorframe. I stepped softly backward across the metal landing of the fire escape, carrying the door with me and gently laying it to rest against the brick wall.

I still couldn't hear anything from inside the building, but I was fully a hundred feet away from the side door used by Skullcap and his goons on the floor below. The hole opened by the gaping doorway was pitch black, the shadows driven back as I pulled the flashlight from my teeth and scanned it across the opening.

There was a worn wooden floor on the other side, and an abandoned metal desk. Papers and rat feces littered the floor, but there was nobody to stop me as I switched the flashlight off and crept ahead.

I was in.

33

The floorboards squeaked a little under my feet, and I still couldn't hear anything from the first floor of the factory. The room around me seemed to be a long-abandoned office, with discarded documents and an outdated computer system heaped in one corner. As my eyes dilated to capture more from the moonlight leaking through the door behind me, I noted a further door opening into a hallway paved in tattered industrial carpet.

And more rat turds.

I traded the Swiss army knife for the switchblade, but kept it closed as I entered the hall. Everything smelled musty, and tiny rodent feet scuttled behind a wall. The hall ran perpendicular to the length of the factory, meaning there was probably a stairwell at one end, but I wasn't trying to go down. I wanted a view from the top, so I turned right.

I found what I was looking for in the next room—another office, probably the foreman's office. It featured windows spread down the length of one wall, several of them gleaming with bright yellow light. I dropped to my hands and knees, ignoring the rat poop and creeping toward the far wall. For the first time I heard sounds—voices, muted but nearby. Heavy items scraping across concrete. Men grunting.

I lay at the base of the wall and looked up to the windows. They were fogged with years of collected grime, rendering them useless for a view of the factory floor. I thought about trying to scrub the dirt away, but I didn't want to risk rattling the metal window frames or breaking the glass.

Instead, I pressed the switch on the Microtech, and the double-edged blade snapped out. I used it to score a line across the wall paneling built beneath the window. It was cheap and flimsy, like the kind you might find in a manufactured home. The razor-sharp blade made short work of it, and I peeled away a ten-inch section, exposing packed insulation on the other side.

I pulled that away also and found sheet metal beyond. It was rusty, with a gap at the bottom opening directly downward. I could hear the voices clearly now—one shouting, the others grumbling.

"Who pissed here? Mop this up!"

Mumbled answers.

"This is a headquarters! This ain't no ghetto club. I oughta bust a cap in yo asses!"

I closed the switchblade and pushed out on the sheet metal with one hand. It was thin and buckled outward, opening up a gap near the bottom. I could see part of the factory floor now. I pressed a little farther and opened up another two inches, then froze as a screw snapped out, and metal scraped against metal.

The grumbling from below continued, the popping screw masked by a heavy box crashing against concrete.

I could see it all now. Skullcap stood on the factory floor, pointing and cursing as his goons hurried to put the building in order under the glare of powerful shop lights. There was junk everywhere—not just fast-food trash, but mechanical garbage. Old machines and rusting conveyor systems pushed against the walls, relics of whatever purpose this building had once served.

Near the end of the factory, opposite the fire escape where I had crept in, two giant rolling doors stood closed, but there was a cleaned and swept stretch of concrete in front of them now occupied by rows of plastic tables. Unopened shipping boxes were heaped on those tables, alongside utility knives and postage scales.

I saw it all with the aid of the binoculars as I lay on the floor just inside the hole. As the guys on the floor finished their cleanup, Skullcap checked his watch and snapped his fingers.

"Now quiet down! Be chill. Anybody screw this up, I'll cut yo throat myself. You hear me?"

Nobody answered. Skullcap walked to the side door, lighting a cigarette as he moved. Two of the goons in leather and bling followed him. The other two stayed back, watching their disgruntled associates with disgust.

I checked my watch. It was five 'til three, and something was about to happen.

I heard tires first, grinding against the gravel outside. I thought about getting up and looking for an exterior view, but decided to stay put. Whoever the new arrival was, it wouldn't be long before they entered the building.

I relaxed on the floor, blocking out the sour stench of rat feces and praying one of the little varmints didn't crawl up my pants leg. I couldn't hear voices through the thick brick walls, but it wasn't long before the door swung open again.

Skullcap and his goons marched in first, followed by a short guy, also in black, with a black baseball cap pulled low over his ears. I couldn't make out his face in the dim light, but he didn't look like he belonged with Skullcap. He walked separate from the rest and scanned the factory with a suspicious glare, his gaze passing right across my position without pausing. I caught his face in the binoculars and guessed his ethnicity by gentle features matched with caramel skin.

He was Hispanic.

The short guy looked back through the door and nodded once; then two more guys shoved inside, looking much like him, dressed in black jackets and dark jeans.

Then came the final guy—taller than the first three, also dressed in black pants and shirt, but instead of a ball cap he wore a fedora resting on one side of a shaved skull like some kind of afterthought.

The newcomer walked with his hands in his pockets, stomping into the place like he owned it. He wore black combat boots, unlaced and flapping open at the tops, and jammed into his belt just above a silver belt buckle was a matching nickel-plated Beretta 92.

He looked like something out of a video game or a comic. Not a real person. More of a caricature. But as he approached the middle of the illuminated space and inspected the factory with a quick sweep of dark eyes, nobody spoke.

Not even Skullcap.

"This is it?" the man said at last. I recognized his accent. It was Mexican, definitely. Specifically northwestern Mexican, from one of the mountain states. Sonora or Chihuahua. I'd heard plenty of that accent in Phoenix.

"Everything we need," Skullcap said. The angry command had vanished from his tone, but he still held his head up. "Let me show you the production line."

Skullcap walked to the line of tables just inside the rolling doors and clicked on more lights. The entire factory was now illuminated like a football stadium, forcing me to squint into the binoculars. Skullcap started at the head of one row of tables, the Mexican at his heels. He flicked out a knife and cut open a box.

"The cans are unmarked and interchangeable," Skullcap said, dumping the box out on the table. A pile of metal soup cans spilled out. They were empty and unlabeled, missing their lids. "We can pack them with as much product as we want, then slap on a label."

Skullcap motioned to the funky-looking machine I had noticed before. Some kind of canning device, apparently, used to apply soup can lids.

"We can have your entire shipment ready to distribute inside of two days, no problem."

"Impressive, *ese*," the Mexican said, rolling a soup can in his hand as though it were a blood diamond. Skullcap opened another case and distributed stacks of labels across the tabletop. I adjusted the binoculars and recognized familiar soup brands printed across each—red and white, a perfect replication of the logo.

"Tell me about your contacts," the Mexican said. "How strong is your network outside of Atlanta?"

"We got markets in Birmingham and Chattanooga," Skullcap said, crossing his arms confidently. "Here in Atlanta, obviously. And big holds in South Carolina. Greenville and Columbia are strong markets."

The Mexican laughed, sifting through the labels with one finger, that stupid fedora still cocked on the back of his head. He shot Skullcap a sideways sneer.

"Birmingham and Carolina...you know that's not why I'm here. You said you could access Washington. *Miami.*"

Skullcap waved his hand dismissively. "It's like a told you before. Gateways, right? We got gateways, bruh. That thing in Greenville? It's a done deal."

The Mexican pocketed his hands and walked to the end of the line, inspecting the canning machine. Then he licked his lips.

"It looks good, amigo. A clean operation. But we're not

talking about smack and crack, here. This stuff is legit, and the DEA knows it. You slip up even once, they'll be down your throat like my ten-inch prick, you hear me?"

Skullcap snorted and shot a sideways glance at one of his goons, then leered at the Mexican.

"Bruh. Chill. You with professionals now, you feel me? We own these streets. You ever even heard of the Squad befo'?"

The Mexican said nothing.

"Exactly," Skullcap said. "That's because we ain't flashin' our colors on every street corner like some kinda dime-bag thugs. We legit. We got networks in five states, and the DEA ain't got a feel on none of them. I mean...that's why you're here, right?"

Skullcap spread his hands, gold teeth flashing in the shop lights.

The Mexican didn't grin back. He stood with his hands in his pockets, staring down the bigger man without a hint of fear. Then a coy smile crept across his mouth.

"Right," he said.

Skullcap smacked his hands together. "So let's get poppin', then. When can you get the stuff here?"

"Soon," the Mexican said. "Later this week. But there's no hurry. I've got a man headed this way. From Los Angeles—a specialist. He'll help you...get oriented."

Skullcap's grin melted in an instant, replaced by a storm cloud frown.

"Hey, cuz. We don't need no damn babysitter. You want us to spread your product, we do it *our* way."

The Mexican said nothing, still inspecting the canning machine. Skullcap took a step forward.

"Hey! Yo, Cholo. I'm talkin' to you, bit—"

I saw it coming, but Skullcap walked right into it. The Mexican's right hand flashed from his pocket and snapped. A collapsible nightstick flicked out and caught the bigger man right across his left knee, hard enough to bruise, not quite hard enough to break.

A muted grunt was followed by a flurry of action around the room. The black gangsters scrambled for knives and handguns, but they were outpaced by the three Mexicans standing in a semicircle around their leader. Uzi submachine guns appeared like snake tongues, spitting out from under leather jackets and settling over the South Atlanta Squad.

Skullcap collapsed like a house of cards, and the Mexican flicked his nightstick, popping the gangster once in the nose before placing the tip of the weapon under his chin and forcing his face up.

Skullcap didn't resist. He saw the Uzis as clearly as I did.

"Listen carefully, *ese*," the Mexican snarled. "You did well with our heroin. Your network is impressive, it's true. But we aren't talking about fifty grand worth of Mexican mud. These M30s are the real deal. You get caught with a load like I'm sending you, and it's not just your Squad the DEA goes after. They come after *me*. After *my familia*. You feel me?"

The Mexican mimicked Skullcap's accent with the final question. The black man remained on his knees, the nightstick still jammed under his throat.

"I don't want any confusion about who's the boss around here," the Mexican continued. "If you or your hombres get any bright ideas about coloring outside the lines, I will send a squad of Mexican soldados up here to carve you apart cartel style. Understand, cuz?"

Skullcap's chin trembled against the tip of the nightstick. He nodded once. The Mexican lowered the stick, then popped the end against his open palm and snapped it closed. His posture loosened immediately.

"*Muy bueno, amigo.* I knew we'd get along." The Mexican started toward the door, pocketing the nightstick. "The specialist's name is Hansley. He's a white boy. He'll be checking into the Westin later this week; then he'll text you."

The Mexican stopped at the door, looking over one shoulder and smirking as Skullcap scrabbled to his feet.

"Make sure he feels welcome."

The four Mexicans disappeared through the door, and a moment later a big engine fired up. Skullcap stood fuming in the factory, wiping his face and glowering at anybody who was dumb enough to make eye contact. As soon as the Mexican's car growled away, Skullcap commenced screaming at his men, throwing cans and daring any of them to speak up.

I didn't stick around for the duration of the temper tantrum. Sliding backward, I returned to the fire escape and reached the ground. Ten minutes later I was jogging alongside the road, the bolt cutters smacking against my lower back as adrenaline-charged blood surged through my veins.

The meeting between the SAS and whatever Mexican cartel the tattooed guy represented hadn't been what I expected. I wasn't sure what I expected.

But it gave me something to work with. A lead to follow.

I hit the door locks on the Charger as I neared the car, already planning my next moves back in Atlanta. The man called Hansley would be the key. He would know enough to bring this whole operation crumbling down.

Assuming I could catch him.

I placed a hand on the door and wiped sweat off my face. As I lowered my arm, I saw my own reflection in the window.

Mine, and somebody else's. I stiffened, already turning. Already reaching for the switchblade and knowing I was too late.

Then something hard and heavy slammed into the back of my head, and everything went black.

34

I awoke in the trunk of a car. My hands were bound behind my back, and there was something soft and dirty crammed in my mouth. A sock, maybe?

I couldn't see. I was blindfolded, but I knew it was a trunk because I could hear the hum of tires from directly beneath me. Rough carpet ground against one side of my face, and when I kicked out with both legs, my feet slammed into hard steel. I tried spitting the sock out, but it was useless. The thing was jammed in deep, forcing my jaw wide and disabling my tongue.

There wasn't even a strip of tape to hold it in place. Whoever had stuffed it there knew what he was doing, and if I tried too hard to dislodge it, I might wind up blocking my own windpipe and suffocating.

I leaned back instead, breathing through my nose and focusing on remaining calm.

Where am I? What do I see?

I twisted my head in either direction, noting the oily smell of gasoline and the creak of old leaf springs. It was pitch black in the trunk, but when I began to calm my own desperate breathing, I heard another sound leaking through the wall to my right, barely louder than the tires on the road.

It was music. Blues music, I thought, with a lot of slow electric guitar and a gentle beat. The sound instantly reminded me of late nights down on Bourbon Street, staggering between bars with Mia on one arm.

It was the first trip we ever took together, down to New Orleans in the heat of the previous summer. Mia wore a skimpy black cocktail dress, and we danced on a worn hardwood floor while a four-piece band massaged a similar melody from acoustic instruments.

The artist singing from the car's cabin was B. B. King. I was sure of it now. But I didn't recognize the track.

My mind snatched back to my predicament, and I felt the bonds that held my wrists together. It was duct tape—a lot of it, wrapped in successive bands around my wrists and forearms, pinching my shoulders together. I was already cramping, and the muscle spasms alone were inhibiting my ability to fight the restraints.

Yeah, whoever this guy was, he knew what he was doing.

The car groaned, and my head smacked against the trunk's floor as we crossed railroad tracks. I recognized the *thump, thump* cadence of the two rails passing beneath the tires, then the muffler rumbled, and we surged forward. Outside the car I thought I heard the occasional rush of passing cars and distant horns, but I couldn't be sure.

B. B. King sang a little louder. The whole track was louder —a more engaged, thumping beat. A dance tune.

"Everyday I Have the Blues". I was sure of it. A damn classic, blaring from the speakers of whatever psychopath had crammed me in this trunk like a sardine in a biscuit.

I kicked out again, pissed off now, but my legs were numb

from being folded up. My feet made barely enough noise to offset the thump of the bass track. The car braked abruptly enough to send me face-planting into the back seat.

My head spun, and the music cranked up. I rolled onto my back again, starting to feel a little desperate now. I replayed the moment I'd blacked out in my mind, picturing the man I saw in the reflection of the Charger's dusty window.

I hadn't actually seen his face. Just a lightning quick flash of his profile right before he drove something across my skull —a bat or a two-by-four. Something hard.

I remembered the blow and right on cue noticed my headache for the first time. The adrenaline had blocked it out before, but the tempo of B. B. King seemed to organize and ignite the pain.

I'd never wanted to shut off a radio so bad in my life—and I like blues.

I settled into the trunk, relaxing to the environment and accepting my fate for the time being. The status quo was out of my control—at least for now. The best I could hope for would be to learn from my environment and prepare for an opportunity.

I rolled left and right, feeling out my pockets against the trunk floor. They were all empty, meaning both of my knives and all my gear had been removed. I had to assume my kidnapper knew exactly who I was, if he had my wallet, but that was logical anyway. He had kidnapped me *because* he knew who I was.

Was he one of Anthony's cousins, from Greenville? One of the Steel Mafia guys I had banged up in south Atlanta?

No. Any of those guys would have wasted me right where I stood. Probably left my corpse to rot behind the gas station.

I clamped my eyes shut, blocking out the headache and

thinking. I remembered the guy at the Skyline Diner the same moment as I remembered his oversized green Cadillac.

An old car. With a big trunk.

The suspension creaked again as we crossed off the blacktop. Dirt and rocks popped beneath me, and the suspension groaned as the driver negotiated a rut. I slammed into the wall again and winced. My whole body felt like it had just survived three rounds with Floyd Mayweather.

B. B. King crooned from the car's cabin, and I cursed his participation in whatever the hell was happening. The moment the car ground to a stop and the motor cut off, however, I would have paid anything to have his smooth voice return.

The dead silence was somehow far more chilling. A door swung open with a groan, and feet hit the ground. I lay still and breathed evenly, feeling around in the bottom of the trunk for anything to use as a makeshift weapon. Not that it would do me a lot of good, tied and blindfolded. I'd lost this battle the moment I allowed my fixation with the conversation at the factory to smother my situational awareness.

Stupid.

The car shifted as somebody leaned against it. Then I heard metal clinking on metal, followed by more footsteps.

Wherever we were, it was dead quiet. No cars, no traffic at all. Only the whisper of the wind mixed with the song of a distant cicada.

Then I heard a sound that chilled me to the bone—the slice and crunch of a shovel biting into soft dirt.

Despite myself, my heart began to pound. I bit down on the gag and struggled to spit it out. I twisted my head and fought to dislodge the blindfold.

Nothing worked. The methodical scrape and slide of the shovel continued, punctuated by dirt piling on top of itself as the digger sank deeper into an invisible hole.

This jackass was digging a *grave*. My grave.

I calmed myself, focusing on the details. I couldn't rip out of the tape. It wasn't possible. I couldn't do anything about the blindfold or gag, either. Not directly.

But he'd left my legs free, and he wouldn't kill me in his own trunk. Too much mess. He'd make me climb out first, and when he did, I'd drive a knee into his balls and make a dash for it.

A bad plan, but the best I could think of.

The guy dug for the better part of half an hour. At times I thought I heard him whistling, and my blood grew colder. Then at last the shovel bit dirt and fell silent. Heavy breathing reached my ears, followed by the scrape of a cigarette lighter. I smelled tobacco on the air.

Another five minutes passed. Then the footsteps approached the back of the car, and I braced myself.

The moment the trunk popped open, I felt the gun against my rib cage. Jammed in, cold steel against tender flesh. The sensation was followed almost immediately by a rough grunt.

"Don't even think about it, kid. Too late for that."

I recognized the voice. It was the man at the diner, and that cold steel beneath my armpit would be the muzzle of a gun.

"Get out," he said. A powerful hand grabbed my arm and hauled me up. I rolled and twisted; then my feet hit the ground. "Stand up."

Smoke filled my nose, and I coughed. He got behind me and shoved with the gun. I couldn't see. I could barely stand straight. I circled to the nose of the car, brushing the long side panel. Then he grabbed me by one elbow, yanking me to a halt.

"Step down," he said.

My heart thundered. I dug my feet in. He pressed with the

muzzle of the gun, and I stepped back. Then he smacked me across the back of the head and shoved hard, right between my shoulders. I toppled forward and fell, landing on my face and knees. Sticky Georgia clay clung to my cheeks, and I breathed hard. I felt a root scraping my forehead, hard and sharp enough to draw blood.

Panic set in, but I shoved it back. Twisting my face, I found the end of the root and pressed it between the inside of my cheek and the mass of the sock. I pushed it all the way in, drawing blood from my lip and tasting mud. Then I twisted and spat. The sock caught on the root and dislodged from my mouth. A moment later I was upright on my knees, gasping for air as I heard the boots crunching in from behind.

"Now, listen!" I said. "We can talk about this."

"We ain't talkin' about nothing," the gravelly voice said. "You had your chance. Now lie down and take it like a man."

I wasn't about to lie down. I twisted toward the voice.

"My fight isn't with you!"

"Shut up, now. And close your eyes. Imma say a prayer."

"What?" I said, genuinely taken off guard.

"I said be quiet! We gonna get you straight with Jesus before he judges your ass."

I didn't know what to say. I choked as I felt the blade of the shovel press against my spine and force me forward.

Then my captor began to pray. Soft and confident, with a lot of profanity thrown in, but an undercurrent of earnest sincerity I'd seldom heard in a prayer. It reminded me of how Mia used to pray before every meal.

She used to ask me to join her. I never would. I didn't know what to say to God then.

I definitely didn't know what to say to Him now.

I leaned forward, shoved down by the blade. Then I heard the click of a revolver being cocked.

That familiar sound from the diner.

"This gives me no pleasure," the guy said.

The shovel moved. I pictured the gun swinging in to align with the base of my skull.

And I threw all my cards on the table.

"Reginald James? I can save your nephew."

35

Dead silence encased the space around us. I didn't move, my face pressed into the mud again, my body ready to receive a mass of copper-cased lead, ripping through my spine and flicking my lights out like a switch.

I imagined Mia on the other side of a misted glass of eternity. I had reached out before, ready to shatter that glass.

In the end I couldn't. Now somebody was about to break it for me. And yet, in this moment, I knew I didn't want to die. I wasn't ready. It didn't feel right.

I gasped for breath as the distant cicada was joined my another. I heard B. B. King still crooning in my head. Lamenting the love who rejected him.

It all blended in my skull as a single hellish Georgian melody.

"What you say?" the man behind me growled. His voice was soft, not strained. I tasted mud on my tongue.

"You're Reginald James, right? Anthony Cox's uncle. You were at his trial."

No answer.

"I saw your name on the court docs," I continued, deciding to press ahead.

No answer.

I hauled myself to my knees, my back still turned to him. "You care about Anthony. That's why you're doing this. They've got leverage on him, don't they?"

I turned my head, looking over my shoulder even though I couldn't see behind the blindfold.

"I can help Anthony," I said. "I can prove his innocence."

"How?" The word was a growl.

"Take the blindfold off, and we'll talk."

"Kid, I ain't takin' *nothing* off. You'll talk now, or you can talk to Jesus."

Fair enough.

I wiped my torn lip on one shoulder, spitting out clay. My face was still coated in black grease, and that grease had collected and retained dirt. I could only imagine what I looked like.

"Anthony took the fall on the Martin killing, didn't he?" I didn't expect an answer, but I phrased it as a question anyway. "Somebody put his prints on the murder weapon and tipped the police off to his location. But that's not enough to keep him silent in prison, is it? Not enough to keep him from filing an appeal. Whoever put leverage over him must still have leverage over him. Something Anthony cares about more than his own life...his little brother, Jalen."

My captor remained silent, but I knew I was right.

"That's why Anthony called his cousins up in Greenville. Had them rough me up. It's why you turned up at the diner, then slashed my tires. You're all trying to run me off before the wrong people find out what I'm up to and make good on their promises to hurt Jalen. Right?"

Boots crunched alongside my shallow grave. I felt the man growing closer. Dirt cascaded against my knees, and I heard him sit alongside the grave, dropping his boots in. Then the cigarette lighter ground again, and once more I smelled tobacco.

He didn't remove the blindfold.

"Who are you?"

"Just a guy," I said. "I met Jalen at the diner earlier this week. He was trying to steal my truck. Then I was arrested by the DEA. They think Anthony is calling the shots from prison, piping messages through Jalen."

My captor snorted a laugh. More confirmation I was on the right track.

"They're gonna burn Jalen," I said. "They'll do whatever it takes to bring down Anthony's gang. It's personal now."

"Tell me something I don't know," he snarled, blowing smoke in my face. I turned away.

"There's a shipment coming. Fentanyl pills, straight out of Mexico. A lot of them. The SAS is establishing a distribution network across the entire southeast. Hundreds of millions in business."

"And?"

"And it's an opportunity. I've already made a deal with the DEA. We bring them the SAS, and they'll piss off for eternity. They'll leave Jalen alone. We might even get Anthony out."

Another disgusted snort.

"I'm serious," I said. "We both know Anthony didn't kill that guy. All we have to do is prove it."

The guy got up. I heard him flick the cigarette butt, and my heart began to race.

"This changes nothin'," he said.

"It changes everything," I retorted. "It's a chance to turn this around."

"Anthony made his choice. Ain't no changing that."

"And what about Jalen? Is he making a choice, working for the SAS?"

Dead quiet.

"What you say?"

"He's dealing weed for the Squad," I said. "Only he doesn't know it. He's raising money for a fancy lawyer."

No answer. Boots crunched in the mud. He was crossing behind me again. I thought about the heavy click I'd heard earlier—the snap of a revolver being cocked. I imagined some oversized Smith and Wesson, nickel-plated and loaded with heavy magnum rounds. Enough to explode my skull like a watermelon.

I remained calm, choosing my words carefully.

"You can bury me here, and it won't change a thing. Jalen won't stop until Anthony is free...or he's rotting in the mud next to me."

I squared my shoulders, twisting in the shallow grave until I faced the sound of his voice. If he was going to kill me, he was gonna have to face me while he did it.

"You don't want to do this," I said.

"You're right. I don't. Now shut yo mouth and get right with God."

I imagined the gaping mouth of the revolver staring down my nose. I thought I heard his shoes shift in the soft Georgia clay. I suddenly realized the cicadas had fallen silent, and the woods around me felt very still. It was as though the world itself had stopped turning. I involuntarily held my breath.

"I warned you," he said, the growl of his voice dropping into a whisper.

I lifted my chin. "You're not gonna do it."

Then I closed my eyes behind the blindfold. Because in truth, I knew he just might.

The world froze. Then the revolver cracked.

36

I felt the muzzle flash on my face as the bullet raced by. It cleared my head someplace left of my skull, but the concussive energy of the racing slug was enough to send me toppling sideways. I hit the mud coughing.

My captor dropped into the grave, and I gritted my teeth, bracing for the next shot. The shot that wouldn't miss.

Instead I felt rough hands on my face, wrenching my head around. Then the blindfold was tugged away, and I looked up into the weathered face of my kidnapper.

He could have been fifty or seventy—I would have believed either one. A bold jawline was accentuated by dark brown skin and deep eyes. He wore a Georgia Bulldogs baseball cap and a tight tank top that exposed bulky arms and a rock-solid chest that would have shamed a man half his age.

In his right hand was clamped an oversized revolver—a Smith and Wesson, just like I thought. Nickel-plated, with powder residue sticking to the muzzle.

He stared down at me for a long while, then switched the gun to his left hand and grabbed me by the elbow. With a powerful heave he hauled my torso up and over the edge of the grave. I kicked out with both feet and wormed my way onto solid ground, still gasping for breath. He followed me, flipping out of the grave with agile ease.

Standing over me, he jammed the revolver into his back pocket, then turned toward the car.

It was the green Cadillac I'd seen before. Up close it was older than it first looked—late seventies, maybe, about a mile long and forest green in color. A nice-looking car, obviously loved and well cared for.

The man reached into the passenger seat and returned with something black in one hand. His thumb moved, and the metallic *click* of my captured switchblade broke the stillness. I flinched involuntarily as he stepped behind me.

"You try to run, and I'll kill you," he growled as he sliced the duct tape. "I only miss on purpose."

Relief washed over my strained shoulders. It never felt so good just to rub my arms.

He closed the knife and circled in front of me, folding his muscled arms. He wasn't tall—barely average height. But from my position on the ground with that behemoth of a handgun tucked in his back pocket, I felt like I was staring up at the Terminator.

"You were right," he said. "I'm Anthony's uncle. Folk just call me Regi."

"Mason Sharpe," I said, wiping mud and grease off my face with the back of one hand. "I wish I could say it was a pleasure."

The flicker of a smile passed across Regi's lips. It didn't last.

"*Who* are you?" Regi repeated the question, and I knew my standby "I'm just a guy" line wouldn't cut it this time.

"I used to be a cop. Before that I was Army. Now I'm just... headed south. Or I was. Then I met Jalen."

"So you just wanderin' around, poking your nose in other folk's business?"

"I mean...not usually. It just happened that way."

"Why you wanna help Jalen?"

I swabbed sweat off my forehead. It felt like a million degrees in the forest. Someplace behind the Cadillac I saw a long winding road, but no people. No lights. We might as well be sitting on Mars.

"I don't like bullies," I said. "I guess I just think he's been given a bad shake."

Regi spat sideways. "Stop lyin' to me, boy."

I looked into his iron face and suddenly felt like he saw right through me. I noted the tangle of dark green and black tattoos on his bare arms and across his chest, and the rippling scar passing down one side of his neck.

This guy was nobody's fool. He'd been around the block —several times.

"I remember what it was like," I said. "To be like Jalen."

"You ain't never been like Jalen. You're white."

"Fair enough. But I grew up without a family. I grew up on the wrong side of the tracks. I know how easy it is to flush your life away. And...I don't like watching it happen. To anybody. Jalen is a smart kid. He deserves a fair shot."

Regi grunted. "So you're a do-gooder."

"No. I'm just a guy passing through. I would have left by now, but the DEA pulled me in on it. Then I banged up some guys at Jalen's place."

"Steel Mafia."

"Right."

"Gutter punks. You shoulda let Jalen handle it."

"Probably. But it is what it is now, and I'm trying to make it right. Are you gonna let me help or not?"

Regi reached slowly into his front pocket and liberated a smoke. It wasn't a cigarette like I'd first assumed—it was a cigarillo. A miniature cigar about the size of a stubby pen. He lit it up with a steel lighter, then folded his arms.

"What you got in mind?"

I thought quickly. My ears still rang from the missed gunshot, and I was no more fooled by it than I was the sliced duct tape. This guy could still kill me. I had to give him a reason not to.

"There's a guy called Hansley coming in from California. Some white guy to oversee the distribution of the cartel's M30s."

"M30s?"

"Fentanyl. Like supercharged heroin."

Regi snorted. "Punks these days. Back in my day we just smoked weed."

I seriously doubted whether that was true but chose not to stress the point.

"These M30s are worth millions. Hansley is coming to make sure they're properly managed. He'll be here this week —at the Westin Peachtree Plaza, downtown."

"How do you know all this?"

"Because I found their operations center. It's not far from where you jumped me, some old factory."

"You mean the lock and key plant?"

"Maybe. It's abandoned now. They're using it to package M30s in soup cans for distribution up the east coast."

"So you just poked around?"

"I slipped inside while they were holding a meeting. There was a Mexican there to inspect the operation. That's when I learned about Hansley."

"Okay. So what's this cracka got to do with anything?"

I shrugged. "Well, we know Anthony didn't kill that guy. And we know somebody's got a gun over his head. We just need to prove it. Like you so eloquently noted, Hansley is white. And I'm white. So..."

Regi squinted; then a dry grin crept across his face. "You must be trippin'."

"Think about it. They've never met Hansley. We know where he's staying. So we jump him, I take his phone, then I take his place inside the gang. Figure out who really killed that fed, and how to prove it. Then we call the DEA."

"You some kind of stupid." Regi snorted. "What makes you think they ain't seen this guy's picture?"

"Because before I was a homicide detective, I was a street cop in one of the most cartel-influenced cities in America. I had more than my share of brushes with organized crime from south of the border. They know how the FBI works. They know the DEA can tap cell phones and syphon data. There's zero chance this Hansley guy allows his picture to be taken, let alone transmitted via cell phone. The Squad hasn't met him before, so it's unlikely they know what he looks like."

"That's thin."

"It's not, but you shouldn't care anyway. It's not your ass on the line."

"Kid, you ain't got a clue what you gettin' into. You know what they did to that fed?"

"Skinned his face off," I said. "I know what they did. They're cartel wannabes. Bloodthirsty maniacs with some psychopath in charge."

"Exactly. And when they bust your dumb ass—"

"*If,*" I corrected.

"*If* they bust your dumb ass, they'll do the same to you."

"Probably."

"That don't scare you?"

I shrugged. "We've all got to die sometime. I'd like to do some good while I'm here."

He shook his head. "You one crazy joker."

I grew quiet, looking into the grave I sat next to. It was

barely two feet deep and just long enough to fit my six-foot-two frame.

"Maybe I just don't have a hell of a lot to live for," I said.

"We all got a lot to live for," Regi said. "That's why we put here."

Hot take coming from the guy who almost murdered me.

I thought it, but I didn't say it.

"I know you care about Jalen," I said. "I may not fully appreciate the difficulties of his life, but I understand the trajectory. He's *obsessed* with proving Anthony's innocence. He won't stop until he's killed or incarcerated. You know that, right?"

I made eye contact as I said it. Regi looked at his cigarillo, rolling it between dirty fingers. He knew.

"How do I know you ain't just tryin' to get loose, then jump me?"

"You don't. Just like I can't be sure you won't shoot me in the back later tonight. Life is full of risks, but here's a guarantee: The longer this rolls on, the more damage it causes. The more likely it ends with Jalen six feet under. You wanna let that happen?"

Regi stood next to the grave, sucking his teeth. His cigarillo had burned out, and I saw something dark behind his already dark eyes. Something deadly. I couldn't tell if it was hostile or not, but there was no doubt in my mind that Regi would have shot me.

He was capable.

Regi flicked the cigarillo butt into the grave, then jabbed his thumb toward the Cadillac.

"Clean off your shoes. No mud in my Caddy."

37

The Cadillac was an Eldorado. I saw the name written in elegant silver script on the trunk lid, just outside where I had so recently been incarcerated. I kicked mud off my sneakers and wiped down the face of my pants before opening the passenger door.

The interior was black leather—immaculate, with stitched carpet and LED lights built beneath the dash, glowing softly in alternating blue, purple, and gold. Regi was already in the driver's seat, situated behind an oversized steering wheel and fiddling with the stereo.

B. B. King came back on. I didn't think I'd ever enjoy his rolling melodies in the same way again.

I cast a suspicious look at the back seat, where the shovel and my captured personal items rode on a folded blue tarpaulin. Regi gestured impatiently, and I smothered my nerves and got in. The heavy door slammed a lot like the doors on my GMC.

"Nice ride," I muttered.

Regi shifted the big transmission into gear. I thought about the soft mud outside, but the Cadillac maintained traction with ease as he swung it around like a battleship. Pretty soon we were bumping back down the same road we came in on, my ride a great deal more comfortable than before.

"So, you're Anthony's uncle."

"That's right," Regi grunted. He was leaned back in his seat now, totally relaxed like he hadn't been about to blow a man's brains out.

"Not Jalen's uncle," I clarified.

"Leroy was my brother," Regi said. "Anthony's father. We don't know who Jalen's father is."

"What about the old lady?" I asked. "The one Jalen lives with."

"His mama's mama."

The stereo clicked, and a new B. B. King track came on. I adjusted in the comfortable high-back seat and tried not to admit how relieved I was not to be in that grave. I didn't want to give Regi the perception of an upper hand in the conversation.

"Help me put this together," I said.

"Put what together?"

"Well, obviously you care about Jalen. Enough to kill a man for jeopardizing his security."

"Right."

"And yet you can't be bothered to involve yourself in his daily life."

The comment was calculated to sting. I hit my target. Regi bristled.

"Excuse me?"

"The single greatest contributor to poverty in America: broken families. That's a proven fact. Jalen is growing up without a father. Seems like you'd step up to the plate."

I was still throwing barbs. I knew Regi was hiding something, and I wanted to flush it out.

"You got a big mouth for a man I almost shot."

"But you didn't shoot, and I was honest with you. So return the favor. Or are we just gonna ride around and listen to crappy jazz?"

"It's *blues*," Regi snapped. "And this ain't no crap. This the King."

"Oh," I said. "All sounds the same to me."

He glared sideways at me as he negotiated a turn in the messy dirt road. We were *way* outside the city. I couldn't even see the glow of urban metropolis on the horizon.

"So?" I prompted.

Regi's hands twisted around the wheel. He sucked his teeth again and shook his head, as though he was more disgusted with himself than with me. He stopped the car at an intersection with a paved road, but he didn't turn down it. He just sat with the powerful high beams blasting back the darkness.

"Years ago, I was a banger like Anthony." He kept his foot on the brake, scratching his cheek. Then he grunted. "Well, not like Anthony. I weren't no petty drug dealer. I was a Crip."

The familiar name sent a dull chill up my spine. It was an involuntary reaction, but a genuine one. Anybody even passingly familiar with gangland warfare had heard of the Crips. A Los Angeles–based, African American gang that spread from coast to coast, locked in an endless war with their archenemies, the Bloods.

Who knew how it started? Who cared. The body count rose, and the hatred only deepened.

"Here in Atlanta?" I asked.

Regi nodded. "It weren't no big city then. Just a big old town, with brothas doing what they had to do. My daddy got popped in 'Nam, so I had a broken family. Like you say."

He sneered at me, exposing a gold tooth in the back of his mouth. I said nothing.

"I was in deep. A lot deeper than Anthony. There was war

brewing. Big showdown with the Bloods, but we had rats in the ranks, you know? People snitching to the cops. There was opportunity for a young banger like me. Chance to rise in the ranks."

Regi looked away, down the silent gray tunnel of the county road we'd stopped against. "I popped a kid one Friday night. Right downtown, in front of a dozen strangers. Thought it'd go down harder that way. Thought we'd make our point. Thought we were untouchable! The Crips, man. Bloodsuckas and head bustas."

He shook his head, then turned the wheel and hit the gas. "I did twenty-two up in Hartwell. Right where Anthony's sittin'."

The Cadillac groaned as it hit the road; then a storm of mud and rocks broke free from the tires and rattled against the undercarriage. Regi leaned back in his seat, one hand riding the bottom of the wheel. He looked like an absolute king. Like he was born in that Cadillac.

I processed the story piece by piece, unsure how any of it had anything to do with Anthony or Jalen.

Then I remembered my earlier challenge, and it all made sense.

"Jalen blames you," I said.

Regi didn't answer.

"When Anthony went down, you stepped back. Skipped most of the trial. Jalen thinks you cut Anthony loose."

Regi leaned his head against the headrest, looking suddenly very tired. I wondered again how old he was. Maybe I'd judged him too harshly.

Maybe I could be forgiven if I had, considering my abduction and planned murder.

"Jalen's just a little sprout," Regi said. "He don't know how the world turns. He thinks enough lawyers, enough acting out, and something will change. But I been on the inside, son.

I seen how these things shake down. I got the picture real quick after Anthony was arrested. I was the first person he called. He let me know straight up..."

Regi trailed off.

"Not to fight it," I said. "To look after Jalen and accept the sentencing."

"Yeah. Coz it's like you say...they got leverage."

"So it was a setup? From the start."

"Look that way. He never shared specifics."

"What exactly does Jalen know?"

"He don't know he's being used as leverage, if that's what you mean."

"But he knows Anthony was burned."

Regi's shoulders sagged. "Seems so. I guess word leaked. Or maybe the Squad leaked it on purpose. Nothing that can be proven. But enough to intimidate some folk."

"So Anthony's got you running interference? Trying to keep Jalen out of trouble."

"Somethin' like that."

"But the Squad has their hooks in him. He's dealing their weed."

"Keepin' him on the line," Regi said. "I known about it for a few days now. I just...don't know what to do about it."

"There's only one thing to do," I said. "We've got to kneecap the Squad. Burn them to the ground. Anything less, and they'll absolutely kill Jalen. No amount of protection will ever be enough. And we've got to get Anthony out of jail, too. Get Jalen off his rampage before he ruins his whole life."

"You make it sound so simple," Regi snorted. "This ain't no one-man job. These killas are for real. There's dozens of them."

"Which is why we're gonna let the DEA do the dirty work. I'll go in as Hansley. Figure out about this shipment. Figure out who really murdered that undercover agent. Then we call the DEA. Game over."

Regi shot me another sideways look. The weariness was still there. And the subdued anger. But I thought I saw something new.

A trace of respect.

I turned the volume up on the stereo. "*My Kind of Blues*," I said. "Nineteen sixty-one. Great album."

"You know BB?" Regi said, his voice turning a little shrill.

"Of course I know BB. Like you said, he's the King."

A grin crept across Regi's face, his lip lifting. He drummed the steering wheel and began to sing along while I just enjoyed not being dead.

Up ahead I finally saw the glow in the black sky. Atlanta, drawing nearer.

Bringing the fight with it.

38

R egi refused to return me to my hotel, muttering something about not letting me out of his sight. Instead he drove me right to his house—a nine-teen-forties-style cottage in Bankhead, not far from A. B. Colby's law office. The house was small, and the street it sat on looked ready to be bulldozed, with dark and unmanaged lots on every side.

But Regi's place was immaculate. The lawn was cut, the driveway pressure washed and patched, and there were even some tulips planted in a little flower bed next to the front steps. He pulled the Cadillac onto the drive and climbed out, grunting a little as he stretched. I looked into the back seat, contemplating a quick retrieval of my personal items, followed by a mad dash for freedom.

I meant what I'd said to Regi. I wouldn't leave Atlanta until Jalen's problems were addressed. But I also didn't like the idea of being under his thumb while solving those problems.

"Don't even think about it," Regi muttered, his back still turned. The Smith and Wesson was crammed into his front pocket now, bulging and gleaming in the dim streetlights. An illegal possession for any convicted felon.

Also not a subject I was willing to raise.

"Go on inside," Regi said. "Clean yourself up. I gotta wash the Caddy."

"You serious?" I asked, reflexively checking my watch. It was almost five a.m.

"Boy, you don't hang on to a jewel like this by mud doggin' her. Gotta get that clay off!"

He was already unwinding a garden hose from the corner of the house. He tossed me the keys, and I shuffled up the front steps, marveling that I had so quickly transitioned from prisoner to trusted houseguest.

I figured that said more about Regi's own confidence than any great trust in me.

The front room was small, but immaculately clean. I was greeted almost instantly by a painting on the far wall, a full two feet wide and twice as high. It displayed a gleaming cross backlit by the light of heaven, with a rolling green field stretching beneath it. Across that field was scattered a flock of white sheep, and written in elegant script at the bottom of the painting were the words:

You are the sheep, I am the shepherd.

I glanced around the living room and noted a couch and an easy chair resting on orange shag carpet. There was no TV, but there were shelves lined with Christian trinkets *every-where*. Little figurines of Christ with His arms spread, children and sheep at His feet. Gold and silver crucifixes, with inscriptions of Scripture engraved into them. Smaller paintings of the twelve disciples alongside a turbulent sea.

An artist's impression of the crucifixion, black clouds boiling behind.

I wasn't sure what I expected at the house of an admitted murderer, but this wasn't it. Especially in context of Regi's recent intentions to leave me rotting in a Georgia grave. I peeled a curtain back and watched him lovingly washing the mud off the tires of the Eldorado, singing softly the B. B. King song we'd been listening to on the ride back into the city.

What the hell?

I moved through a dining room set with a four-person table, and around a small corner cabinet loaded with polished china dinnerware. My confusion intensified as I reached the kitchen and found a little breakfast table spread out with that day's issue of the *Atlanta Journal-Constitution*, the crossword half filled out.

Suddenly, I wondered if this was really Regi's house. Was this some kind of prank? Had he led me here to be arrested for trespassing? That would get me off Jalen's case well enough.

Then I saw the photograph.

It was framed on the wall next to an old-fashioned corded telephone. Faded in color, taken sometime several decades prior, it displayed a handsome African American couple standing at the base of a Ferris wheel at some carnival. The man was young and healthy, strapping with big muscles and a bulging chest. He stood with his arm around a beautiful young woman, her face glowing with the promise of a lifetime of love and happiness.

I didn't recognize the woman, but the man was most definitely Reginald James.

A footstep rang against the kitchen linoleum behind me. I twisted to see Regi standing there, wiping his hands on a kitchen towel. He wasn't looking at me, though. He was looking at the photo.

"I'm...I'm sorry," I said. I wasn't sure why, but I suddenly felt like an intruder.

Regi put the towel down and walked to a puke green fridge that looked as old as the house. He unlatched the heavy door and reached inside, withdrawing two icy-cold bottles of Coors Light. I caught one and twisted the cap off. Regi swallowed half of his and wiped his mouth with the back of one hand.

"We were married six months when I capped that sucka," he said quietly. "She divorced me while I was in prison. Left our apartment and everything in it. Moved right out of town."

He scraped a kitchen chair back and settled in with a soft grunt.

"I'm sorry," I said again. I didn't know what else to say.

Regi shrugged. "It was murder, what I done. She didn't know how deep I was with the Crips. Had every right to split."

"Did she ever remarry?"

He smiled. "Naw. Been single ever since."

He tapped the bottle, his gaze falling across the newspaper. Then he snapped his fingers.

"*Nightingale*. A bird with eleven letters."

He filled out another bar on the crossword, then drained the beer. "Fourteen hundred thirty-two days. Almost four years I been doin' the crossword, and it ain't whipped me yet!"

His grin exposed the gold tooth again, and I smiled, my shoulders relaxing a little. It wasn't the beer.

Regi went to the bathroom, and I busied myself at the kitchen sink, scrubbing away the remnants of Georgia clay and black grease. When he returned, he tossed me a blanket.

"You got the couch," he said. "No pissing, and no masturbatin'. Breakfast in three hours."

I kicked my shoes off, glancing again at the painting as I re-entered the living room. It was so bright it almost hurt to look at.

"Hey," I said. "What's with...all this?"

I gestured openly to the display of trinkets and paintings.

"What about it?" Regi asked.

"Are these...I mean, were these your wife's things?"

He scowled. "These are my things."

"Oh."

I didn't know what else to say. He raised an eyebrow.

"Oh *what*?"

I shrugged. "I guess I just didn't expect...you know."

"A gangbanger to love Jesus?"

"Well."

"It's a rough world we lives in. If I didn't have Jesus, I'd have punched my own ticket by now."

"And yet you see no problem punching somebody else's ticket," I said. I couldn't help it.

Regi snorted. "I was never gonna kill you, fool. Just gotta put the fear of God in you."

He flicked the light out and started down the hall. "Get some sleep, and don't lay a finger on tomorrow's paper."

39

I didn't think I would sleep, but I slept like a baby, only awakening four hours later to the smell of sizzling bacon and hot coffee.

I rolled off the couch and put both feet on the shag carpet, rubbing my eyes and inhaling the heavenly scent. The first thing I saw was one of Regi's golden crucifixes, wrapped in thorns and polished until it gleamed.

I blinked, then heard a soft whistling from the kitchen. Another B. B. King tune.

Pulling my shirt on, I stumbled through the little dining room to find Regi shirtless at the stove, his taut muscles rippling beneath tight, healthy skin. He was covered from the neck down in tattoos—many of which were irregular shapes all colored in with black and green. Only one image was clear. It was a replication of the cross painting in the living room, filling his back from the shoulders down in vivid detail.

Regi looked up from his frying pan, noting my fixation with his tattoos.

"Be not conformed to this world, but be ye *transformed*," he pronounced.

"Huh?" I was still sleepy.

"I had to transform this body into a temple for the Lord," Regi said. "Some of this gangsta ink weren't edifying."

I looked again at the irregular blotches of color and suddenly realized they were cover-ups for previous artwork. God only knew what lay beneath.

"Where's the coffee?" I said.

He handed me a cup, and I helped myself to the pot.

"Eggs?" he asked.

"Over medium."

Five minutes later we were sitting at the breakfast table, and Regi was busy working his crossword while I stuffed my face with bacon, eggs, toast, and enough coffee to wash it all down. I hadn't eaten anything substantial since the pasta at Metro Diner, and Regi was a good cook. The food was perfect.

"Seven letters," he said. "Sports stars...middle letter is a T..."

He trailed off. I held my fork in midair.

"Montana," I said. "Joe Montana."

The paper crumpled as Regi wadded it up, his face blazing with indignation.

"I weren't asking *you*."

"My mistake. Geez. Don't shoot me."

He shot me a sideways glance, and I saw a smirk rippling at the corner of his mouth. He smoothed out the paper and wrote Montana down anyway, then sipped his coffee.

"All right, hotshot. You drinking my beer and eating my bacon. What's the big plan?"

I wiped my mouth. Sipped coffee. "We'll get to the plan. First, I want to know about Anthony."

"What about him?"

"Everything about him. Who he is. Where he came from.

What his family's like. And most importantly, what his involvement with the SAS was."

"How would I know that?" Regi said.

"Well, you're the number one person Anthony trusts to look after Jalen. And Jalen seems to be the number one person in Anthony's life. So valuable he's sacrificing his own freedom to protect him. I'm guessing you and Anthony are pretty tight."

Regi looked away. Swirled his coffee. Then he nodded. "Yeah...I guess you could say that."

"So talk to me."

"Ain't much to say, really. Another sad story. I already told you his daddy was my brother. Leroy never married Anthony's mama, so Anthony had her name, but Leroy was always the better parent. He managed a gas station. Got held up and capped by some dumb thugs when Anthony was, like, fifteen. Anthony's mama got pregnant again with Jalen, then ran off not long after he was born...wouldn't surprise me none if she's dead too. She liked the smack. So I kinda looked after the boys comin' up. Did what I could."

"When did Anthony join the gang?"

"Sheesh...young. Seventeen, maybe. I didn't know about it until it was too late to turn back. It was just some petty street gang back then, but it blossomed into the SAS. Anthony got in on the ground level. Was banging with them for 'bout fifteen years."

"So he was a boss?"

"I guess. To be honest, I didn't really want to know. Anthony and I talked regular. He'd come over to my place, and we'd grill out. That kind of thing. But he was always real respectful about his line of work. Didn't want to bother me with it none. Given my faith and whatnot. At least, not until...well."

"What?"

Regi shifted uncomfortably. Slurped coffee.

"What changed?" I prompted.

"Fentanyl," Regi said at last. "I don't know what the Squad was slinging before then. Smack and crack, probably. But they got in on some fentanyl. Started selling to rich white kids in the suburbs. Lots more money to be made. That fentanyl...sheet. Ain't no joke."

"I know."

"Anthony started seeing what it was doing to kids. Some of them pop a couple of pills, first time, and drop dead. Maybe a bad batch. Maybe too strong. You just don't never know."

"He had second thoughts?"

"He was worried about it. Didn't think it was a good business. Too much risk. Too much heat."

"Did he try to leave the gang?"

"Nah. He just wanted to cut out the fentanyl. But there was some guy, some other boss. He wouldn't have it. Said the money was too good. Apparently there was some big expansion plan in play. Something Anthony had facilitated. I don't know details, but he was all kinda stressed about it."

"How long was this before they burned him?" I asked.

"Not long. Few weeks. He called me drunk one night, all tore up about it. I...well, I was a little lit myself. Not much I knew to say. I wish..."

He looked away. His eyes watered, and he cleared his throat a few times. I withdrew my burner phone from my pocket and called up the same photo I'd showed Feldon.

"You ever see this guy?"

Regi gave the phone a good squint, then shook his head. "Nah."

I returned the phone to my pocket and poured myself more coffee, giving Regi time to get himself straight. He finished off his own cup and sat up.

"So. The plan."

"First thing we've got to do is call the hotel and confirm this reservation for Hansley. Then we can nail down a plan to accost him and, well..."

"'Nap his ass," Regi said, looking at the crossword again.

"Yeah. Exactly. Does that...conflict?"

I looked toward the living room. Regi smiled.

"Brotha, you got all kinds of mixed-up ideas about faith, don't you?"

That wasn't a question I was even remotely interested in evaluating, least of all with a semi-stable psychopath who had so recently "'napped" *my* ass with the intention of terminating me.

"I just want to know where you stand on this," I said. "It's a good plan, but I wasn't looking for an accomplice. It seems like you've done a pretty good job of keeping your nose clean. I'm not here to disrupt that."

Regi took his time in responding.

"You were a cop?" he said at last.

"Yes."

"A good one?"

I wasn't sure how to answer that. I'd been an *effective* cop. I closed cases. But the file of excessive force citations on my record argued I wasn't a *good* one. I'd been a soldier too long to understand the value of respecting red tape while bad guys trampled innocent people.

"I got the job done."

"You know how to get Anthony off?"

"I know how to try. If we find evidence, I know a lawyer who will file the appeal for free. She's good."

"See..." Regi hesitated, looking awkward for the first time since I met him. "That's stuff I don't know nothing about. I never finished high school. Not too good with no books or legal stuff. If I knew how to get Anthony off, I already would have. I just...don't know where to start."

"I do," I said. "I just need to know where you stand."

He faced me. "Right behind you."

"All right, then. Let's get it done."

I USED the outdated phone book in the kitchen drawer and the even more outdated phone on the wall to dial the Westin Peachtree Plaza in downtown Atlanta. I recognized the tower pictured in the phone book as a member of the Atlanta skyline—very tall and round, encased in plate glass with a black ring near the top—a restaurant, maybe. Only a couple of blocks from the Sheraton where I'd been staying.

When the receptionist picked up, I asked to be transferred to reservations. Then my ruse kicked in, and I assumed the identity of Hansley's personal assistant.

It was a onetime trick. If the woman on the other end of the line didn't buy the ploy, I was out of ideas about how to nail down Hansley's travel plans.

"Peachtree Plaza, this is Samantha. How may I help you?"

"Hi, Sam. I'm calling on behalf of my boss, Mr. Hansley. I just needed to confirm his reservation for this week."

Long pause. I leaned against the wall, desperately hoping she didn't ask for a first name.

"You said this week?" she asked.

"That's right."

"L. Hansley?"

"Right."

It was a roll of the dice. I couldn't imagine more than one Hansley being booked at the same hotel for the same week.

"I have it right here. Check-in is at two p.m., and we have him booked through the end of the month."

I frowned. "Two p.m.? What day?"

"Um...this day?"

I thanked her and hung up the phone. Regi was just walking down the hall, freshly showered and dressed in another tight tank top and Bulldogs hat. He looked as lithe and ready as ever.

"Come on," I said. "We gotta roll."

"Where?"

"Downtown. To the hotel."

"Huh? Why?"

I slid my shoes on, grabbing Regi's Cadillac keys from the rack by the door. "Because Hansley isn't arriving later this week. He'll be here *today*."

40

"What exactly is your plan, here?"

Regi drove the Cadillac, one hand riding the bottom of the wheel while his oversized Smith and Wesson sat jammed against the seat next to him. He looked remarkably cool considering the illegal activity he had just committed to.

B. B. King's musings about why he sang the blues probably didn't hurt.

"I need you on the street across from the valet stand," I said. "Look for California plates. I'm going to stake out in the lobby near reception and listen for the name."

"Seriously?" Regi shot me a disappointed look. "That's the best you got?"

"Ninety percent of good police work is boring as hell. The Mexican guy at the factory said Hansley was driving in, and he's from California. There shouldn't be too many California plates checking in with the valet. Look for a flashy luxury car, probably black, probably European. These guys have the imagination of rookie athletes."

"What happens when you find him?"

"I'm going to invite him to lunch in your trunk."

Regi's lips twitched. I snorted.

"Oh, *now* you've got a problem with shoving people in your trunk?"

Regi cranked up the stereo.

We reached downtown and circled the Westin Peachtree Plaza twice, giving me a complete view of the property. The tower was tall and cylindrical, with a secondary cylindrical shaft sticking to one side and running all the way to the top. A glass elevator, I figured.

The base was much less interesting to look at. A simple concrete building that consumed the bulk of the block, with steps leading to a main entrance on the east side and the entrance to the valet stand on the north. There was no place for Regi to stop the car, but on the south side of the hotel, a micro block was built into a simple park.

"Find street parking and stake out at that park," I said, digging through my pile of equipment still riding in Regi's back seat. I found the binoculars and handed them off to him, then took my burner cell phone, wallet, and both knives.

"Where's my money?" I demanded. Regi jammed a thumb at the glove box without comment. I opened it and found my dwindling supply of running money resting on top of two Glock handguns and four boxes of 9mm ammunition.

"Holy cow," I said. "Aren't you a felon?"

Regi snorted. "Rather take my chances with the law than some of these thugs."

I took the cash and snapped the glove box closed. Regi pulled off the street half a block from the Westin.

"Give me your phone," I said. He handed off a simple cell not unlike my burner, and I entered the burner's number into the contact list.

"Call or text," I said. "And don't get spotted."

"A black man scoping out expensive cars with binoculars? What could go wrong?"

I ignored the complaint and swung out of the Caddy, the switchblade ready in my front right pocket. I scanned the block quickly for any sign of Feldon's unmarked Ford, but for the moment the DEA seemed to have lost me.

That was just as well. They didn't need to see this.

Jaywalking to the hotel's front entrance, I straightened my collar and ran a hand through my hair. I saw the reflection of Regi's long green Eldorado rolling across the tinted hotel glass, and I drew a deep breath.

Then I pushed inside like I owned the joint.

The hallway ahead was quiet and almost empty. On both sides doors opened into conference and ballrooms, and directly ahead the mass of a spiraling stairwell led to the second floor of the block building. Everything smelled very clean and sterile, and the hotel staff I passed all wore vests and little black ties.

None of them spoke to me as I stopped at the base of the stairwell and quickly scanned the main lobby.

To my right lay a gift shop and the entrance to the glass elevator. Directly ahead was a field of couches and lounge chairs, with the reception desk and a bank of elevators beyond them.

Perfect.

I circled the stairs and scooped a copy of the *Atlanta Journal-Constitution* off an end table. A crowd of people stood at reception, slowly filtering through check-in as luggage carts rolled across cold tile and elevators dinged.

I sat on a couch and opened the newspaper, scanning the headlines before adjusting my seat for a better view of the reception desk.

I saw a lot of jerseys—Boston Celtics jerseys, mostly, with a few Atlanta Hawks thrown in. I glanced back down at the newspaper and reinterpreted the headline I had initially ignored.

Can Atlanta Win It All? Hawks Advance to Conference Semi-Finals.

Well, that explained the crowd checking in at reception. The additional witnesses weren't going to make my job any easier.

I alternated between the newspaper and surveying the people incoming from the valet stand, eventually settling on the crossword puzzle Regi had been working on over breakfast. Nobody seemed to notice me sitting by myself on a lonely couch. The hotel staff were swamped by the influx of guests. The elevators almost never stopped, shuffling loads of basketball fans as dozens more poured in from the garage.

I checked my watch. It was well past two p.m., and I still hadn't heard anything from Regi. I shot him a quick text.

Anything?

The reply was almost immediate and as blunt as I expected.

No.

I folded the paper in my lap and wondered if I'd miscalculated. This whole harebrained scheme of mine was a stretch at best. Assuming Hansley showed up, and assuming I successfully singled him out, and assuming we then successfully sidelined him and accessed his phone to arrange a meetup with the SAS, it was still a big leap to uncover evidence of Anthony's innocence before my cover evaporated.

Regi was right. It was a crazy plan. But my window of opportunity to do anything on Anthony's behalf was closing quickly. As soon as the promised load of M30s arrived in Atlanta, I'd have no choice but to tip off the DEA. I couldn't stand by and watch that much poison stream across a brand-new market of unsuspecting victims, even if a DEA bust would almost certainly destroy any chance I had of exonerating Anthony.

It was now or never.

My phone buzzed, and I glanced down to see a message from Regi.

Black Jag. Cali plates.

I tossed the newspaper aside and walked to the coffee stand near reception. It cut my distance from the valet entrance in half and gave me a clear view of the check-in desk.

I poured coffee slowly and fumbled with sugar packets.

Getting out.

Regi's next text flashed across the screen, and I pocketed the phone. Glancing through the double glass doors to the valet stand, I recognized the elongated trunk lid and rounded taillight of a Jaguar XJ—a big sedan, with inky black windows and gloss black wheels.

No imagination.

I stirred my coffee and took a protracted sip. Then I reached for more sugar.

A new crowd of Celtics fans poured in from valet, all bustling together wearing team hats and bright green shirts, but I picked Hansley out of the crowd like a fly on a wedding cake.

He was tall—almost as tall as me—and dressed head to toe in all black. Black shoes. Black slacks. A black shirt covered by a black jacket. Jet-black hair and dark black sunglasses. He looked like a freaking undertaker, wheeling an all-black suitcase behind him and pressing through the crowd of Celtics fans like they didn't exist. He pushed right into the lobby and turned for the reception desk without bothering to apologize to the people he cut off.

His face was stone cold. Complete iron, scraped clean of facial hair with no hint of a smile as he acknowledged the receptionist with a simple nod, then laid down an ID card.

The man looked like a cartoon. The bad guy from a *Batman* comic.

Target acquired.

I texted Regi, then moved directly to the elevator and pressed the button. A knot of tourists gathered at the door, and I politely volunteered to wait for the next car as Hansley completed check-in.

He wheeled in next to me, and I smelled the hint of cologne. He still wore the sunglasses and glared ahead at the door as though it had killed his dog.

I said nothing as we both stepped inside the car amongst a crowd of college kids all shouting and swapping jokes. Hansley pushed the twenty-second button. I remained quiet as the elevator rose, noting another text from Regi.

What's the play?

I pocketed the phone and stepped out of the car at the twenty-second floor. Hansley was the only other passenger to exit. He moved directly to room 2207 and withdrew a card key. I kept walking and turned the corner, drawing the phone again.

Get the car. Meet me at the service entrance. I'm bringing him.

41

I checked for the switchblade in my pocket and wished I'd taken one of Regi's guns. Hansley would almost definitely be armed—probably a full-sized handgun concealed beneath his jacket and maybe another on his ankle. I would need to get the jump on him.

Turning back down the hall, I walked directly to room 2207 and rapped on the door.

There was no answer, and I knocked again.

"Read the sign," a voice called from the inside. It was cold and irritated. I looked down to see the *Do Not Disturb* sign swinging from the handle.

"I hit your car," I said.

Long pause. Footsteps tapped across the carpet, and I watched the peephole. It didn't darken.

Smart man.

"Who are you?" Hansley asked, still not opening the door.

"Hey, buddy. I smacked your car at the valet stand. They gave me your room number to call, but I figured we could work it out in person. Maybe you'll take cash?"

The door slid open, but only a couple of inches. Hansley's

face appeared in the crack, and he surveyed me with a quick squint. I was still wearing the black clothes from my covert operation the night before and knew I looked somewhat conspicuous. There wasn't much to be done about that.

Hansley's sunglasses were gone. His eyes were ice blue. Somehow, I expected that.

"What car?" he asked.

"Black Jag," I said. "California plates?"

"It's a rental," he said. "Don't worry about it."

He moved to shut the door. I spoke quickly.

"I just want you to know the trunk won't close. All your stuff is gonna get wet."

That got him, just like I knew it would. The car was too customized to be a rental, and any cartel associate traveling across country was sure to have illicit materials in his trunk. The kinds of things he didn't want just anyone seeing.

The door swung open, and Hansley stood glowering death at me.

"Where is it?"

"Outside," I said, jabbing my thumb in the general direction of the service entrance on the west side of the building. "They're calling a tow truck."

"*No*," he snapped, shoving by me and hurrying for the elevator. "Stupid fool. What the hell were you thinking?"

"Sorry, man. Foot just slipped off the brake, you know?"

I joined him in the elevator, and he fumed as we rode downward, checking his watch twice.

I made note of the impatience as we stepped out, but I turned right and motioned him toward a hallway. "This way."

He squinted, momentary doubt flashing across his face. Then he followed me, down a long hall past more conference rooms and a laundry center, toward a glass door that opened directly onto Carnegie Way NW—the street running alongside the hotel's parking garage.

I walked ahead, keeping my hands loose at my sides, my fingers within easy reach of the switchblade.

Don't let him draw.

I reached the door and saw Regi's Eldorado waiting at the curb. The muscular ex-gangster leaned against the rear fender just behind the passenger's door, smoking a cigarillo, his hands poked casually into his pockets.

The door was closed, but the front passenger seat was already rocked forward—ready to receive a passenger into the back seat.

Not a bad plan, on Regi's part. Except for Hansley's guns.

I pushed the door opening, motioning ahead of the Cadillac to a spot Hansley couldn't yet see.

"Right there," I said.

He followed me through the door and onto the sidewalk, rocking his head toward the spot and frowning.

"Where?"

"In front of the Suburban," I said, motioning again. Hansley took a step forward, crossing in front of me, only six feet from the Cadillac. I checked quickly for pedestrians or passing cars—potential witnesses.

Then I drew the switchblade and closed behind Hansley in one fluid motion. The blade snapped open against his lower back, and I pressed hard enough to pierce his suit jacket—right above his kidney.

"Stay loose," I said, hearing the Cadillac's door swing open behind me. "Get in the car."

Hansley stiffened, a look of complete disgust washing across his face. He looked down at me with those ice blue eyes, and I didn't see a trace of fear. Just disdain.

"You have no idea who you're messing with."

"Yeah, whatever. Get in the car."

I prodded with the knife. He turned slowly toward the Cadillac. Regi lifted the tail of his shirt to expose the Smith and Wesson tucked into his pants. Hansley stopped short of the Caddy and snorted.

"Seriously? What is this?"

"We'll chat in the car, Hansley," I said. "Now move it."

I prodded with the knife, a little harder this time. And then I felt it. The tip of the dagger blade penetrated the suit jacket and stopped cold. The hint of a smirk flashed across Hansley's face, and I looked down at the knife.

Kevlar.

I saw the elbow flying back at my face only a millisecond too late. The joint collided with my mouth and sent me flailing backward, the knife spinning across the sidewalk as Hansley broke into a sprint. Regi shouted and lifted the gun. My head spun, and I wiped blood from my mouth, scrambling to get up.

"Don't!" I shouted. Regi hesitated, and Hansley rushed around the corner of the hotel. I snatched up the knife and snapped the blade closed, already breaking into a mad dash.

"Follow me in the car!" I said.

Then I was around the corner, headed east along the south side of the Westin as I saw Hansley bolting fifty yards ahead. The man ran like a leopard, his long legs consuming concrete as he swerved to dodge an oncoming streetcar. The car rushed toward me on sunken rails, forcing me to swerve back onto the sidewalk as it clacked past in a long stream of sleek blue. Looking ahead, I saw Hansley cross behind the tail of the car and then turn right onto Peachtree Street—now a hundred yards ahead and gaining steam.

I stretched out and leveraged every inch of my long legs, breathing deeply and embracing the sprint. I reached the intersection of Peachtree Street and dashed to the right, casting a quick look down the sidewalk for the man in all black.

Hansley was gone. I looked both ways down the street

and through the glass doors of a hotel situated at the intersection. The Californian had simply vanished.

Then I saw the sign. Small and subdued, hanging from the roof of a squat brick building with escalators shooting into the ground directly beneath it.

MARTA—Peachtree Center Train Station.

I dashed across the street, holding out a hand as a taxi blared its horn. At the train station I ran down the moving escalator, shoving past other pedestrians with mumbled apologies and jumping the final four steps.

A bank of turnstiles blocked my path to another pair of escalators, leading deeper beneath the city. But they weren't waist-high rods—they were head-high gates held closed by automated arms and impossible to jump.

I slid to a stop at the ticket kiosk, and then I saw Hansley. The tall Californian had just passed through a turnstile, the gates smacking closed behind him. He looked over his shoulder once, his face encased in sunglasses again, and I saw his lips tighten when he saw me. He broke into a run for the second escalator, and I barged for a turnstile, shoving against a gate.

It wouldn't budge. The automatic ticket reader built next to the gate buzzed and flashed red. I looked down the line of turnstiles, watching as a middle-aged guy in a business suit passed a plastic card across the reader. A green light flashed, and I bolted, shoving ahead of him and blasting through the gates. He stumbled and shouted a profanity. I ignored him, taking the escalator steps two and three at a time. I saw Hansley stepping off at the bottom, his coattails flapping as he broke into a jog. Someplace deep below, a train screamed against metal rails, and a rush of subterranean air washed across my face.

I saw the train as I reached the bottom of the escalator. It had already stopped, and passengers were packing in along a wide platform. I searched the faces, but I didn't see Hansley until the bulk of passengers were already on board.

Hansley had taken the car to my far right, sixty or eighty yards away from the escalator. I could see him just inside a narrow train window, but I would never reach that car before the train departed. I dashed straight ahead as a bell rang and the doors began to close. My feet skipped over the edge of the platform, and I slid inside, sweat streaming across my face as the doors clapped shut. A grandmotherly old woman seated across from me raised both eyebrows like I was crazy, but nobody spoke as the car lurched.

I braced myself against an overhead rail, breathing heavily as I worked my way to the end of the car, where a steel door connected to the next car. I grabbed the handle and turned, but the latch stuck. Then I saw the sign pasted beneath it:

WALKWAY CLOSED.

I stepped back, casting a quick glance around the car, but nobody was paying any attention to me. Everyone was lost in a sea of electronic devices.

I moved back to the door, finding a map glued to the wall displaying the train route. According to the overhead display, we were traveling south on the Gold Line, toward the airport.

The train began to brake, and an electronic voice spoke from overhead: "The next station is Five Points Station."

I took my position next to the door, ready to sprint. Up ahead I could see only one platform, meaning that Hansley would have to exit on the same side of the train as I if he wanted to escape. I already knew he couldn't transition between cars.

He was trapped.

The train stopped, and I bolted. Up the line of cars, shoving between passengers and searching for Hansley. I couldn't remember which car he was in. The last one? The next to last?

Fresh passengers packed in on the southbound train, and I thought I saw a black sleeve through a window in the last car. I made a split-second decision to dive back on board a second before the doors closed; then we were off again, surging south.

"The next station is Garnett," the voice said.

I pulled the burner from my pocket. There was no signal, but I typed a message and hit send anyway, hoping it would transmit to Regi once I returned to the surface.

Garnett Station.

I felt the floor rising beneath my feet and looked out the window to see light shining from someplace ahead. The train was emerging out of the rock, reaching back for surface level.

Garnett would be above ground. That was perfect.

The train began to slow as the computerized voice listed off local attractions at the next stop. I pressed against the door again, the knife closed but clasped between my fingers, my thumb on the switch.

He wasn't getting away this time.

The train slowed to a stop, and the doors rolled open. I broke out and turned left.

And then I saw Hansley, already free of the car, sprinting across the platform for the exit.

42

I dashed through the crowd, heedlessly throwing people aside as I cleared the platform and reached another set of escalators. Hansley was already near the top, flashing a plastic card to pass through another row of turnstiles. He was fifty yards ahead, and I didn't have a chance of catching him. I ran up the escalator and swept my gaze across the crowd of commuters, selecting the nearest guy with a MARTA card clamped in one hand, ready to exit.

I snatched the card and bolted for the gate before he could stop me, smacking it against the automatic reader. A light flashed green, and the gates parted. Then I was out onto a concrete deck, running out from under the train station's roof and dropping the card behind me.

Ahead I saw Hansley, turning off the raised deck onto a set of spiraling stairs that led down to street level. I could hear the city now, car horns blaring, another train rushing in from the south. My pocket buzzed, signaling an incoming text from Regi, but I ignored it. I zeroed in on Hansley and sprinted like my life depended on it, stretching out and throwing myself at the stairs. He was already near the bottom, running for the half-empty parking lot waiting there.

I made it halfway down, then grabbed the rail and flipped my legs over, dropping the final ten feet.

A shock wave radiated through my knees on impact, but I maintained my footing, hitting the switch on the Microtech and pivoting toward the bottom of the stairs.

The gun almost hit me in the face. I saw the gaping mouth of a .45 caliber sweeping toward me like a pit of hell, and shot my hand up, closing my fingers around the muzzle of the weapon and pressing.

It was a lightning-fast, instinctual move. Hansley pulled the trigger, but nothing happened. My hand had driven the slide back a quarter inch, bringing the gun out of battery and instantly disabling it.

I swept up with my knife hand, stabbing him right in the elbow and sinking the blade a full inch. Hansley grunted, and the gun dropped from his fingers, clattering on the concrete. He stumbled back and I drove my knee into his face, closing his jaw with a crunch of teeth. His head snapped back, and his eyeballs rolled. Then he collapsed, his skull cracking against the concrete.

He was out cold, limp on the sidewalk.

I flicked the knife closed, glancing quickly around me. To my right was a liquor store with a trash-infested lot behind it. On my left was a public parking lot, mostly empty, with an unmarked brick building beyond it.

Empty soda bottles and abandoned fast-food wrappers skittered across the concrete under a light breeze. There were no people.

I pulled the phone out and dialed Regi.

"Where you at?" he said.

"Parking lot next to the train station. Hurry."

I hung up and scooped the gun off the concrete. It was a

Glock 30, chambered in .45 ACP, as I'd initially guessed. Dropping the mag, I confirmed the presence of ten rounds of hollow-point ammunition, with an eleventh round resting in the chamber.

Not a bad weapon. I shoved it into my pocket and grabbed Hansley by the arms, dragging his inert body behind the liquor store before anyone could see it.

Regi arrived two minutes later, rolling the Eldorado into the parking lot like a cruise ship. He got out and grabbed Hansley's feet without hesitation or question, helping me to haul him to the open trunk.

The big Californian fit easily into the even bigger trunk, and Regi slammed the lid. Five seconds later we were rolling again; Regi leaned back and relaxed, me scanning the street for possible witnesses.

I had no qualms about what I was doing. But I couldn't easily finish the job from jail.

"What happened at the hotel?" Regi demanded.

"Kevlar body armor," I said. "The knife was worthless."

"Shoulda let me cap 'im," Regi said.

"Really? And then where would we be? Prison?"

Regi snorted and turned up B. B. King. I wiped more sweat off my face. It wasn't hot outside, but my heart still thumped from the exertion of running Hansley down.

"Where to?" Regi asked.

"Someplace quiet where we can search him."

Regi took the highway, the Cadillac floating on its heavy-duty suspension and squatting a little in the rear. The city passed outside my right window, and then we were back in Bankhead, navigating to Regi's house.

"This the best you've got?" I asked as we pulled up in front of the eighty-year-old cottage.

Regi shrugged. "I got a storm cellar in the back. Nobody will hear him."

I got out and surveyed the street. It looked a lot less sinister in broad daylight. Most of the houses were old, but many were occupied and semi-cared for. Regi pitched me a pair of keys for the privacy fence gate leading to the backyard; then he backed the Cadillac into the driveway. He stopped the car with the bumper just inside the gate, and I stepped into a clean and landscaped backyard complete with a koi pond and a little rock garden with two decorative metal chairs.

Regi got out and moved to the trunk, catching me staring at the manicured haven.

"What?" he said.

I shook my head, using the gate key a second time to unlock the door to an exterior-access storm cellar.

"I don't get you," I said.

"Don't get what?"

"You love Jesus and crosswords, but you don't mind kidnapping people and tossing them in your basement."

"You expect me to be perfect?"

"No. I guess I just don't see the correlation."

"Maybe I'm working on it. Maybe imma rusty old sinner who don't blame Jesus for my methods. Now help me with this cracka."

Hansley was still unconscious—maybe I'd hit him harder than I realized. We hauled his limp body out of the trunk, then dragged him across the gravel to the storm cellar. The steps were steep, and we almost dropped him halfway down. In the bottom I found a concrete floor with brick walls, a couple of folded metal chairs, and some storm supplies. We propped Hansley up in a chair and taped his hands behind his back, running a few strips around his mouth before I went to work searching him.

There was another handgun on his ankle, which I should have expected and removed prior to locking him in the trunk.

It was a Glock 43 subcompact chambered in 9mm. In his pockets I found a wallet, a couple of thousand dollars in cash, keys for the Jaguar, a valet ticket, his hotel key, and an iPhone.

I flipped the wallet open and dumped out a mess of credit cards before finding a California driver's license.

Lawrence Hansley, of Los Angeles. He wore black in his driver's license photo and didn't smile.

"Hold his eyes open," I said, scooping up the iPhone.

"Huh?"

"Hold his head up and pin his eyes open."

Regi grabbed Hansley by the hair, lifting his face before using two fingers to open his eyelids. His eyeballs rolled back in his head, still unconscious. I woke the phone up and held the facial-recognition camera in front of his face. It unlocked without protest.

Regi snorted. "Technology's beyond me."

I unfolded another metal chair and sat, navigating first to the text message menu. There was a slew of conversations, and more than a few of them were completely in Spanish. I made note of that and switched to the search feature on the messaging app, typing in the word "Atlanta."

The search produced over a dozen results, but most were only mentions within greater conversations. Only two were addresses.

210 Peachtree St NW, Atlanta, GA. CHK in APR 17.

That would be his hotel reservation at the Westin. The second address was for a street name I didn't recognize, but it sounded familiar. I tapped the address, and the phone automatically called it up in the map application. I zoomed in and switched to satellite mode, and then it clicked.

It was the club. The one I had traced Jalen to only two nights previously. Someplace off Cleveland Avenue.

I looked back to the text message. It was in English, but the contact was labeled *Garcia*. A quick survey of the thread's contents confirmed that Garcia was some sort of boss. All of the messages consisted of either questions or directions from Garcia, answered by mostly "yes" or "no" from Hansley.

A man of few words.

Beneath the nightclub address was a short message from Garcia.

April 17. 5 PM.

I checked my watch. It was four p.m.

"Find anything?" Regi asked.

"He's meeting with the SAS at a club in one hour. Help me strip his clothes."

Regi stood near the stairwell, arms folded, not moving. I peeled Hansley's coat back and began to unbutton his shirt.

"You'll have to drive me. We don't have time for public transit."

Regi didn't move. I looked over my shoulder.

"What?" I demanded.

Regi sucked his teeth. "You sure about this?"

"Sure about what? About kidnapping a guy and stealing his clothes? I guess I'd better be."

I resumed work on the buttons. Regi stepped in next to me and put a hand on my arm. The grip was gentler than I expected. I looked up.

"You were right about Jalen," Regi said. "I shoulda stepped up. I shoulda been there after Anthony went away. I don't blame Jalen for hating me."

"He's young," I said. "And ignorant."

"And right," Regi said, eyes dropping.

I straightened. In the dim light of the cellar, Regi

suddenly looked older. A lot older. And broken someplace deep inside.

"You can't change the past," I said. "But we can change the future. I need to know you've got my back."

I held out a hand. Regi clasped his powerful fingers around my palm, and as we shook, I saw the strength return to his haggard face. I turned back to Hansley.

"Why do you need the clothes?" Regi asked as I finished unbuttoning Hansley's shirt. He was still hopelessly unconscious.

"Look at his driver's photo. This guy always wears fancy black clothes. It's part of his brand."

"I thought you said they won't have seen a picture."

"They shouldn't have, but that doesn't mean he won't have a reputation. A signature people are expecting. I don't want to take unnecessary risks."

We stripped Hansley down to his underwear—which were also black—and I pulled his clothes on. The pants were a little snug, and the shirt an inch shorter than I would have liked. Otherwise, everything fit reasonably well. I tucked both Glocks into the same holsters Hansley had worn them in, then slid the jacket on and checked myself in the reverse camera of his phone. I had already disabled the automatic sleep mode. So long as I didn't hit the power switch or run down the battery, the phone wouldn't lock again.

"What do you think?" I asked.

Regi swept his sharp eyes over me and snorted. "You look like an asshole."

"I feel like one. Let's roll."

43

I used the map on Hansley's phone to navigate back into south Atlanta. Before leaving, Regi had double-checked the Californian's bonds, then locked the outside of the storm cellar. He didn't seem the least concerned about having a captive under his sanctuary living room, and I made a mental note to find a way to hand Hansley over to the DEA without incriminating Regi when all this was over.

It should have felt ironic for me to feel protective over a guy who had so recently tossed me in a shallow grave and put a gun to my head, but there was something about Regi that was nothing short of likable. He was easy to ride with. Easy to be around.

The kind of guy who was in no denial about exactly who he was, and if not comfortable with it, he was at least at peace with it.

"I won't have the burner while I'm in there," I said. "If I have to contact you, I'll do it through Hansley's phone."

"You save my number?"

"Yeah."

"What about the guns?"

"What about them?"

"You don't think they'll give you away?"

"They're Hansley's guns. I doubt he went anywhere without them. We've got to stick to character."

Regi steered the Cadillac off the highway and onto Cleveland Avenue. It wouldn't be long before I had him pull over, and I walked the rest of the way. I couldn't risk a member of the SAS recognizing him.

"How will you get it?" Regi asked.

"Get what? Evidence?"

"Right."

I pocketed the phone and watched an apartment complex roll by. It was massive—sprawling. Spilling out across an entire block, surrounded by a high metal fence and littered with trash. Entire portions of roofs were covered by tarps, while occasional windows were boarded over.

This wasn't Atlanta's garden community.

"Gangsters like to brag, right?" I asked.

"I guess."

"So I'm gonna get them bragging, and see what spills. All we need is something tangible. Anthony's whereabouts at the time of the murder might suffice."

"They ain't gonna just hand that over," Regi muttered.

I gritted my teeth. "It's the best I've got, okay? We can keep fooling around trailing these people and harassing Anthony, or we can take the bull by the horns. What do you want?"

Regi held up a hand. "All right, all right. I'm sorry."

I motioned to the curb, and he pulled off. I double-checked the Glock in my belt and the switchblade in my pocket. I wasn't in a hurry to use either.

But I would if my back was against the wall.

I reached for the door handle.

"Hey, Mason."

"What?"

Regi faced me from the driver's seat. "I'm praying for you."

I wasn't sure what to say to that, so I simply nodded and got out of the car. The Cadillac pulled away, and I adjusted my suit jacket, wriggling my broad shoulders to find a little room in the tailored cut.

It was hot. The sun would set in another half hour, and already the city smelled like evening. The start of another long night, full of God only knew what.

Turning down the sidewalk, I followed the streets by memory, thinking back to Jalen and his buddy rolling up on the club with their bicycles. The supply Skullcap had given him looked large enough to keep Jalen busy for a few days. Hopefully he wouldn't turn up tonight.

As I passed disheveled houses, I noted faces peering out at me from behind grimy windows. Curious eyes watched as I walked with my head up, my shoulders back. Like I owned the city. Walking like Hansley had walked. I wore his aviator-style sunglasses, encasing my face behind a shield of shadow and adopting as much of his detached persona as I could manage.

This whole gambit depended on the guess that none of the SAS had seen Hansley before. It was a reasonable assumption. My logic was sound.

But as I approached the two-story club at the end of the street, I began to doubt. My stomach churned, and my back raced with chills. I saw the big guys standing outside the iron-gated door, slouching against the blocks, then straightening when they saw me.

I picked out the silhouettes of handguns beneath their tight shirts. I knew a few dozen more weapons would lie inside, alongside plenty of gangsters ready to use them.

If I rolled the dice and lost, there wouldn't be another turn. I'd be finished, right here on the spot.

I stopped at the street, and for a split second I almost

turned back. My knees felt rigid, and I saw both big guys step to the edge of the curb, defying me to cross.

I crossed anyway. Not because my odds were any better now than they had been thirty seconds prior.

But because Jalen's odds hadn't improved either. Not unless I took control.

I reached the far side of the street and moved to circle the two bouncers. The one on the left cut me off while the one on my right raised the tail of his shirt and placed his hand on the exposed grip of a Smith and Wesson M&P.

I stopped, but I didn't say a thing. The guy with the Smith stood back while his buddy leered down at me from the advantage of the raised sidewalk.

"*Roll*, white boy," he snarled.

I didn't move. The bouncer shot his buddy a disbelieving grin, then clenched his fist.

"You hear me, cracka? You on the wrong side of the tracks."

"Get your boss," I said, my tone perfectly flat. "Tell him Hansley is here."

The guy stiffened, confusion and then concern flashing across his face. "What you say?"

"Get your boss," I repeated, dropping my tone a notch. "He's expecting me."

It was that last bit that got through to them. Sudden clarity shone behind stoned eyes, and one guy jerked his head toward the door. The second man went inside, leaving me on the street, stone faced and silent. Channeling Hansley.

The second bouncer was gone only sixty seconds before he barged back out. This time he wasn't alone, accompanied by two more big guys openly wearing handguns, and a third guy dressed in tight black leather.

And a black skullcap.

Skullcap took the lead, his dark eyes narrowing as he

stopped five feet short of the curb. The sidewalk became suddenly very still, and I surveyed the three of them behind Hansley's dark sunglasses.

The two men standing behind Skullcap were absolute killers, I had no doubt. I could see it in their confident stance, their dead eyes. They were both high as hell, but that didn't necessarily dampen their capacity to be dangerous.

Skullcap took a step forward, lifting his chin. "Hansley?"

"That's right," I said, voice cold.

He squinted. "We weren't expecting you 'til tomorrow."

"Surprise inspection," I said. "Garcia sent me early."

It was a BS line. When I saw the appointment in the text message, I rolled the dice and assumed it was a pre-arranged meeting between the SAS and the cartel's representative. Apparently, that wasn't the case. But I was here now. I had to own it.

Skullcap looked to one of his lieutenants, uncertainty and the hint of discomfort crossing his face. Then he seemed to decide to roll with it, much as I had. He offered his hand.

"Darius Carter. I'm the Squad boss."

His grip was like iron, bending around my hand and crushing down. I took it without comment, squeezing back as Darius advanced to the edge of the curb, staring at me as though I were a prize painting. The moment lingered a beat too long, and red flags shot up in my mind as a cruel grin spread across Darius's face.

He shook his head, still clenching my hand. "You ain't Hansley."

44

Ice flooded my veins, but I didn't freak out. There would be no point. Darius clamped down on my hand and tilted his head to his guys. They moved in and swept my body, quickly finding and seizing both handguns and the switchblade. I remained cool, not bothering to fight. It wouldn't do any good, and I couldn't afford to look desperate.

Once they were done, somebody closed behind me, and I felt a gun press against my kidney.

"Why don't you step inside?" Darius sneered. He released my hand and motioned to the club as though it were a palace.

I stepped through the door and was immediately swallowed by a dark interior. A hallway stretched ahead, filthy with footprints and grime, battered walls marked by shoe scuffs. The place reeked of marijuana smoke and body odor. Someplace ahead dull green lights shone, and I heard thumping rap music.

The door smacked shut behind me, and I was propelled into a small coat room. Leather jackets lay everywhere amid empty beer cartons. A single incandescent bulb flickered overhead. Darius and his goons crowded in around me.

"Who. Are. You?" Darius punctuated each word with a jab to my chest. I stood tall and took it, evaluating my options quickly.

Darius had never met Hansley. I already knew that. If he had, he would never have shaken my hand, let alone taken me inside. This was some kind of bizarre test, or at the least a pissing contest.

There was only one way to deal with it.

I slowly removed the sunglasses, revealing my iron gaze. I didn't have Hansley's piercing blue eyes, but I felt confident I was delivering at least half of his ice-cold hatred.

I folded the glasses, not breaking eye contact, then slid them into the interior pocket of my jacket.

"I'm only going to say this once," I said, my tone flat. "If you touch me again, I'll break your arm."

Darius's eyes widened, just a little. His lips parted, but one of his goons moved first. A hard hand closed on my shoulder, nails biting down.

I moved like a striking snake, grabbing the guy by the wrist and the elbow. Then I twisted, not unlike I had done with the Steel Mafia kid at the basketball court. Before he knew what was happening, the elbow joint popped like a gunshot, and everybody freaked. Guns flashed, and I released the injured gangster, closing on Darius until our noses almost touched, but not putting my hands on him. I didn't blink, didn't so much as twitch. I just leaned in until Darius took an involuntary step back, uncertainty flashing across his face.

The field of handguns around me remained trained on my skull, but I knew they wouldn't shoot.

They didn't know who I was.

"You wanna play games?" I kept my voice low and angry, like Hansley. "I'm not here to play games. I'll get back in my car and go right back to Cali. Tell Garcia he's got the wrong distributor. There are a million outfits begging to move our product. I don't *need* the drama."

Darius stood with his feet splayed apart, his head tilted back just a little to make eye contact, his breath rank as it washed over my face. My heart thundered, and I felt a muzzle brush the back of my head. For a split second I felt like I was back in that shallow grave outside of town, with Regi bearing down on me.

Darius could blink, and one of these thugs would blow me away.

But the room remained still. Darius made eye contact with the man behind me and shook his head once. The guns slowly lowered, and I took half a step back.

Darius ran sweaty palms across his jeans and swallowed involuntarily. He looked ready to burst, like he wanted to gut me right there on the grimy concrete.

But he couldn't afford to. We both knew that.

I straightened my suit jacket and made a show of pulling my sleeves out to my wrists, one at a time. Then I ran a hand through my hair and sneered at the sniveling gangster with the wounded elbow.

"Are we done here, or should I break something for real?"

A flash of fire ignited behind Darius's dark eyes—a split second, come and gone. Then his shoulders relaxed, and a broad grin broke across a mouth filled with gold teeth.

"Sheesh, bruh. We just messin' wid yah. It's all good."

He kicked his fallen soldier in the ass, and the guy scrambled to his feet.

"Your elbow is dislocated, and the tendons torn," I said coolly, not bothering to look at him. "I recommend a hospital."

Then I gestured to the door, looking to Darius. His grin widened, but it didn't reach his eyes. He tilted his head to his remaining goons, and the guns disappeared. Then he led me down the hall, walking loosely and willingly turning his back to me.

A sign of trust, however empty it might be. If I made a move, I'd be gunned down before I reached his neck.

Near the end of the hall I heard music thumping behind a heavy door, and alternating blue and green lights glimmered from beneath it.

"Welcome to the club, bruh," Darius said. "I think we could all use a drink."

I tilted my hand again, and Darius pushed the door back.

Club was a loose word. The interior of the block room was windowless, paved in dirty shag carpet, and occupied by an assortment of sagging leather couches and easy chairs. There was a bar in one corner laden with glass bottles of liquor, flashing LEDs mounted to the ceiling, and oversized speakers blasting subdued hip-hop music.

And there were women. Four of them, all topless, long black braids draping over their shoulders as they lounged on the couches. A cloud of weed smoke hung in the air, rendering everything a hazy gray color. I felt the burn in my lungs, and almost immediately my head began to float.

"What can I get you?" Darius asked. "You a tequila man?"

"Beer," I said. "In a bottle."

I really wasn't interested in drinking anything, but at least beer would come from a sealed bottle. I couldn't expect this jackass to talk if I didn't prime the pump.

Darius snapped his fingers to one of the women, and she got up with a seductive sweep of her braids over her shoulder, fully exposing her chest.

I met her gaze and held it, conscious that everyone was watching me. Then I accepted Darius's invitation to take her place on the couch. He sat next to me and produced a joint from one pocket, wetting it with his lips.

"We don't get a lot of white folks 'round here," he said. "But if you see something you like...help yourself."

He shot me a knowing wink. I said nothing, waving my hand when he offered me the joint.

"Not a weed man?"

"More of a coke guy," I said, regretting the words even as they left my lips. The gold teeth flashed again, and Darius snapped his fingers. Another one of the girls got up and stepped through a door into a side room.

"You're in luck, bruh."

I felt cold glass on my neck, and condensation saturated my shirt collar. I took the beer as the woman leaned close, her cheek brushing mine, her body pressed against the back of the couch. She kissed my neck, and I tried not to stiffen.

Darius was still watching me. I took a long swig of the beer as the second woman returned with a wooden cigar box. I could already see the white powder smeared across the lid.

"Straight out of Colombia," Darius bragged. "The good stuff. Help yo'self."

The box hit the table. I set the beer down.

"Why don't we talk business?" I said. "I didn't come here on vacation."

Darius laughed but didn't answer. He flipped the box open, exposing half a kilo of smooth white powder. It piled up in the box like a snowy mountaintop, as innocuous looking as baking soda.

Darius dug his wallet out and used a credit card to scoop out a small pile. He then cut it into lines, scraping across the glass table, his dilated eyes fixated on the stuff like it was pure gold.

"You know the key to good coke? It's gotta be sticky. It's gotta cut."

He completed four rows of packed white powder, then rolled a twenty-dollar bill out of his wallet and proceeded to snort an entire line. One quick swipe. An energetic inhale, one finger closing off a nostril, the other sucking up coke like it was going out of style.

His eyes rolled back in his head, and he rocked against the couch, blinking several times, his arms tense. The coke hit like a train, and I saw his back go rigid. The grin returned, and he sat up with a shrill whoop.

"*Sheet*, bruh. That's strong!"

The girl who brought him the coke sat cross-legged next to him, running one nail-polished hand over his chest, grinning also, but not seeing. Her eyes were glassy and lifeless, her mind saturated in something a lot stronger than coke.

Darius wiped his nose, then offered me the rolled twenty.

"Why don't we talk business?" I said again, keeping my voice cool and flat.

His lip twitched rhythmically, and he didn't blink. I looked into his eyes and saw a fraction of the man I'd spoken to only sixty seconds earlier. He was hyped as hell.

"Take a line," he said.

"I'm good."

His lip twitched again, and the flash of fire I'd seen earlier returned to his gaze. He jabbed with the twenty.

"This is the South, bruh. We take it personal when a man refuses hospitality."

I felt the woman on my neck again, her breath hot and sour only inches from my face. In the corners of the room Darius's gangsters stood smoking joints, their eyes fixed on me.

Watching. And ready.

Darius jabbed with the twenty. "You gonna refuse my hospitality?"

The woman's sharp fingernails gripped my arm, and I gritted my teeth. Darius's wolfish grin returned.

"Take a line."

I accepted the twenty and tapped it twice against the table, knocking off damp coke from the tip.

Then I put it to my nose and leaned over the table.

45

I 'd snorted cocaine before—once, when I was sixteen. Not long before my career as a wannabe gangster earned me a one-way ticket to Army Basic Training.

It set me on fire then, and it set me on fire now.

The fine white powder shot up the makeshift straw and flooded my sinus cavity. In an instant my face went numb, my heart rate spiked, and then it was like a thousand fireworks detonated in my head. The edgy nervousness I'd felt only seconds before melted under a flood of hot euphoria. My fingers tingled, raw energy raced up and down my spine, and I wanted to freaking punch a bear.

All the anxiety was gone. All the fear evaporated. Confidence overtook my mind as my vision blurred and then slowly returned to focus.

Darius was right. It *was* good stuff. Premium white gold.

I sat upright on the couch and gasped for breath, flicking the rolled twenty back onto the tabletop. Darius slouched back with the woman still slouched against his shoulder like a sloppy teenager.

"He ain't no cokehead." Darius laughed. His goons joined

in, but I didn't care. All my trepidation was gone. He could have pulled a gun on me, and I would have told him to go to hell. Nothing concerned me anymore.

I was *Hansley*, dammit. A freaking cartel soldier. The might of Garcia and his mob of soldados stood behind me. This street thug could get in line.

I drained the beer, conscious of the fact that alcohol and coke don't mix, but not caring. I didn't care about anything other than what I came for—finding the truth about Anthony.

"You ever snort junk like that?" Darius asked.

"It's all right," I said with a dismissive shrug. "I'll have Garcia bring you something real."

Darius's mouth dropped open, and he laughed from his gut, tears streaming down his face. Then he retrieved the twenty and ran another line. The music pounded in my skull, and marijuana haze wafted around the room. I knew I was crossfading—hard. Beer, coke, and enough secondhand weed smoke to knock out a linebacker. It was a dangerous cocktail, easily capable of overwhelming my system and shutting down my heart.

But I was in this far. No turning back now.

Darius handed me the twenty. I waved him off. "You tryin' to kill me? Let me get another beer."

I knew he would send the woman. I wanted her off my shoulder. She brought me another icy-cold bottle and thankfully stumbled off to a different couch as I tipped it back.

"Talk to me about your network," I said. "You're shipping in soup cans, right?"

Darius was fiddling with the credit card again, cutting new lines. He looked up, eyes narrowing.

"Who told you that?"

"Garcia," I said, as if it was obvious. His gold teeth flashed.

"Oh, right. Yeah. Soup cans, bruh. Can ship it anywhere,

nobody knows. Put a little mustard in there and even the dogs can't smell it. We learned that from the amigos."

"Right," I said, joining in his dry laugh.

Darius collapsed into the couch and looked at the ceiling, the grin still covering his face. He was crossfading, also. Caught someplace between uppers and downers, not sure which way to turn, playing jump rope with his moods.

A deadly mix.

"I hear you have contacts in South Carolina," I said. "Greenville."

He didn't seem to hear me. He just stared at the ceiling. I remembered the guys who jumped me after leaving the prison—Anthony's cousins. Anthony had people in Greenville. An entire network of friends and family, willing to mug a random stranger on his behalf.

It was easy enough to believe they would also have helped in the distribution of incoming M30s. Was that why Anthony had been in South Carolina when he was arrested?

"Are we shipping M30s into Greenville?" I pressed. "Who's your contact out there?"

Darius sat bolt upright as the jump rope crossed into an upswing, the coke overwhelming the weed.

"Why you want my contact?" His voice carried an edge.

I kept calm, still feeling endless, drug-induced confidence. "I just like to know who I'm working with. That's my job."

Darius blinked rapidly. "Right..."

He looked away, and I knew I'd lost him. He started making out with the half-naked woman sitting next to him, her body almost limp from her own overload of drugs.

I felt sudden anger. This wasn't why I was here. I snapped my fingers.

"Hey! I'm talking to you."

Darius picked himself up, wiping his mouth and looking

toward me. His gaze turned hard, and two of the guys in the corners stiffened. A break in the music brought sudden calm to the room, and nobody moved.

"Why don't you take another line?" Darius said, handing me the rolled twenty.

"I'm good."

He smiled, his lip lifting over the gold teeth, and didn't lower the twenty. The music resumed, but the two guys across the room kept their eyes on me. I thought I felt somebody behind me, also. A room full of sharks circling my position.

"Nah, bruh. I think you aren't," Darius said. "You all business, but we barely met."

I remained calm, but already the high of the coke was starting to fade. I suddenly wondered if I'd overplayed my hand.

"This is a business trip," I said. "I've got a boss breathing down my neck."

Darius smiled. "Don't worry, we'll get to all that. First, we gotta get acquainted. It's like you said...you gotta know who you're working with."

He held out the twenty. "Take another line, bruh."

Every eye in the room rested on me. I could feel the tension like a rubber band, stretched and ready to bust.

It wasn't an invitation. It was another test.

I took the twenty.

46

I awoke eight hours later, unsure of whether I'd been sleeping or simply blacked out. My head floated as I sat up, checking my watch and looking across the crowded room.

Everybody was passed out. Cocaine smeared the tabletop, while half-naked women flopped across couches, and Darius lay snoring next to them. The air stilled reeked of marijuana smoke, and my head pounded.

I was still high. Or drunk. Or otherwise intoxicated. Stumbling to my feet, I almost fell over a field of empty beer bottles, freezing as glass clinked on glass.

Nobody got up. The music had died sometime during the drug binge, and nobody had turned it back on. I navigated around slouched gangsters, retrieving my two Glocks and the switchblade from a nearby table before pushing through the door into the relatively clean air of the hallway.

I felt ready to collapse. All the high of the coke was long gone, and my right nostril was clogged with congealed snot. More snot ran down the back of my throat, tasting of cocaine, and my stomach churned.

I'd never felt so sick in my life. It was like a bad case of the flu, without a fever. I reached the exterior door and barely made it onto the sidewalk before I puked. Bile and the remnants of my last meal sprayed across the concrete, and I supported myself against the side of the building.

It was still dark outside. A few hours before sunrise, and the grungy neighborhood was fast asleep. I saw no one as I stumbled across the street to the sidewalk and began to head south. I wasn't sure exactly where I was going, but I knew I needed to get away from the club before Darius awoke. I didn't need him catching me this messed up.

Nobody as deep in the drug trade as Hansley would be this ignorant about how to handle a crossfade.

Blasting out my clogged nostril, I fished for Hansley's phone. It was still unlocked, still glowing with only five percent remaining on the battery bar. I called Regi, praying he would pick up. It took four rings, but he finally did.

"Mason?"

"I need you to come pick me up."

"Where are you? You good? You sound like hell!"

I leaned against a stop sign, another wave of nausea washing over me. It was like being an Army private on leave all over again, stumbling home from a late-night bender with the guys. Except this was worse. So much worse.

I puked a second time, wiping my mouth as Regi called desperately through the phone. "Mason? Where are you?"

I looked up at the street sign and started to read off the intersection. Then I stopped. I couldn't risk any of Darius's associates seeing me getting into a car with Regi.

"Call me a cab," I said, adding the name of the intersection. "Have them drop me off downtown. You pick me up there."

"Okay. Hang tight. I'll be right there."

He hung up, and I slouched against the signpost. Looking

at my feet, it felt like the sidewalk was made of water, rising and falling with every passing wave, leaving me awash in dizziness. This wasn't the coke, I knew. Cocaine doesn't leave you hungover like this. It was the alcohol and the second-hand weed smoke blended together with the coke.

I should have simply taken the joint Darius first offered me. *Stupid.*

The cab arrived half an hour later. The driver didn't ask questions as he drove me into the heart of the sleeping city, dropping me off at the Five Points train station where all four MARTA lines converged.

It was a smart spot for Regi to pick. Nobody would suspect a guy stumbling out of a cab here.

The dark green Eldorado rolled up two minutes later, and I slid into the passenger seat, scrubbing my face with the back of one hand. Regi cast me a sideways look, his dark eyes widening with concern.

"What the hell, man."

I waved him off, and he began to drive. It felt good to sit. My stomach was starting to stabilize, but my head still pounded like a drum.

"What happened?" Regi demanded.

"Cocaine. Beer. Marijuana. Bad rap music. A lot of things happened."

"Did they bust you?"

"No. They tried to rattle me though. I don't think Darius is convinced."

"Darius?"

"Squad boss, apparently. A real piece of work."

"But you didn't get anything? Nothing about Anthony?"

Regi didn't mean to push, but I couldn't help snapping.

"Pardon me for getting sidetracked! He was shoveling booze and blow down my face the moment I walked in."

Regi held up a hand apologetically. I collapsed in the seat and crossed my arms. The sky was starting to brighten in the east. The city was awakening. How long before Darius reached out?

Or Garcia. That was another possibility.

I really hadn't planned on this harebrained strategy stretching out this way. I hadn't planned on snorting five lines of coke, either.

"Where to?" Regi asked, a little subdued.

"Back to your place. I need four Tylenols and a gallon of water. Then breakfast. Then I want to talk to Hansley."

Regi grunted. "Yeah, he wants to talk to you."

"So he's awake?"

"Oh yeah."

"What did you do with him?"

"Tried to give him some water. That boy is mad as a hornet."

Regi couldn't resist a chuckle. I indulged in a dry grin. Of all my problems right now, a cartel logistics officer wasn't high on the list. There were probably a few thousand people suffering from crippling addiction thanks to Hansley's work. I wasn't overly concerned with his outrage.

We reached the house just as the sun crested the Atlanta skyline. I hurried inside before any of Regi's neighbors could notice me, proceeding to the bathroom and ramming my fingers down my throat until I puked again. Then I scrubbed my face and washed out my nose.

Whatever it took, I wanted to be as toxin-free as possible.

I swallowed Tylenol next, to fight the headache, and guzzled water. Then, while Regi heated up a skillet and scrambled eggs, I dug an iPhone charger out of a junk drawer and left Hansley's phone charging before proceeding to the back of the house. My head still floated, and I lost my balance at random intervals, but overall I felt okay for having just indulged in a multi-drug spree. My symptoms had faded to little more than a bad hangover, and the painkillers would kick in soon.

I stepped carefully into the dank confines of Regi's storm cellar. I was still wearing Hansley's ill-fitting black suit, now stained by a dusting of white powder and the splash of various body fluids.

My prisoner sat tied up in the corner, right where I'd left him. I could tell by scrape marks on the floor that he'd done his best to break free, but Regi was good at restraining people. He'd wrapped enough tape around Hansley's legs, arms, and chest to subdue a Bengal tiger.

Clicking the overhead light on, I watched as Hansley's eyes snapped open; then he turned his head away from the blaze. I walked right to him, keeping the bulb over my head to prevent him from looking straight at me.

It was an old-school interrogation technique. It kept him disoriented.

"Enjoying yourself?" I asked. "Maybe you'd like some fentanyl."

It was a cheap jab. I couldn't resist.

I grabbed the edge of the tape covering his mouth and spoke quietly only inches from his face.

"If you scream, I'll knock you out. Got it?"

Bloodshot eyes blinked up at me. He was breathing hard, but he nodded once. I tore the tape away, and even I winced at the rip of adhesive pulling at tender flesh. Hansley gritted his teeth. He didn't scream.

I returned to the light. I could smell bacon frying from upstairs, and my stomach growled.

"You work for a guy named Garcia?"

I already knew the answer, but I wanted to start with something easy. Hansley didn't answer.

"I know you're from California. I know you came here to

advise a local gang on fentanyl distribution. And I know it's only a matter of time before your absence is noticed."

I stepped across the basement floor, kneeling in front of him and dusting off my knees.

"So. I've had a rough night. Let's make this easy. I want to know when the shipment will arrive."

Hansley didn't answer. His jaw twitched. His bloodshot eyes blazed. But he said nothing.

I reached beneath the suit jacket and wrapped my fingers around his Glock 30. It was already chambered with a heavy .45-caliber round. I drew the weapon and rocked the muzzle toward Hansley, watching as his neck tendons grew rigid. But I didn't place the gun against his head.

I moved it instead between his legs.

"Talk," I said.

Hansley didn't so much as twitch.

"You're a long way up the ladder, aren't you, big chief?" I said. "Nobody's gonna mess with you. Not with an army of soldados at your beck and call. Am I right?"

Hansley sneered, and at last, he spoke.

"You have no idea who you're messing with."

"You said so before. Actually, I'm quite familiar with the handiwork of your bosses. You know we all looked the other way about the weed. Heroin was a bigger problem. But fentanyl? You guys are really pushing the envelope."

"You some kind of cop?" Hansley said.

"It doesn't matter what I am. It only matters that you're here, and that five pounds of pressure will turn your balls to paste."

Another twitch of his neck tendons. I pushed the gun farther between his restrained legs. He gritted his teeth.

"Go to hell," he snarled.

"When does the shipment arrive?" I said.

No answer. I pushed the Glock.

"Last chance, jackass."

I wasn't going to shoot him. I didn't want to deal with the mess right now. But he didn't know that. All covered in cocaine residue and smelling like vomit, I knew I looked crazy. I was counting on it.

"*When?*" I demanded.

The storm cellar door saved Hansley. It smacked open, and Regi's voice shouted from the top of the stairs.

"Mason! Somebody's calling his phone."

"Who?"

"Garcia! Wait...it went to voicemail."

I withdrew the gun and walked to the bottom of the stairs. Regi tossed me the phone. I noted the missed call, and my heart rate accelerated.

It was a problem. I could bump Garcia for now, but it wouldn't be long before the cartel boss moved from frustration to concern. One call to Darius would be all it took to derail everything.

I looked back to Hansley. Saw the hint of a smirk on his lips. He thought this was a *good* thing. An escalation I couldn't control.

I returned to the darkened corner of the cellar and jammed the Glock under his chin, rocking his head back. Then I hit dial on the phone.

"You wanna talk to your boss? Okay, then. Let's talk."

47

The phone rang. I hit the mute button.

"Tell him everything is on schedule. You met with Darius last night, and it went well. You say *anything* off color, and I'll shoot you right here. Understand?"

I pressed with the Glock. Hansley gritted his teeth.

"Hello?" The voice sounded familiar. It was the Mexican guy I'd seen at the factory. I turned the volume all the way up and held the phone an inch from Hansley's ear.

"Tell him you were in the shower," I said. Then I took the phone off mute.

"Hansley?" Garcia pressed.

"Sorry," Hansley mumbled. His voice was dry. "I was in the shower."

"You never called. What happened?"

I hit mute. "You got in late and went straight to meet Darius."

I kept the Glock pressed against his neck as Hansley regurgitated the line. Garcia sounded pissed, but not suspicious. He asked about Darius, and I coached Hansley through a spiel about a crazy cocaine party. I wasn't sure if

Darius had a reputation for drug-heavy receptions, but I wanted to check the box just in case.

Garcia snorted. "Stupid fool. You should know better than to mess with crackheads."

"Ask him about the shipment," I prodded.

Hansley's eyes narrowed. I thought he was about to act out, and I kept the phone on mute, waving the gun in front of his face. He dropped his gaze.

"Darius is ready to distribute," Hansley said. "When's the shipment getting in?"

"That's why I'm calling. We're loading the truck now. Should arrive around noon tomorrow."

Tomorrow. Thirty hours, give or take. Assuming two drivers who rotated and kept the truck moving through the night, it could be coming from as far away as San Diego. With one driver, maybe it was coming from New Mexico or west Texas.

Either way, this development accelerated my timeline considerably.

"Tell him it's good," I said. "Tell him you're meeting Darius this afternoon."

Hansley repeated the message without objection and wound down the call. I hung up and backed away from the chair, running one hand through my hair.

This wasn't how I pictured my scheme playing out. With Garcia's shipment rolling east, I was running out of time to exonerate Anthony. If I couldn't squeeze something tangible out of Darius in the next few hours, I'd have no choice but to go ahead and call Feldon.

"Are you trying to jack our shipment?" Hansley asked. His voice was toneless. I turned back.

"What?"

"Who do you work for?" Hansley pressed. I didn't answer.

A slow sneer broke across his face. "You're not a cop."

"What if I am?"

He laughed. "No way. And if you are, you're way off the reservation. No...you're local competition. Somebody trying to dethrone the SAS."

I tapped the phone against my open palm, ignoring him. Still thinking.

"We can deal," Hansley said. "If you've got something Darius doesn't...we're listening."

"Shut up," I said, growing irritated.

Hansley leaned back in the chair, his face dripping with condescension. "Let me give you a nickel's worth of free advice. You'd better cut me loose now, or my balls won't be the ones blown to paste. When Garcia finds out, you think he'll stop with you? That's not the cartel way. He'll find your family. Whoever you love. Anybody you've ever known. You ever heard of a cartel barbecue? He'll put them in barrels, then—"

My right hook caught him right across his left cheekbone, snapping his head back as my knuckles plowed through his nose. The nose broke, and blood flowed. I wrung my hand and grabbed the duct tape off the floor. Two layers across his lips terminated the flow of free advice.

"*Shut. Up,*" I said. Then I dropped the tape and returned to the backyard. Regi met me as I closed the storm cellar door.

"What did he say?" Regi asked.

"A lot of nothing, but I found out about the shipment. It's getting here sometime tomorrow morning—a whole truck-load. Enough fentanyl to service the region."

Regi fiddled with a cigarillo, but he didn't light it. He looked more nervous than I'd seen him yet. Maybe it was having a cartel thug tied up in his basement.

Maybe it was the prospect of an unraveling plan sliding out of control.

"Man, we gotta call the police. Cut this fool loose and wash our hands."

"If we do, we'll never exonerate Anthony. He'll rot in that prison."

"Maybe that ship has sailed. Look, I appreciate what you tryin' to do. But if we call the DEA and hand them this, they won't mess with Jalen no more. Then we can do something about Anthony."

"If the DEA sweeps in and busts the SAS, there's zero chance you exonerate Anthony. Nobody they arrest will admit to anything, and any chance of finding concrete evidence in his favor will be gone. Trust me, I've seen these busts go down. They get what they need, and the rest burns. Anthony will die in prison."

Regi muttered something unintelligible and turned away, still fiddling with the cigarillo.

"What's that?" I said.

"Maybe he *should* be in prison!" Regi snapped, whirling on me. "Anthony ain't no saint. He may not have kilt that fed, but he done plenty of rough things. He was a gangsta, hardcore."

I folded my arms. "Like you?"

Regi flushed, jabbing at me with the unlit smoke. "Hey. I done my time! Anthony gotta do his."

I said nothing. I knew I'd hit a sore spot, and I had a pretty good idea why. But Regi needed to say it himself.

He rolled the cigarillo between his fingers, then lit it and took a long drag. His eyes rimmed with red, and he looked haggard. Not like the beefy, hardened gangster who had kidnapped me. More like a tired old man, broken by life.

"These streets take everything," Regi rasped. "My ole man died fightin' the Bloods befo' I could even walk. Got my first gun before I got my first car. It ain't nothing but a cycle. Took my youth, took my wife, took my brother. Now it's takin' his son..."

He looked away. I softened my voice.

"What happened to Anthony wasn't your fault. We all make our own choices." I took a step closer. "But if you stand back now and do nothing, what happens to Jalen will be on both our heads. Those feds can piss off, and he'll still wind up in jail or in a ditch. He needs a father. He needs *you*."

Regi blew smoke. "Don't you think I've tried? That kid don't want nothing to do with me."

"And that's why we need to exonerate Anthony," I said. "It's not just about keeping Jalen out of trouble. That kid needs something to believe in. He needs to understand why you didn't fight Anthony's conviction. He's not stupid. He sees the world for what it is and draws his own conclusions. Show him a side of life that breaks the cycle, and he'll let you back in."

Regi sucked on the cigarillo. I saw tears rim in his large eyes, and he scrubbed a thumb over his face.

"Man, why you care so much?"

I pocketed my hands. Thought about that judge. Thought about Sergeant Smiles at Fort Benning.

"Because people cared about me," I said. "And Jalen deserves as much."

Regi nodded a couple of times, still tugging on the smoke. His gaze was lost on the koi pond, his fingers trembling but growing gradually still. At last, he cleared his throat.

"All right, then. What next?"

I looked back at the cellar doors, thinking about Hansley. Whatever happened next, our prisoner was a time bomb. We needed to wrap things up and wash our hands of him before we both wound up in jail for kidnapping.

"I'm gonna call Darius and arrange another meetup. With the shipment on the way, we're short on time, but that should also set the table for Darius to talk business. As soon as I have something, we'll ring up the lawyer and notify the DEA about the shipment."

"What about him?" Regi said, jabbing a thumb at the storm cellar.

"We'll knock him out and leave him someplace where the DEA can find him. Make sure there's nothing to lead back to you. Like you said, you've done your time."

"And what if you can't get anything concrete out of Darius?"

I hesitated, evaluating my options. But in truth, there was only one.

Brute force. Violence of action. Squeeze the tube until something came out.

"Let me worry about that," I said. "You keep Hansley quiet while I get back to the hotel and clean up. I have a feeling I'll need Hansley's car."

Regi opened his mouth with another question, but just then the kitchen phone rang—long and shrill. He flicked the cigarillo into the koi pond and shuffled inside while I checked on our prisoner.

Hansley's face and chest were covered in blood trails, but his nose had stopped running, and he was still very much alive. He glowered at me with enough hatred to set something on fire. I blew him a kiss before turning back for the door.

"What? When?" I heard Regi shout from the kitchen. A few mumbled words were followed by the phone hanging up; then he appeared at the cellar door, beckoning to me.

"I got to go. Jalen got nabbed."

I hurried up the steps and followed him into the house. It still smelled of bacon. Regi was busy shuffling through his freezer, digging out ice cream cartons and packages of frozen vegetables. They rained over the floor in a heap before he located a white paper package marked *steak* in black marker.

It didn't look like steak.

"What happened?" I said.

"Jalen got busted," Regi muttered, moving to the sink and flicking on the hot water. The package was encased in ice.

"Cops?"

Regi nodded.

"Weed?" I guessed.

"Backpack full of it. They got him downtown."

"He called you?" I was surprised, but it was a good sign.

"He called his grandmama. She called me. I gotta go get him out."

The ice began to crack away from the package, and he tore the paper back. Inside the package was a plastic bag loaded with cash—two or three grand in small bills. Regi's fingers shook as he switched the water off.

I put a hand on his shoulder. "Take a breath. This isn't the end of the world. How much is bail?"

"Five Gs. I think I got three...I'll have to go to the bank for more."

"Don't worry about it," I said, digging in my pocket. "Hansley will cover the rest."

I peeled out Hansley's wad and dropped it on the counter.

The moment I said it, Regi cursed again.

Hansley.

We couldn't just leave him here, unattended, all morning long. It had been dangerous enough to leave him in the middle of the night.

"Somebody has to look after him," I said.

"I can't leave Jalen downtown," Regi objected. "He already feels abandoned. If he starts spilling to them cops—"

I held up a hand. "Slow down. We're not leaving him anywhere." I scooped up the cash and shoveled it into my coat pocket. "Call the jail. Tell them a family friend is coming to pay his bail. I'll pick him up and get him back to his apartment, then get back to the hotel and hook up with Darius. Just call me a cab."

Regi looked hesitant. I wet a rag and got busy scrubbing cocaine residue off my jacket.

The last thing the Atlanta PD needed to see was blow on my collar.

"It'll be okay, Regi. We've got this. Call the cab."

48

R egi called a cab to take me across town to the Home Depot where I'd left the GMC. I now had a number of vehicles at my disposal, but the GMC would raise the fewest questions from Jalen, and at the moment I wasn't interested in answering his questions. I had a few of my own.

Back in the old truck, I was surprised by how much the sagging seat and musty smell felt like home. I enjoyed its rumbling rattle as I drove into northwest Atlanta to the Fulton County Jail. I still didn't have details on what had happened—Regi's conversation with Jalen's grandmother had been short and confused. Understandably, the old lady was distressed. All I really knew was that Jalen had been picked up for possession. The expense of his bail indicated he'd been in possession of quite a large amount, and they probably assumed he was dealing.

Not a great day for a fifteen-year-old.

Parking at a city meter, I walked the two blocks to the jail with nothing in my pockets save my wallet and the bail cash. I still wore Hansley's ill-fitting suit, having scrubbed it down with a wet towel and sprayed it with fabric softener to remove the trace and smell of narcotics.

After passing through a metal detector, I was directed to a service desk, where the duty cop asked me to present ID and sign in before stating the purpose of my visit.

"I'm here to pick up Jalen Powell," I said. "I understand bail has been set."

The guy ran a search on his computer, then gave me a sideways glance. I knew what he was thinking. Black kid, white adult.

"Forty-eight hundred," he said. "We don't take checks, but there's a money order place—"

I plopped the wad of bills on the counter. "How about cash?"

His eyes narrowed, but he accepted the bills, counting them one at a time and running a counterfeit pen across each one. Then he reached for more paperwork.

"What is your relationship to Mr. Powell?"

"Guardian," I lied. I knew they wouldn't turn him loose to just anybody, but guardian should be a persuasive enough title to give me access without a need for proof.

I completed the paperwork, noting the terms of Jalen's bail. He was charged with possession with the intent to distribute, just as I suspected. A court date had yet to be set. He was permitted to leave jail but must remain within Fulton County and make himself available to phone calls and visits from law enforcement at all times.

Typical stipulations. I imagined the Fulton County Sheriff's Office printed off a few dozen of these per week.

I signed the paper and pushed the clipboard back. The desk guy sighed like a man who hated his job. "All right. I'll get him."

Half an hour passed before Jalen appeared. He was dressed in loose jeans and another Hawks jersey—nothing if not a man of consistency. I noted the absence of any back-pack, and the presence of a new cop. An old guy, with sergeant patches on his arms.

The three of them stopped behind the desk, and momentary surprise flashed across Jalen's face. But he didn't say anything, waiting for the sergeant to jab his clipboard at me.

"You know this guy?"

Jalen hesitated. I remained relaxed, conscious of the original cop watching me closely.

"Yeah," Jalen said, shoving his hands into his pockets. "I know him. Thanks for showing up, bruh."

"He some kind of relation to you?" the sergeant prompted. "We can't turn you loose to just anybody. You're a minor."

Jalen shrugged. "He's my auntie's boyfriend."

Smart kid, I thought.

"I thought you said you were his guardian?" the desk cop asked.

"He is," Jalen said quickly. "Look, can I go now?"

The cops exchanged a weary look. The kind of look that said neither one of them really cared who I was, or what happened to Jalen. They just wanted to cover their asses.

Then the desk guy opened the secured door to allow Jalen to pass through. He approached me awkwardly, as though he wasn't sure how to perpetuate the ruse.

I decided to take control before he said something stupid.

"You're in one heap of trouble, young man. Come on."

I put my arm behind his shoulders and propelled him ahead, down the long hall and back onto the street before anyone could change their mind. Neither one of us spoke until we were back at the truck. Jalen had to squeeze into the middle seat, my mountain of camping gear still piled up near the passenger's side. I slammed the heavy door but didn't immediately reach for the key.

"What the hell you doin' here, man? I called my grammy!"

I rested both hands on the steering wheel, clamping my eyes shut as the remnants of a headache fought to overcome the power of the four Tylenol I'd consumed. I was still tired. Still hungover.

Very much *not* in the mood for any of Jalen's childish outbursts.

"A simple *thank you* would suffice," I said. "I just paid your bail, dude."

"Yeah, well, nobody asked for that. I was just fine on my own."

"Like hell you were," I said. "If you were fine, you wouldn't have been caught. And even if you were caught, you wouldn't have dialed up an old woman with health problems. You got up the creek without a paddle, kid. Amateur move. You keep this circus going, and you'll be dead before you're old enough to drink."

I hit the clutch and twisted the key. Jalen said nothing. Turning south, I navigated amid a maze of concrete buildings and traffic lights, headed back toward his apartment complex.

We had crossed through another five blocks before Jalen broke the silence.

"Why are you here? Why can't I get rid of you?"

"That's a good question. I wish I had an answer. I guess I'm just a nice guy, huh? Truth is you were right before—I'm damn near homeless. But I was hanging with your uncle Regi when your grammy called, and we scraped some cash together. So again. Any time you want to express some gratitude, I'm all ears."

I wasn't feeling half as aggressive as I sounded. I knew I was being hard on Jalen. But I also knew what it was like to be a kid brushing up with some really bad decisions. Jalen didn't appreciate the gravity of where his life was headed. Somebody needed to impress that upon him.

"What you doin' hanging with that old thug?" Jalen demanded.

I snorted. "Thug? Really? Who got picked up with a pound of weed in their backpack? It's none of your business what I was doing with your uncle. If I were in your shoes, I'd stop looking a gift horse in the mouth."

A long, protracted pause. Jalen looked out the window, turning his head away. He didn't realize it, but I could see his face in my right-hand mirror. I saw the tears in his eyes, and how hard he was fighting to hold them back. Something twisted in my stomach, and the face in the mirror morphed.

I didn't see Jalen anymore. I saw myself—looking every bit as embarrassed and helpless.

I pulled the truck off the street at a Burger King and cut the engine. We sat in silence while the muffler cooled, ticking softly. Then I ran a hand over my tired face.

"You know what? You're right. You don't know me from Adam. I'm just some guy who keeps turning up at all the wrong moments. If I were in your shoes, I'd have some questions of my own."

Jalen scrubbed a hand across his face, trying and failing to make it look like he wasn't wiping tears away.

"I was a cop," I said. "In Arizona. I worked homicide investigations. Last fall..."

I stopped. This wasn't something I relished discussing. But if I wanted Jalen to let me in, I owed him some reciprocation.

"Last fall my fiancée was killed. School shooting. Senseless thing. I was shot up, too. Since then, I've been...I don't know. Kind of wandering around. I was passing through town when you jacked my truck. After I dropped you off, I...stumbled into some information about your brother. About Anthony."

Jalen stiffened just a little. I faced him.

"You think he's innocent, don't you?"

Jalen didn't answer, but I saw the truth in his eyes.

"You're right," I said. "Your brother was set up by the South Atlanta Squad to take the fall for somebody else. I'm not sure who. Regi and I are looking into it."

"Why?"

"Why was he set up?"

"Why are you looking into it?" The question was blunt. I could hear the frustration still boiling beneath the taut words.

"Because I don't like bullies," I said. "And I like injustice even less. But mostly...because I don't like the path you're on. I know where it leads, and you deserve better. I know I made things worse for you at the basketball court the other day. So I feel obligated to make things right."

"By pounding the people who set up Anthony?" Jalen snorted.

"No. By proving that he's innocent."

Jalen didn't blink. I saw the disbelief in his face—like he wanted to buy what I was selling, but wouldn't allow himself. He'd been down this road before, with A. B. Colby and then with Sarah Dalton. Neither had helped.

"You stacking up cash, aren't you?"

Jalen didn't answer.

"Saving for a fancy lawyer?" I prodded.

He looked at his hands, shifting uncomfortably. I nodded.

"I thought so. I wish it were that simple, kid. Anthony's problems are bigger than money. I'm going to do what I can to help him, but you've got to meet me halfway. Slinging dope for these thugs is a fast track to winding up just like them. Is that really what you want?"

Jalen avoided my gaze, but the obstinance had faded from his shoulders. Now he just looked tired and maybe a little scared. I considered telling him who he was slinging dope *for*, but it seemed like too great a risk. A kid as angry and irrational as Jalen could take that information and march straight back to Darius's club with a gun in his pants.

"What else am I supposed to do?" Jalen mumbled. "It ain't like I gotta lot of options."

"I realize that. But you do have potential. I saw you shooting hoops with those boys. You've got real skills. A kid like you could land a scholarship if he worked hard. Play for a nice school. Get an education."

Jalen snorted and looked out the window. I placed a gentle hand on his shoulder and gave it a soft squeeze.

"Jalen."

He looked at me, his face still hard. But he didn't pull away.

"I may not know what it's like to be you, but I know what it's like to be at rock bottom. And I promise you...life is worth fighting for. Let me prove it."

49

I bought Jalen breakfast at the Burger King, then
dropped him off at his apartment. We didn't talk any
more about Anthony or Jalen's run-in with the law. We
argued about basketball and whether the Hawks would win
it all.

Jalen doubted.

I told him it was a done deal.

The moment his door closed, I spun the truck back
around and headed for downtown. Hansley's phone had
already buzzed twice since I'd left Regi's house. The first was
a message from Garcia, letting me know that the shipment
had departed El Paso and was on its way.

One driver, then. He'd have to overnight somewhere.

The second message was from Darius. The gangster
wanted to meet. He wanted to take me on a tour of his facility.

Rolling back into downtown, I drove the GMC to the valet
stand at the Westin Peachtree Plaza and checked it in without
comment, then proceeded directly to Hansley's room on the
twenty-second floor, using his key card to gain access.

The room was clean and undisturbed, with a large suitcase resting on the bed. I peeled quickly out of my soiled clothes and showered, scrubbing away the scent of drugs and vomit before rifling through the suitcase to inspect what Hansley had brought with him.

The clothes were all black—every stitch and thread. Black socks and underwear joined black pants, shirt, and jacket. I found spare magazines for both of Hansley's Glocks, along with bath salts and a Jane Austen novel.

Weirdo.

Re-dressing, I was digging through fresh socks when my fingers touched something stiff beneath the synthetic floor of the suitcase. I dumped the clothes out and found a zipper to open the false bottom of the case.

Twenty thousand dollars spilled out—two banded stacks of Benjamins, clean but not new, banded together. I flicked my thumb across the end of a stack and smirked as I thought of my depleted checking account.

Thanks, Hansley.

I replaced the cash in the suitcase for the time being. Once I was finished dealing with the SAS, I'd return to confiscate it. I figured I would have earned it by then.

Pulling a black jacket over my shirt, I double-checked the presence of both Glocks before exiting the hotel room. Then I was off, down the elevators to the valet stand.

But when I presented the valet with my ticket, it wasn't for the 1967 GMC I'd just exited. For my trip back to Darius's club, I'd ride in style, compliments of Hansley's brand-new Jaguar XJ.

THE CAR RAN like the cat it was named for, gobbling up the highway with a throaty roar, sucking closer to the asphalt the harder I pushed the big engine. The seats were large and comfortable—and everything was black. Even the pouncing cat emblem on the steering wheel had been blacked out.

Hansley needed a psychiatrist.

The text message from Darius directed me to meet him at the club, but when I was only ten minutes out, he texted again and changed the rendezvous to a house two miles away. The Jaguar's built-in navigation handled the switch with ease, and I rolled up on the house with a gentle rumble of British horsepower.

The property sat on a slightly gentrified side of the ghetto Darius's club was located in. Sitting back off the street with a black metal fence staked around it, the home was old but well kept, updated with a new metal roof.

The Mercedes S-Class sat on a narrow driveway, and two of the big guys who had accosted me at the entrance of the club now lounged on the home's sprawling front porch.

I cut the motor but didn't immediately exit, taking time to put myself in Hansley's head, remembering how I had confronted Darius the night before. The cocaine-fueled bender was a demonstration of poor judgment on my part, but nothing could be a demonstration of weakness.

This might be my last opportunity to find tangible evidence of Anthony's innocence prior to the shipment arriving.

Stepping out of the car, I shut the door with an authoritative shove, then pushed through the unlocked gate onto the concrete walkway leading up to the house.

The two big gangsters saw me coming and stood but didn't move to block my path. As I reached the foot of the porch steps, the front door opened, and Darius stomped out.

If I hadn't been witness to the crazed partying of the night before, I would never have believed Darius was a participant. He stood tall and clear-eyed, not the least bit hungover, dressed in fresh clothes with a fresh skullcap covering his head. When our gazes met, I saw something sinister flash behind his dark eyes. He stopped at the top of the steps.

"Nice whip," Darius said.

"Thanks."

"You know, I like the German cars, myself." He tilted his head toward the Mercedes. I said nothing. Whatever Darius's reason for summoning me to his personal residence, I knew car talk wasn't it.

Darius held out a hand, and one of his men passed him a blunt. He lit up and sucked down a deep lungful of reefer. His eyes dilated as he breathed out through his nose. Then he offered me a drag.

"I think we've had quite enough of that, don't you?" I said.

Darius squinted, and I thought an outburst was coming. Or maybe a bad joke.

Instead, he simply flicked the joint onto the sidewalk and jerked his head toward his men.

"All right, white boy," he said, starting down the steps and drawing the Mercedes keys from his pocket. "Business, then. Let's roll."

50

D arius offered me a ride, but I firmly declined and started up the Jaguar. Whatever came next, I was done being pushed around. Hansley was here to inspect, after all. Not to take orders.

The big Mercedes roared onto the highway and took off south. I pushed the Jag to keep up, the two black cars weaving in and out of traffic without any particular effort to avoid drawing attention. I thought it was sloppy on Darius's part, and decided it meant only one of two things: either he was trying to impress me with his flippant disregard for local law enforcement, or else he was as dumb as a fence post.

Maybe both.

I followed close to the S-Class as though I were brand new to the city, but in truth I was growing familiar with the path to the abandoned lock and key plant outside of town. Everything looked a little different in broad daylight, with lots of landmarks I had previously missed now fully visible. We blazed past the gas station where Regi had jumped me, and I noted that the rental car was already missing. It must have been towed—something to sort out later.

We reached the gravel turnoff and the slouching fence. I remained in the Jag as one of Darius's goons unlocked the gate. Then we were rolling through, over the lip of the shallow valley, and down toward the factory.

The building looked a lot older and in worse condition under sunlight, with faded paint outlining the name of the company that once owned it. Dust clung to busted windows, and one corner of the metal roof was all but rusted away.

Darius stopped in his usual parking place, and I parked the Jag just behind.

This is your first time, I reminded myself. *You've never been here before.*

Stepping into the Georgia sunshine, I pushed Hansley's sunglasses up my nose and adjusted my sleeves. They were too short, and I hoped it didn't show.

"Welcome to SAS headquarters," Darius said, slamming the Mercedes door. "This is where the magic happens."

The two beefy SAS goons fell in behind me as Darius led the way, unlocking the side access door and flicking a switch to turn the lights on. All the musty smells of old grease and decades-old grime greeted my nostrils, reminding me of two nights previously when I'd first snuck in via the fire escape. I deliberately avoided looking toward the overhead office and the small hole in the wall, slowly sliding the sunglasses off instead and folding them into my pocket.

I swept my gaze across the factory floor, surveying the array of tables and the canning machine. Then I wrinkled my nose.

"This is it?"

Darius looked to his goons, cutting loose with a nervous laugh.

"*This is it?*" He mimicked my voice. "Is this cracka serious?"

I said nothing. His shoulders bristled. Apparently, whatever mellowing effects the blunt had produced were now long worn off. He looked like a caged bull, ready to fight.

"Look, bruh. You're here on a courtesy, see? I'm getting tired of—"

I turned for the door, showing him my back and walking with purpose. My heart thumped as the two goons and the guns they carried disappeared from my view, but I didn't show it.

I couldn't afford to.

"Hey!" Darius called. "Where you goin'?"

"Back to California," I said simply.

I reached for the doorknob. Darius closed his fist and smacked it against the all-metal door.

"Excuse me?" he snapped.

I pursed my lips. "Clearly, you're not the kind of organization we can do business with. Thank you for your time."

I spoke with my back straight, my chin up. Acting and sounding like there weren't two oversized goons breathing down my neck. I knew I was pushing the envelope. I knew everything I said was calibrated to send Darius into meltdown mode.

But I also knew that this wasn't about Hansley. This wasn't even about Garcia or M30 fentanyl.

This was about money and power—a metric ton of each. The kind of money and power Darius would never taste apart from a successful partnership with a Mexican cartel.

Darius's lip trembled. I could tell he wanted to throat punch me.

But he didn't.

"What are you saying?" he growled.

"I'm saying I'm done with the thug act," I said. "The distribution networks I advise experience one to three hundred percent revenue growth in the first six months. I'm incredibly good at what I do, Mr. Carter, but I don't waste time. So you can either start answering my questions, or you can move your fist off that door and get the hell out of my way."

I kept my words flat and cold, channeling Hansley. Not the man tied up in Regi's basement, but the man I imagined Hansley to be. Big and tough, totally fearless, a weapon of the cartel.

A man who didn't step aside for anyone, least of all a petty dope dealer.

Darius looked momentarily unsure, as though he couldn't decide whether he wanted to jump me right on the spot. I knew he was thinking about the goons behind me, and what he looked like if he cowered.

Then he lifted his chin. Took a half step back and dropped his fist off the door with a sheepish shrug. "Man, homie. It ain't like that. We can deal."

He gestured toward the production line and the canning machine. "You got questions, I got answers."

I SPENT the next two hours running Darius through the wringer about his operation, asking a lot of meaningless questions about product storage and shipment as I wove around the questions I *really* wanted to ask—questions about networks in South Carolina and a former Squad soldier named Anthony Cox.

The longer I played my fictitious vision of Hansley, the more comfortable I became in his shoes. I pushed on Darius, but also gave him room to flex his personality. It was a balancing act of demonstrating who was in charge while also protecting his ego.

While he was giving me a demonstration of the canning machine, several more Squad members rolled up. I recognized many of them from the drug-fest of the previous night, and none of them looked hungover. They worked like a well-oiled machine, prepping the assembly line with boxes and cans, eager to package the product the moment it arrived.

It reminded me of Darius's earlier claim to Garcia that he could repackage the entire shipment within a couple of days. The DEA needed to pounce *before* the drugs left the building. It tightened my timeline and further frustrated my fruitless efforts to organically raise the subject of Anthony Cox. I couldn't think of a plausible reason why Hansley should ask about Cox, and Darius had given me nothing to work with.

We were standing over a table overlooking a detailed road map of the southeast as Darius's crew packed up and began to leave. Darius had marked the map in several places with key distribution hubs—Birmingham, Chattanooga, Macon, Montgomery...and Greenville.

It was the last city that rang a bell in my mind. I remembered what Regi had said about Anthony facilitating the distribution of a growing fentanyl trade, then getting cold feet.

If Anthony had associates in Greenville, maybe that was the market he had been facilitating. Maybe after he argued with Darius about the fentanyl, Darius had sent him to Greenville on some petty assignment. Getting him out of the way while Martin was tortured, murdered, and dumped.

It would be easy enough for Darius to obtain Anthony's fingerprints and DNA. Easy enough for him to gain access into Anthony's apartment to leave a shirt stained with Martin's blood.

But how did I get Darius to admit to it?

"Garcia wants to move up the east coast," I said. "Charlotte is our next target. Talk to me about your people in South Carolina. Who do you have to grow that network?"

Darius drew breath to answer. Then one of his goons

stuck his head through a factory door, calling across the room.

"Hey, boss! We ready."

A strange light crossed behind Darius's eyes, and his lips rose into a wolfish grin, exposing gold teeth. He tilted his head toward the door.

"Got something to show you, Hansley. Special treat."

I didn't like the way he used the word *special*—with just a tinge of sarcasm, but no shortage of excitement. I motioned back to the map, but Darius shook his head.

"Later. Come on...you'll enjoy this."

A sinister undertone slipped into Darius's voice, and a tingle ran up my spine. I left the table and dutifully followed him outside, where the gleam of the sun still beat down on the crushed gravel parking lot. The two goons who had originally accompanied him in the Mercedes now led the way around a pile of busted cinder blocks to a trail running behind the factory. It was overgrown here, with tall grass and tangles of brambles beaten back to expose the path. I saw boot marks and scrapes in the dirt, with a trace of dried blood on a passing thorn bush.

My tingling spine turned to a full chill as the lead goon pushed aside a low-hanging tree branch, exposing a rust-red metal box resting in the mud beyond.

It was a shipping container, like the kind used for global trade. Built of heavy metal, capable of being stacked on a ship, loaded on a train car, or pulled by a semitruck, the container now lay sandwiched between the back wall of the factory and the rising hillside beyond, covered by trees and encrusted by rust.

The doors were chained shut, but even as the goon stuck a key into the padlock and wrestled it open, I had a pretty good idea what lay inside.

Darius looked up at me, that thirsty fire still alive behind his gleaming eyes.

"Call it a new business celebration," he said. "A little *welcome to Atlanta* gift."

The goon hauled the door open. It ground and squealed on rusted hinges, exposing a dark interior. Then the big guy flipped a flashlight on and flooded the container with cold blue light.

Only one thing occupied the space—and it wasn't a thing, it was a person.

The woman sat tied to a metal chair, gagged with duct tape, her face bloodied and bruised. Pure fear consumed her wide eyes as the light glared into them. It reflected off something lying on the floor, also. A bloody chunk of metal about the size and shape of a wallet, resting near her feet.

It was an FBI shield.

51

D arius chuckled like a demented movie villain as he led the way into the container, taking the flashlight and pointing it directly into the woman's eyes.

She was young—early thirties, maybe. African American and very attractive. As the light hit her face, she turned her head away, trembling.

I followed Darius into the container, the stench of urine and human excrement assaulting my nose. The chair the woman sat in was slick with refuse, as was the floor beneath her. Purple and black bruises covered her neck, and the button-down shirt she wore was torn down the front, barely covering her chest.

She'd been raped. It wasn't hard to guess that. Her pants and underwear were missing, and her upper thighs were bruised also. She kept her knees clamped firmly together, attempting a weak cry through the gag as Darius approached.

It was a pitiful and worthless sound. Darius leaned over her, his face alight with a wolfish grin. He kicked the bloodied FBI shield across the container floor toward me. It scraped through a puddle of urine and came to a stop at the toe of Hansley's black dress shoe.

"A fed!" Darius said it as though he were announcing the species of a trophy fish. "Caught her sniffing around last week. On the *prowl*." He grabbed her face, wrenching her jaw around and prizing her mouth open. She coughed and jerked, but she couldn't move. Her hands were bound fast.

"Stop," I snarled.

Darius looked back at me, the wolfish smile still consuming his face. He ran his tongue across gold-plated teeth.

"Oh, you want some, don't you? Ha. I wish you got here last week, bruh. It was *good* then. A little torn up now. But hey. I'll share."

He licked his lips, his eyes wide and crazed, his fingers still clutching her jaw.

The edges of my vision turned red, but I fought to keep my mind in check. I could take him, right here, right now. Put my hands on his throat and snap his neck. Or, better yet, draw Hansley's Glock and take a shot at all three of them before they could reach their weapons.

I liked my odds. But killing Darius would bring my whole crusade crashing down.

I had to keep playing Hansley.

"Are you out of your mind?" I almost shouted. "We don't mess with feds! They'll have people looking for her!"

My voice boomed off the enclosed walls. Darius's grin faded. He looked back at the sobbing woman barely hanging on to consciousness, and I saw indecision in his face. I couldn't decide if he was conflicted about what I was saying, or about me.

I closed the distance between us. Darius bristled.

"This is what I was talking about," I said. "You think you

can build a billion-dollar drug empire by kidnapping feds? Were you born yesterday?"

"She found *us!*" Darius retorted, releasing the woman and snapping upright.

"Even worse. They're on your trail. That's a *liability*, fool. It's something you should have told Garcia! Now we've got to clean this up."

I turned away, like I was too angry to even look at him. In reality, my mind was spinning, desperately trying to concoct a way to manipulate both myself and the woman out of this container. She was still alive, but she wouldn't be for much longer if she remained in this baking hot box, slowly drowning in the fumes of her own refuse.

Think, dammit. Think.

"You don't come down here and tell us how to run our city!" Darius shouted. "This *my* hood, bruh. We run it *my* way."

I heard the whisper of metal against cloth. I turned in time to see Darius drawing a handgun from beneath his shirt. It was a 1911, nickel plated with pearl grips and a gold hammer. His knuckles turned white around the weapon as he stepped toward me.

"Stop playin' like you the king of the world. You here because we got something you need. We got the network, right? Worth driving all the way from Cali for!"

"And it won't be worth *anything* if you go to war with the FBI!" I screamed. The rage I channeled had nothing to do with the circumstances of a cartel partnership, but I let the anger flow anyway. I saw the woman out of the corner of my eye, cowering in shadows. Piss raining from the chair as her bladder gave way under a wave of panic. Her whole body shaking.

An undercover agent. Probably working a case that had nothing to do with Darius and his drugs. Just caught in the wrong place at the wrong time. A woman with a family, maybe. A woman whose life would never be the same.

I had to get her out. Somehow, some way. Even if I blew my own cover.

"You're gonna give her to me," I snarled, leaning over Darius like a punk kid on a street corner. "You're gonna tell me everything you know about her investigation. I'm gonna clean this up!"

Darius shook. I saw his goons take a half step back, maybe reading warning signs I wasn't familiar with. His face strained, and his jaw began to work, teeth grinding. He looked like a helium balloon, overinflated and stretching to its limit.

I lowered my voice, the anger still there, but the rage under control. I had to de-escalate. I had to get her *out* of this box.

"Put her in my trunk," I said. "I'm gonna deal with this."

"Oh, you gonna deal with it?" Darius hissed. His voice verged on shrill.

"That's right," I said. "I'll clean it up."

"You can clean it up?" he asked. I couldn't tell if he was crazed or desperate. What I saw in his eyes could be either.

"I'll clean it up," I repeated. Drawing the Jaguar keys from my pocket, I flipped them to one of Darius's goons. "Get my car."

Darius continued to pant, breath whistling between his clenched teeth, the pistol trembling in his hand. The goon didn't move, looking to his boss.

"Trust me," I said, my voice now calm. "I'll erase her like she never existed. We'll get the FBI off your back. I've done it before."

Darius's shoulders began to steady. He wiped his lip with the back of one hand, scrubbing sweat away. Then he shot a sideways glance at the goon and nodded once.

The man headed for the door, and I breathed an invisible sigh of relief. Darius tilted his head back, his face still stone cold, but steady now.

"You've done it before?" he asked.

"Plenty of times."

"Make her disappear?"

"Like she was never born."

He grinned. Shrugged like it was all just a bad joke.

"All right, bruh. Whatever you say."

He gestured to the door. I started toward the welcome promise of fresh air, my head still spinning. Darius walked beside me. His second goon fell in behind.

Halfway there Darius stopped, holding up a finger. "Oh... just one other thing."

The polished 1911 flashed as Darius whirled. My heart leapt into my throat as I instinctively raised a hand, a shout building in my gut and boiling out.

It was all too late. Darius fired. Once, twice, three times. The gun belched fire and spat empty casings out, so loud it deafened me. He fast-walked toward the FBI agent, still firing, unloading into her face and chest and blowing her backward onto the floor. The gun locked back over an empty magazine, and Darius screamed, throwing his head back and howling at the metal ceiling.

Then he kicked her, smashing his boot into her face again and again. Dancing around her and raining down kicks across her lifeless body, still howling like some primeval animal.

I stood frozen at the entrance of the container, heart thundering, ears ringing. I could barely hear. Bile convulsed in my stomach, and I almost puked, my mind screaming at me to grab Hansley's Glock.

To gun Darius down in a maddened rage.

But I didn't move. It was too late for that now. It was too late for anything.

Darius stopped over the body and shrieked, saliva running from his lips, a hungry grin plastered across his face. He looked down at the body and spat; then he just laughed as the goon came barreling back to the container, the Jaguar keys in one hand, panic crossing his face.

Darius stepped through the blood and marched straight for me. Still grinning. Still crazed.

"There you go, Hansley! *Cleaned up!*" He jabbed me in the chest with the muzzle of the pistol. I said nothing, still fighting back the urge to vomit.

Darius dropped the empty magazine and rammed a fresh one home, chambering a round and returning the weapon to his waistband. He walked right past me, out into the open sunshine, and drew a deep breath.

I followed, snatching the Jaguar keys from the goon on my way. Head spinning. Ears ringing.

Darius dug a joint out of his pocket and lit up. His shoulders still shook with maddened energy, but as gray-green smoke swirled around his head, he began to calm. He took a long drag and closed his eyes. Then he spoke in what might have been a shout, but to my ringing ears it sounded like a whisper.

"You ever question me in front of my dawgs again...I'll freakin' kill you."

He took another drag, his shoulders falling loose. Then he grinned at me and offered the joint. Totally calm. Like old buddies.

An absolute psychopath.

I shook my head, and he simply shrugged.

"Suit yourself, white boy."

Behind me I heard scraping on the metal floor of the container. The goons were hauling the lifeless FBI agent out, dragging the chair. She was still mostly naked and coated in blood, her head rolling. They didn't so much as close her eyes.

Darius headed down the trail, back to the front of the factory building. I followed him as he finished the joint, stopping by his Mercedes and dropping it in the gravel.

"You were askin' about Greenville," he said, the rage evaporating from his tone as if nothing had happened. "We had a boy from there. One of my men. Had a hookup with the local railroad union. Got guys ready to move our product anywhere you need, inside the cars. My boy got locked up, unfortunately." Darius said it with a little shrug, as though it wasn't that unfortunate at all. "But the network's still there. The thing about Greenville, it ain't just the local market. We put those little green pills on them trains, and that's your avenue right into Washington."

Darius grinned, flashing that wolf smile. "Worth driving from Cali for?"

He hit the unlock on his car and slid in, apparently unconcerned about leaving his men behind. They had work to do.

"I'll see you when the truck arrives, Hansley! Don't get no blood on that nice suit jacket."

52

Darius barely made it out of the valley before I let myself go. My eyes blurred, and the world around me swayed. My hands knotted into fists, and I slammed the hood of the Jag hard enough to leave a dint.

All I could see was the FBI agent in the shipping container. Bloody. Hanging on to life by a thread. Beaten and violated.

And then blown away.

Throwing the Jaguar's door open, I fired up the big motor and slung gravel as I hurtled out of the parking lot. Up the hill and back onto the blacktop, I kicked the AC on but still felt hot. Hansley's shirt stuck to my chest, and I struggled to breathe in the confined space.

I heard the screams over and over again—muffled by the gag, echoing inside that makeshift prison. I saw the maddened panic in the woman's eyes and heard the gunshots. A full magazine dumped into her body like so much trash.

And it's my fault.

I should have killed him. I should have drawn Hansley's

Glock and blown them all to hell, Anthony Cox and the DEA investigation be damned. Finished this thing off right then and there. Sent Darius cartwheeling into Hell.

My knuckles turned white around the leather-wrapped steering wheel. I reached the highway and took the fast lane, roaring toward Atlanta. Digging Hansley's phone out, I dialed Regi.

"Mason? Where you at? Where's Jalen?"

I suddenly remembered that I hadn't updated Regi after bailing Jalen out of jail. It had only been a few hours ago, but it felt like ages. It also felt meaningless.

"He's fine," I said. "I just left Darius. I think I've got something to work with, but it's gonna be tight. Go find the pants I was wearing when I changed into Hansley's clothes. I left my burner phone in the front pocket."

"Wait. Slow down. What the hell happened?"

"I don't have time, Regi. Find the phone!"

I heard the creak of the outdated curly wire straining against the handset, and the phone smacked against a counter. I waited. Then Regi returned.

"I got it."

"Look through the contacts and text me Sarah Dalton's number."

"Who?"

"The lawyer, Regi. Just do it."

I hung up and hit my brakes as a line of backed-up Atlanta traffic gathered in front of me. Somewhere beyond I saw the flashing lights of an ambulance, and a police car screamed by. I twisted my hand around the wheel and tapped the gas, easing forward.

Hansley's phone buzzed, signaling a text from Regi. I dialed Sarah.

She didn't pick up on the first attempt or the second. I kept trying.

I got her on the fourth dial. Sarah answered with the subdued outrage of a woman ready to fight a telemarketer.

"Who the hell—"

"Sarah, it's Mason. I need you at the Westin Peachtree Plaza, room 2207, ASAP. Bring a notepad."

"Wait...what?"

"I can prove Anthony's innocence," I said. "But the window is closing. If you really care about that kid, meet me at the hotel. I'll be there in twenty minutes."

"Mason, I'm in the middle of a deposition! I can't just leave."

"Then I guess you're not the lawyer I'm looking for. Thanks for nothing."

I reached for the red button. Sarah's voice broke through.

"Just calm down, jackass. What do you mean you can prove his innocence? Prove it how?"

"I mean I can prove he wasn't in town the night that DEA guy was killed. But I'm not talking over the phone. Room 2207. Get there."

I hung up and hit my turn signal to migrate around the wreck, then punched the gas as the Atlanta skyline broke through the clouds.

I still saw red. I still saw the slain FBI agent dragged out on that chair like a side of beef.

And I saw Darius.

A dead man walking.

53

I left the Jaguar at the valet stand and called for my
truck, grabbing my road map out of the glove box
before instructing the valet to return the vehicle to the
garage. He looked pissed, but I didn't give him time to fuss,
checking my watch as I jogged to the elevator. It was three
p.m.—twenty-one hours before Garcia's shipment of M30s
arrived, give or take.

Cutting it close.

I'd spent the entire drive back to the Westin calculating
every which way the next phase of this chaotic game could go
down, and I could think of only one series of events wherein
Anthony's innocence was proven while Garcia's shipment was
also captured. It would require careful orchestration.

And the willing participation of one Sarah Dalton.

Back in my hotel room, I shoved Hansley's luggage off the
bed and spread the road map over the mattress. It was a large
map, covering Georgia and both Carolinas, with a little bit of
Tennessee and Alabama thrown in for good measure. Atlanta
sat as a nest of tangled highways right in the center, with free-
ways leading off in every direction.

Clicking a hotel pen open, I marked the approximate spot on the map where Darius's headquarters lay. Then I moved northeast, one hundred fifty miles along I-85 to Greenville, South Carolina.

The key to this entire puzzle.

A soft knock rang against my door. I dumped the pen and checked the peephole to confirm the visitor. Sarah stood outside in a conservative pants suit, her purse held over one shoulder, a semi-irritated look on her face. There was a box of something held in one hand, and even as she glowered at the door, she chewed methodically.

She looked good. Even in the fishbowl distortion of the peephole, I couldn't deny how the suit clung to her curves and accentuated her natural complexion.

I drove the thoughts away and opened the door. The irritation on Sarah's face intensified immediately into a frown.

"What the hell are you wearing?"

I waved my hand dismissively and ushered her inside. "Come on in."

She didn't look enthused, but she stepped inside, feeding clusters of popcorn into her mouth from the box. I bolted the door and returned to the bed, retrieving my pen.

"Where have you been?" Sarah spoke through a mouthful of popcorn. For anybody else, it would have been gross. For her it almost looked cute.

"Inside," I said.

"Inside what?"

"The South Atlanta Squad."

I bent over the map and traced the outline of a railroad line leading out of Greenville—southeast to Columbia. Another headed southwest to Atlanta. A third headed northeast to Charlotte and then on to Greensboro, Raleigh, and Richmond.

And then D.C. It was just like Darius had claimed. Greenville was a freaking goldmine of distribution potential.

You only needed a man on the inside.

"Wait. You infiltrated the SAS?"

Sarah stopped chewing, her voice edging beyond admiration into simple disbelief.

"Right," I said. "Did you bring a notepad?"

She deposited her purse and the popcorn box on the bed, but she didn't produce a notepad. She just folded her arms.

"I'll give you five minutes," she said. "Why am I here?"

Fair enough.

I gestured with the pen to the map, jabbing at Atlanta.

"The Squad has a distribution monopoly on most of Atlanta—but that's not why they're branching into fentanyl. They've connected with a Mexican cartel for exclusive distribution of M30 pills because they also have networks in Birmingham, Chattanooga, and most importantly, Greenville."

I tapped the South Carolina city.

"Hold on. They're working with a cartel?"

"Exactly. Some group out of north Mexico. A truckload of fentanyl is headed this way as we speak."

"Are you kidding? How do you know this?"

"Because I was there when they planned it. Look, that's not important. What's important is Greenville."

I tapped the city again. "The SAS has an established connection with railroad workers at the Greenville train depot. People who can seclude shipments of fentanyl aboard railcars headed out of town."

I traced the train lines. "Columbia. Charlotte. Up the east coast. It's a foolproof system, really. It's not easy to gain access to a locked boxcar, but once you do, nobody is gonna notice a small package hidden inside. Plus, shipping is free. You just arrange pickup on the other side. All you need is an inside man."

Sarah held her hand up again. "I'm still confused. What does any of this have to do with Anthony Cox? You said you could prove his innocence."

"I can. Because Anthony Cox was the inside man."

"What do you mean?"

I capped the pen. "Anthony was born in Atlanta, but his father was from Greenville. Anthony Cox Senior died young and hard—a gang shooting. Extended family in Greenville took Anthony in. Gave him a home. He split time between South Carolina and Atlanta, eventually coming up in the SAS. But those Greenville contacts were still there."

"He was arrested in Greenville," Sarah said.

"Exactly. And that's my entire point. Assume for a moment that Anthony was set up. Assume he was framed by another gang member. How did the cops find him so quickly, in another state?"

"They were tipped off," Sarah said.

"That's logical. But I'll do you one better. What if the people who set Anthony up didn't just happen to know where he was? What if they *sent* him there?"

"To Greenville?"

"Right. So then he's out of the way while they set him up, and after he's arrested, they tell him not to fight it or Jalen gets skinned alive like that DEA guy."

"That doesn't make sense. Even if you knew that to be true—"

"I do. The Squad leader told me himself."

She put up a finger. "*Even if you knew that to be true...*why would they kill their golden goose?"

"They didn't. They just locked him up. The DEA thinks Anthony is still calling the shots from jail. He may well be. But not for the SAS. He's just negotiating shipments out of Greenville."

"Why would he do that if the SAS burned him?"

"For the same reason he went along with being burned in the first place—to protect Jalen."

I laid the pen down, still surveying the map. "They have a choke hold on Anthony. He already lost both his parents. The only thing he has left is his half-brother, little Jalen. They were close before Anthony went away. The SAS is now threatening Jalen's life if Anthony doesn't go along with it. He's SOL."

"But he was a willing participant prior to being burned, right? He was already a gangster. Already arranging shipments out of Greenville. Why turn on him?"

"Because he was getting out," I said. "I spoke with his uncle. Somebody who knows him well. Anthony was having second thoughts. He saw what the fentanyl could do. It was too much for him. He was jeopardizing the SAS's entire growth scheme."

Sarah looked at the map. Pursed her lips.

"You know...this is a good story. A great movie, maybe. But this isn't a court case. You said you had *proof*."

"I do."

"Where?"

"In Greenville." I pointed back to the map.

"What are you talking about?"

"Anthony was in the city at the time of his arrest. It's reasonable to conclude he was in Greenville at the time of the crime, also. All we have to do is prove that, and it's a done deal. Hard evidence."

"A witness?" she asked.

I shook my head. "Not a human one. His extended family has already declined to testify on his behalf, probably at his request. You need something more irrefutable than that. You need Anthony on camera, at the rail yard, time-stamped for the time of the murder."

Sarah squinted at the map. "Wait. Are you serious?"

LOGAN RYLES

"There has to be a tape," I said. "All these places keep security cameras. They might never check them, but if Anthony was anywhere near the rail yard at the time of the murder, that recording should still be on file. It should be digital."

"Mason..." Sarah let out an exhausted sigh. "You're asking for a needle in a haystack. Do you understand that? Even *if* there are cameras, and even *if* he was there, do you know how hard that tape would be to obtain? They're not just gonna hand it to you."

"Which is why I won't be the one asking."

"What?"

"I need you to go to Greenville—to the rail yard. These guys don't see women like you every day. Be nice. Use honey not vinegar. You already have the dates. All you need to do is review the footage for that period. It's easy."

She let out a short laugh, grabbing her purse. "You're out of your mind, you know that?"

Sarah started for the door. I cut her off, my heart rate spiking. I wasn't thinking about Greenville anymore. I wasn't even thinking about Anthony.

I was thinking about the FBI agent. About DEA Special Agent Martin's skinless face.

About all the devastation Darius was about to unleash across the east coast.

"*Look,*" I said, blocking the hallway with one arm. "If the SAS set Anthony up, it's reasonable to assume they sent him to Greenville to get him out of the way. They couldn't do that without a pretext. Something like *go check on the guys at the rail yard*. I know it's a long shot. One in a million. But that's what you *do*. You take the cases nobody else will take. You stand up for the helpless. Right?"

"Anthony Cox isn't helpless. If anything you said is true, he dug his own grave."

"Maybe. But Jalen didn't. And this is our best chance to reverse that curse. I need to know you'll make that happen. With or without me."

Sarah's brow wrinkled. "What does that mean?"

I looked away, realizing I'd said too much.

"What are you doing?" she pressed.

"That truck isn't going to stop itself. I can't let that much fentanyl spill across the state. And somebody has to deal with the Squad—permanently."

"*So call the DEA. This isn't rocket science!*"

"I will call them. Just as soon as I know where the shipment is."

And as soon as I have my hands around Darius's neck.

I thought it, but didn't say it. When I made my deal with Feldon, I'd intended to let his guys do the dirty work. Find evidence of Anthony's innocence, pin down the Squad someplace where the DEA could catch them red-handed, then stand back and watch the fireworks.

But that was before I got to know Darius. That was before I watched him slaughter that FBI agent.

No way was I standing back now.

"There's a chance this goes sideways, and I don't make it out," I said. "If so, I need your word that you'll look after Jalen. Whatever it takes."

This time it was Sarah's turn to look away. She bit her lip, appearing uncertain for the first time since I'd met her. Thrown off balance by everything I'd slung at her.

"I know you care about people, Sarah. You've dedicated your life to helping the helpless. There's nobody more helpless than Jalen. His entire existence is one train wreck of bad luck and worse decisions. If Anthony broke the law, he'll serve time for that. But nobody should serve time for crimes they didn't commit. Jalen needs to see justice. He needs to believe."

Long pause. I gave her arm a gentle squeeze.

"It's one in a million," she said.

"So bet on yourself. Take that shot."

Another protracted pause. She bit her lip so hard I thought it would bleed.

Then she nodded.

"Okay. I'll do it."

54

Sarah left with the address of the rail yard in Greenville, promising to update me the moment she found anything concrete. She warned that it could take a while—there might be gatekeepers in the way. Secretaries or security officers who wouldn't want to simply surrender proprietary security footage. She might need a subpoena.

I left those complications in her expert hands and turned my mind immediately to what came next—burning the SAS to the ground.

I called Regi and gave him the address of the factory, along with the cell phone number listed on Feldon's card. Regi would dial that number only after I saw the fentanyl truck arrive at the factory. Only after I knew for sure that the Squad was present, cornered and ready for slaughter.

Only after I carved Darius apart. One bloody piece at a time.

"After you call in the tip, load Hansley in your trunk and dump him someplace outside of town," I said. "We'll make sure the DEA finds him. I don't want any of this blowing back on you."

Regi was quiet for a long while, and I couldn't tell if he was uncertain about my instructions or my general strategy. At last, he grunted an acknowledgment.

"Keep me posted," he said.

"I will. Stay by your phone."

I hung up and stripped out of Hansley's uncomfortable black clothes, ready for a very long shower. I couldn't get the grisly images of the murdered FBI agent out of my head, and just picturing the foul interior of her makeshift prison cell made me feel filthy. Standing under the hot water with both palms on the wall, eyes closed, I tried not to think about the hail of lead tearing through her chest.

Or what had happened to her in the agonizing days leading up to that moment.

She'd probably been there when I first infiltrated the factory building. Only a few yards away, tied up in that shipping container, the ravished plaything of Darius and his thugs. I wondered what her name was, and what her story might be. How she was caught, and what she was investigating. Who her family was, and if they had been notified of her disappearance.

I also wondered who else had died. Darius had proven himself to be the kind of guy who didn't mind shedding blood. He felt invincible at the top of his little empire. He didn't know just how vulnerable he was.

I was going to be the one to teach him.

Outside the shower, I sat on the end of the bed with a towel around my waist, putting off wearing Hansley's undersized clothes for as long as possible. I didn't have my own bag—it was still a few blocks away in my other hotel room.

I missed the violin and wished I could distract myself with another attempt at that Zac Brown Band song. Or maybe I would just sit quietly and page through Mia's Bible. Try to make sense of the confusing passages again.

Instead, I was left to stare at the floor, slowly drying under the blast of the air conditioner, and picturing what I would do next.

This was the hardest part of my plan by far. Just sitting and waiting, counting the minutes as Sarah drove to Greenville, and early afternoon dragged into evening. Waiting for the dark of night to arrive, and Garcia to text.

When the truck neared Atlanta, I would head for the factory. I already knew how I wanted to deal with Darius. All I had to do was separate him from his thugs. Get him one on one.

He wouldn't stand a chance.

Lying back on the bed, I crossed my hands behind my head and closed my eyes. I knew I wouldn't be able to sleep, but I wanted to unwind the best I could. Recharge a little.

Think of Mia. I hadn't pictured her beautiful face all day. I'd been too distracted by the unfolding horrors around me. But now I saw her at our little Phoenix home again. Curled up on the couch, working on a painting. Humming along as I played my violin.

It was something out of a cheesy movie. Now so far away it felt like make-believe. I focused on the rise and fall of the music and let myself slip deeper into the daydream.

When Hansley's phone rang, it sounded like gunfire in the stillness. I sat bolt upright, eyes snapping open, and scooped it off the nightstand, ready for a call from Garcia. Recalling Hansley's voice and wondering if I could fake it.

But it wasn't Garcia. It was Regi.

"Hello?"

"Any update?" Regi asked.

"No. Just waiting on the truck."

Long pause.

"I been praying," Regi said at last.

"You think that helps?"

"I hope so, Mason. I've got bigger problems if it don't."

I indulged in a dry smile. "Well, pray for the both of us. I could use a little divine favor."

"I been praying for you since the day we met. I was praying for you while you was rolling around in the trunk of my car."

"I don't think I have to tell you how messed up that is."

Regi laughed. "It's a messed-up world, Mason. Thank God it ain't the end."

He grew silent, but I could tell there was something on his mind. I gave him time.

"You gonna kill this fella, aren't you? Darius."

"Yes," I said simply.

"Can I give you some advice, Mason? From an old man."

"Okay."

"You can't wash blood with blood. I tried. It just makes everything red."

"You're looking at it backwards, Regi. I'm not the one spilling blood everywhere—he is. And I'm going to stop it."

Regi didn't argue. He only grunted.

"Well...call me when it's time. I'm waiting by the phone."

I hung up and checked the clock. It was nearly five, growing dark outside. I envisioned Garcia's truck rolling across Mississippi or maybe north Alabama by now.

Drawing near. Bringing death with it.

I walked to the window, still wearing nothing but the towel. My nerves felt raw. The vision of Mia in our living room was long gone now, leaving only the picture of Darius hopping around the dead agent.

Smashing her face with repeated kicks. Howling at the ceiling.

A sudden chime from Hansley's phone shattered the nightmare. This time it was Garcia—a text.

I opened the message, and adrenaline rushed up my spine.

Replaced driver in Jackson. Truck will arrive at 10PM.

My gaze snapped back to the clock. Ten p.m. Only four hours away. Earlier than I had expected.

But it changed nothing.

The phone rang again, signaling a call this time. It was Darius.

"Hello?"

"You hear from Garcia?" Darius asked. I heard the crinkle of a burning joint as he spoke. He was high again.

Garcia is texting Darius? I wasn't sure if that was a new development or not.

"Yeah," I said.

"Be here at nine," Darius said. "We'll work all night."

I hung up and looked back out the window. Thought about the darkness and the way it would close around the factory.

This would be a good thing. It would make it that much easier to get the jump on Darius.

I opened a new text message and typed in a cell phone number from a card in my wallet. Feldon's number. Then I punched out a short message.

Assemble a team and stand by.

I signed it with my initials and pressed *send*.

55

I left the hotel at a quarter to eight. It was already dark outside as I re-dressed in Hansley's godawful wardrobe, triple-checking both Glocks to ensure they were chambered and ready for action. I placed the switchblade in the small of my back, held in place by its built-in pocket clip, ready for emergency use if the bullets failed.

Then I took the Jaguar keys and the valet slip, and I stepped back into Atlanta.

The ride to the factory was nerve-racking. My body felt supercharged with adrenaline, and I couldn't find a comfortable position in the leather seat.

I saw the FBI agent. I saw Anthony seated behind bullet-proof glass at the prison. I saw Jalen surrounded by Steel Mafia gangsters, getting the snot pounded out of him.

And I saw Darius strung out on coke, eyes dilated, that hideous grin stretched across his ugly face.

Karma was overdue.

I reached the factory turnoff at eight thirty. It was as early as I thought I could arrive without raising eyebrows, while still leaving as much time as possible before the fentanyl truck reached the building. A shipment this large would certainly come guarded by heavily armed soldados—at least a couple of them. I didn't want Darius to have any help when it came time to take him out.

As soon as I topped the edge of the valley and looked down on the factory, I knew I'd miscalculated. In addition to Darius's Mercedes, the Escalade had returned to the valley, promising additional muscle and firepower. I couldn't be sure how many, but at capacity, the two vehicles could easily transport eight or ten people.

It was more than I was prepared to handle. I stopped the Jaguar at the mouth of the drive and looked quickly around the valley perimeter. I thought about positioning myself among the shrubbery with a high-powered rifle or at least an AR-15. Trimming down my competition prior to infiltrating the building.

Evening the odds.

But I didn't have an AR-15, and I didn't know where to get one at eight o'clock at night. And besides, I didn't want to do this long distance. I wanted to be close.

I wanted to look Darius in the eyes when I killed him.

Hansley's phone buzzed one last time. It was a text from Regi.

Godspeed, Mason.

I switched the phone off, then started back down the drive. At the side door I saw two of Darius's muscle-heads, both slouched against the wall smoking. As I parked the Jag and switched the lights off, they both stood and flicked the smokes away, looking tense and alert. Hands dropping near their hips.

I sat with the keys in one hand, red flags flashing in my mind. Something was wrong. I could feel it. These guys had never given a damn about me. Why all the sudden alertness?

I checked the presence of both handguns one more time; then I swung the door open. Gravel crunched under Hansley's dusty black dress shoes. I locked the Jag and started toward the door, leaving my jacket unbuttoned for easier access to the Glock.

"Where's Darius?" I demanded, slipping back into the character I had built for Hansley.

"Inside," one guy grunted. They both stared at me, unmoving.

I squinted. "You boys need a joint."

The guy on the left cracked a smile. The guy on the right only reached for the door.

I walked in, greeted by a blast of bright light. The floor of the factory was illuminated like a football stadium, with half a dozen gangsters hustling around the field of tables, constructing boxes and lining up soup cans. Two more of the beefy guys lounged against the far wall, strapped up with handguns and smoking cigarettes.

I didn't see Darius.

"Who's in charge here?" I demanded. Nobody answered. Nobody so much as looked up from what they were doing.

It was odd. The uneasiness in my stomach grew. It had been only a few hours since the FBI agent's execution, but the entire tone of this place had changed completely.

I took another step inside. Then the door slammed shut behind me, and cold steel pressed against the back of my skull. I froze, hands at my sides as the muzzle of a gun scraped around from behind my head, circling over my ear and coming to rest against my temple.

And then I saw Darius. He stood next to me, tilting his

head back to make eye contact, his scalp encased in a fresh white skullcap.

His mouth spread into that wolfish grin, gold teeth glistening.

"Wassup, Mr. Sharpe?"

56

My right arm dropped to my side. Darius's gun shoved against my skull, and a heavy hand descended on my shoulder from behind. One of his goons.

"Take it easy," Darius warned. "Hands up."

I lifted my hands, my face turning hot. Feeling like a complete fool.

Something had gone sideways. I wasn't sure what yet. But if Darius knew my name, the game was up.

What the hell had happened? Who had blown my cover? I considered Garcia or one of the Steel Mafia punks. But neither of them would know my real name.

Meaty fingers clawed beneath my jacket. Both Glocks were removed, along with my cell phone and wallet. Darius's goon did the work while Darius kept the gun pressed against my head, the grin not wavering for a moment.

Just looking at him made me want to rip his throat out.

My arms were wrenched behind my back. Darius circled in front of me, his 1911 now trained on my chest as my hands were crossed and bound with duct tape.

"You one slick joker," Darius sneered. "You almost had me."

"Whatever you're doing, don't," I said. "When Garcia finds out—"

"Oh, Garcia done found out. He got all kinda plans for you, but we gonna negotiate." Darius stepped forward, running his tongue over his lips, leering up at me. "Because I got some plans of my own."

The goon finished with the tape, my hands now firmly secured behind my back. Then Darius jabbed with the gun, pointing to the back of the warehouse.

"Back there! Move it."

I took one stumbling step forward; then I heard tires grinding against the gravel outside. Darius looked over his shoulder, and the door shoved open. It was another one of his thugs.

"They here!" the guy said.

Darius's grin widened, and his greedy eyes flashed. He held up a hand to the guy dragging me.

"Hold up. He'll wanna see this."

Feet hit the dirt outside, and doors slammed. I heard a scrabbling sound, mixed with a moan. Somebody grunted and cursed. A fist met flesh with a muted thud.

Then gravel crunched. The door blasted open.

And Sarah was shoved inside. She was bound hand and foot, gagged with more tape, kicking and writhing like a restrained dragon, her face already red with welts. She was hauled by two overweight guys in tight black shirts.

And she wasn't alone. Just behind her, wrapped in tape and being dragged by one arm, was Jalen.

My stomach convulsed, and I tried to jerk free. My efforts won me a fist to the gut and another to the jaw, snapping my head back. The world spun, and I almost fell. Sarah and Jalen were hurled onto the concrete next to me, both writhing. I regained my balance and looked up just in time to see another figure step through the door—a familiar face.

He was short and wiry. White with black hair, wire-rim glasses, and a narrow face.

A ratty face.

It was Special Agent Randy White, Drug Enforcement Administration.

"Long time no see, Sharpe," White quipped cheerfully. "Guess you should've cleared out while you had the chance."

The agent wore civilian clothes, but his DEA-issued handgun was still strapped to his hip. He walked among the SAS gangsters like an old friend, relaxed and smug.

"You son of a bitch," I snarled.

White shrugged. "Call me anything you want. Just so long as the check clears."

"Let them go," I said. "They don't have anything to do with this."

"Au contraire, they've got everything to do with this. You see, when Ms. Dalton turned up at the rail yard in Greenville, she had a four out of five chance of drawing a supervisor that Darius here didn't own. But wouldn't you know it, fate was against her. So Darius got a call from his man in Greenville about a lawyer poking around, and he phoned me. Since I'm his buddy, and all. Asked if it was a DEA thing. I said, 'No. No DEA thing.' But then I remembered what our guys said—you know. The guys we had following you. About how you met with Ms. Dalton at that deli."

White shook his head, his ratty face contorting into what might have been a smile, or possibly a grimace. It was ugly as sin either way.

"I have to tell you, buddy. That's when I knew something was up. So I tell Darius, I'm like, 'Darius, you'd better look out for this Mason guy.' Then I send him a copy of your driver's license photo, and what do you know, you've already met!"

White smacked his hands together with an obnoxious laugh, like the drunk guy at a party who just repeated a lame joke nobody else found funny.

Darius shoved between us, jabbing me in the chest.

"Now you got *all kinds* of explaining to do. Starting with where the real Hansley is, and movin' on to what you know 'bout my business. But unfortunately, that gonna have to wait. Come on!"

Darius's men closed in, grabbing me by the arms. Somebody snatched my jaw open, and before I could bite his fingers, I felt tape slide over my teeth. Sarah got manhandled, hoisted over the concrete like a dead animal, while Jalen was simply dragged. I looked down to see maddened panic in his dark eyes—panic and maybe a little anger, too. I couldn't blame him.

If I thought for a moment that Darius had a DEA agent on payroll, I would never have sent Sarah to Greenville. But there was no reason for Darius's men to kidnap Jalen as well.

That was just pure spite.

Darius's army of goons towed us to the back of the factory, where a wall built of faux wood paneling blocked off a small room. It might have been an office or a filing closet at one time—now it was just dusty and hung with cobwebs. Darius hauled the door open, and the three of us were dumped inside, rolling on a bare concrete floor. No sooner had I fallen than a boot collided with my stomach, hard enough to blast the wind right out of me. I choked, and Darius grabbed me by the arm, lifting me onto my knees and driving his knuckles right into my left eye. My head snapped back, and pain exploded through my skull.

Then Darius dropped me and shouted at his men. They crowded in, and the three of us were forced into sitting positions and shoved against one wall. Exposed two-by-fours blocked off another section of the room, with gaps between them wide enough to pass a roll of duct tape through. Darius's thugs made short work of taping us in place, wrapping strips of tape first around our chests and then our foreheads.

Locking our faces in position, pointed at the far wall where Darius stood, grinning again.

There was something about his smile that was creepier than before. More sadistic. It was like the very soul had left his eyes, leaving nothing but empty pits in its place.

When the gangsters finished, Darius motioned them out of the small room, then ran his tongue across wet lips, like a snake.

"We're all gonna get real acquainted here shortly," he said. He knelt in front of Sarah and traced her cheek with a thick finger, reaching her neck and squeezing just a little. She jerked and tried to break free. My heart thundered, but I was locked against the two-by-fours by multiple strips of tape.

"Oh, I got special plans for you," Darius whispered, drawing his lips close to Sarah's cheek and kissing her. She tried to jerk her head away, but the tape around her forehead held it in place.

Darius winked at her. Then he looked down at Jalen.

"You all kinds of trouble, kid. I woulda capped your ass months ago if you weren't so useful."

Jalen's eyes blazed hatred at Darius. The big gangster turned to me.

"And *you*. Mr. Sharpe. Well, I don't know what you doin' fooling around my business, but it's gonna cost you, bruh. By the time I'm finished with you, you gonna wish you'd never been born."

The grin returned. "Like I said before, I got business to

attend to. But I don't want y'all to get bored or nothin'. I got a little feature film for you to watch."

He called through the open door, and one of the gangsters returned, carrying a small flatscreen TV and a DVD player. Darius directed the man to position the TV on the floor, directly in front of us. Right where our restrained heads were forced to face it.

Darius had the man plug it in, then motioned him off as he used the remote to turn on the unit. The DVD player spun to life next to the TV, and the screen flashed. Then it became a distorted blur as Darius paused the playback and leaned close to my ear.

"This a little taste," he whispered. "This what's comin' to ya."

Then he stood, squeezing Sarah's cheek as he passed.

"Enjoy the show!"

As he left the room, he hit the play button. My stomach knotted, already having a pretty good idea what I was about to see. My suspicions were confirmed as the video clarified around a man tied to a chair. His arms and legs were restrained, and his head was tied to a post with more tape.

It was a face I recognized from newspaper images I'd viewed at the library.

Special Agent Drew Martin.

57

The next hour was the most ghastly of my life. Nothing—not Afghanistan, not murders in Phoenix, not the worst horror movies I'd ever watched—could prepare me for what I saw on Darius's home video.

Drew Martin sat facing the camera while Darius skinned his face off.

The process was excruciatingly slow, with Darius taking frequent breaks to snort cocaine and swig liquor. There were others in the background, at times laughing and other times groaning as Darius went about the grisly work.

Martin screamed at first, thrashing and fighting to jerk free. Then his body seemed to give out. His face was exposed. His eyes looked ready to pop free, and he simply shivered in place. Groaning endlessly. Teeth coated in blood, his cheekbones gleaming bright white.

And eventually choking to death on his own blood.

Sarah and Jalen clamped their eyes shut soon after the video started, but I kept mine open. Even as my stomach boiled and I fought back the urge to vomit, I wanted to see it.

I wanted to experience every horrific detail, because some-how, someway, I was going to kill Darius.

And I was going to rip him open when I did.

When the video finally ended, the screen went blank, but nobody came to bother us. A short while later I heard one of the rolling doors rattling open at the end of the factory, and then the slow beep of a truck equipped with a backup alarm. Tires ground on the concrete, and I twisted my head sideways against the tape holding my skull in place.

Behind the TV there was a hole in the faux wood panel-ing, about the size of an orange. Jagged and torn, it gave me only a partial view of the factory floor. I could see the tables, with the back corner of a moving truck barely visible beyond them. Darius's thugs passed back and forth behind the truck, and then I heard new voices—voices speaking Spanish with heavy Mexican accents.

Garcia's shipment had arrived.

The door rolled shut, then the truck was opened, and the soup can machine began to hum. My heart thumped as I calculated the time it would take for a truckload of fentanyl to be packaged.

It wouldn't all be completed tonight. At some point they would have to stop.

At some point Darius would return to deal with his prisoners.

My fingers felt numb as I fought with the edge of the tape constraining my hands. Both arms were tied off to the two-by-fours, leaving me incapable of rolling to either side and stretching out the tape around my wrists.

I twisted my hips to relieve the strain on my back and felt something hard and metal biting into my ass.

The switchblade.

Darius's goons had missed it when they took my weapons. The slim knife was pressed so close to my skin they must not have felt it as they patted me down. Now, with my hands restrained behind my back, I pictured the weapon clipped to the inside of my waistband. And I strained for it.

Momentary hope ignited in my mind as my fingertips brushed hard steel. Twisting to one side, I jammed my tail-bone toward the two-by-fours and reached again. I felt the tip of the glass breaker built into the tail of the handle, and adrenaline surged through my chest.

Sarah's gaze flicked toward me, her head still strapped to the wall. Sweat streamed down her face, but she wasn't panicking. I couldn't see Jalen as I strained against the tape and clawed for the knife.

It was still held in the small of my back by the pocket clip, but my pants had slipped down a little as I was thrown to the floor, moving it farther out of reach.

I closed my eyes, blocking out the noise of the factory floor and focusing every fragment of my strained mind on one thing—reaching that knife.

My fingers touched the grip, and in my mind I saw Mia. We were on Bourbon Street again, and she was drunk. She stumbled out of a bar and onto the sidewalk, giggling and calling for me to catch her.

Her foot hit a mud puddle, and she staggered backward. I saw the oncoming taxi, but she didn't. Surprise consumed her face as she began to fall, her hand still reaching for mine.

Desperation overtook my mind, and I lunged forward.

My fingers closed around the knife grip. I tugged it free, almost dropping it as the pocket clip broke loose of my pants.

I held on by sheer willpower, gritting my teeth around the gag and staring directly ahead. Wiggling the knife backward in my palm, I found the switch and deployed the razor-sharp blade. It snapped out, and I rolled the knife in one hand.

Boots hit the concrete outside. The blade touched duct tape, and I began to wiggle the handle. The angle was all wrong—I couldn't put any pressure on the knife. All the work was left to the sharpness of the blade alone.

I wiggled the grip a little faster, wincing as the knife tip stabbed my forearm. I felt hot blood dripping down my palm, but I didn't stop.

The footsteps neared. Heavy and purposeful, headed straight for the door to our little prison. Through the hole in the wall, I could see men lined up at the production tables, unpacking cardboard boxes while the canning machine hummed. Near the edge of my little portal into the outside world, I saw a Mexican soldado smoking alongside one of Darius's goons, a shortened AK-47 slung over one shoulder and riding next to his hip.

A shadow crossed the hole as the approaching man reached the door. I thought it might be Darius, but I couldn't tell. The knob on the cheap plywood door twisted, and I fumbled desperately with the knife.

Then I heard something else. Distant, but growing louder. Tires grinding amid gravel, and music playing. The tune carried through the brick walls and broken windows of the factory, rolling across the valley floor with lots of guitar and a smooth, rolling beat. A voice crooned amid the melody, gentle at first, then growing into a triumphant shout.

The voice of blues legend B. B. King.

"What's that?" Darius shouted. It was him standing just outside the door. The factory fell silent as heavy Cadillac tires ground against the rocks outside. BB kept singing, even louder now, mourning love lost and the melancholy he felt. Nobody in the factory moved.

"What the *hell* is that?" Darius demanded.

The Cadillac's engine died, killing the music with it; then a heavy door slammed. Someplace outside the factory one of Darius's goons shouted.

"Hey! Who th—"

His voice cut off amid the thunderous boom of a shotgun, and panic broke out inside the factory. I could see them dashing back and forth across my viewing portal, the soldado racking a round into the chamber of his AK and taking a position behind the canning machine.

My heart began to race, and I sawed with the knife. I could feel the tape giving—just a little at first, but I was gaining speed. I could hear the individual threads snapping as my wrists began to loosen. I cut my arm again, and my fingers became slick with blood. I didn't stop.

It was quiet outside now. Everybody had taken position inside the factory and was anxiously watching the door. I could see the soldado kneeling with his AK-47 riding at shoulder level.

And then the door burst open. It slammed back against its hinges, and boots scraped the concrete. Somebody sobbed and mumbled a desperate plea.

"Shut up, fool!"

I recognized the voice immediately. It was Regi.

"Stop right there!" Darius shouted. Whoever Regi held prisoner continued to sob. I pictured him on his knees, Regi holding a fist full of his hair with one hand while he used the other to thrust a shotgun against his face.

Old school. A real gangster.

The switchblade slipped in my bloody fingers, but I caught it. I kept sawing.

"Which one of you fools in charge of this mess?" Regi shouted. His voice carried, echoing against the brick walls. The factory had suddenly become very silent, everybody waiting for somebody else to confront the elephant in the room.

Then Darius spoke. "Who are *you*?"

He didn't sound panicked. He just sounded annoyed and more than a little incredulous.

"Don't matter who I am. Only matters that I got a shotgun at this fool's head. Where's Jalen?"

Long pause. Then a slow laugh. It was Darius.

"You shoulda stayed home, old man."

Darius started across the concrete. I made one more pass with the switchblade; then my wrists broke free. Grabbing the knife with my unfettered hand, I slashed the strips binding my chest, followed by those restraining my head. Finally I tore the gag out, still tasting sour adhesive from the underside of the tape.

Breaking free of the wall, I moved immediately to Sarah as the arguing outside continued. Regi demanded to see Jalen. Darius just laughed.

I cut Sarah free. The moment the tape left her mouth, she started talking.

"Mason! They jumped me at the railroad. I never—"

"Quiet!" I hissed, moving to Jalen. "Listen carefully. I'm gonna cut him loose. Wait until I create a distraction, then exit through the back. There's a broken door and a loading dock. Don't stop running until you reach the gas station up the hill. Find a phone and call the cops."

"What about you?" Sarah protested.

"I'm staying here. Regi's gonna get himself killed if—"

I was cut off by a shout from Darius.

"Get on your knees, old man!"

Regi snorted. "I don't kneel to nobody but Jesus, young buck. Where's my nephew?"

I cut Jalen free, pulling the tape out of his mouth and holding a finger across my lips. The poor kid looked ready to faint. His face was one solid mask of fear, tears streaming down his cheeks. He shook as he broke free of the wall, and then to my surprise he threw himself at me, wrapping both arms around my neck. I awkwardly patted his shoulder with one arm. I could feel him shaking.

"It's okay," I whispered. "Go with Sarah. She'll get you out of here."

He shook his head. "Come with us!"

I opened my mouth to argue. Then Regi shouted.

"I'll kill this mofo!"

Darius laughed. "Who? Him? I'll save you the trouble."

A gun barked. Once, twice, three times. A body hit the floor. My heart raced, and I shoved Jalen toward Sarah, rising to my feet and hurrying to the door. Through a crack in the faux wood paneling, I could make out Regi standing just inside the side door, a shotgun in one hand, a dead gangster at his feet.

Darius stood ten feet away, his 1911 raised, a sneer on his face.

"Adios, old man."

Then he fired.

58

T hree rounds struck Regi, right in center mass. He went down, and I blew out of the little room like a wrecking ball.

I caught the first of Darius's men from behind, grabbing him by the face and yanking his head back. The switchblade tore through his windpipe in a gurgling spray of crimson. I caught his Glock as he tumbled, then slung myself behind a mountain of boxes packed with soup cans.

The soldado was the first to respond. He pivoted the shortened AK-47 toward me and unleashed the magazine, dumping thirty rounds of 7.62 ammunition through the cardboard in an endless stream. Paper and shreds of metal exploded only inches over my face as I rolled onto my back and kicked toward the far wall, drawing fire away from Sarah and Jalen.

Darius was gone, but another SAS gangster appeared next to Regi's fallen body. I shot him twice in the head from fifteen yards, and he crumpled to the ground. Then I swung the Glock to the left and delivered three more rounds into the breaker panel mounted near the door. The lights died in a flash of electrical sparks, and I was back on my feet, rushing for Regi's side.

The factory was alive with muzzle flash. It illuminated the space near the parked fentanyl truck, but most of the confused fire was still directed at the shredded mound of soup can boxes. Nobody saw me as I reached Regi's side and grabbed him by the collar, dragging his wounded body toward the side door. I knew he was still alive because he clung on to the shotgun, its shortened barrel scraping the concrete.

A bullet kissed my arm, and somebody screamed as they fell victim to friendly fire. Darius shouted for the shooting to stop, and I reached the open door. Jerking Regi out, I tasted fresh air and looked across the valley to see two darkened figures dashing for the hillside—Sarah and Jalen.

Pulling Regi near the exterior wall, I laid him next to the obliterated face of the man he'd shot upon arrival. His head hit the ground, and he shook, wheezing and coughing. I ran a hand quickly beneath his jacket, searching his chest. I had to stop the blood flow. I had to somehow stabilize him long enough for first responders to arrive.

But I couldn't find the entry wounds. I couldn't even find any blood. Regi wheezed, his hand shaking as I probed his ribs.

"Ow! Stop it, already. I'm fine."

I tore his shirt back and touched Kevlar.

"Hansley's vest," Regi rasped with a grin, his white teeth flashing in the darkness.

"Damn you, Regi," I muttered. "Are you okay?"

"Fine. Just a few broken ribs."

Momentary relief melted in an instant as the pound of boots filled the factory floor beyond the doorway, headed our way.

"Go!" Regi said, shoving his shotgun into my hands. I

jammed the Glock into my waistband and wheeled toward the door just as the next gangster appeared. I blew a hole in his chest the size of a grapefruit, and he tumbled backward.

Racking the slide, I leaned next to the door, measuring my breaths and willing my eyes to adjust to the darkness. I heard men shuffling inside. Muted Mexican voices spoke in Spanish while Darius cursed for his men to keep quiet. The noises gave me a rough idea of where everyone was dug in, but it wasn't enough to act on.

I needed to find Darius.

"Hey, asshole!" I shouted.

"That you, Sharpe?"

"You're damn right it's me. You gonna come out here and fight like a man, or would you rather I was tied to a chair?"

A string of profanity was joined by a short burst of automatic gunfire. Heavy bullets blasted through a window to my left and blew out the windshield of Regi's Cadillac. I didn't so much as flinch.

"Imma skin you alive, Sharpe!" Darius howled.

I drew breath to reply, and then I felt a slight tremor beneath my feet. It was faint—barely perceptible. A Californian might have confused it for a minor earthquake. A Midwesterner might have called it distant thunder.

But a U.S. Army Ranger knew that tremor like he knew the rifle in his hands and the man at his elbow. I looked to Regi, and he shot me a wink.

"You'd better hurry!" I called. "You're short on time."

The chopper broke across the valley mouth like a lunging jungle cat, flooding the valley with the piercing beam of a spotlight. Dust exploded from the gravel, and the aircraft spun sideways, exposing bold yellow letters printed across its tail: DEA.

I shot Regi a thumbs-up, and he flashed a weak grin as he held his rib cage with one arm. The chopper circled, the high-powered beam cutting swaths across the valley floor as a loudspeaker ordered everyone in the building to come out with their hands up. I could hear sirens now, screaming toward us from down the road.

And then automatic gunfire. It exploded from a second-floor window of the factory, directed skyward toward the aircraft. The chopper swung violently to the left to avoid the blast, and I whirled around the doorjamb and back into the darkness, leading with the shotgun.

DEA or no DEA. Darius was mine.

59

I collided with another soldado almost immediately, and he took a load of buckshot to the gut before collapsing in a heap. The inside of the factory now resembled a crazed nightclub—all dark save for the irregular flashes of gunfire spraying toward the windows. I navigated around the guy Darius shot, then found cover behind an upturned table.

Soup cans and packages of M30 fentanyl lay everywhere. The helicopter's spotlight cut through the windows, exposing an SAS gangster drawing a bead on me with a handgun. My final round from Regi's shotgun took most of his head off. I drew the Glock and dropped the mag, quickly checking the load. Five or six rounds of .40-caliber remained, plus the bloody switchblade in my pocket.

And somewhere in this hellhole, Darius was hiding.

Lunging back to my feet, I rushed for the side of the fentanyl truck as an automatic AK-47 opened up someplace overhead. Bullets pinged off the concrete, and one of them skimmed my shoulder blade, laying the skin open and leaving a stream of blood to run down my back. Sliding into cover, I opened up on the catwalk where I'd seen the muzzle flash. I emptied the Glock to the sound of a muted scream; then the AK-47 tumbled off the catwalk and hit the floor ten yards away.

Long before I could make a move on the weapon, Darius appeared. I saw him at the nose of the truck as flashing blue lights blazed through the shattered factory windows. A bull-horn ordered all occupants to drop their weapons and walk out.

We both ignored the call. Darius's eyes were wide and crazy, dilated with whatever pollutant he'd most recently ingested. His gold teeth glimmered with blood, and his right hand shook as he raised his polished 1911.

I dove left as the gun cracked. The first round missed me. I hurled the empty Glock at him full force. The weapon spun toward his face, and he ducked. I rolled to my feet as he fired again, blindly this time. Desperate. The .45-caliber slugs struck the concrete, and I hurtled forward, exploiting the momentary confusion to close the distance between us.

My shoulder hit him in the chest and drove him back-ward, slamming his back against the rolling door of the factory. It rattled, and his head left a dint in the thin sheet metal. He fumbled with the gun and fired again, blasting a hole through Hansley's suit jacket but failing to hit me.

I doubled up my fist and drove a right hook straight into his jaw, sending his head slamming against the door again. He dropped the gun and struggled to grab hold of my left arm as I closed my fingers around his throat.

I saw red. I saw the FBI agent. I saw Drew Martin.

Darius thrashed and reached for my face, but my arms were longer than his, and I was a lot stronger. I kept him pinned against the door with one hand and drew the switch-blade with the other. The blade snapped open with a harsh *click*, blue light shining on the bloodied edge. Darius's eyes went wide as he struggled to breathe, clawing at my throat hand with one arm and automatically raising the other to deflect the knife.

But I wasn't going for his face. It would have been poetic, but I didn't have the time.

I went for his gut.

I stabbed, driving the knife up to its hilt just above his pelvic bone. Darius gasped and attempted to double over, flailing at the wound. It was too late. I dragged the switchblade across his stomach, tearing and slicing the whole way, laying his gut open. His eyes went wide, and he choked. I relaxed off his windpipe, allowing him a desperate gasp of air.

Enough to keep him alive another agonizing minute.

I yanked the knife free and let him go. Darius slumped to the floor, both arms clamped over his stomach as blood surged out. His eyes rimmed red, and his shoulders shook as his body entered shock.

I squatted, bringing my eyes back into line with his. I saw death in his gaze, creeping in from the edges. Only minutes from consuming him altogether as he quickly bled out.

"This is for Jalen," I snarled. Then I grabbed him by the neck and shoved his head back.

Flipped the knife and caught it by the handle, point down.

And then drove the blade through his eye and straight into his brain.

Lights out.

Darius collapsed against the door, and I left the knife in place. Boots thundered across the concrete behind me, and I stood, automatically raising both arms.

"Turn around!" somebody yelled. "Keep your hands up!"

The man behind me wore full tactical gear, a shortened M4 carbine trained on my chest, his face hidden behind a gas mask. Standard equipment for a drug bust.

Feldon had done his part when I texted him. He'd prepared a team. When Regi called in the tip, they were ready.

I kept my hands up, but I didn't kneel when ordered. I squinted into the light and watched as the last of Darius's thugs were corralled into a corner and quickly handcuffed.

The Mexicans were all dead. They had fought to the end, hundreds of fallen rifle casings gathered around their bodies like confetti. Real soldados.

"On your knees!" the guy nearest me shouted again.

I kept my hands up and spoke two words. "Get Feldon."

60

It took a while, but Special Agent Mark Feldon was eventually found. I sat in a chair next to a table laden with enough fentanyl to kill anything breathing, and ignored the two men with rifles trained on my head.

Feldon looked just as I'd last seen him—dressed in a shabby suit, a little dirty, and exhausted. His tired eyes surveyed the carnage around me, then came to rest on the disemboweled gangster slumped against the rolling door. A switchblade rammed to the hilt in his right eye.

I tilted my head toward White. The traitorous DEA agent had been shot in the shoulder sometime during the raid, and was now being hauled out on a stretcher, handcuffed and protesting.

"Seems you had a rat," I said.

Feldon swept his gaze across the truckload of spilled fentanyl and slowly shook his head. "You've got some serious explaining to do."

"Actually, it's a pretty simple story."

"Is that right?"

I shrugged. "I was kidnapped. I broke free. Some people died. These things happen."

Feldon narrowed his eyes. I stood up, and the two agents with guns on me tensed.

"Sit down!"

I ignored them, pocketing my hands and turning to Feldon.

"In the back room, next to the TV on the floor. There's a DVD player and a disc."

Nobody moved. I tilted my head toward the room, and Feldon nodded. One of his men lowered his gun and went for the disc. When he returned, he offered it to Feldon.

"Cox didn't do it," I said. "Too bad you wouldn't listen."

Then I turned for the door.

"Where do you think you're going?" Feldon demanded.

I stopped. Looked over one shoulder. Shrugged. "Wherever I want."

"We've got questions," Feldon snapped, jabbing the disk at me. "We've got a *mess*."

I looked around the room. Noted the puddles of blood and the field of spent brass. Then I turned back to Feldon. "What you have is a mountain of fentanyl, a busted double agent, and a pile of dead cartel thugs. Don't look a gift horse in the mouth, Feldon."

"Sir, you need to sit down!" one of the men barked.

I looked to Feldon. Cocked my head. Shot him a knowing look. A look that reminded him of what I knew, and of the deal we'd made.

He glowered at me, then turned to his agents and shook his head.

"Let him go."

"But, sir—"

"I said let him go, dammit! Don't you have something better to be doing? We gotta process this whole mess."

I left them to argue and stepped outside into clear Georgia air. All around the factory an armada of cop cars sat with their headlights blazing in my face, patrolmen and DEA agents rushing about like little ants, caught someplace between horror at the bloodshed and euphoria at a successful bust. The dilemma of every victorious cop.

I saw an ambulance parked near the factory, its rear doors open. Regi lay inside on a stretcher, leaned back and handcuffed. They probably thought he was a gangster. All of that would be cleared up soon enough, but for now the slow wheels of law enforcement bureaucracy must be allowed to grind.

I would deal with it later.

Weaving through the cop cars, I found the Eldorado covered in dust from the helicopter, the windshield shattered by gunfire. The driver's door groaned on its hinges, and I raked glass cubes out of the driver's seat before piling inside.

The keys were still in the ignition. When I started the car, B. B. King blared to life.

He said he'd made a lot of mistakes. But he never made his move too soon.

I looked up to see Feldon stepping out of the factory building. He met my gaze and held it, then nodded. Just once.

I shot him a two-finger salute; then I shifted into gear and ground back to Atlanta. One last time.

61

ONE WEEK LATER

I spent the next six or seven days doing what I should have done from the start—enjoying the city. I ate all the local food, visited all the local museums, and bought myself a new wardrobe of jeans and comfortable shirts.

All compliments of Hansley's cash. I doubted whether the Californian would need it. After driving the Cadillac back to Regi's house, I had manhandled our hostage into the trunk, drove him to an abandoned grocery store, duct-taped him to a light post, and then called in an anonymous tip to Feldon's office.

I ended the tip with a snippet of good advice: Don't look a gift horse in the mouth.

Feldon didn't.

Back at the Westin, I took the cash and retrieved my truck. Then I returned to my own hotel and stripped out of the bloody black clothes. I was pretty sure I'd never wear black again.

Feldon's bosses had questions, of course, and I submitted to the interview, spinning an elaborate tale about being kidnapped, breaking free, and fighting for my life. It was all

BS, but Feldon did his part to control the questioning, ensuring that topics such as Jalen, Cox, and his own illegal investigation were never raised. With nobody but Regi and a heap of bodies to contest my version of events, I was released in time for lunch with a handshake and a hearty thank you from the Drug Enforcement Administration.

Regi himself spun an equally tall tale about passing by in his Cadillac and hearing gunfire, so he stopped by to lend a hand. When asked why his fingerprints were found on a pump-action shotgun, he claimed he found it on the scene. When asked why an average citizen was wearing Kevlar body armor, he said it helped with mosquitoes.

In truth, it was Darius's own stupidity that had tipped Regi off. Squad members had broken into Jalen's apartment to kidnap him, knocking his grandmother unconscious and leaving her amid a field of shattered glass. It took a while for a neighbor to pass by and notice the busted window, but when the police arrived, they called Regi. Apparently, he was listed as the old woman's emergency contact. Regi quickly guessed who was responsible, and when I didn't answer Hansley's phone, he took matters into his own hands.

An old-school gangster. A real tough SOB.

In the end the DEA didn't press Regi about the shotgun or the Kevlar. They were too busy reveling in the capture of twelve million dollars' worth of fentanyl, not to mention the DVD with Martin's murder documented on it. That bombshell alone would shake the agency and keep the news media hopping for months, not to mention the discovery of the slain FBI agent buried behind the factory. I'd clued Feldon in on her murder, and he had transferred the information to the right people. Her name was Julia Jenkins, and I hoped that having her body would bring some small comfort to her family.

At least she could be buried properly, and her name placed on the FBI's Wall of Honor where it belonged.

The Saturday morning following the shootout at the factory, I woke early and checked out of the Sheraton. Packing all my luggage into the truck, I bumped across town to a Burger King and ordered two sausage biscuits, with bottled water. Then I turned south, back on the highway, passing the Skyline Diner on my way.

Taking an exit near the neighborhood of Pittsburgh, I navigated amid the faded homes and worn streets until I found the government housing complex with the dirty sidewalks and boarded-up windows. Parking behind a Chevy Caprice on blocks, I left the truck and took the biscuits. I met Jalen at the foot of the steps outside his apartment, dressed in another Hawks jersey, a new basketball cradled under one arm.

He grinned when he saw me and reached out for his complex handshake. I'd been practicing it all week, but I still hadn't mastered the sequence of bumps, grips, and high fives.

I was a long way from the athlete Jalen was.

He bounced the ball as we walked, chewing his biscuit and talking at ninety miles an hour about the latest Hawks game. Atlanta had squeaked by Boston and would now face the Toronto Raptors on its quest for a championship.

I couldn't be sure, but I thought there was more behind Jalen's increased animation than enthusiasm about basketball, or even comfort with me. What had happened in that factory and what he'd witnessed on that TV would haunt him for the rest of his life. At some point, he'd need therapy.

But for now, the kid just needed to talk. I was happy to listen.

We reached the basketball court in the middle of the complex, by which time Jalen had finished the biscuit. He bounced the ball against cold concrete and shot me a devilish grin.

"You ready for this, white boy?"

I snorted. "Larry Bird is white. Didn't bother him any."

"Who?"

I bristled. Jalen laughed. He dribbled the ball and sprinted to my offside. I moved to block him, and he dodged me with ease. Three seconds later he scored, and I was left chasing the ball like an idiot.

We played for the better part of an hour, running up and down the court, working up a good sweat. I used my height at times to block some of his more ambitious shots, but could do nothing about locking him down. A takeaway was completely out of the question as he passed the ball between his legs, behind his back, and faked shots like an absolute wizard.

The kid was good. With a little work and focus, he could play for college. He could get an education.

I called it quits sometime after he hit triple digits on our invisible scoreboard, and the two of us found the park bench where I had watched him play the previous week, slouching down and sucking on the water bottles. The apartment complex was quiet for a Saturday morning, but everybody who passed by waved. Apparently, Jalen had made it known that the outsider was a friend of his, and that carried some weight.

"I've got something for you," I said, finishing my bottle.

Jalen squinted. "Do I want it?"

"I imagine so. It's not easy to get."

Digging into my pocket, I found the envelope I'd received at State Farm Arena. I passed it to him, and he rolled it over in his hand suspiciously.

"Oh, give it a rest," I said. "Just open it."

He opened the envelope. Two tickets fell out—nosebleeds

for the opening game of the conference finals. Not great seats, really. They still cost an arm and a leg.

Jalen's eyes went wide, and he almost dropped the tickets. He fumbled to catch them, then looked up.

"Are you serious, bruh?"

"Yeah, bruh. I'm serious." I laughed. "There's just one condition."

"What?"

"You gotta take Regi."

The elation that had consumed his face only moments prior faded almost completely. He looked back to the tickets in his hand and chewed his lip. When our gazes met again, he didn't look like a kid anymore. He looked like a young man.

"I don't know if I can do that," he said simply. "Me and him been cold for a while. I don't know if he'd wanna talk to me."

"That's funny. He said something similar."

I put the cap back on my bottle and rested my elbows on my knees. Some other kids had started playing in the basket-ball court. I recognized one of them as a kid who'd been playing skins the day I roughed up the Steel Mafia punks. He might have recognized me, but he didn't say anything.

"There's some bad blood there," Jalen said.

"I know. And for what it's worth...I get it. But can I tell you something?"

He shrugged, still looking at the tickets.

"Regi's a good man. He's made mistakes in life, same as all of us. He held out on your brother, and maybe he shouldn't have. But he was only trying to protect you. Regi cares about you, man. He wants to be in your life. And honestly...I think you could use that."

Jalen fingered the tickets. Then he slid them into the envelope, closed it, and held out his fist.

"Okay." We bumped knuckles, and I liked the look in his

eye. For all the damage this past week had done to him, maybe it had done some good, also. Maybe he was growing up.

He pocketed the tickets carefully. When he looked up again, I thought I saw something glimmer in his eye.

"You leaving?"

"Probably. Headed south, I think. I'd like to see some Georgia pines."

"Pines? Like pine trees?"

"Right."

"Bruh, you trippin'."

We both laughed, and he looked away.

"You know...if you ever pass through again..."

"You'll be my first stop," I promised.

Jalen nodded once. Then he reached over and wrapped his arms around me. I hugged back, and this time it didn't feel so awkward.

62

My last stop before hitting the road was the headquarters of the Atlanta Social Justice Coalition. I parked on the street and texted Sarah to let me in. Because it was a Saturday, the building was locked, but I knew she would be there.

She'd be working overtime for the considerable future. It was the biggest case of her life.

Back in her office I was greeted by the smell of Chinese food and found a carton of half-eaten lo mein growing cold next to her computer. There were notes everywhere—scattered across the desktop and littering the floor. Heaps of printouts and law books, with pens and empty take-out containers littered amongst them.

A *lot* of take-out containers.

I shoved a mess out of a chair to find a seat, and Sarah retrieved the lo mein, working the chopsticks like a ninja. For a moment I just sat and marveled at her grace and speed. Even stuffing her face, Sarah looked good. Really good. For weekend work she'd traded her business suit for a tank top and yoga pants, and the change suited her.

I recalled my momentary fantasy of her in the shower and again felt guilty. But then I decided to give myself some grace. I was tired of thinking so hard. I was ready to just exist for a while.

"So, we're making headway on the appeal," Sarah said. "Anthony has officially contracted me as his attorney, and he's willing to work through the process."

"What happened to A. B. Colby?"

She shrugged. "Apparently, he wants nothing to do with it. Suits me fine; this is the biggest case the ASJC has ever taken. When we win, it could mean a lot of free publicity and more donations. That means more cases. More good work."

"You never slow down, do you?"

She shrugged. "What else are we here for? Anyway, the DEA has already volunteered a copy of the DVD from the drug bust. We haven't received it yet, but we may not even need it. I was able to obtain the security footage at the rail yard in Greenville. Check it out."

She rotated a laptop screen and hit the space bar. The video was black and white and grainy, but Anthony Cox was easily recognizable. The time stamp matched the date and time of Martin's death.

"Your instincts were good," Sarah said. "Of course, this only proves Anthony was involved in *another* crime, but considering time served, I think he'll be out in a year or so. A big win!"

She shoveled in the rest of the lo mein. I looked around the room and for the first time took notice not of the trash and legal material piled on every available surface, but of what was missing.

No personal trinkets. No sports memorabilia or hobby paraphernalia. No vacation photos.

Only the single picture framed on her desk. The one of the middle-aged man pushing a little girl on a swing set.

A little girl who looked like her.

"I have a question," I said. "But I won't ask it if you don't want me to."

Sarah grew still, slowly poking the chopsticks at a stray noodle in the bottom of the carton. Not looking up. At last she gave up on the noodle and set the carton down, smoothing her hands over her yoga pants. Avoiding my gaze.

"You want to know why I'm like this," she said.

I had a pretty good idea why. Barring the existence of any boyfriend or lost lover, I could think of only one emotional driver sufficient to motivate a person to work ninety-hour weeks for twenty percent of what she was worth.

"Your father?" I asked.

Sarah looked at her hands. "He was charged with murder. First degree. He didn't do it, but I can't deny the circumstantial evidence was ugly."

"Was he convicted?"

"Yeah...just before I went to college. I was gonna be a marketing major, but I switched to law. Wanted to prove he didn't do it."

"Did you?" I already knew the answer. The outdated photograph told the story, to say nothing of the tears bubbling up in her eyes.

"I did," she said with a soft smile. "But not soon enough."

"Illness?" I asked.

"Prison riot. Some guy knifed him over twenty bucks. All I could get was a posthumous acquittal."

I let the room grow quiet while Sarah wiped her eyes. There was nothing for me to say. We both knew that. But I wanted to say something anyway.

"I'm sorry."

She smiled. "You know, I wasn't going to say this before. But you remind me of my daddy, a little. He never could turn a blind eye to injustice."

And neither can you.

Sarah reached for a tissue, and I looked out the window to give her time to wipe her face. The sprawling Atlanta skyline stretched away toward the horizon, looking brighter and more welcoming than it had since I arrived. I watched the sunrise glimmer off the distant silhouette of the Westin Peachtree Plaza, and for the first time since I rolled into town, a new thought flashed across my mind.

What if I stayed?

I never intended to be here for long. I never intended to stop at all. The traffic and bustle of the metropolis didn't suit me. If I wanted more of that, I could return to Phoenix.

And yet...Atlanta wasn't like Phoenix. It was new. I had made new friends here, and I didn't have any of the trappings of my old life surrounding me as haunting reminders of all that I had lost.

It could be a fresh start. It could be...

I looked back at Sarah, and just for a moment I pictured a front porch. Someplace where the two of us could enjoy a nightcap, snuggled up next to each other on a bench swing, her head on my arm...

I winced, and Mia flashed into my mind. In an instant I saw her on Bourbon Street again, laughing as I yanked her into my arms, narrowly missing that rushing cab. I saw her smile light up my world like a million stars, and I felt her in my arms.

The memory sent an ache through my chest unlike anything I'd felt all week. More painful than the bullet that had grazed my shoulder blade. More real than the beautiful woman sitting right in front of me.

I looked away from the window and saw Sarah staring at me. She looked suddenly awkward, rolling the chopsticks in one hand.

"You know...I don't know what you've got planned next,

but it's a nice city. I'm sure I could help you find a place. Maybe we could talk about it over dinner?"

Her voice softened as she finished the line. I looked into her eyes and saw a mirror of myself.

I wasn't the only one who felt the attraction.

I stood up slowly.

"I wish I could. But..."

I looked back out the window. Then I pocketed my hands.

"I'm just not ready for that."

I could tell by her puzzled squint that she didn't understand, but she didn't argue either. She stood and offered a hand, then flushed and wrapped me in a hug.

It was my second unexpected hug of the day, and I liked it even better than the first.

BACK IN MY TRUCK, it took a while to reach the highway. I rode with the windows down, polluted city air wafting in around my camping equipment, my wallet-sized photo of Mia smiling up at me from the dash. The truck ran well, seemingly happy to get back on the road.

As Atlanta faded behind me, I let go of memories of Jalen, Regi, and Sarah. I looked ahead, and then I flicked on the radio and surfed through some stations. The audio was predictably unreliable, but I didn't mind. I heard a familiar blues riff—lots of guitar and a smooth rolling beat. It brought on a smile, but I kept scanning.

It wasn't long before I landed on a good country track. It was the Zac Brown Band, crackling through my outdated truck radio in full harmony.

Singing about Georgia pines.

ABOUT THE AUTHOR

Logan Ryles was born in small town USA and knew from an early age he wanted to be a writer. After working as a pizza delivery driver, sawmill operator, and banker, he finally embraced the dream and has been writing ever since. With a passion for action-packed and mystery-laced stories, Logan's work has ranged from global-scale political thrillers to small town vigilante hero fiction.

Beyond writing, Logan enjoys saltwater fishing, road trips, sports, and fast cars. He lives with his wife and three fun-loving dogs in Alabama.

Did you enjoy *Take Down?* Please consider leaving a review on Amazon to help other readers discover the book.

www.loganryles.com

ALSO BY LOGAN RYLES

Printed in Great Britain
by Amazon